When Joni Died

By

Steven Bailey

For anyone who's ever been through something like this, this one is for you.

Summer of 2013

1

"I think it's a terrible idea, Joni."

You would, Joni thought to herself.

"I don't know, Mom. What if it would actually be good for her?"

Joni paced around her living room with the phone to her ear. It was Friday evening, and the sun was just starting to go down outside. Fireflies danced about the silver maple tree in her front yard. Aside from the occasional car driving by and a few crickets chirping, her neighborhood was quiet. Joni pulled the blinds down on the window to the right of the front door. To the left of the front door was a smaller window and her laptop desk. Dozens of unorganized motel reservation papers lay sprawled about her laptop, which itself sported a dozen open internet tabs.

She'd been dreading this phone call all day. Fridays at *Chemical Supplies and More!* were usually her victory lap days: she would update the inventory databases, enjoy a small lunch, try to strike up a conversation with Emily, address any pressing inventory issues, and then embrace the weekend like an old friend. But this particular Friday had been more stressful. She'd known that at the end of it, she would have to call her mom.

She just needed her Aunt Dottie's number. But asking for it meant revealing so many things. It meant telling her mom that she was taking a long trip out west, that she was going to do something adventurous, and that her daughter wanted to invite the aunt that they'd disowned over twenty years earlier.

As Joni had expected, her mom listed all the reasons Joni should not follow her instincts.

"Think about it, Joni. She's sleazy, washed-up, does drugs. Drinks and swears like a sailor. She wouldn't be a good travelling companion. Why would you ever want to travel with someone like that?"

Joni observed a crack between two of the floorboards underneath her desk. She stuck the tip of her toe in the space, feeling for any dirt. *I need to sweep.*

"You know she's an atheist," her mom said.

"I know." *I don't really care, though.*

"You'd be spending, what, two weeks? Three weeks with her? You'd be subjecting yourself to all that worldly influence. You don't want that. That wouldn't be walking in wisdom, Joni. You'd want someone who would help guide you spiritually, not hinder you."

I just need her phone number.

"Well, I'm not worried about that so much," Joni said. "I mean, you never know! Maybe this would be good for her." Joni laughed, hoping to steer the conversation away from a monologue about what God wanted.

"Trust me, Joni," her mom said. "She is a wretched woman, and you'd just be exposing yourself to her sick worldviews for several weeks. But back up just a minute. Why are you taking a trip out west?"

Joni looked at her desk and noticed how disorganized her travel papers were. She started stacking them in a pile, arranging the motel bookings and receipts in the order she'd be staying at them. She started to think that maybe she should've secured a travelling partner before reserving so many rooms for two.

"Well, it's something I've really wanted to do for a long time. My friends and I used to talk about taking a trip like this in college, but we never could because, you know, we were too busy or whatever. But now, it's like . . . whatever. I've got the money. I've got the time. I'm doing this. And I planned it so that I'll be back in time for Violet's birthday party, too."

Joni's sister Violet was busy getting ready for college. She would be attending a freshman orientation program and buying up school supplies for dormitory life soon. The vacation was set to end just two days before Violet's eighteenth birthday party, so inviting her sister had been out of the question.

"But, Joni, what I'm saying is what if something happens to your car? What'll you do if it breaks down in the middle of nowhere?"

"Mom, I'll be fine. I'm getting the car tuned up before—"

"But listen, what if something happens? Have you thought about that? Oh, hold on . . . yes, good point . . . your dad just asked if you're staying at hotels. What if there aren't any hotels when you go out there? What if they're all booked up?"

"I've already booked them in advance, so I'm good to go there."

"Are you sure? Have you researched them all enough? Sometimes they rip people off, and then you'll be stranded. You could be attacked by homeless people. Sometimes they're really dangerous. Really sinful places where drug deals and adulterous affairs go down. You see what I'm saying? Plus, it's the west. Lots of liberals and druggies out there, Joni."

The questions were suffocating Joni now. "Mom, I'm not touring drug dens or hooking up with people. I'm just seeing more of the country. You know, Grand Canyon, Horseshoe Bend . . ." She flipped through her hotel papers to see any other major landmarks that might resonate with her mom. "The cliff dwellings at Mesa Verde."

"But it's so far away," her mom said. "Wouldn't it be easier to do something simple like the beach? You know, the Campbell's have a nice beach house down in Charleston. I'm sure if you called them, they wouldn't mind letting you stay there for a few days. Save you some money on hotels."

They were getting off-topic, and Joni wanted this call to end.

"Thanks, Mom, but I'm definitely going west. It's a long trip, and that's why I'll need a travelling companion. Someone to help navigate. I really do want to ask Aunt Dottie. Do you have her number?"

"Why don't you ask some of your college friends? Why don't you ask Amy?"

It was a simple question, but it stung.

Once she had decided to start planning this trip back in March, Joni had sent out messages to see which of her friends from college wanted to tag along. This was going to be that one big trip that they'd spent so much of college talking about taking together one day. She sent out messages to Jodi, Tia (her husband and kid could come along, too), Chris and his wife, Elin and her husband. Even Amy got invited, though Joni was careful to word her message so that it was clear the invitation did not extend to Amy's husband Frank.

She wanted out of South Carolina for a bit, wanted to do something daring and new. It felt so freeing to plan such a huge road trip. Joni just needed at least one companion to make it happen. If they could all somehow go together, it would have made the whole experience perfect. To her, this was it. This would be the trip that reunited them. It was finally happening.

Only it wasn't.

She didn't know exactly what she expected. She knew they all had lives now. It had been nearly two years since they'd made any effort to reconnect with her, and it had been over a year since she'd given up trying to contact them. Her westward invitations were a final attempt to reunite with her college friends. But when no one replied to any of her messages, she wasn't ready for how badly it hurt. Their uniform silence on the trip, without so much as a text back to say, "Sorry! Wish we could make it!" made her realize that she had no close friends anymore. Even though they were only two years out of college, they were already on vastly different tracks in life that didn't allow time for staying connected.

The painful realization that the season of life with her college friends was now over led to Joni doubting herself and growing very discouraged. She felt alone. She felt as though her friends had abandoned her to the maelstrom of life. She felt as though her parents had done her a great disservice by homeschooling her and raising her in a fundamentalist church. She felt that it was a cruel irony that her reward for a four-year degree in English was not becoming a writer, as she had always wanted, but rather getting a dead-end job at a chemical factory.

It was in this hurt, anxious mindset that Joni decided to do something drastic. She wanted a change. She wanted a friend. She wanted to really live her own life. She wanted to be creative and free. And that's when the idea of reaching out to her estranged Aunt Dottie came to her.

Joni couldn't bring herself to dredge all of this up for her mom, so she said, "I did ask them, but they're all busy."

"Well, you know, I'm sure there's someone at the church who might be willing to go with you. Caroline might be able to. You remember Caroline Messer? The Messer family? She might be able to go."

Shit. Here it comes.

"Maybe you could come to church this Sunday and ask her?"

God damn it.

"Maybe."

"Swing by and we'll go together as a family. What else have you got going on?"

"I might be going to a friend's church this weekend, actually." Joni hoped the lie wouldn't necessitate a follow-up excuse.

Her mom was silent for a moment. On the other end of the line, Joni only heard, "Hmm." It was sinking in now that Joni was not going to get the number from her mom. That uneasy feeling that Joni knew all too well was starting to grow. That feeling that she'd made an irredeemable mistake, that she'd violated one of the sacred tenets of eternal salvation by declining to go to her parents' church and was now risking an eternity burning in Hell, was building within her. She could sense it morph into that ethereal phantom that crippled her ability to think, that made her doubt her own gut feelings. He had done so ever since she was little.

The Blue Ghost.

As if being directed by this phantom personification of her anxiety, her mom said, "You know, Joni, you're an adult. You can make your own decisions now. But I really think you'd be better off coming back to our church. I don't know what they teach you at these other churches you've been going to, but you know at least that at Elohim, you get the true Word of God. Pastor Greg's a good man. You know him. You know he'll never lead you wrong. And to be honest with you, Joni, I think if you'd been coming here, you wouldn't be making these rash decisions like trying to invite your aunt out on a trip with you. I mean, we don't talk to her for a reason, Joni. You know that."

Joni walked over to her kitchen sink. She noted that the dishes were starting to pile up and probably needed cleaning soon. It was better than listening to the Blue Ghost, who was reminding her that she hadn't actually gone to a church in several years.

"What exactly happened, Mom? Why don't we talk to her?"

Joni started stacking the plates up on the counter and readying the glasses. She set all the dirty silverware in the pot she'd last used for couscous. She did this slowly to avoid making too many clinking noises over the phone. *I really need a dishwasher.*

"She's just a liberal atheist who got too worldly, Joni. It's not worth jeopardizing your soul to associate with her."

"Yeah, but, I mean, is that all? I feel like we'd have shunned a lot more people and places over the years if that was it. Was there something specific? Like, did she do something bad?" Joni really didn't know the exact cause that led to Dottie being disowned by her family, and part of the reason she'd ultimately decided to reach out to her aunt was to find out. She was tired of the vague reasons she'd been fed her whole life and lately had begun to think there was more to it.

"It's just . . . it's different when it's family, Joni. When you're out in the world trying to reach lost souls, it's fine. You know what you're getting into. But when it's family, they know you. They know how to hurt you. They can betray you and get to you first. Yes, she betrayed us all with her worldly ways, and we didn't want you growing up around someone like that. We didn't want her to hurt you or Violet with poison and false teachings. We wanted you to grow with the seeds of the spirit, not the weeds of the enemy. And I really think, Joni, that you wanting to invite her back into your life is just giving that poison an open door. Seriously, you should come back to Elohim this Sunday. Let's find someone else for you to travel with."

Joni wanted to scream. She wanted to scream that she didn't care whether her Aunt Dottie had religious beliefs or not. She wanted to scream that she was twenty-four years old and could do whatever she wanted whenever she wanted. She wanted to scream that she would never go back to Elohim Creation Salvation Community Church even if God himself came down and ordered her to. She wanted to scream at her friends for abandoning her. She wanted to scream at her parents for raising her in toxic Christian fundamentalism that now manifested itself in shame and guilt every time she tried to be herself.

But she couldn't do any of this. The fear of her parents' judgment and possibly God's wrath for crossing that line held her back. The Blue Ghost had done his job well.

Holding back angry tears, all Joni could muster when speaking to her mom was a non-committal, "Well, maybe I'll figure something else out. Maybe I could still ask Dottie. Maybe I could reach her, you know? Be a positive influence on her?"

"Joni, you have a good heart, but sometimes the risk isn't worth it to yourself. Remember, she's an atheist who hates God. She's a liberal hippie with no morals. She does drugs and sleeps around. She's low-life trash, Joni. We don't associate with her anymore because of that. You know we don't associate with people like that at all."

It was as much a reminder as a warning. Joni knew the subtext all too well: *If you become like her, you'll be disowned too.*

She remembered what had happened to Mr. Bridges.

"Alright, well, thanks for your time, Mom. I better let you go so I can go figure something out."

"Alright, Joni. I'll pray for you."

"Thanks, Mom."

"I love you, Joni."

"Love you, too. Bye, Mom."

Once she hung up, she let the tears fall down her cheek. She hated herself. *Why can't you just tell her the truth? Who cares what they'll say? They didn't go through what you went through. They have no clue how badly they hurt you.* She moved over to her computer desk, leaned on it, and breathed slowly and deeply to calm down.

On cue, the Blue Ghost started assaulting her with guilt.

How dare you think about doing this. You knew what was going to happen. You have an option before you, and you're willingly disobeying God. You're letting the world guide you, not Him. You're not a real Christian if the world guides you. You're scum. You're worthless. Your friends hate you. You're a disappointment to everyone. You deserve to burn. You're trash.

The shame and guilt tormented her. She doubted herself, wondering if this trip was too big for her to handle. She felt an uneasy pain in her stomach at even considering inviting her aunt. But the thoughts gave way when she remembered her college experience, how the church had hurt her, and how these thoughts were nothing more than gaslighting traps meant to make her run back to the snakelike embrace of her fundamentalist church. Something familiar, sure, but ultimately toxic. She couldn't go back to it. She wouldn't go back, no matter how hard the Blue Ghost screamed at her.

Suddenly, she found herself on her laptop and typing in her aunt's name.

Dottie White, Greenville, South Carolina.

There were several Dottie Whites listed in the area. Joni didn't know her aunt's exact age, but she narrowed it down to the only two in their late forties. She figured out which Dottie was most likely correct by finding the one that listed her parents as relatives. *Tim and Laura Arable. That's gotta be her.* She found the number and grabbed her phone.

That was easy. I should've started with this instead of calling Mom.

It was now about ten after eight. Wiping away her tears, she dialed the number. She didn't care if it was too late to be calling or not. She wanted to do this. She wanted to know the truth: What was Dottie really like? What was so awful about her? And most importantly, why did they really disown her? What had she actually done?

Joni didn't know what to expect, and for once she was glad to be stepping into an unknown. The dial rang three times before someone answered. Joni heard a cough, then a woman said, "Hello?"

"Hi, this is Joni Arable. Is this Aunt Dottie?"

She heard another two coughs, then, "Who'd you say you were?" The woman had a slightly raspy voice that sounded vaguely more midwestern than southern. Joni cleared her own throat and spoke louder and more clearly.

"Joni Arable. Is this Aunt Dottie?"

There was a moment of silence that grew into being uncomfortably quiet. Joni thought the woman on the other end was going to hang up. Then, just as Joni started to wonder whether the woman had even heard her, there was a laugh on the other end.

"Oh my God, holy shit. Joni! Is that really you?"

"Yes, it's me," Joni said, relieved. "Surprise!"

"Well, how the hell are you? God, it's been a long time!"

"Yes, it has! I'm good, how are you?" Joni said. She wasn't quite sure how to jump into her question about the trip just yet. She was surprised how ecstatic her aunt sounded, though.

"Man, it's been what, twenty years? Goddamn!" her aunt said. "You sound all grown up now. Oh, wait. Hold on." Joni heard what sounded like a fork or spoon being tossed into a sink.

"So Joni! It's a real shock to hear your voice. How's Laura?"

Mom's name. It's definitely her.

"She's good!" Joni lied. "How are you doing? It's been a long time."

"I'm alright. Just settling in for the night." More coughing. "What's been up with you? What are you up to these days?"

"Not too much. I'm working at a chemical plant as a database and inventory manager. Living on my own, paying bills. The life, you know?"

"Chemical plant, huh?"

"Yeah. It's called *Chemical Supplies and More!* I didn't go to college for science or anything. I studied English, but it's the job I landed. Life, I guess."

"I see. Interesting!"

"Yeah. The reason I'm calling—I know this is weird. It's been like twenty-one years since I saw you. Gosh, I was just a toddler—Um, the reason I called is because I've been planning a trip out west recently. And I needed a travelling partner to help me navigate and figure things out as we go. And I was calling because I was wondering if you would actually like to join me as a travelling companion."

"Oh, I see. Wow! That sounds fun! Where we headed?"

So far, so good.

"The plan is to head out west and just see the country. We'd leave June 25th and head out to the Grand Canyon. From there we'd also go visit Horseshoe Bend, Mesa Verde, which are cliff dwellings, and just, I guess, see a lot of the country. We would see other things along the way, too. Think of it as an all-American road-trip to get out of the south and have fun adventures out west! We'd be back by July 5th. So about a week and a half out there. Um, eleven days in total, I think."

"Sounds fun! Okay, I'm in!"

Joni was taken aback. She'd expected some sort of resistance or hesitancy to the idea. After all, this was the niece whose family had shunned Dottie for just over two decades. She hadn't expected her aunt to simply agree to go with her like this. For all Dottie knew, this was some scam artist playing a sick joke. She wondered if her aunt was high or drunk at that moment.

"Are you sure? I mean, I know I'm asking a lot. You're probably wondering why I'm calling you after . . . well, my parents and all . . ."

"Are you kidding? It's not every day you get a phone call from your long-lost niece!"

The plan evolved so that Joni would pick Dottie up from her apartment the day they were to set out. When she hung up the phone, she felt as if a huge burden had suddenly fallen off her shoulders.

She sensed the Blue Ghost screaming at her that this was a huge mistake.

Good. I don't care.

Just over a month later on June 25, Joni pulled her red car into her aunt's low-rent apartment parking lot and parked in front of the 1700 building. At that moment, the sky was a faint purple with the first hints of sunlight beginning to illuminate the trees. The apartments, which were situated near the community college, were all a distinct 1980's blue and surrounded by tall pine trees.

Joni hadn't ever seen these apartments up close before, though she had passed by them many times in her life. The main road and her car were separated by an apartment building and a thin line of pine trees. Traffic on it was already starting to pick up, but everything was silent in the parking lot. Even the wren flittering about on the sidewalk where Joni sat seemed too afraid to chirp just yet.

Joni sent her aunt a text message: "I'm here."

The last time she had seen her aunt, Joni was about three years old. She had vague but fond memories of her aunt. She remembered holding her hand once. She remembered Dottie had puffy blonde hair, like someone out of an eighties' fashion poster.

Joni heard a door snap shut followed by someone stumbling into a trash can near one of the apartments behind her. Turning around, she saw her Aunt Dottie, wearing cheeseburger-themed pajama bottoms and a white bra, staggering while trying to realign the trash can. She'd been in the 1900 building.

"It's good!" Dottie shouted to no one in particular. She was thin and almost as tall as Joni. Her hair still had that eighties' puff to it, though it seemed more gray than blonde now. Dottie began walking towards the 1700 building while rubbing the sleep out of her eyes. Just then, a shirtless man with a beer gut and handlebar mustache stepped out of the 1900 building.

"You thirsty?" he said.

Rubbing her eyes with one hand and waving him away with the other, her aunt called, "No, no, it's cool. Don't call me. I'll call you." The man shrugged his shoulders, picked at his belly button, belched, and walked back inside.

Oh, God. Was mom telling the truth?

Joni slowly got out of her car and waved. "Hey, Aunt Dottie!"

Dottie seemed too tired to realize what was happening, but after a few very intense moments of hard concentration, she realized she was looking at her niece Joni.

"Joni!" she yelled, coming over and throwing her arms tightly around her niece.

She's hugging me in her bra. She's hugging me in her bra. She's hugging me in her bra.

"Holy shit, you've grown up," Dottie said, releasing her niece. "Last time I saw you, you barely reached my hip! Now you're taller than me!" Dottie coughed. Joni smelled alcohol and cigarettes on her breath.

"Thanks!" Joni replied. "Yeah, how are you doing? Are you ready to hit the road yet?"

"Ah, no. Not just yet," Dottie said. "I gotta go get some clothes on. I am anything but ready. As you can see, I'm underdressed." Dottie started fumbling in her pockets for keys. "I need to clean up, I think."

"Who was that guy? With the mustache?" Joni said.

Dottie looked back at the 1900 building. "You know what, I have no idea. I forgot to ask." Laughing, she said, "I just said I'd call him back. I don't even know what the hell his phone number is." Dottie found her keys and walked inside the 1700 building, leaving Joni to wonder if she hadn't made a huge mistake. The Blue Ghost crept into her soul with all the warnings her mom had given her: *She's drunk. She's worldly. She's trash.*

It's not too late, Joni thought to herself. *I can hop in the car and leave. She looks so wasted that she'll probably crash and think the whole thing was a dream.*

Joni, clutching her phone tightly, took a deep breath and dismissed the anxious thoughts. *No. I'm not gonna be like my parents. Drunk or not, we're doing this.*

While she waited, Joni started the car back up. She rolled down her window and enjoyed the gentle morning breeze. The air smelled slightly like gasoline mixed with spring water. *I wonder what the desert will smell like.*

When Dottie eventually came back out, she was now fully dressed in long pink pants and a red and yellow Hawaiian shirt. There was no indication that she'd just awoken from a booze-fueled one-night stand. She had a purse, a large green suitcase with two silver clasps and a brown handle, and a blue messenger-bag draped over her right shoulder. When Dottie stepped off the sidewalk, Joni heard the distinct sound of glass bottles clinking together in the messenger-bag.

Joni opened the trunk and made room for her aunt's stuff.

"I ain't been out west in a long time," Dottie said. She heaved her green suitcase into the trunk, shut the door, and they both climbed into their respective seats.

Dottie looked at Joni. "You ready for this?"

"I'm ready, Aunt Dottie."

"Well, where to first?" Dottie said, reaching into her messenger-bag.

Joni pulled out her phone and began plugging in directions for her GPS app. "A motel in Jackson, Tennessee. Never really been through Tennessee. The mountains should be something to look at. By the way, do you need breakfast or anything?"

"Miles ahead of ya," Dottie said, pulling a bottle of whiskey out of the messenger-bag. She popped the top off and started drinking.

Joni began signaling for her to stop. "Aunt Dottie! Whoa! You can't drink in the car!"

Dottie wiped away some alcoholic dribble on her chin and said, "Says who?"

Joni blinked, amazed. "The law."

Dottie rolled her eyes. "Oh my God, you are definitely your mother's child." She took another swig of the bottle.

"It's against the law! If you start drinking in here, I'm the one who gets punished!"

"Yeah, yeah."

Joni decided to get firm. "You can't drink in here."

Dottie hiccupped and laughed. "Now you sound like your father!" Her aunt laughed and put the top back on. "Alright, alright. I'll stick it in the trunk and save it for Jackson."

It's not too late.

Joni opened the trunk for her aunt.

No.

After hiding the bottles and the messenger-bag, they returned to their seats.

"Shoot. I almost forgot," Dottie said, pulling open her purse. To Joni's dismay, Dottie pulled out two silver flasks. Joni was almost too stunned to open the trunk again for her aunt. When her aunt returned from putting these in the trunk, Joni decided to be firm about the drinking.

"Do you drink a lot?" Joni asked. Dottie looked at Joni. Rolling her eyes, her aunt assumed the sort of position a teacher might when trying to explain something. "It helps soothe the nerves."

"You might need help," Joni said, again trying to be blunt.

"And you need to shut the hell up and start driving. We got a long trip ahead of us, and we ain't gonna start it out with you telling me what you think about alcohol."

"Well, alcohol is fine, but . . . I mean, you're not gonna drink in the car, are you?"

Dottie laughed, then put her right hand over her heart and raised her left hand. "I solemnly swear not to drink in Joni's car ever again on pain of death 'til death do us part. Forever and ever, amen." She put her hands down and looked at Joni. "Feel better?"

"Yes, that's fine," Joni said, though she wasn't entirely relieved.

As she pulled out of the parking space, she wondered if this really was, as her mom had said, a terrible idea after all.

2

It didn't take too long before they hit I-40. The moment the "Welcome to North Carolina" sign appeared, the hills swelled up into lush, green mountains, leaving the foothills of South Carolina behind. Joni saw out of the corner of her right eye how far below the valley was.

"High drop," she said. "The guard rail isn't very reassuring."

Dottie, enjoying the view, turned to her niece. "You ever been through the mountains before?"

"I've been through here before with my family, but it was a long time ago," Joni said. "I was really little."

"Are you scared of heights?"

"I didn't think so, but then again, I'm not used to mountains. I've spent pretty much my whole life in South Carolina."

Dottie laughed. "Oh, South Carolina! With your majestic flat lands and little green hills."

"And bumpy roads that are forever under construction," Joni said. "I guess we'll see how well I handle mountains as we go." She took some comfort whenever they began passing trees growing on the other side of the guard rail. Obscuring the valley made her feel a little more protected from the cliffside.

"Don't worry," Dottie said, taking out a cigarette and lighting up. "Tennessee is full of them!" After a puff, she rolled her window down a bit and added, "And so is the west. The ones out west are larger, too. Well, most of them anyway."

Joni shifted uneasily in her seat. "Great. That'll be a fun challenge."

"So you've never been out west?"

"Never."

Dottie cocked her head curiously. "What's the furthest you've travelled before?'"

Joni thought for a moment. "Just Georgia, I think. And North Carolina. I know we came through Asheville when I was younger, but I don't remember being this uneasy about the mountains."

"Your parents don't travel much, do they?"

"No, I guess not. Dad doesn't anyway. He's never been beyond North Carolina or Georgia. I think he said that once, actually."

"Jeez, Laura's been out further west than that," Dottie said, taking another puff of her cigarette and blowing the smoke out the window. "I know she's been to Oklahoma. We had a friend's funeral out there one time. That was a bit before she met your dad. When she was younger, she liked to travel."

"Yeah, I knew she had been to Oklahoma before," Joni said. "I know she hasn't been further north than North Carolina. Like Dad."

"Well, now you're going to outdo them both."

"Yeah! I guess I am. I hadn't thought of that."

Dottie leaned back in her seat and watched the traffic ahead. Joni heard her aunt cough. She tried to gauge her aunt's expression using the peripheral vision of her right eye but couldn't quite see her aunt's face. Under the guise of checking out the scenery again, she got a better look.

"The mountains do look pretty."

Her aunt was looking out the window too, but Joni saw that she seemed to be enjoying the drive. *As long as she doesn't drink and keeps the window down, I can handle the smoking.*

A driver in a white minivan merged in front of them going about ten under the speed limit, forcing Joni to slow down too. Before long, the mountain road disappeared into another expanse of forest with tame hillsides surrounding them. Joni breathed a sigh of relief. Dottie puffed a huge cloud of smoke out the window, blowing it back into the windshield of the driver behind them. "So tell me about yourself, Joni. Whatcha been up to all these years? You said you studied English?" Dottie asked.

"Yes. I studied English Language and Literature. Got my bachelor's degree. I also minored in Creative Writing. I want to be a writer."

"A writer! Nice! Have you gotten anything published yet?"

"Just a few poems and essays in the college journal, nothing big yet. That was a few years ago. They weren't very good poems, to tell you the truth."

Dottie puffed her cigarette again. Joni failed to suppress her cough as the scent of tobacco plunged into her nostrils.

"You like poetry? You write like the Beats?" Dottie asked.

"The Beats," Joni said, thinking. "No, not really. I mean, I write some poetry. Not often, though. I have a hard time with poetry. I really just want to write novels and stuff. Try to, anyway. I was hoping to spend some down time on this trip working on an outline for a book."

"Oh, okay," Dottie said. "What's it about? Or do I need to wait to read it?"

Joni laughed. "I don't have an exact idea yet. Just images, really. Vague ideas. I wanted to sift through them, see what works, I guess. See what doesn't work."

"Hmm," Dottie said. "Well that's neat, you want to be a writer. Last time I saw you, you wanted to be a ninja."

Joni thought for a moment, remembering with some effort. "Say what now?"

"You were a ninja for Halloween."

Joni remembered. "Oh yeah! I remember that. That was the only time I can remember my parents doing Halloween. How old was I? I had to be really little."

We're going there.

"Gosh, you couldn't have been but about three. That was about the last time I saw you. How old are you now?"

"Twenty-four."

Dottie whistled. "Damn. Twenty-one years. My God, time flies. You've grown, girl. You used to be as plump as a watermelon!"

"Gee. Thanks."

Dottie laughed. "Now you're taller than me! And skinny, too!"

"Yep."

"I don't think you were a brunette, either."

"It was probably more blonde then. My hair just turned color over time. I think it started when I was around ten or so. Eleven, maybe?

Violet joked that I was going to turn into a unicorn with rainbow-colored hair eventually, and then I could be her noble steed. She was only like five or six at the time. I think she was going through her princess phase."

"How's your sister doing?" Dottie asked.

"Violet's good. She just graduated high school. She's about to turn eighteen. In fact, I wanted to get a souvenir for her while we're out west. She's having a birthday party when we get back."

"She a straight-A student?"

"I guess. Well, homeschool straight-A. Does it really mean anything?"

Dottie ran a hand through her thick gray hair, scratching her scalp. "You know, I never got to meet Violet."

In spite of the steady hum of traffic, the rumbling of the car engine, and the bass of the rushing wind through the open windows, it got really quiet. Until this moment, it hadn't really dawned on Joni that Dottie had never met Violet.

"Your parents stopped talking to me before they had her. Man, I missed out on you two. Now you're all grown up. You want to be a writer, and Violet's becoming an adult. How did I miss out on you two?"

Joni realized that Dottie was looking right at her as she said it. She wasn't quite sure how to respond without bringing up potentially hurtful memories for Dottie. *I need her as my travelling partner. I can't start this trip by offending her.*

"I guess . . . I don't know. I mean, my parents disowned you. I know they didn't like you being a liberal atheist."

Dottie roared with laughter that turned into coughing. Joni thought she could hear her aunt's lungs gasping for oxygen. When Dottie regained her breathing, it turned back into laughter. "That does sound like something your parents would say! Liberal atheist. What a serious charge."

"Well, aren't you, though?" Joni asked. "I'm not trying to pry or anything. I've only ever heard them say that's why they disowned you."

"You tell me," Dottie said, flicking ashes off her cigarette out the window. She took another puff. "I'm curious. What are they saying about me that makes me a liberal atheist?"

"Well," Joni said, deciding to merge back into the left lane to pass the minivan, "I know you smoke. And drink. And apparently sleep with strange men."

"Right, because no true Christian has ever smoked, drank, or slept with strange men in history." Dottie looked at Joni with a crooked smile.

Joni couldn't help but smile at that. "Hey, it's their words, not mine! Although—and again, not trying to judge—but seriously, who was that guy? You didn't even know his name?"

Dottie took another drag of her cigarette. "Not to judge, but I'm going to judge you anyway," she said, mocking Joni. "That's basically what you just said."

"Sorry. I wasn't trying to. I just thought—"

"You just thought that a real Christian wouldn't smoke or drink or bang outside of marriage. Is that it?"

Joni shifted in her seat. "I didn't mean to suggest that."

"But it's what you were taught, right?"

"Well, yeah. I was definitely taught those things growing up. But I don't exactly agree that that's true now."

Dottie chucked her cigarette out the window and pulled out another one. As she lit it, she said, "I take it pointing that out to your parents wouldn't convince them that a person could engage in that sort of behavior and still be a Christian, would it?"

"No, I don't think they'd agree."

Dottie took a puff of her new cigarette, then continued. "Tell me if this sounds right, Joni. If you tried arguing that a person could smoke and drink and fuck and still be a Christian, they'd say that person wasn't really a Christian to begin with. They'd say either her heart wasn't really in it, or she just lives for the world. She cleans up on Sundays so she can live in sin all week. Then she just rinses and repeats on Sundays and does the whole thing over again. Or maybe, if they're feeling extra compassionate, they don't blame the person. They blame the church she goes to. Says that her church is run by false prophets. They teach her to live for the world's pleasures and so she never spends enough time in the Word. She's led by the flesh, not the spirit. Does that sound about right?"

Joni was impressed. Even as her aunt was laying out the scenario, Joni was thinking of how her parent's church would argue against the person. "Jeez, that's exactly what they'd say," Joni said. "They've said it before. And so do a lot of people at their church."

Dottie continued. "I figured. I guess they haven't changed one bit. Still judging other people's hearts. Like they'd know. Like anyone could really know another person's heart. I mean, yeah, actions speak louder than words, but shit. They're human too! Same as you and me. I just think it's better to be honest than pretend to be some perfect saint who's really no better than anyone else."

"Well, that is true," Joni admitted. "Lots of Christians do fail at their own moral compass. It becomes a problem when they think they have some moral superiority over others."

Dottie clapped Joni on the back. "You agree, huh? I'm surprised to hear that kinda talk coming from you. I figured your parents would've beaten that sort of thinkin' outta ya a long time ago."

"Well, for many years, they did. There was no room for nuance like that. It was always 'a real Christian is led by the Spirit, not by the world. By their fruits you shall know them.' That sort of thing. But that's partly why I'm undertaking this trip," Joni said. "To escape that sort of thinking."

"Really?"

"I realized that I've never actually had a life of my own other than what my parents set up for me, and honestly, after . . . well, a lot of things through the years . . . I'm just done with it. I want to see the world. I want to see other people and how they live. I want normal things. I want to get a good job. I want a boyfriend. I want to be a good writer. I just want a normal life where I don't feel like I'm going to Hell every time I even remotely enjoy myself."

"Sounds like you know what you want. What'd you fight over?"

Joni briefly let off the gas. "Sorry?"

"With your parents? What'd you fight about?"

"Okay, are you psychic? How'd you know we fought?"

Dottie shrugged innocently, smiling. "Dottie's intuition."

Joni couldn't grasp how Dottie had guessed about the fight. "Well, it's complicated."

Dottie waved her hand, and a fleck of ash fell onto the seat. "I mean, we've got time. Might as well talk about something." Dottie picked up the ash and flicked it out the window.

Eight hours. Guess I better just be honest.

"We fought about me inviting you as my travelling companion."

"Ouch."

"It wasn't really a fight, per se. I spoke with Mom. She was kind of passive-aggressive, I guess. Suggesting that I wouldn't have been so reckless if I'd still been going to their church regularly. Which of course led to me having to dance around the obvious."

"Which is?" Dottie asked.

"I stopped going to their church halfway through college."

"You stopped going to Elohim Creation Salvation?"

"Yeah. I don't feel strong enough to tell them why. I just keep playing it off like I'm busy and looking for other churches. The truth is I don't like going there. If I'm being totally honest, I don't like going to church at all anymore. But I can't just *tell* them that. They'd freak out and tell me I was walking with the devil. Worst-case scenario, they'd probably disown me. Anyway, after having to dodge going into all that, she turned the conversation to why they didn't think me travelling was a good idea. They said I'd end up in a sketchy part of town with no clue where I was and get attacked by homeless men. Or something ridiculous like that." Joni found herself squeezing the steering wheel tighter as the memory of the phone call came back to her.

"That certainly sounds like Tim and Laura to me. Shit, they really haven't changed at all, have they?"

"They definitely still talk like that, if that's what you remember of them," Joni said. "But you know what? I'm an adult. I can make decisions for myself, so I told her not to fret. I played it cool and got it across to her that I was going through with the trip regardless. It's over and done with, so thank you, Aunt Dottie, for agreeing to be my travelling partner. Despite whatever worldly influence you intend to have over me."

Dottie laughed. "My pleasure," she said. The wind at sixty miles an hour wasn't too bad, but when the road reached seventy, Joni had to roll her window back up.

Why is it seventy through here?

She looked in her rearview mirror. "Uh-oh."

Joni saw there was now a long line of cars behind her that were now switching into the right lane and passing her. When the fifth car in less than fifteen seconds had passed her, she said, "Wow. Is seventy too slow for these people?"

"No, but you sure as hell are," Dottie replied.

"How? I'm going seventy!"

"Yeah, but you're in the left lane."

"So?" Joni replied. "I know it's the fast lane. That's why I'm going as fast as the law allows. Besides, this road feels like it should be sixty-five, not seventy."

Dottie looked at Joni in disbelief. "Wow, your parents really did shelter you, didn't they? Honey, get in the right lane."

Joni did so. "Why? Now I'm in the slow lane."

"Look, forget the speed limit signs," Dottie said. "On the open road, there are two speed limits you need to worry about: *slow-as-hell* and *fast-as-fuck*."

Joni braked as she came upon a station wagon going about forty miles an hour. "This is the slow lane."

"The slow-as-hell lane." Dottie exhaled more smoke. Despite Dottie's open window, the car was really beginning to smell like an ashtray. Joni cracked her window open again to ventilate the car more.

"I don't get it. Why post speed signs if no one is going to obey them?"

"Just maintain the flow of traffic," her aunt said, casually puffing streams of smoke from her mouth.

"So which is it? Follow the speed limit or maintain the flow of traffic?"

"Both."

Joni groaned. "I'm going to have to stay out of the fast lane, aren't I?"

Dottie chuckled. "Stay out of the fast-as-fuck lane unless you need to pass this bozo here." Joni looked and saw Dottie staring at her. She couldn't read the expression. Dottie finally rolled her eyes and said, "What I'm saying is you should pass this bozo here."

"Oh. Right. Gotcha."

Joni passed the station wagon going forty. There wasn't another car for at least a mile ahead, so Joni sped up comfortably back to about sixty-eight and decided to take in the scenery. The green forests were steadily rising, but they weren't entirely in the heart of the mountains just yet.

"Didn't your parents teach you how to drive?"

"No, not really. Dad thought that I wasn't mature enough to handle it. He said they only had the one car, and if something happened to it, we'd be sunk as a family. So they never helped. Never even let me practice in a parking lot. I had to go to Grandma Sue for it. She taught me right before going off to college."

"She did? Jeez, I never figured Laura would go fascist on something as basic as driving. Well, your Grandma Sue taught me too. And I know she understood how speeding on the road worked. Did she not teach you about the fast and slow lanes?"

"She did. She said follow the speed limit, use the left to go faster, and the right lane for going slower. That was it. Makes sense. But the DMV handbook said follow the speed limit and also maintain the flow of traffic. But no one gave me a clear idea of what to do if the flow of traffic wasn't following the speed limit. Like, what should I do if everyone is speeding? Do I speed, too? It's like the law of the jungle at that point. No consistency."

"I can't believe your parents didn't teach you driving. That's like a rite of passage, you know?"

"Yeah. They didn't teach me much of anything except how to pray, how to avoid worldly temptations, and how to dress properly. Okay, reading and writing properly. I guess they kind of winged math. No idea how to do taxes. They homeschooled me the whole way through."

"Jeez, that sucks, kid," Dottie said, sounding depressed. "How do you feel about that?"

"I feel . . . I mean, it was irritating, but I guess I understand why they didn't let me—"

Dottie *tsk*ed, accidentally dropping her cigarette in the process. After picking it up and brushing the ashes from her lap, she said, "Okay, Joni. There you go, talking the way they trained you. Look, if I'm gonna travel with you, let's get my demands out of the way. The first and only rule is you gotta be honest with me. That's it, okay? I want you to be honest. I really do. You ain't gotta hide nothing. You said yourself this is some big spiritual quest to discover yourself and write a book, right? Well, the only way that's gonna happen is if you're honest. With yourself. With me. Everybody. And look, you ain't got nothing to be afraid of, either. It's not like I'm gonna pick up the phone, call my sister and be like, 'You'll never guess what Joni said today!' Just be your fucking self. Come on. How does being homeschooled and getting fucked over when it came to driving make you feel?"

"It makes me mad."

"The fucking truth, Joni."

"It makes me *really* mad."

"Have you ever cussed in your life, girl?"

"Around friends, sure. I don't usually do it around—"

"Cuss, girl! Damn! Stop playing teatime. Let it out! You're not going to Hell for saying how you feel. Get creative with it! That's half the fun."

"It pisses me off!"

"There you go! Now you sound like a niece of mine!" Dottie laughed. "What about it pisses you off? What about it is so god-damned unfair?"

Joni let the wave of frustration burst out. "Everything! All my friends could drive, but I sure as hell couldn't. I was the most responsible kid I knew, but I wasn't allowed to drive. I wasn't allowed to even question it. It was bullshit! I was told by my parents and the youth minister that I set an *unholy example* for Violet by questioning authority. Their words. Not mine. Well, actually, their church's words. Like, what a bunch of shit! I had to learn from Grandma before heading off to college."

This kind of feels good.

"And being homeschooled, I feel like I was just sheltered from so many things. From a normal life. I was just raised to accept that questioning them was a bad thing, and I had to just obey. If I questioned them on driving, it was like questioning God. And I couldn't argue whenever something happened at their church that made me feel like shit, either. I was just taught to accept it as what God wants. It wasn't until college that I was finally able to stop going to their church," Joni said.

"What made you realize you wanted to leave their church?" her aunt asked.

Joni thought for a moment. "There were a lot of reasons, most of which happened when I was in college, but if I had to narrow it down to a moment that started me on that path, it would have to be when a deacon yelled at me for wearing sandals in church."

"For doing what now?" Dottie asked in disbelief.

"For wearing yellow sandals. I was twelve years old."

"Because it was too casual?" Dottie asked, confused.

"No," Joni said. "Because it was too slutty."

"Wait, *what!?*"

"Yeah." Recalling the incident, Joni decided to get creative and let her anger shine through. "I was yelled at by a god-damned deacon for wearing god-damned yellow sandals!"

Dottie smiled. "Atta, girl!"

"Sandals!" Joni continued. "Yellow sandals! Who gives a shit about yellow sandals? They're sandals! I didn't have anything else to wear to church that day, so I threw on my yellow sandals. I'd worn them to church several times before, so I didn't think anything of it. But no. This deacon—his name was Mr. Northen. Creepy old bastard. We called him Merv the Perv—came up to me before the main service and said I was tempting the boys by wearing revealing footwear and should be ashamed of myself. I was so embarrassed. I couldn't bring it up to my parents I was so embarrassed. I was twelve years old, Dottie."

"That's seriously fucked up," Dottie said.

"You think?" Joni continued. "And because of that, my whole teenage years were spent living in fear of tempting guys with how I dressed. Like, who the hell cares how I dress! But I had to live in constant fear of *tripping up men trying to walk for God.* If they lusted after my body, it would be *my* fault. So during my teen years and on into college, I had an embarrassing wardrobe. Loose skirts that couldn't be any higher than halfway up my calves, no jeans or pants, layered shirts that weren't tight or showing cleavage, oversized coats. Low-heeled pumps. I was too scared to wear a comfortable Spring-time dress. I didn't want to incur God's wrath for tempting the men around me. I looked like a weirdo. I was literally the stereotypical image of a weird homeschool child. But hey! At least I wasn't giving pervy old bastards boners with my bitchin' yellow sandals!"

"Got some alliteration going on there. Nice!" Dottie said.

Joni triumphantly shouted, "Woo!"

Looking at her aunt, Joni could see that Dottie was smiling and sitting up in her seat as if she had just accomplished some great task.

"Did that feel good?" Dottie asked.

"Hell yeah! That was fun to get out. I usually filter my thoughts before saying them."

"You should let those feelings out more often. Bottling up how you really feel can drive you crazy. Wanna smoke?" Dottie said, offering Joni a stick.

"Ah, no thank you," Joni said. "I definitely have no desire to become a smoker."

"I'm feeling called out," Dottie said, sticking the pack back in her purse. "That sounds rough, Joni. For what it's worth, I think you're a fine driver. Even if a bit of a slow one."

"Slow, huh?"

"You drive like my mother."

"Well, she is the one who taught me."

"Touché, Joni. Touché."

Dottie reached over and observed the GPS. They still had 374 miles left until they reached the motel. The Tennessee line wasn't too far away now. Mountainous rock was appearing more frequently now alongside the roadway.

"Where are we heading again?" Dottie asked.

"A motel in Jackson. I found it for pretty cheap."

"Nice."

"I just hope it's not sketchy. Like, really sketchy."

"How much did you pay for it?" Dottie asked.

"About forty-seven, I think. Wasn't too bad. Why?"

Dottie chuckled. "Trust me: anything under fifty is gonna be a dive. I stayed in a motel one time in Mississippi. Cost me forty-two bucks. The place smelled like ass. The bed was directly under a leaking ceiling, so the corner of the bed was wet and smelled like mildew. The TV only had one channel that kept advertising how great the hotel was. There was no soap, there was one towel, a broken toilet lid, a cracked window. It was bad. And this was in the summer, too, and the air conditioner was broken. I went to go complain at the front desk, ask for a better room, and there wasn't anybody in there! So I waited. Must've been two hours, and nobody ever showed up. They didn't have a ringer to call anyone. They didn't even have security cameras! So I said what the hell and lit up a joint right there in broad daylight. I flicked it over the counter when I finished and went to my room and made the best of it."

Joni tensed up. The thrill of being free to cuss had been scary, surreal, exciting, fun. But now, Dottie's simple confession made her anxieties come screaming back into the forefront of her mind.

Oh shit. Is she carrying drugs now?

Dottie must have sensed Joni's concern, because she laughed and said, "Don't worry. I'm not packin' the good stuff. That was a long time ago. I was a different kid back then. Now I'm reformed!" Dottie coughed. "But I tell ya, that hotel wasn't worth the forty-two. I could've spent an extra ten bucks elsewhere and slept with the knowledge that I wouldn't get rabies of the butt. I mean, there were so many cockroaches, I swear they must've been having a cockroach convention going on. Oh, by the way—not to change the subject or anything—but do you like music?"

"Yeah. You want to see what's on the radio?"

"Do you like violin music?"

"I don't really know anything specific. You have a suggestion?"

"Here." Dottie started searching through her purse. "Ever heard of Lukaas Bennett?" Her aunt pulled out a CD. "Here's some of the finest pieces of violin music you'll ever hear." Her aunt put the disc in the car CD player.

The violin music provided good background noise to nod her head to as Joni drove through the ever-increasingly tall mountains. The drop-off of the cliff was to her far left now. It comforted her that the other side of traffic was closer, but the feeling of being so high still made her nervous. *Why is this making me so nervous?* She tried not to think about it. The swing from comforting to upbeat rhythms on the violin CD helped take her mind off of the height.

Before long, they passed the blue and white *Tennessee – The Volunteer State Welcomes You* sign. Just as they did so, a semi-truck came barreling down the left lane at over eighty miles an hour. It merged without warning in front of Joni and nearly clipped her fender in the process. A jolt of panic surged through her as she slammed the brakes. "Whoa, dude! What the hell!?"

Turning to Dottie, she said, "I cursed."

Dottie laughed. "You sure did. Give it time. You'll get better at it."

Joni derived a little pleasure about a half hour later when she saw that the semi-truck had been pulled over by a police officer and the driver was being ticketed.

"Welcome to Tennessee," Dottie said, giving an obligatory one-fingered salute to the driver as they passed him.

3

They stopped for food and a restroom break. In her trunk, Joni had packed two coolers. One was stocked with pre-made ham and cheese sandwiches, crackers, chips, breakfast bars, gummy candies, and drinkable fruit and veggie juices in squeezable pouches. The other cooler was filled with ice and water bottles. When she opened the trunk, she was reminded with sudden horror that her aunt's open liquor bottles were still in the back here. They had rolled out of the blue messenger-bag. She had an impulse to throw them out, but her aunt was returning from the restroom. Quickly throwing a blanket over them (and hoping no one else in the parking lot had noticed them), she grabbed two sandwiches, two fruit pouches, and two bags of chips. She closed the trunk and joined her aunt back in the car.

The traffic didn't improve. There were still many drivers going faster than the speed limit. One was a semi-truck driver with a popped tire that flapped violently as he sped past them. Joni, meanwhile, embraced defensive driving and stayed in the slow-as-hell lane. As the rumble of traffic droned on, the sky slowly turned a dark purple. Around seven, Joni took the exit to Jackson. Dottie looked at the directions on Joni's phone, telling her when to turn next.

"I love phones. I remember the good ol' days when we just had paper maps with roads that didn't exist," Dottie said.

"Sometimes you still get the non-existent roads, unfortunately," Joni said.

Not long after, Joni pulled into the motel parking lot, scraping her rear bumper on the unusually high entrance hump. The motel was two-stories tall and sat like a giant L-shaped building before them.

"Here we are!" Joni said. "The Glad Pine Express Inn!"

The first warning sign, as she parked in front of the motel's check-in office, was that every window on the surrounding buildings was barred.

The second warning sign, as they got out of the car and walked up to the lobby entrance, was a notice posted on the door that read:

HIDE YOUR VALUABLES! HIDE YOUR KEYS! WHATEVER YOU DO OR DON'T NOT DO, LOCK YOU'RE DOORS! THUGS CAN PROWL AND STEAL WHATEVER THEY YOU HAVE!

The typos alone overwhelmed Joni. The third warning sign was a loud, pulsating bass that emanated from a windowless building attached to the side of the motel on their left. In pink neon lights, the words *Pick-Me-Up Lounge* flashed on and off. Joni felt a headache starting because of the flashing glare.

"Oh my God, what is this place?" was Joni's first question, but her aunt shouted with glee.

"This place has a club? Oh, hell yes!" Turning to Joni, she said, "Quick! Let's get checked in so we can scope out the joint for some action!"

Joni looked at her aunt with bewilderment, wondering if this all hadn't been one big, giant, fast-as-fuck mistake.

"Are you serious? No, no way, I'm good. Let's just get checked in."

Fuck. This is exactly the sort of place my parents said I'd end up in.

"Oh, come on! Live a little, girl!" Dottie said.

"I just want to check in, Dottie," Joni said, though every instinct in her body screamed that she should move on to find a better place to stay. The seedy nightclub, the barred windows, the ominous posting with bad grammar . . . To Joni, it felt like the start of an actual horror movie. With her travelling companion being totally entranced by the nightclub, Joni felt a knot forming in her stomach. She sensed the Blue Ghost awakening within her.

The situation didn't improve when they went inside.

"Oh God," Joni said. "It smells like a daycare center where the children eat nothing but vanilla wafers."

"That's an oddly vivid description," Dottie said. "But so what? Let's get checked in. Then we can leave this nasty lobby and hit up the lounge." There was an unpleasant stickiness on the faux-marble floor beneath their shoes, making a *stick-stick-stick* sound as they walked. No one was at the desk, but there was a security monitor hanging up on the wall. It was in black and white, and it displayed a view of the pool area. The screen showed several adults staggering around the pool with martini glasses. One guy puked into the pool. Another woman fell in, spilling her drink. Joni could hear their laughter all the way in the lobby. To the left of the check-in counter was a long hallway with green walls and flickering fluorescent lights. At the end of this hallway were two heavy wooden doors with a small black chalkboard. Written on it in neon colors were the words:

PICK-ME-UP LOUNGE – ENTER HERE. NO ONE UNDER 21 PERMITTED.

Along with the foreboding blast of continuous bass that was threatening to make the security monitor fall off the wall, the sounds of laughing came from behind the lounge doors. Joni looked for a bell to ring. She couldn't find one.

"You didn't tell me this place had a pool! This place has got everything!" Dottie reached into her purse and dug out her phone. "Wait'll Dolores hears where I am now!" she laughed, sending a text message.

"I don't know, Dottie. This place kind of scares me. Maybe we should find a better place?"

"Oh, we'll be fine. An establishment like this can't last long if it were really all that bad. Live a little! We'll be fine. Trust me."

At that moment, a short, burly man of about thirty-five in a gray polo shirt and khakis walked in from a hallway adjacent to the green one. He was using a walkie-talkie. "Janice, I'm gonna need backup," he was saying into it. "We've got six or seven guests in the pool. Drunk." He set the walkie-talkie down and faced Joni.

"Hi! Can I help you?"

"Yes, I have a reservation," Joni said, getting out her confirmation ticket. The man took it and started typing her information into a computer. "Name?" he asked.

"Joni Arable."

He continued to type away. "I'll need to see a photo ID. Driver's license?"

Joni handed it to him. As he started comparing her ID to notes on the ticket, his walkie-talkie clicked. "What am I supposed to do about the pool?" Janice said.

He picked up the talkie. "Just get them outta there! They're fucking up the pool!"

"But there's seven of them and one of me! What am I supposed to do here, Gary? Seems like they outnumber me seven to one. Can you come help me?"

"Oh for God's sake, Janice. Grow a pair and kick them out!" As he hung up, he muttered, "Fuck, fuck, fuckity-fuck."

I don't feel safe here. I've made a huge mistake.

Joni didn't know of a good way out of it though, especially since she'd already paid online. Too late for a refund and too late to find another motel, she took comfort in that it was only forty-two dollars for one night.

God, is my life only worth forty-two dollars?

The man handed her back the driver's license along with two card keys. "It's room 238. First floor, about the middle of the building to your right. If you need anything, just call the service desk." With that, he grabbed the walkie-talkie and stormed back down the hallway. "I'm gonna fuck someone up tonight!" he yelled.

Joni stared in horror, but Dottie laughed. "This place is awesome, Joni."

They went back outside and found the room. It had two beds, a television, an air conditioner unit, a bathroom, and a sink. Unlike the lobby, it was much quieter here. She could no longer hear the music from the nightclub. Feeling a little easier, Joni thought to herself, *Okay. This is doable. We can do this.*

Joni, back at the car and with her purse slung over her shoulder, pulled from the trunk her suitcase and her laptop bag. Dottie pulled her own green suitcase along but left the blue messenger-bag behind. Joni thought she heard wine bottles clinking together within the suitcase. Once they had everything in the room, Joni plopped down on her bed.

"I am dead. You need the bathroom? I think I might take a shower," she said.

"I'll tidy myself up a bit," Dottie said, grabbing some brown lipstick, some mouth wash, and a hairbrush. "I wanna check out that club."

"Dottie," Joni pleaded, "are you sure that's a safe idea? You could get mugged. What if you get shot? Seriously, this place skeeves me out."

Dottie laughed, going over to the bathroom. The top of her Hawaiian shirt was already unbuttoned. "What if I get laid? Kiddo, relax. I'll be fine. I speak their language." When her aunt disappeared into the bathroom, Joni looked up at the ceiling.

She's reckless. I'm reckless. We're just two peas in a fucking pod, aren't we.

As her eyes adjusted to the dimness of the motel lighting, she started counting the brown stains that decorated various sections of the ceiling. Outside, a car drove by, blaring something vaguely heavy metal. The shrill guitars and amplified drums made the window vibrate. Joni wondered if the windowpane would fall out.

Have I really lost it? Were Mom and Dad actually right? I have no idea what's out here, and the world's just an evil, wicked place?

Joni swatted at a fly that landed on her nose.

No. That's stupid thinking. They sheltered me from too much. I have to see it for myself, crappy motels and all.

When Dottie left the bathroom, she said, "Hey, Joni! I want to thank you, by the way, for allowing me to tag along. I don't get invited to go places too often. Just remember I'm paying for gas, 'kay?'"

Joni smiled. "Thanks, Dottie."

"Are you sure you don't wanna tag along? You look like you could use a little relaxation."

"I'm good. I guess I can't talk you out of going, can I?"

"Nope. I'm on vacation, and I'm going to have some nighttime fun."

Joni rolled her eyes, too tired to really protest. "Please be safe."

Grabbing one of the card keys, Dottie waved goodbye and walked out the door. Joni then went to the shower. After stripping, she fumbled with the nozzles for a long time. When she turned the nozzle marked *COLD*, scalding hot water blasted out against her skin. She yanked her arms back with a yell. When she figured that the nozzle had been improperly installed, she decided to try the nozzle marked *HOT* to compensate. The water just got even hotter. Turning off the hot nozzle, she played around with varying degrees of turning the cold nozzle until she finally got a temperature her skin could withstand.

Then she had to figure out how to get the water to come out of the showerhead. To this extent, she had no idea what to do. There was a little button on the wall. *Is that it?*

When she pushed it, the toilet to her right flushed.

There was a thumb-sized lever on top of the bathtub spigot. *Is that it?*

All it did was plug up the tub and prevent the water from draining.

Joni went back and forth, hating the water, hating the designers, hating this motel, hating Jackson, hating her parents, hating herself, and all the while having no clue how to take a simple shower.

Then, quite by accident, her arm brushed against the cold nozzle, turning it farther than she realized it could go. Now the nozzle was pointing up, and water burst forth from the showerhead. Unfortunately, the water was now freezing cold and pelted her bare back like a thousand tiny icicles.

Jumping out of the way, she realized her discovery and adjusted the hot nozzle as well. When she got the temperature just right again, she hopped in and thought, *Why'd they have to make that so difficult? Who the hell designed this shower system?*

The shower felt good. She washed the frustration of driving through Tennessee traffic and mountains out of her hair, scrubbed the sweat and grime off of the rest of her, and took deep breaths. As her mind began to clear, a thought came to her. *You said you were gonna write on this trip. Might as well try tonight.*

After her shower, Joni threw on a white t-shirt and pink pajama-bottoms. Dottie wasn't back yet, the alarm clock read ten, and she didn't feel like calling it quits for the night. Opening her folder of travelling notes and travel reservations, she saw that their next day's destination was a motel in Okemah, Oklahoma. She'd done enough research to know that once they hit Oklahoma, it was best to be on the lookout for gas stations whenever possible because they would eventually disappear for many miles at a time.

I'll cross that bridge when I get to it, she thought. *Alright. Time to write.*

Sitting on her bed, she opened her laptop, opened a new document, and cleared her mind. Joni stared at the blank page on her computer screen. At first, an exclamation mark appeared in her mind, but it quickly turned into a *Fuck. I got nothing.*

Images appeared in her mind. *A girl. Brunette. Athletic. Thirteen? No, fourteen. Fifteen. Yeah, fifteen. Sixteen. She gets cancer. No. Scratch that. It's cliché. Start at the beginning. Who is she? What does she want to do?*

Joni started typing some nonsense, and then erased all of it. *Start with her name. Gotta give her a name. Gotta give her a history. Okay.*

With both forefingers, she rubbed her temples and closed her eyes. A sea of faces from the lunch tables back when she was at college appeared in her mind—a mental supply box of countless names and circumstances. *Tina, the perpetually popular cheerleader. Lisa. Lisa always throws a pity party despite having everything handed to her in life. Claire, ballerina with a heart of gold. Claire, who tutors young kids when she can.*

She decided she sort of liked Claire. Now she needed something for Claire to do. *But what?*

A dozen landscapes raced through her mind. *A steam-punk dystopia? A Norwegian landscape in the middle-ages? A Japanese okiya? A lost island with dinosaurs?*

She pictured the judgmental blank face of the Blue Ghost, as she often did whenever she tried to start a new creative writing project. He was trying to stir something up about how dangerous this motel was, and maybe she would've been better off going with her parents' church friends to the beach or something.

Not tonight, man. I'm doing this.

The Blue Ghost wouldn't be ignored. *What about the mummy story?*

Joni shut it out, not wanting to give him any more attention. *Not tonight. Not tonight.*

Joni decided that she needed an extra dose of literary inspiration. *I need Cate.*

After typing in the motel's internet password, she went online and found an old creative writing conference video that Cate Marlington had hosted some years earlier. Set up as a Q&A, audience members would ask Cate for advice on various issues facing inexperienced writers, and Joni felt comforted watching this video every time she got stuck herself.

This'll help. She's a genius.

About four minutes into the video, someone from the audience asked Cate what they should do if they get stuck trying to figure out how to advance their story.

Pacing the stage with her microphone, Cate brushed back her curly black hair and said bluntly, "You need to allow yourself to write shit first. Just go ahead and fling as much shit as you can on paper." This led to roars of laughter from her audience. "I'm serious! I'm not saying don't plan out your outline. Obviously, do that, too. But get a draft out first before you start getting bogged down with technical details and stuff. For me, that usually comes in the form of flinging as much shit onto the page as I can. I outline, of course, but then I cram every idea, good or bad, in-between my outline. And I never look back while I'm writing it. As a result, I usually get to use even more wild and fun ideas than I'd originally intended. Think of it like painting walls in a house. You can't paint the walls of a house until you've put the walls up first. So, I put up every wall, don't think of whether it's good or not. I just get it done. Then I can go back and fix whatever isn't working. I pull back the walls until I have just the walls I need. My advice here would be don't wait for the inspiration to hit you, because by the time it does, someone else will have written your story. And someone else will have turned it into a soulless movie with three sequels on the way."

As Joni sat on the motel bed watching the conference, she thought to herself, *Pastor Greg would say that a real Christian is doing what they do for God, so everything should be perfect from the start.* She could sense the Blue Ghost at the edge of her mind screaming and throwing a tantrum as she watched this video.

"When I was finished throwing shit on the page," Cate continued, "I had about five-hundred pages of garbage. But you know what? When I went to revise, I at least had a garbage pile to sift through to find the treasures within. Got it down to about 250 pages or so in the end. And that's the point. You need something to work with before you try to revise. So before you even think about revising so much as a typo, write down the garbage first. Fix it all later. Fixing is a separate step entirely in the writing process."

Joni had read Cate's book, *One More thing Before You Die*, six years earlier when she was still a college freshman. She knew all of these ideas from Cate pretty well by now. But somehow hearing Cate herself say them in a video helped calm her mind enough to accept that she didn't have to be perfect. She didn't have to write something that would be honorable before God, which really meant something that would just please Pastor Greg or her parents.

I don't have to worry about how godly they are or aren't.

She imagined shoving the Blue Ghost into the closet, throwing in a tank of gasoline, lighting a match, and blowing him the hell up. While he evaporated into an ethereal nothingness for the night, Joni found herself distracted from the video, wondering. Wondering if Dottie was okay. Wondering why she'd ended up travelling with someone so reckless. Wondering why none of her friends had responded to her when she'd invited them to come along. Wondering if she would ever get a career that was suited to her abilities. Wondering if her friends even cared about her existence anymore.

Yawning, Joni closed her laptop, zipped up her bag, set her phone alarm to sound off at seven the next morning, turned out the lights, sprawled out on her bed, and shut her eyes. As her muscles relaxed from the day's events, she thought about what kind of story she really wanted to write about.

Maybe I can send the girl on the road like me, Joni thought. *I can write about her travelling the states, seeing the countryside.*

She pulled the blanket up to her chin and curled up onto her side.

Actually, that might be kind of boring.

The last thing she dimly remembered was the hum of the air conditioner before drifting off to sleep, wondering what time Dottie would return.

Joni was awakened by a violent banging on the door. The clock read 2:30. It was pitch-black in the room. At first her head was so fuzzy, she thought it was part of her dream. Then her eyes adjusted, her sleepiness left her, and the banging happened again.

No, this is real.

Bang. Bang. Bang.

Maybe they'll go away.

"Hey, Vince! Open up!" a man yelled. More banging.

What the hell?

Tossing the blanket aside, Joni leapt off the bed. Dottie's bed, she noticed, was still empty and perfectly made up. Looking around the room, she saw that her aunt was nowhere to be found.

Great. I get to deal with this on my own.

Joni went up to the door peephole. Peering out through the fish-eye lens, she saw a bald, twenty-something man in a white t-shirt and jeans, holding *Oh my God, is that a gun?*

"Yo, Vince! Open up, bitch! You're not gonna gyp me again. Let's go!" He banged on the door next to hers, revealing his weapon of choice in his other hand.

Oh, thank God. It's just an ice drink. Wait . . . what?

Joni continued to peer through the hole. The man was now leaning against her door, slurping his drink and rapping his knuckles on her neighbor's door. "I know you're in there, dick. Not leaving without my money."

Without warning, the man drove his fist into her door out of anger, then turned around and started kicking Vince's door. The impact of his fist had pushed the door back into her face. As she rubbed her forehead, she noticed how flimsy the lock looked.

"Get the fuck out here, dick! I'm gonna knife a bitch if you don't!"

Joni backed away from the door and ran to the bathroom. The knot in her stomach was so tight and painful that she threw up. Grabbing her phone, her breathing started coming heavily. *Oh my God. Oh my God. They were right. My parents were right. This is stupid. I never should've gone out here. What the hell was I thinking. Oh my God he said he was gonna knife someone. Is he gonna knife me? What do I do? Do I call the cops? They said never call the police unless it's a real emergency. I feel scared, God, what do I do? Does this count as an emergency? He hasn't really attacked anyone yet. What if he's joking? What if they're friends? What if this is a false alarm? But he said he'd knife someone. What if he hears me and breaks in and kills me before they get here? Oh God, what do I do!*

Tears starting to roll down her face, she accepted that she didn't know what to do. She was paralyzed by fear. She wondered where Dottie was. *Where the hell is she? Why was I so stupid? Why did I bring someone so fucking stupid? My parents were smart for abandoning her drunk ass. Maybe they're right about everything. Here I am, about to die in a strange place while she's out playing grab-ass.*

The man continued kicking Vince's door. "Open up, Vince! I'll break the window! Man, I'll break the goddamn window!"

Collecting her nerve, she inched back towards the door. She had to see. Looking out the peephole, she saw him drinking his ice drink and staring at the ground. His eyes were filled with a bored sort of anger, frowning but clearly tired.

Maybe he's high?

Joni wasn't sure what the exact symptoms for being high included. Her parents never really taught her. When she'd asked, her father unhelpfully said, "Black people."

This guy isn't black. He's white. He's bald, he's skinny, and he's white. Thanks for nothing, Dad. Fucking racist. Her phone became slippery from the sweat collecting on her palms.

Her phone.

Do I call the cops?

Another kick. "Open up! I ain't messin' around!"

Emergencies only. This has to be an emergency. Is this an emergency?

Another kick. "Gettin' real tired of your shit, Vince! Open up!"

Joni recalled a story Pastor Greg once told about a guy who jokingly called the cops, so they threw him in jail for a few days. The pastor had used it as a metaphor for why people should feel guilty praying empty prayers to God. Joni was about thirteen when he'd delivered that sermon. Even though the guilt-trip didn't stick with her, the part about being thrown in jail for wasting the cop's time did.

I can't get thrown in jail. Not here. I can't prove my parents right. This has to be the right time to call them, right? I feel threatened.

Just as she started to get out her phone, the banging stopped.

Flashing through the curtains were the familiar blue lights of a police car. Peering through the peephole, she saw the officer stop his car just outside her door. The man who'd been kicking the door turned and drank his ice drink casually, then tried to walk away. The officer approached him, led him back to the cop car, cuffed him, put him in the back, said some inaudible things, and drove off.

And that was it. Vince would not be getting knifed that night.

Joni let out a huge gasp of air, breathing heavily as she caught her breath. She didn't realize that she'd been holding it in the entire time. Feeling woozy, she stumbled back to the bathroom and threw up again. With her breath smelling foul now, she brushed her teeth and threw water in her face. As she tried to collect herself, her door opened. Spinning around, she was relieved to see it was Dottie. Then she got angry.

"Where were you!? I could've been killed just now! And you could've been killed—"

Dottie didn't seem to be paying her any attention. She moved to her suitcase.

"Well, I'm glad that problem's taken care of. You alright, kid?"

"What?"

That's when Joni noticed that not only did Dottie have her phone in hand, but she also seemed perfectly sober.

"Bubba Joe there ruined a perfectly nice evening for me, banging on the door. What an asshole! I called the cops because I didn't think I could take him."

Joni was trying to wrap her head around it all.

"Wait, so *you* called the cops?"

Dottie looked at her. "Damn right I did! When some skinhead is threatening your niece's general vicinity, what the hell else would you do?" Quickly throwing her belongings back together, she said, "Now let's get the hell outta here!"

4

It was about three-thirty in the morning when they finished packing. Once they checked out of the motel, they pulled out of the parking lot. The *Pick-Me-Up Lounge* sign was still flickering, and steady beats of bass still pulsed from within that made the car windows rattle. The sky was now a brownish purple, casting a little more light on the area, and Joni saw clearly that every small business and house within sight had barred windows, not just the ones in the immediate area. There was a stationary train with lots of colorful graffiti sitting just behind the motel.

Maybe I can write about graffiti art.

The idea didn't have time to form. She was so busy still collecting her breath and hoping to God they weren't shot at driving away that the idea quickly fizzled before reaching long-term memory.

"Wanna grab some food? Breakfast?" Dottie suggested.

"Maybe in the next town?" Joni pleaded.

"Fine by me," Dottie said.

They continued until they found I-40 again, headed west, and left Jackson behind.

They grabbed some fast-food biscuits and coffee about twenty-minutes later, took time to collect their thoughts, and continued driving. The mountains were far behind them now, and the land was getting flatter. Dottie asked to put on some music, and Joni agreed. *Maybe it'll help calm the nerves.*

Dottie put on the electric violin music from the day before. Joni tried to remember the name of the artist. "Who is this guy again?" she asked.

"Lukaas Bennett. He was a genius."

"How'd you discover him?"

Dottie thought for a moment, furrowing her brows. It seemed as if she was really exerting great mental effort over the question. For a moment, Joni thought that maybe her aunt hadn't heard her or was simply ignoring the question. Then her aunt finally said, "At an art museum. At a concert of his."

"You went to his concerts?"

"Oh yeah," Dottie said, proud to see Joni so surprised. "What's with that look?"

"You just didn't strike me as the kind of person who went to art museums."

Dottie smiled. "You didn't strike me as the sort of person who judges others before getting to know them."

Joni's face reddened. "I don't judge people."

"Maybe not intentionally, but you do in ways you probably don't realize."

"How did I judge someone before getting to know them?" Joni asked.

"Just now. You said I didn't strike you as someone who went to art museums," Dottie said. "Then again, you don't know much about me other than that I drink and go to clubs. Don't worry. You're not in trouble. I'm not mad at you for it. You weren't the one who chose to pretend I didn't exist."

"You blame my parents for it?"

"Sort of. Truthfully, I lay a lot of the blame on their crazy-ass pastor. But they share the guilt. They're adults. They ought to have known better."

With that thought, Joni felt a little bit of the burden fly away. "Well, I'm sorry. I didn't mean to judge you. I blame their church, too." As they listened to the sounds of Lukaas Bennett on the violin, Joni drove on. The rays of dawn were beginning to poke through the clouds.

Joni then said, "Okay, but the *Pick-Me-Up Lounge*? Really? I mean, weren't you afraid of getting shot or something?"

Dottie laughed. "I had a great time last night with a fellow named Gary. You want the details?"

"Oh please God, no."

"Well, I guess I should say I had a great time *until* Asshat started banging on your door. We were literally one floor right above you. But that jackass's banging could be heard everywhere."

"Yeah. He kept going on about some guy named Vince. I think he was trying to get into the neighbor's room, too." Joni didn't mention throwing up to Dottie.

"Until that point, I had some fun last night. What about you? What'd you get up to before he showed up?" Dottie asked.

Joni sighed. "I tried to do some writing. I didn't get very far, though."

"You get stuck?"

"Yeah. I just couldn't think of anything to write."

Dottie looked straight ahead out the window and appeared to be in deep thought. "What kind of stuff do you like to write?"

"Different kinds of things, I guess. I like to write fiction. Maybe fantasy stuff."

Joni debated whether she should tell Dottie what was really keeping her stuck. Dottie seemed to sense that Joni's struggles weren't limited to mere writer's block. Her aunt said, "So you're an English major who struggles with writing. Are you a perfectionist or do you worry what others will say about what you write?"

She's good.

"Maybe a little of both, but definitely the latter. As you probably guessed, it wasn't easy being a creative writer growing up in my parents' house."

Dottie lit a cigarette and cracked her window. "That doesn't surprise me. Did something happen?"

Joni thought for a moment. She'd only ever really talked about why she struggled with creative writing to Amy, but that was back in college. With Dottie, she wasn't even sure which incident to start with.

"There were several things that happened. I guess a good starting point would be Violet's seventh birthday party. I was thirteen at the time, and by that point I knew I wanted to be a writer. I loved writing and storytelling."

"What happened?"

"Violet had her birthday party and celebrated by having a sort of girl's campout in the backyard with some friends. Mom and Dad set up a big camping tent in the backyard. She had a few friends over—friends from the church—and they had a campout after the party, so Violet asked me to tell them a ghost story."

"Uh-oh," Dottie said. "I have a feeling I know where this is going."

"She knew I liked telling stories, and she thought I told really good scary ones. So later that night, I went out and told the girls a ghost story. They were all like seven, eight, nine-year-olds. I figured I'd tell them one I'd been working on for a while. I told them one about a dead girl who'd come back as a vengeful spirit and needed to kill Christians so she could regenerate and stalk the earth forever with evil."

"Oh shit!" Dottie said. "I bet that went over well with the church crowd!"

"Yeah," Joni said. "Remember that little detail for a moment. So anyway, I finish telling the story. I thought the kids really enjoyed it. They jumped a few times, so that was good. I left them, they were all laughing and chatting about whatever in their tent, so I went back inside thinking everything's cool. Well, I go inside and take a shower. When I get out of the shower, I get dressed, open the bathroom door, and there's my mom on the other side with a cell phone in her hand. She's glaring at me with, like, the eyes of death. She's giving me the death stare. I ask her 'What's wrong,' and she just holds up a finger to me, like daring me to move. Then she says, 'Yes, I'll speak to her' into her phone, and now I know I'm trouble. She sounds super-pissed. I had literally never seen her have so much anger in her eyes before. She finally hangs up and says, 'I bet you think that was real funny, don't you.'"

"Man, like an order? Not even a question?"

"Yep. I asked, 'What did I do?' She responds, 'Don't give me that! You know *exactly* what you did.' I'm not making the connection yet, so I ask her to clarify. She goes, 'Okay, your little story? It scared those kids to death. Half of them are crying, and their parents are on their way to pick them up.' I froze. I mean, I had no clue it had freaked them out that badly. I thought they loved it!"

Dottie clicked her teeth. "Yikes."

"I didn't understand what was going on. The last I'd seen of them, Violet and her friends were laughing and seemed to be having a good time. Now they were going home because I'd traumatized them? It didn't make any sense. I mean, I loved stories with monsters and ghosts, so I didn't think it'd be a huge problem. But anyway, then my mom goes, 'Congratulations, Joni. You ruined your sister's birthday party.' So I started arguing with her. I told her I thought they enjoyed it, but she countered with, 'Yeah? What was the part about killing Christians? Did you ever stop to think that maybe that wasn't appropriate for them?' We just argued for a bit. And then the parents came and took the kids home. Violet was pissed. And I wish I could say that was the end of it."

Dottie chuckled. "I kinda wish I could've seen Laura's face, now. Sorry. Continue."

"A few days later after the church service, Pastor Greg asked to see me in his office. He asked me about the story, the camp-out, and why I did it. I mean, I thought I was just telling a ghost story for entertainment. But then he said something to the effect of, 'Ghost stories aren't the best way to honor God, and maybe instead of frightening the girls with ghosts, you should've told them about Jesus.' Something like that. 'Your writing can be a gift,' he said, 'but you've got to hone it, sharpen it up for God. Otherwise, it's a wasted gift. And remember that you should be glorifying Him in *all* things you do, not just your writing.' I mean, something in the way he said that last part really struck fear in me. Like anything I did or didn't do, it was disappointing to God. So I left feeling guilty, and not just for ruining Violet's birthday party. That sense of always failing to glorify God just followed me. No matter what I did, or how well I tried, God was disappointed in me. And this is really where the second story comes in."

Dottie didn't say anything but continued to look and listen as Joni explained. The more Joni spoke, the more comfortable she felt telling Dottie her story.

It's nice to be listened to.

"There was that twinge of shame for ruining Violet's birthday party, but I found a way to convince myself that maybe it was just because I had the wrong audience. So I continued writing more secretly. I mean, writing is what I wanted to do. I knew that from a young age. Didn't mean I had to share it with them. At that point, I didn't really make the connection that they wanted me to not write scary stories. I just figured they didn't want me sharing it with my sister or any church people. After the birthday incident, I was fine with that."

"So you kept writing?" Dottie asked.

"Yes, I did. Around that time, I was working on a horror novel about a group of people unleashing a flesh-eating mummy who couldn't be destroyed by man-made weapons. No guns, no knives! I got pretty far, too. Fifteen chapters and 175 pages. Only had about five chapters left to go. This was just a few months after the ghost story incident, too. I was nearing the end of the mummy story when, one day after church, I went over to my computer and discovered that the entire manuscript had been deleted."

"Oh that sucks," Dottie said.

"I panicked. I scanned every inch of my hard drive. I learned how to search for hidden folders. I even looked up older versions of the story on floppy disks—yeah, remember those?—only to discover that those, too, had been wiped clean. It was as if every non-school or church-related thing I'd ever written had been wiped from existence. So I went downstairs to ask Violet or someone about it. But when I went downstairs, I found my parents with the youth leader in our living room sitting on the couch."

"The youth leader?" Dottie asked. "Were they going to exorcise you?"

"Kind of!" Joni said. "I walk in the living room and the youth leader was all smiles and waving his Bible and says in that fake-welcoming tone, 'Hey, Joni! Your parents and I were just talking about you.' Dad just goes, 'Sit down, Joni,' and now I know I'm in for some sort of lecture. He looked upset, just rubbing his temples and looking everywhere in the room but at me. Mom wasn't smiling either. But since I had to be obedient, I went into the living room and sat."

Joni enjoyed being listened to so much that she'd almost forgot how painful this memory was for her. But now that she was here, she slowed down her voice, not eager to recount it. *She's listened this far. May as well tell her.*

"Then the youth leader guy—I forget his name—starts in on me. He goes, 'Joni, your parents are very concerned about you. They saw your story about the mummy and something about a curse? Lots of dark stuff in it, you know! Lots of witchcraft and magic!' Now, I'm more upset at this point because all my work is missing. I'm not even thinking about holiness or whatever at this point, so I asked if they knew where my story was. My mom then says, 'We deleted your story.'"

Dottie's eyes widened. "Oh, that's fucked up."

"I can't tell you how angry that made me. I mean, I worked my ass off on that story, and they erased it just like that." Joni snapped her fingers for emphasis. "But then Mom continued. She goes, 'Violet told us about your story, Joni. So we investigated. She told us about it, how you had curses? And human sacrifices? It didn't sound good, but we wanted to give you the benefit of the doubt. And so we saw it. We read some of it for ourselves and, you know, I just couldn't believe . . .' Something like that. The youth leader jumped in to lecture me. 'Joni, your parents shared the story with us, and frankly, it was very disturbing. Do you know what the *occult* is? The occult involves magic stuff, you know? Witchcraft, sorcery, voodoo, and in your case, curses, hexes, resurrection of sinners, and human sacrifices. Now Joni, the Bible tells us that God condemns such practices. We're also told that the world will know us by our fruits. That is, the works we create and our actions, as well. Now Joni, you believe in God, don't you?'

"By this point, I kinda knew what was coming. As it turned out, they'd deleted all of my stories. Not just the mummy one, but everything. I had one with a lighthouse being invaded by zombies that was kind of far along, too. I had a lot of other stories in various stages of completion. Probably about four years of work. Gone. But they were gonna push this idea that I was the one who'd done wrong. I was the one who'd disobeyed God.

"So they continued. The youth guy said, 'Now think about what you put in that story. You put things in there—the resurrections, the human sacrifices, the curses—you put things in there that God calls abominations, right? So now think about that. You were writing about things that God hates, Joni. You understand, right? He *hates* this stuff. You need to think about how that might reflect on God. What it tells the world about Him. See, if you're writing about it, it tells the world that He's okay with it, and the Bible tells us He's not. Do you understand what I'm saying?'

"'You claim to be a Christian,' Dad jumps in, 'but yet you're putting devil stuff in what you write. You are bringing the devil into my home, and I will not allow it.' I'm shook at this point, Dottie. The youth guy, probably seeing the fear and shock in my face, continued. He said, 'You know, Joni, you don't have to look at this as bad. This is a good thing! You're learning, and you've just gained wisdom. Now you're a little wiser! You're at least aware that you disobeyed God. All you have to do now is pray for forgiveness and you know, it might hurt, but look at it this way. You like to write, so why not write stories for God? Write stories that show his goodness, not stories about the devil or devils.'"

"God, what an ass. I bet he had a punchable face. So he said all that?" Dottie asked.

"More or less. That was the gist of it from what I can remember," Joni said. "But it was a lot to take at once. I was still angry and hurt that my parents had erased all my work. I was horrified that they were now acting like I'd engaged in some unholy act by writing. But . . ."

Joni hesitated. This was the part of the story she was deeply ashamed of. She imagined the Blue Ghost sitting in the back with arms folded, not saying anything but daring her to question what her parents and the youth leader did next. Daring her to tell Dottie what had happened as if it hadn't been the correct thing to do.

No. I don't care. She asked, so here goes.

"It took me a moment to realize that this wasn't just a meeting with the youth leader to reprimand me. No, they were actually telling me to repent. Right then and there. In front of them. They wanted me to pray to God and ask forgiveness for writing scary stories. I tried arguing with them, said all the magic stuff was the bad guys doing it. The good guys weren't bad. But they didn't care. Mom and Dad said that if I didn't repent right then and there, they'd take my computer away. The asshole youth leader goads them on. He said, 'Very good thinking, Tim. Stay with her. Stay on it. If you let one sin go, it'll lead to another, and another. Best stop her now and set her on the straight path.'"

"I wish I could go back in time and punch this youth leader guy in the face," Dottie said.

"Me too," Joni said. "I was furious. I was hurt. I couldn't believe my parents were doing this to me. But I didn't see a way out, so I said, 'Okay, I'm sorry.' But Mom then said, 'Not to us. To God.'"

Joni swallowed back some tears as the pain and humiliation came back.

"I had three sets of adult eyes boring into me, pressuring me to actually pray to God. I didn't want to, but it was so uncomfortable. So I said a quick silent prayer to myself, asked for forgiveness for writing occult-themed stories. When I finished, I told them. 'There. I prayed. I'm sorry.' Dad then says, 'So we can hear you, Joni.' So I prayed again out loud. 'Dear God, I'm sorry I wrote about witchcraft. I won't do it again.' Then Mom says, 'Say it like you mean it.' Dottie . . . I must've said that prayer out loud five or six times before they were finally satisfied. I was on my knees literally weeping. I'd never felt so humiliated before. And then there was the following Sunday!"

"Jesus, there's more?" Dottie said. "Oh God, child. I'm so sorry this happened to you."

"At church," Joni said, "when I went to youth group, the kids refused to sit with me. One kid—I think his name was Norman—told me that his parents thought I was a bad influence now, and so he couldn't talk to me. When we got to the big service, I found out that my parents had shared my story with the deacons. Mr. Northen—you know, the guy who freaked out about my scandalous yellow sandals—came up and started calling me a witch and told my dad to keep me on a leash or some shit like that. Another deacon named Derek came up and told my parents to keep an eye on what I was reading. He went on about secular literature giving me bad ideas. And then he says, 'And you know, it's not like it's any different from when we were growing up. We read Satanic books too, like *The Wizard of Oz*. It had the Occult and devilish stuff, too, but we just didn't have the internet to let us know these things back then.' He said it without a trace of irony, too."

Dottie burst into laughter. "Because the internet is always so accurate!"

"Yeah, he said the quiet part out loud."

"Oh man. Okay, so why did your parents send your manuscript to the deacons?"

"That's just what they did. They probably wanted some spiritual guidance from the church leaders or something. Pastor Greg is always good about preaching that: seek accountability from God-ordained leaders, but really it was just giving that church an extra pathway into your personal life. So yeah, while they gave my parents the advice to bully me into begging for forgiveness for nothing, they also got a sneak preview into the private lives of the Arables."

Dottie looked overwhelmed by this story. She stared straight ahead with her mouth open in shock, as if trying to think of the right thing to say. Finally, her aunt said, "I'm really sorry you experienced this. How did it make you feel? All that weird shit?"

"I felt betrayed. Plain and simple. But I also felt that God wanted me to obey my authority figures, so I just had to comply and go along with it. Questioning it was tantamount to questioning God himself, and I didn't wanna go to Hell. The worst part of all was that all my hard work was gone, and now . . ." Joni hesitated again.

She'll probably think I'm crazy.

Joni sighed. "Now I have a crippling anxiety every time I try to write something new. I felt so thoroughly betrayed by everyone, and yet I couldn't say anything. They'd associated my work with devil-worship and threatened that my writing wasn't Christian enough and therefore I might not really be a Christian and was going to Hell. I didn't want to go to Hell, so I panicked. Every time I tried to write, my creativity was stifled. I didn't want to offend God, but it felt like anytime I had a burst of creativity, God was ready to smite me down and send me to Hell. I just kept having this image of—do you remember those old religious comic book tracts? They were, like, small and had freaky illustrations of people sinning and going to Hell?"

Dottie thought for a moment. "Oh, yeah. I remember those. You still see them every now and then stuck behind a can of peaches at the grocery store. Yeah, those were creepy. I didn't like those."

"They were very creepy. The church used to have a giant magazine rack filled with them. I remember reading a lot of them as a teenager because of some sick, twisted idea that I wasn't Christian enough unless I was in a state of constant panic for my soul. Anyway, a lot of them ended with the sinner being sent to Hell by God who always looked like this faceless blue ghost. Over the years, as I continued to try to write creative fiction stuff, I just kept feeling this shame, this guilt that whatever I did, there'd be this faceless Blue Ghost waiting to judge me at the end of it all. And no matter how many times I begged for forgiveness, no matter how many times I prayed the Sinner's Prayer, it just keeps feeling like it will never be good enough, and this Blue Ghost will be waiting for me ready to yell, 'Depart from me, ye cursed!' and down to the flames I go."

"But didn't you have to write in college?"

"Essays, sure. But I'm talking about creative writing. Like creative fiction stories."

Dottie looked a little confused. "Are you actually seeing a blue ghost thing?"

"No, not literally. It's more like . . . it's my anxiety about spiritual damnation, but I'd read somewhere that assigning a name or a face to your anxiety can help you cope with it."

"Did assigning your anxiety the image of a blue ghost from creepy religious tracts help?"

"Not especially, but it seems better than not doing that."

For a while, Dottie said nothing. There was the hum of the vehicle as it pressed on, but otherwise things were quiet. Traffic was beginning to pick up, but it was still really early in the morning. Joni wondered if she had revealed too much and weirded her aunt out. She imagined the Blue Ghost screaming at her for recounting this story as the traumatic experience it was and not as the enlightening moment of devotion that her parents imagined it to have been.

Finally, Dottie said, "I'm sorry you had to go through that. That was a real shitty thing for Tim and Laura to do." Dottie looked as if she wanted to say more but decided not to.

"Thank you," Joni said. After that, Dottie pulled out her pillow and reclined her seat back. "I need to take a nap. I didn't really get any sleep."

"Alright."

The sun was higher now, and the traffic was getting thicker. Before long they were passing through Memphis. Buildings on all sides, there didn't seem to be as many semi-trucks as there had been earlier. *I think the general color of this town is blue*, Joni thought to herself.

"Hey Dottie, we're in Memphis."

Her aunt sleepily looked up from her pillow. "Hot damn, we are. Lukaas recorded his last album here."

"Yeah?"

"Yep."

Just above the line of skyscrapers, Joni saw the metal arches of the suspension bridge. As they drove towards it, the vast Mississippi River came into sight. It was much larger than she had expected it to be, stretching nearly half a mile wide at this point. The water was blue and gray under this sky. As they crossed, Joni felt a moment of euphoric honor.

"Dottie, this is the same river Huckleberry Finn and Jim crossed."

Dottie cocked her head to the side. "Who the hell are they?"

Joni smiled. "Characters in Mark Twain's novel *The Adventures of Huckleberry Finn*."

Dottie waved her hand in defeat. "Well, no shit. Obviously. It's just you spoke about them like they were real people."

Underneath was nothing but water. Overhead were clouds and sky. Home was behind her. Ahead would be either fear and doubt or opportunity. Joni hoped for the latter.

5

As soon as they crossed the bridge, the landscape changed completely. Gone were the rolling hills and tall buildings of Tennessee. They were now replaced by the distinctly green and mild flatness of Arkansas. The flat grasslands were decorated on either side by a few trees, some houses, and the occasional sign. There were a few other drivers keeping pace with them now.

"It's like even the landscape wants to leave the southeast behind," Joni said.

Okay, we made it through the mountains. Nothing but flat land coasting from here on out! Well, maybe until we get to Colorado, but it's okay, she thought.

A while later, they pulled over for gas and a restroom break. They were in no hurry since they had left so early in the morning. When Joni had originally planned out the trip, she measured about seven to nine-hour trips for each day. Today, they would reach Okemah, Oklahoma. Tomorrow, they'd reach Santa Rosa, New Mexico, which was supposed to have an old, abandoned church she wanted to visit. The day after that, they'd reach Flagstaff, Arizona. Finally, on the fifth day of their trip, they'd reach the Grand Canyon Village where they would stay for a day and a half before heading on. The plan was to curve back on a more northern route to see the historic Horseshoe Bend, a canyon-like formation carved in the shape of a horseshoe by the Colorado River. From there, the route would continue back through Colorado, Kansas, Missouri, Illinois, and on until they finally made it back home.

Dottie used the bathroom as Joni pumped the gas. Flies buzzed around her head. The heat was intense, and humidity fogged up her sunglasses. Taking them off, she wiped a bead of sweat trailing down her forehead. A gentle wind was the only reprieve from the heat.

Joni finished pumping the gas and closed the hatch. Yawning, she realized that she'd only had about three hours of sleep, and she felt incredibly tired. She went inside the gas station and bought a soda hoping the caffeine would help. When she got back to the car, Dottie still wasn't back. Joni put the drink in her cupholder and went to the trunk. Opening one cooler, she grabbed a gummy fruit-pouch and two packages of salted crackers. In the other cooler, she grabbed a bottle of water for her aunt. Between the two coolers were her aunt's green suitcase and blue messenger-bag.

She looked over the top of the car to check for Dottie. Seeing that her aunt was nowhere to be seen, she quickly looked in the blue messenger-bag. She saw that it was now empty, so she opened the suitcase. The smell of old strawberries greeted her nose. Sitting on top of piles of clothes were the half-empty bottles of liquor and flasks of whiskey.

Okay, we need to do something about this.

Joni had heard horror stories of how unforgiving the police could be when catching drivers with open liquor in their car. She remembered hearing that it was illegal to have it even in the trunk. She started to grab the containers to toss them when her aunt came strolling out of the gas station. Setting them back down and quickly zipping back up the suitcase, Joni decided she'd have to confront her aunt about it. She headed back to the driver's seat.

This just won't do.

"How many miles left?" Joni asked Dottie as her aunt fastened her seatbelt.

"Two-hundred and forty-four miles," Dottie said, looking at the GPS. "About three and a half hours if we don't stop. We should be there around two or so."

"That's better than seven," Joni said.

"These for me?" Dottie said, pointing to the bottled water and extra crackers.

"Yes."

"Thank you!" Dottie said, taking the cap off the water and drinking. Joni couldn't think of a way to bring up the alcohol without admitting that she'd snuck a peek in her aunt's suitcase. *Okay, time for some reverse psychology.*

"Unless we stop for drinks, better get used to water," Joni said. "It's all I brought for the trip."

Dottie laughed, then took another drink of the water. After a curiously loud gulp, her aunt said, "I got stronger stuff in the trunk. Life's not so desperate yet."

Joni looked at Dottie. Her hand was on the gear lever, but she kept it in park. "Yeah, but we can't drink in the car. We can't even open them in the car."

A little heavy-handed, but that's the point.

Dottie looked at Joni with a curious glance. Leaning towards Joni on the arm rest, Dottie said, "Well, they're in the trunk, so we're good."

"You do know it's illegal to have open bottles in the trunk, right?" Joni said.

Dottie raised a skeptical eyebrow. "No, most states are okay if it's in the trunk."

"That's not what I was taught."

"I think we've established your education about the road was uneven at best," Dottie laughed. "Just drive the speed limit, don't swerve, use your turn signal, don't hit anyone, and you'll be fine."

"But what if they have a random license check down the road?" Joni said, trying not to sound desperate. The last thing she wanted to do was tick off her road companion so early in the journey. "If we get caught, I'm the one who gets in trouble."

"They won't do that," her aunt protested with a crooked smile on her face. "We got nothing but desert and grasslands ahead of us! Besides, it's seventy through here. They're only gonna pull the people going slow-as-hell or speeding. You typically fall between the two of those, so you're good."

Goddamn it. Okay, let's do this.

Joni sighed in exasperation. "Dottie. Can you please dispose of those bottles? I don't want to risk it, and I don't feel comfortable with open liquor in the car."

Dottie looked at Joni and sat back as if making an approval of something. To Joni's astonishment, Dottie said simply, "Okay. Your car, your rules. I'll pour 'em out. For the record, I think you're overreacting to nothing, but I'll pour them out if it makes you feel better."

Dottie got out of the car as Joni popped the trunk open. She watched as Dottie made a huge show of lifting the bottles in question, flittering over to the gas station trash can, and gracefully dropping them into the bin as if they were burning matches. She then pulled out the flasks and poured them in the trash as well.

After shutting the trunk and returning to her seat, Dottie said, "I put the flasks in my suitcase. If we stop at a fine restaurant, please do me the courtesy of not freaking out if I order some wine."

"Thank you," Joni said. Maybe it was the years of being too afraid to ask for much out of fear that it would somehow displease God, but Joni felt good at how simply this conflict had been resolved.

The road stretched on. The sun was now high, and clouds dotted the blue sky. The air conditioner was on full blast. Joni occasionally sipped her soda while Dottie munched on crackers. Her aunt's steady crunching added a much-needed break from the hum of the tires on the bumpy road beneath them.

Having gotten the weight of the Blue Ghost off her chest, Joni thought that maybe she could get her aunt to reveal more of what happened between her and the family.

"So, I was wondering. What happened between you and my parents? Why'd they disown you?"

Amidst the sound of chewing crackers, Joni heard what she thought was her aunt giving a low chuckle. When Dottie finished chewing her crackers, she said, "How is Laura these days?"

She definitely doesn't want to talk about it.

Joni shrugged. "I mean, Mom's good, I guess. I don't really see her much these days. I don't live with them anymore."

"On your own, huh?"

"Yep. I talk to them every now and then. And I'll be seeing them shortly after we get back. Violet's party."

"Wow. Time flies," Dottie said. "I remember when Laura gave birth to you. They stopped talking to me by the time Violet was born. You were born in '90, right?"

"1989. April 11."

"I got a call from Laura in the middle of the night. No, wait, not Laura. Your dad. Tim. Tim called. Said she was in the delivery room. You didn't want to leave the womb until after I got there. You were an early-morning baby."

Joni laughed. "I guess I just liked the comforts of the womb."

"Yeah! And you were born, and your mom and dad were crying and hugging. Everybody was proud of them. Your Grandma Sue and Grandpa Dale were there, and your grandpa on your dad's side."

Just then a semi-truck appeared in Joni's rearview mirror, blaring horns and speeding way faster than seventy. Its grill was decked-out with the visage of bared fangs. Joni, going sixty-eight in the slow-as-hell lane, waited for him to pass her. As he did so, she saw that the right side of his cargo trailer had a massive dent in its side as if from some earlier collision.

When it bull-dozed its way in front of her without a turn signal, Joni saw the most bizarre graphic she'd ever seen on a semi-truck. Its cargo doors were painted with a black outline of a stern-looking caricature of a man pointing and glaring at her. Underneath the drawing of the man were the words *HAVE YOU FOUND GOD YET?*

Attached to the trailer hitch beneath that was a metallic testicles accessory dangling beside a mud flap with a sticker that depicted the silhouette of a naked woman. A Confederate flag bumper sticker was right beside the Tennessee license plate.

"Wow," Joni said. "I thought we were out of South Carolina?"

"Yeah, but we're not out of the south yet. I expect we'll see a lot more Confederate chode gobblers," Dottie said. The truck driver sped off down the road, disappearing into the traffic ahead.

"I love how he's telling me to find God while rocking the metal balls and naked bimbo on the back of his truck," Dottie said.

"And promoting slavery," Joni added.

Dottie pulled out her phone. "I'm taking a picture. Dolores'll get a kick outta this!"

"Who's Dolores?" Joni asked.

"She's my neighbor. We go for drinks all the time. That and the occasional graffiti binge whenever one of us has a bad break up with someone."

I have no comment for that. Please ask a question before my silence makes the car ride awkward.

"You got a special friend?" Dottie asked.

Thank you for your compliance. Happy to do business with you.

"Um, not really. I used to. She's married now. Haven't really spoken to her in a while."

"No, no. A boyfriend."

Hmm, I don't know if we should go there.

"Oh. No. Uh, haven't really found someone yet."

"Ah," Dottie said, smiling mischievously. "So we'll need to get you hooked up with some western boy."

Joni laughed. "No thanks. I'm good."

"You have any boyfriends in college?"

"Two. Didn't work out."

"Why's that?"

"Well," Joni began, "it's complicated."

"Oh, you mean there's another story here?" Dottie said.

"Yeah, there is. I went to a Christian university, so of course it's gonna be a story! First one was just a dud, a freshman thing. Lasted maybe two weeks. The second one, though. That's the story. I was a sophomore studying English. He was a junior studying Christian Ministry. It just seemed like something my parents would go for."

"Wait a minute, that's a thing you can major in? Christian Ministry?"

Joni nodded. "It is when you're at a Christian liberal-arts school. How do you think people become pastors?"

"Didn't realize it required a college degree, I guess. So what happened?" Dottie inquired.

There was no hint of mockery or contempt in Dottie's question, just curiosity. Joni knew this, but answering it would require her to admit to one of the things that started snowballing her change of opinions on the church.

"It's complicated. We were just on different paths in life."

Dottie pulled down her sunglasses and stared at Joni. "Joni, fast-as-fuck or slow-as-hell. C'mon. We got all day. Let's talk about something."

Joni sighed. "Alright."

Well, she did throw out the bottles when I asked her.

"His name was John. I started dating him because he was training to become a pastor. I figured that if I ended up with a guy like him, my parents would support it."

"Was that important to you?" Dottie asked.

"Kind of," Joni said. "Remember, I was in that mindset that everything, including relationships, had to be honorable to God. At the time, I thought parental approval went hand-in-hand with that. A pastor-in-training just seemed like the way to go. So we dated for about three months. It was nice at first, I guess. We went out and stuff. But issues started to show, and I got real nervous. The main problem was he was just looking for a trophy wife. There I was, having just barely grasped the concept of writing a coherent essay, and all he kept talking about was getting married and having lots of children to raise and becoming a pastor and following God's will for our lives. He already had like three Bible studies he was leading and expected me to attend all of them with him. It was all way too much and way too fast for me. I knew I wasn't ready for any of that. Oh, and we made out a lot. Like, seriously, a lot."

Dottie chuckled, seemingly unsurprised. "I'd have figured they'd have an issue with those kinds of shenanigans."

Joni nodded. "You'd think. But for all his Bible study talk about how everybody needs to be abstinent and maintain their purity, he certainly had no problem making out with me and putting his hands everywhere. Don't get me wrong. It was consensual. We never, like, you know . . ." Joni wasn't sure if she was oversharing or not, but it felt good to get this off her chest.

"Banged?" Dottie said.

"Yeah, no. We never had full-on sex, but what about all that purity stuff? Every time we made out, all I could think about was if this was a sin or not. Are we doing something wrong? Was I leading him into temptation? Honestly, it wasn't fun for me. I just kept feeling shame. Like God was mad at me for not staying utterly pure."

"You felt you should've been waiting for marriage?"

"At the time," Joni said. "Just to be clear, I don't feel that way now, but at the time, that's what I thought I was supposed to be doing. Not just abstaining from sex, but anything physical. I felt like a hypocrite who preached purity by day but made out with John by night, and I definitely didn't feel ready to get married and have kids. Shit, I still don't feel that way. So I tried talking to him about how I felt. How I didn't feel ready for the things he wanted, how everything felt like it was moving too fast, how I felt constant shame just for making out. But any time I brought up my feelings on it, he just shrugged and would say, 'It's fine. We're not going too far.' And that was that. He didn't seem to care that I was having a moral dilemma over it. He didn't see the hypocrisy in what he preached. He knew what he wanted, and my feelings didn't matter to him. He was entitled. He was arrogant. He was basically a young Pastor Greg."

"Damn," Dottie said. "That's not good. So, okay, you were in college by now. And you were still having these existential worries? Like were they the same as the ones you had when your parents destroyed your writings?"

"Yes, but magnified times a hundred. They'd raised me with such a one-path mindset that now that I was on my own, it felt more important than ever that I maintain the values they'd raised me with. I was too scared to question any of it because of the fear of God, even though I knew it was a bad relationship. John didn't really care about anything I was interested in or what I wanted to do. I wanted to be a writer, but he seemed more interested in showing me off to his friends than learning about what I wanted to write. I didn't want to become some trophy wife with a guy who barely seemed to notice anything about me other than my boobs."

Vivid yellow-green bushes zipped past on either side of them as they continued down the road. Tucked away beyond the shrubs and trees were some trailers and small, old homes. "I decided that I no longer wanted that life."

"So you broke up with him?" Dottie said.

"As gently as I could. We were on the library steps one day. I told him how I thought we were two different people on totally different paths in life. He wanted to be a pastor with a wife, and I didn't want that. I even added 'You're a nice guy' to soften the blow."

Dottie nodded. "That didn't do the trick?"

Joni held up a hand. "Oh, it went downhill really fast from there."

"Ugh," Dottie said.

"For all my niceties, John—the pastor-in-training—started screaming at me. He started shouting how this would affect his reputation. Said I was a slut for leading him on and probably slept with guys behind his back. He started throwing his backpack and books out of rage." Seeing Dottie's concern out of the corner of her eye, she added, "Don't worry. Not at me. But real husband material, right? He's freaking me out, so I grabbed my backpack, said, 'See ya,' and was outta that circle. And then his bible study friends swooped in."

"Oh no," Dottie said.

"Yep. Almost immediately after I broke up with John, the rest of the ministry students started cornering me, like at lunch or after class, trying to convince me to take him back, that I wasn't praying enough about it. They kept calling me, leaving text messages wanting to know why I broke up with him and if I'd get back with him. He kept texting, too. Kept demanding an explanation, even though I'd already told him the reasons. His buddies kept hounding me. It was like I broke up with the guy! I shouldn't have to justify that to these clowns! When they finally realized I wasn't going to cave, they started giving me the cold shoulder and refused to talk to me. Friendships were over. If they ever existed in the first place. But guess what? It got even worse!"

"Jesus," Dottie said. "Worse?"

"They started spreading rumors that I'd cheated on John. They really ran my reputation into the ground with a lot of our mutual friends. It got so bad that a few days later, one of the ministry counselors called me into his office to try and gauge what had happened. Not to see if I was okay, but to see if I'd really been sleeping around, why his star pastor-in-training was so depressed and suddenly lacking a potential wife, and if I had prayed about it to see what God wanted for my love life."

"Christ, what an ass," Dottie said.

Joni was relieved. She felt certain that if she ever told this story to her parents, they would have repeatedly corrected her on her own actions and choices. They would have put the blame on her: *Shouldn't have been making out with him. Shouldn't have been leading him on into temptation. What were you wearing at the time? Could your tone have set him off?* Those would have been their concerns. But not Dottie. Dottie was listening, and Dottie didn't seem too surprised to hear how the story was playing out.

"I was like, 'Trust me, buddy. I've been praying more than you know!' There I was, having a spiritual crisis of faith, and now this authority figure was prying into my personal life and wondering why I wasn't about to submit to some arrogant prick. Like, obviously I didn't, but even if I had cheated on John, that wouldn't be this asshole's business. The worst thing about it, though, was that I didn't know how to respond. At that point, everything I'd been taught suggested that I'd had no right to break up with John. And yet, common sense said I had to. I didn't want to be a pastor's wife. I didn't want to be John's wife. That should've been enough, but this counselor kept bringing up the Bible and God's expectations for women and submitting to husbands and . . . God, he just would not leave it alone. In the end, he told me to pray about it."

"That meant *reconsider* it," Dottie said.

"Yep," Joni said. "Screw my feelings. It was whatever John wanted, because he was the man with God on his side. I had to respect it because I was supposed to be the lowly, submissive woman. You know, come to think of it, this was the same counselor who told one of my friends to get married after she and her boyfriend had sex."

Dottie almost spit out her drink. "Wait, what?"

"Yeah! One of my college friends, Amy, had sex with her boyfriend. They went to this counselor douche feeling all guilty about it, and his advice to them was basically, 'Get married as quickly as possible.' So they did. They got married like two weeks later."

Dottie laughed. "What, like before God found out or something?"

Joni laughed. "Yeah, I don't know! It was messed up."

"That's fucked up, Joni. How the hell was this guy a licensed counselor?"

"For real. I think he went on about something like it being better to unite as one in matrimony than engaging in the sins of the flesh, but what the hell? This guy had no business getting in on people's personal relationships like that!"

"Did you report the counselor?"

"What?"

"Did you report him? To like a human resources person, or whatever they have in college."

Joni shook her head. "No. Remember, questioning authority and deciding to make my own decisions was all new to me. I didn't know necessarily at that time that this counselor had no right to pry into my personal life like that. I'd been raised to always submit to authority figures in a Christian setting. I saw him as just trying to help, but for the first time, I really hated his advice. I didn't know I could report him. Even if I did, I didn't know who to go to. I'd never learned that."

"Was your school accredited?"

"Somehow, yes."

"That's really messed up, Joni."

"Hell yeah, it's messed up! Think of how many other girls were— hell, *are*—in that position. Can't stand up for themselves because they've been told it's a sin and God will punish them with Hell for disobedience. It was a really difficult time for me. The ministry students and John kept spreading the lie about me cheating on him."

"This Christian Ministry group sounds like a real cult."

"It was," Joni said, seeing some hills and forests starting to spring up again along the highway. "They had each other's backs whenever one of them did something morally reprehensible. Seeing that kind of moral hypocrisy justified by groupthink up close is what finally got me to question the whole idea of church itself. I mean, I'd been questioning the church we went to growing up for a while by then, but this was the make-or-break point, the moment when I realized the sad truth of it all. I actually went and spoke to some of the counselors at Elohim Creation Salvation about the break-up not long after, and they gave me basically the same shtick. They even went further and asked about how I was dressing."

"So no help there, either," Dottie said.

"None. It felt like a reality wake-up call. Christianity, fundamentalism, whatever we're gonna call it, had enabled John's behavior and his buddies' behavior towards me. I started seeing John as basically a young version of Pastor Greg. Pastor Greg is entitled, controlling, knows when to use the guilt-trip, and can simultaneously say he is blessed while his critics are evil. With Greg's followers, there is no correcting him. If you call him or anyone like him out—privileged dudes in a place of Godly leadership—then they retaliate. It's like, 'Everyone else is a lustful sinner, but I'm a pastor, or a pastor-in-training. I'm good.' He has God in his life, so some bending of the rules is okay. For him. Nobody else. His followers do the heavy-lifting and harassment for him. I was now seeing it clearly in John."

"And you recognized that in your home church?" Dottie said.

"I did. Between that time Greg talked down to me in his office and how the church reacted when a former member wrote an article criticizing the church, I realized there were two sets of rules at play. It was the same now with John. I realized that my entire upbringing had been one that valued my submission and sacrifice, not me as a human being. I stopped going to church not long after that. I stopped going home as frequently just to avoid having to go back to my parent's church. I questioned the church. I questioned religion. I questioned God's existence. It was like a domino effect. Once one piece fell, the rest of it started to crumble. And I just started feeling like . . . I don't know. The seams that covered the hypocrisy started to unravel, and I felt like I was the only one who could see it. I couldn't talk to my parents about it because they'd never understand what I was going through. Hell, they'd probably disown me for talking like this. Questioning the ethics of the church is not something on their radar. Never has been. Let alone the bigger question of whether God is even real or if the whole thing is just a social construct meant to control people. And I didn't want to burden them with my feelings."

"How did you convince them that you couldn't go back to their church without telling them the truth?" Dottie asked.

"During a college semester, it was easier. I just pretended that I was going to other churches. During the summers at home, I was stuck and had no choice really. By my senior year, I was able to get by under the guise that I had a lot of life changes, like moving out and getting a job and such."

Dottie scratched her arm, looking ahead. "That must really suck, Joni. Everyone should be able to talk to their parents."

"Kinda hard when you just get Pastor Greg's mouthpieces. That's all they are now: total devotees of Pastor Greg. Pastor Greg knows all and is never wrong. Pastor Greg's views aren't that different from John's. And I kinda realized that I needed to figure it all out on my own."

"So," Dottie said, "what about now? Where do you stand on the whole issue of God?"

"What do you mean?"

"Do you believe in God? Do you think it's all made up?"

Joni felt a wave of panic come over her, but almost as suddenly it vanished. She knew the correct answer if she were answering her parents or someone from their church. But somehow not knowing Dottie's stance on the issue made it easier to be herself and speak what she truly felt. For once, the Blue Ghost seemed muted and unable to monitor her response with a checklist for Hell-bound sinners.

"I . . . I just don't know. I'd like to think God's real. I'd like to think Jesus died and saved us from some great separation from God. But each day it seems less and less likely. I just don't know. And honestly, I'm okay not knowing."

"Okay, so sort of like an agnostic Christian?"

Joni shrugged. "I guess. I hadn't really thought of a label for it. A few years ago, admitting that would have freaked me out. But that sounds about right for me."

"But you feel sure that's not something your parents would be happy to hear? That you have some agnostic leanings?"

"No, definitely not. They would not be happy about that at all."

Dottie lit another cigarette. Cracking her window, she said, "Joni, you've told me quite a bit about yourself today. You've got a common thread in all your stories. How your parents destroyed your stories because they were ungodly. How your college harassed you for turning down this guy. How you've always been expected to act holy when no one else seemed to care about what that actually means. Well you know what? Have you ever tried not giving a fuck what any of them expect you to do?"

"I think so."

"No, no, no. I mean, really, actively do what Joni wants to do. And *only* what Joni wants to do."

"This trip is kinda like that. My parents were against the idea of me inviting you, but I did it anyway."

"And how'd that make you feel? Making that decision for yourself, consequences be damned?"

"I felt good."

"Yeah. You need to chase that feeling more. Whenever you want to write, you write whatever you fucking feel like writing. Whenever that blue whatever . . . what was it?"

"The Blue Ghost."

"Yeah, whenever you get that feeling of that Blue Ghost, just say the hell with him. He's not real. He's just some fucked up concept of guilt set up for you by all these assholes in your life who clearly think nothing of their own guilt but love using yours to hold you back. If you let them, Joni, they'll control you until you get to be seventy years old and realize you've wasted your whole life serving assholes who feared what you could become in your own raw strength. That's why they held you back. So don't let 'em!"

Cate Marlington was the only other person Joni had ever heard talk like this. There was something both terrifying and exciting in Dottie's advice. The longer Joni thought about it, the more it made sense. In the end, all she could say was, "Thank you." She couldn't quite unveil all the complicated thoughts she was thinking about to Dottie just now.

As they drove on, Joni felt a little braver about re-asking Dottie the question that she'd dodged earlier. "So why did my parents disown you?"

Dottie smiled and inhaled her cigarette. She blew the smoke out calmly, flicked her loose ashes out the window, and folded her arms. She furled her brows as if trying to think of where to begin.

"I have no fucking idea." Dottie said nothing more.

Joni could sense that some deeply unpleasant memory was circling around in her aunt's mind. Joni recognized the look because she had used it many times in her own life. It was the look that said, "How much should I tell?" She was annoyed that she'd shared so much, yet Dottie had shared so little. However, she also didn't want to be pushy and bring up a potentially painful memory for her aunt.

I'll have to figure out another way to learn what happened. Dottie is a closed book, but I don't want to pressure her if she's not ready to tell me.

If Dottie were going to reveal it at all, it would need to be in her own time. Joni decided to change the subject. *Maybe she'll reveal something that way.*

"So you do volunteer work?"

Dottie nodded. "Every Saturday and Sunday. Lots of people are hungry at the shelters. Sometimes it's cleaning up the park. Sometimes it's entertaining the old folk's homes. I figure it won't be too long before I go there, so I better make something of a good reputation beforehand."

"What do you do for a living?"

"DMV. It sucks, but work is work, I guess. At least I can get—"

"Something's wrong."

"What?"

Joni peered on the horizon. Beyond the trees and houses and small towns in the distance, she saw mountains. They were long masses of green forest, and with each subtle bend in I-40, they slowly shifted from left to right in front of their path.

"I thought we left the mountains behind us," Joni said.

"We did."

"What the hell is that up ahead?"

"I guess another mountain."

"But I thought it was all flat throughout here?"

"It is."

Joni looked at Dottie. "Are we going to have to drive through that thing?"

Dottie looked ahead. "Hmm. Maybe." Dottie pulled out an old map from the side of her door. She began unfolding it, searching for information. "I feel like I should know what those are."

As they approached it, Joni wrote it off as an illusion. What appeared to swell up like a long, green, flat mountain sank back into the earth as her perspective improved with the road. Joni tried to figure out what had happened to it. It wasn't long after that when another seeming-mountain appeared away in the distance to their left beyond a small town. This one was even larger and longer, and it was also covered with greenery.

"What are these?"

"The Ozark Mountains, maybe?" Dottie was at a loss. "They aren't that big."

But Joni's mind was reeling. "Are we driving through mountains?"

"No, we're not. It's all flat through here."

"I'm not imagining these things, Dottie."

"They're just hills, Joni. Just like back home. They don't even compare to the Tennessee mountains."

"Why is it seventy through here?" Joni asked, feeling suddenly anxious. She realized that the speed limit hadn't changed in some time. To her left, nothing seemed out of place. There were the other two lanes of traffic and the steady lining of trees.

But beyond that?

She realized that all she could see were the tops of the trees and clear blue sky.

Are we on a mountain now? Why is it seventy through here!?

An uneasy feeling swept over her. It was as if her entire left side felt vulnerable. In her mind, she imagined the car sliding off the side of a mountain. She knew it was a ludicrous thought. She knew it was impossible. But she still imagined the tires blowing out. She imagined a semi-truck smashing into her. She imagined blinking at precisely the wrong moment and veering off into the traffic, tumbling over the side.

That's why the mountains seem to disappear. The road is cut into them. The trees hide the elevation. My perspective's changing with the rise and fall of the road.

Her mind raced. Suddenly she didn't like the heights.

"I need to pull over."

"You sick?" Dottie asked.

"No, I just . . . Goddamn it!" she suddenly screamed.

Dottie held up her hands. "Whoa! Okay! What's wrong!?"

Sweat began collecting in her grimy hair. Her sunglasses started fogging. *It's too damn hot*, she thought. Sweat accumulated in her palms on the wheel making it slippery. The other cars were going too fast.

A rest stop. About a mile. I think that's what the sign said.

"I'll pull over at the rest stop."

"Is everything okay?" Dottie asked again, clutching the coat hanger for support.

Joni shook her head. "I think I'm afraid of heights. And I'm only just now realizing it."

Dottie looked at her niece as if she'd just jumped into traffic. "Heights? Joni, it's all flat here."

Joni laughed maniacally. "No, it's not, Dottie! See that!? Over there on the other side of the road!? That's a sheer drop off!"

Dottie looked. "No, sweetie, it's not. That's a gradual decline with lots of trees and a gentle hill. We're not in the mountains."

"I need to pull over."

Once they reached the rest stop, Joni looked for an open parking space. Joni had to collect her nerves and focus on not running over the large number of people who'd decided to visit Arkansas that day.

After parking, Joni turned the car off. She took deep breaths, counted to ten, and didn't want to think about what Dottie's take on this sudden panicking was all about. It had surprised Joni. *What the hell was that? Everything was going fine. I made it through the Tennessee mountains okay. What the hell is wrong with me?*

"I need to pee," Joni said, irritable. She grabbed her empty soda can and got out. "Okay!" Dottie called after her. "I'll just wait here and defend the car."

Once in the stall, Joni rested her hand against the barrier. She didn't care that it was probably crawling with flesh-eating amoebas. She needed it to stabilize herself, to reassure herself that she was standing on solid ground.

Against all her logic and instinct, she felt as if her body were being drawn to the edge of the cliff. She'd seen what Dottie had seen: a little height, probably a grade of about thirty feet. And yet her mind had convinced her that the road was tilted towards that grade, that she would somehow slide right off. She couldn't shake the feeling.

Joni's mind raced for the term. *Vertigo. Do I have vertigo?* She remembered reading something about it in college. *Psychology class. Disorientation, being dizzy from the heights.* She'd never been tested for it.

She'd never had a reason to be tested for it, considering her family had rarely travelled through the mountains. She remembered being a little girl going to see Grandpa Dale in Asheville. The mountains had scared her, but she wasn't the one driving then.

You've got to do this on your own.

On her way back to the car, she bought another soda at the vending machines. She arrived back just in time to see Dottie finish tossing some trash in a nearby garbage can. Once they both were seated in the car again, neither said a word. Joni sipped her soda, and Dottie was silent.

"Dottie, I swear I'm not crazy, and I'm sorry for my freak-out back there. I just didn't realize we'd be going through mountains."

Dottie bit her lip. "Sweetie, these aren't mountains. But if they freak you out, I can always drive for you."

She knew her aunt had good intentions, but this wouldn't work. Joni shook her head.

"That's okay, Dottie. I'll drive. This feeling is new to me. It's like I have to be the one behind the wheel, or I don't have any control. I have to have control over this . . . this . . . whatever . . . this fear of heights, I guess."

Dottie didn't say anything, but instead looked down at the floor, crossing her arms. She extended her arm, appeared to be inspecting her wrist, then folded her arms again. After a few awkward moments of silence, Dottie said, "Well, I just need to know my niece isn't going to flip out and cause a wreck with me in the car."

"I won't. I promise."

Dottie nodded her head slowly. "Okay. Just take a deep breath and continue when you're ready to."

Joni grabbed the keys and started the ignition. The AC came to life, and she decided to hit the play button on the CD player for extra comfort. Lukaas Bennett greeted her ears with a soothing violin solo.

Thanks, Lukaas. You really know how to calm a girl's nerves.

Joni pulled the car out of the rest stop, waiting for another car to zip past them before merging onto the highway and continuing. As she sped up while simultaneously breathing heavily and sweating, Dottie leaned over and said, "You know, it is okay to go slow-as-hell sometimes. Just make sure you're in the right lane when you do."

Joni settled on a comfortable pace of sixty-five, and for once, she didn't mind that virtually every car and semi-truck was passing her by. She didn't know how she would cope with the heights at the Grand Canyon, or Horseshoe Bend, or even the mountains on the route back home. All she knew was that she had to keep going. She would not be deterred from seeking out the truth with Dottie, figuring out her own novel, and seeing the country while at it.

This fear of heights would not be going away, though.

6

In time, the road flattened out, and the trees became less dense. Even the green seemed to lighten up, and the two suddenly found themselves surrounded on either side of the road by lots of grass and farmland.

WELCOME TO OKLAHOMA read a big, blue, and white sign. Underneath it read *"Discover the Excellence."* Joni noted how vastly empty everything looked. Aside from the occasional abandoned truck or distant house, it was all pretty much grass, trees, and farmland.

"Welcome to Oklahoma," Dottie said. "They have cows here."

Joni was still shaking. She knew it was flat here. She knew the mountains were far behind. But she had never seen a landscape so flat before. However, being unable to see the distant land over the bushes and trees along either side of the road made her feel as if she were driving on top of a mountain.

This makes no sense! What the hell's wrong with me? If I keep complaining, Dottie's gonna take the wheel.

Away in the distance behind her, she saw a dark cloud.

"Great," she said.

"What?" Dottie replied.

"Storm cloud behind us." As Dottie looked behind them, Joni said, "You don't think we'll run into any tornadoes, do you?"

Dottie turned back in her seat. "I doubt it. We're more likely to run into a cow than a tornado."

"But this is Tornado Alley. Don't they have tornadoes out here all the time?"

"I'm sure the storm is heading away from us. Probably leftovers making their way to Arkansas. Besides, people out here have storm cellars. They know the land. They're better prepared for tornadoes than people in South Carolina are."

"Are you sure? I mean, we're on the open road, and—"

"Jesus, Joni, relax! I ain't ever seen a more jittery, nervous-wreck than you!"

Joni stopped talking, considered that point, and took a deep breath. "You're right. I know. My mind is playing tricks on me with the height and everything."

"Still flat, child. This is farmland. Mountains are behind us."

I know it's flat. Maybe it's because I can't get a good vantage point to orient myself that's throwing me off. Wait!

Joni thought that if she could just reorient her bearings with the land, she'd be fine.

The fields stretched on and on and on. Joni noted a certain weariness to the landscape. Even the trees seemed tired. Nothing was quite as green as the mountains had been. The grass was a little more yellow with some brown thrown in the mix. It was almost like a tired green.

As they drew nearer to the motel, Joni realized that she hadn't seen many exits lately. *Where do people live out here? It's all trees and flat farmland.* Every now and then they'd pass a road that led away into the heart of some farm territory or distant group of houses, but she hadn't seen many buildings in a long time. Aside from the vividly blue sky, it was all mostly long stretches of grass and the occasional red cedar or row of shrubbery. In one hour, she could count on one hand how many distant houses she had seen.

Four.

Thankfully, their exit existed, and it didn't take long to find the motel afterwards. Joni parked the car at the entrance gates and headed to the check-in. It was a stand-alone walk-in booth no bigger than a horse trailer. Going in, she pulled the usual paperwork and reservation tickets out of her travelling folder. *Mom taught me how to be well organized. Have to give her credit for that.* Inside, there was just enough room to approach the counter.

There was a fairly squat teenage boy with blonde hair sitting at the counter. He was working on what appeared to be algebra homework. When she approached, he looked up at her as if she were lost.

"Hi!" she said. After an awkward four seconds of silence, she added, "I'm checking in. I have a reservation."

The light bulb seemed to come on, and he said, "Oh! Okay." He took her confirmation ticket and studied it thoroughly as if looking for a forgery. He turned to her and said, "I need to see your driver's license."

Joni gave it to him. He clicked away on a computer, looking at the monitor, then at her license, then at the monitor again. "Alright, Joni, here's your room keys. You're on the second floor, right there in the middle." Giving her two card keys to room number 288, he went back to his algebra homework.

Joni returned to the car and pulled through the gates. "I hope this place isn't full of drug dealers."

"I think we're fine," Dottie said. "It looks nicer. How much did this place cost you?"

"About sixty. Sixty-something. I forget."

"And you paid forty-seven for the one in Jackson?"

Joni parked next to the stairwell leading to the second floor. "I think so, yeah."

"Yep," Dottie said. "That's the trick. Forty-seven or less'll get you exactly what you pay for. Keep it above fifty, though, and you should usually be okay."

"Well, now I know."

Room 288 was situated directly at the top of the stairwell. Joni put the card in the reader and pulled it back out but was greeted with only a beep and a red light. Confused, she looked at the card. *It has an arrow pointing down with a black strip. What'd I do wrong?* Troubleshooting, she turned the card around and tried it with the black strip facing her now. Now she got a green light.

"Key-card people need to get their shit together," she said. Dottie laughed behind her. Opening the door, they saw a much cleaner room than the one in Jackson. With two freshly made beds and a new-looking flat-screen television, the room smelled of sweet candles.

After bringing in their suitcases and the coolers, Joni fell back onto the bed closest to the bathroom. "I feel like I've been hit by a truck."

"Probably because we need something to eat. More than the snacks you brought. I saw a deli shop across the street. You want me to pick us up something?" Dottie set out her suitcase on the other bed. Opening it, she pulled out a phone charger. "I don't mind getting it if you're okay with me driving your car."

"That sounds tubular," Joni said, not caring if she ate or not. Staring up at the ceiling, it looked as if it were slowly trying to zoom away from her. *I'm more exhausted than I realized. I just used 'tubular' in a sentence.*

When Dottie finished plugging her phone in, she went over and turned on the television. Tossing the remote to Joni, Dottie said, "You watch something fun and relax while I go get us some food. Anything you want on your sandwich?"

"Lots of good vegetables, turkey, and cheese. Just no mayonnaise."

"Alright."

Joni tossed her the keys and shut her eyes. "Thanks, Dottie. You're awesome."

She didn't see Dottie smile, but she did hear her aunt say after a pause, "No problem," and walk out the door. Joni took deep breaths, trying to force her body to rest and recalibrate its balance.

You are not on a mountain. You are not about to fall off a cliff. You are in the middle of America where everything is flat.

She sat up and looked at the television. Some cartoons were on. Switching the channel, she came across the weather. It looked like it was clear in her area for today and tomorrow, but there were storms in other parts of the state. The weatherman gave his commentary on the developing storms as Joni tried not to think about tornadoes. She recalled there had been an EF5 in Moore just over a month earlier that had devastated the area. Unnerved by the thought, she turned off the television and went over to the window. Looking out, Joni saw there was not a cloud in the sky.

That strange feeling of disorientation lingered, even though the landscape was as flat as she could hope for.

I could call Violet.

Right now, her family would be an hour ahead. Figuring that to mean about three-fifty for her family, she plopped down on the bed again and pulled out her phone. She wanted to catch her sister up on all that she had experienced so far, and she hoped that maybe hearing a familiar voice would help reorient her a bit.

As she pulled up Violet's number, Joni hesitated. There was always the risk that her mom or dad would want to talk to her, too. They hadn't spoken since that last phone call. Joni knew that they would be convinced they had been right. She also knew that they would be completely oblivious to how they had hurt her. She wanted to talk to Violet but not them.

Risk it.

Shutting her eyes and leaning against the surprisingly soft pillows, she let the hum of the dial tone reset her pace. She breathed in and exhaled to the same rhythm as each ring. Then, on the fourth ring, her sister answered.

"Hey, Joni!"

"Hey, Vi! How's it going?"

"Going good. You at the Grand Canyon yet?"

"Not yet. We're in Oklahoma. Just calling to see how you're doing. Hear a familiar voice."

"I've been doing good! Just counting down the days until my birthday. You coming to the party? Mom and Dad invited a lot of people."

Joni smiled. It dawned on her that she hadn't really spoken to her sister in quite a while. It didn't matter, though. They'd both grown up having to learn to walk on eggshells together, having to learn how to survive a world ruled by Elohim Creation Salvation Community Church. Over time, their bond grew so that they knew that they could speak to each other freely whenever. No legalism or sacred truths or Pastor Greg mandates would ever take that from them.

"Of course! I wouldn't miss it for the world. It's gonna be awesome. Are you ready to turn eighteen?"

Violet laughed. "Yes and no. Yes, I can't wait to get out and be an adult. But I'm also kinda worried."

"Why's that?"

"I don't know," Violet said. "I'm worried I'm gonna get to college and discover I have the worst social skills imaginable."

"You'll be fine," Joni said. "Don't worry. Somehow, I survived. It helps having an open mind and a willingness to learn."

"Really? The years of indoctrination from Elohim Creation didn't screw you up in the social life department?"

Mom and Dad must not be in the room.

"Um, yes. It did screw me up very much. But hey! You can learn from my mistakes! Rule number one: don't date a douchebag Christian ministry major," Joni said.

"Noted. Although if I do date someone, I'd better keep it a secret from Mom and Dad," Violet said.

"Why?"

"Well . . . okay, so story time."

"Oh! Something happened?" Joni asked.

"Yeah. So I got asked to go to prom this year by Gabe. Do you remember Gabe? Did you ever meet? He's in the youth group."

"I don't remember meeting a Gabe," Joni said.

"Well, he asked me out. I said yes, but Dad called the church about it, and the deacons wanted him to pray with me about it and see if that was a good idea. He said there might be some lustful intentions, so I needed to be guarded."

"Whoa, that's weird."

"I know, right? Like, why? Why did I have to do that? No one else's kids have to go through that. It was stupid."

"Did you get to go to the prom with him?"

"Yes," Violet continued, "I did go to prom with Gabe. At his actual school. Maybe that's why they freaked out. Because he wasn't homeschooled. But Gabe was a nice guy. It didn't work out after that, but I'm glad I went. At least once. I just . . . when I go to college, I don't want to come across as some awkward homeschool kid. I mean, it's probably too late for that, but you know."

Joni felt two emotions. One was jealousy. Her younger sister had gotten to experience something she never did. Another was anger. Their parents had gotten more extreme over the years. When Joni was a teenager who merely expressed interest in going to prom with Adam, her parents only asked questions about the guy to see if he was a good person or not. He ultimately never asked Joni out, and she felt like a loser. When Violet actually got asked, it sounded as if they turned it into a purity crusade.

"Man, that sucks. I'm sorry, Violet."

"No, it's okay. I just don't want to go to college being a weirdo. I want to be normal."

"I know what you mean. It took me a while to figure that out for myself, but at least you know that going in."

"It's so weird the things they choose to fixate on," Violet said. "They ignore real problems and keep their blinders on. They don't see the problems at the church, and they don't see the big picture of how it's affected us."

"Again, you're doing well for recognizing that now instead of halfway through college. Are you thinking that once you start college, you might stop going to their church?"

"Um, yeah! I'm not like them. Not really. I think they believe some things that Jesus specifically taught against. Jesus said to love your neighbor, and Pastor Greg preaches to be wary of your neighbor "lest he leads your house away from God" or something like that. I feel like when I read my Bible, I'm reading things very differently from how Pastor Greg teaches it. Jesus seems like someone who loves everyone, faults and all. But this church makes it seem like everyone who doesn't fall in line with their exact beliefs is somehow not a real Christian. I just don't feel like I can say any of this out loud because you know how intense Dad gets. He really acts like if you disagree with Pastor Greg's version, then you've got something bad influencing you. And Mom's no better. She parrots everything he says. If you criticize Pastor Greg, it's like you're criticizing God or something."

Joni smiled sympathetically. Hearing her sister put to voice so many of her own frustrations had now replaced her own worries about feeling disoriented and off-balance.

"It would be nice to talk to them," Joni said.

"About what?" Violet said.

"About everything. I'm like you, I don't think their beliefs are healthy. It'd be nice to talk to them about how I'm not like them. About how I think their church and their beliefs are really more destructive than helpful. How it all really hurt me, how it makes me feel. I'm just . . . I'm tired of walking on eggshells every time I talk to them, too, you know? I'm an adult. I shouldn't have to justify who I am to them anymore."

"Amen," Violet said. "You're lucky, though. You have that kind of liberty to do that if you want. I'm still living in their house. Their house, their rules, you know? If I try to say anything now, they'll freak out and think I'm turning against the faith or something. They could do anything: pull my funding for college, not drive me there, send me to church counseling. It's almost better to just keep my opinions to myself until I'm free of them."

She knows the game. God, this sucks.

Joni sighed. She knew of another reason why keeping silent might be best. "Violet, do you remember Mr. Bridges? From the church?"

There was silence. "I remember hearing that name, but I can't put a face to it. Who was he?"

"He was one of the deacons. You would've been about five years old," Joni said, trying to recall the exact order of events. "He stepped down as deacon because he didn't like some of the teaching he saw going on. He thought people were being led to advertise the church rather than actually preach the gospel. Like you know how every time they show a video of someone confessing their sinful life before Pastor Greg led them to Jesus? They always mention how the pastor or how Elohim Creation Salvation led them to Jesus. It's never really about Jesus. It's always an ad for how great the church is."

"Yeah, that's a good point. I hadn't realized that until you said that," Violet said.

"Well," Joni continued, "he didn't like that. He stopped going at some point, then he wrote an opinion piece in the paper about the teachings. Actually, no, I think the article he wrote was about how they shouldn't be tax-exempt because of some of the hateful things they were preaching. I think he just mentioned the other stuff, but the tax-exempt stuff was the main point he was making. The church obviously didn't like that, so two thugs—I forget their names, they were on the staff at the time—started harassing him. They slashed his tires, made threatening phone calls in the middle of the night from blocked numbers. They got caught eventually breaking into his house. It broke out into the news, and he swore it was the church coming after him. Pastor Greg fired the two guys doing it and said he had no knowledge or hand in it. But here's the thing: I was eleven at the time, and looking back, the whole thing just felt like a big warning. Like Pastor Greg seemed less concerned that a former member had been harassed, and more concerned that everyone look at the church as the victim in the situation. I remember him giving a sermon about how the two guys had been fired for misconduct, but he didn't apologize to Mr. Bridges. He didn't say anything to validate Mr. Bridges's concerns or try to make amends. If anything, it almost felt like he was suggesting that 'This can happen to you if you act like Mr. Bridges.' I don't remember exactly what he said. I just remember it came across that way. And I was too young to get it."

"Wow," Violet said. "I guess I'm screwed, huh?"

"Hang in there," Joni said, hating herself for giving the failed advice she knew she'd clung to for years. "You're almost free." *One day, you'll be twenty-four like me, and you'll still be too scared to speak your mind freely around the parents.*

"Has anything else major happened at the church recently?" Joni asked.

"So you'll be at my party, then?" Violet said suddenly, a sudden enthusiasm in her voice.

"What? Of course."

"Awesome! Lots of people coming over."

Oh. I bet the parents showed up.

"Joni," Violet said.

"Yes?" Joni replied.

"I'm talking to Joni."

Yep. She's talking to either Mom or Dad.

"Hey, Dad wants to talk to you," Violet said.

God damn it.

"Alright. Good talking to you, Vi," Joni said.

"You too. Talk to you later, Joni!" Violet said.

Joni felt a sinking feeling in her stomach. She took a deep breath to prepare. She was not in the mood for a lecture.

"Hey, kiddo! How are you doing?" It was her father.

"Hey, Dad. I'm okay. I—"

"Are you at the Grand Canyon yet?"

"Not yet. We're in Okemah right now."

"Okemah? Where's that?"

"It's in Oklahoma. We just got to the motel."

"Okay! Is it flat out there?"

"Well . . . yes, I guess, but not as flat as you'd think. There's some hills."

"You're in Tornado Alley, you know." Joni knew what this comment meant. He was building up to a point about she hadn't thought this through. She decided to counter the fear he was trying to build.

"I know. No storms here today, though, so I think we're safe for the night. I got through the mountains okay, but then we came across these bizarre smaller, flatter mountains in Arkansas. They weren't that large, but I felt weird driving through them. Dizzy."

"Dizzy?"

"Sort of. Like my vision was fine, but I felt sort of light-headed. My hands started sweating, and I felt like the car would just magically slide off the side of the mountain."

Her dad was silent for a moment, then said, "Hmm. Maybe you're afraid of heights?"

"I guess so." Joni mentally kicked herself. She regretted mentioning the dizziness since it now meant her dad would have some ammunition to guilt-trip her. Almost as if on cue, he used it to make her doubt herself.

"Could be vertigo. If you have vertigo, it might not be the safest idea to keep driving."

"I'll be fine, Dad."

"I don't know. I think you should have listened to your mother on this one. You could've been down in Charleston at the Campbell's place. Much closer to home, a lot safer than wherever you are now. Oklahoma. Not a good time or place to get vertigo, you know? I think you bit off more than you can chew, Joni."

Joni felt her cheeks begin to flush with anger. She clutched the phone tighter, controlling her tone.

"Dad, it's fine. I just got a little—"

"Oh, hang on. Your mom wants to talk to you."

Joni felt her heart leap into her throat. This conversation had gone south quickly, and all she'd really wanted was to talk with her sister. Now she had to guard everything she said. Joni knew if she said too much, her mom would catastrophize. This dizziness would spell certain doom and indicate a health problem and she should never have gone on such a trip without someone reliable and they'd be right back to where their conversation left off when they'd spoken to each other last.

"Hi, Joni."

"Hi, Mom."

"What's this about you being dizzy?"

"Oh, just that I got a little disoriented after driving through the mountains. I'm fine now."

"Well, you know, Joni, if you get dizzy or your head starts spinning, pull over to the side of the road. It's not worth it if your vision gets blurry."

Here we go.

"I know, Mom."

"And with your Aunt Dottie, you'll need to be extra careful."

No. I'm not going to let you throw Dottie under the bus like that.

"Actually, Dottie's been very helpful so far. She's been reading the GPS for me so I can concentrate on driving." *Better not mention Jacksonville. Or the drinking. Or the one-night stand with Beer-gut McGee.*

"Okay, but be on your guard, Joni. That's how they get you. They lure you in with a false sense of security, making you trust them. And what you don't realize is that they're actually influencing you with their godless liberalism."

"Um, she's been okay so far." *She's also one of the few who's ever listened to me.*

"I still say it was a bad idea to take her with you."

Joni sighed. "I know, but really she's been a good companion so far."

"She's going to get you in trouble, though! Joni, I'm really worried for you."

Joni hesitated. Deep down, she knew that this is what her parents did: sew doubt in people not like them. Joni had been thrown off by the casual drinking and the casual hook-ups. But Dottie had also been the one to call the police when Joni had frozen. Dottie had tossed the alcohol when Joni asked, regardless of whether it was legal or not to be open in the trunk. When it came to Joni's safety, Dottie had Joni's back.

"She's been fine so far, Mom. Although she did go into a bar already." The words were out before she realized what she'd just opened.

"She *what?*"

"Well . . ." *Damn it, Joni. Just shut-up for once.* She decided she'd have to tell the story now. "We stayed in Jackson at a motel that had a club attached to it. She went in."

"You didn't go in, did you?"

"No, of course not. I was exhausted and went to bed."

"Oh, that's good. I was trying to warn you before you up and left, but Dottie's no good. She drinks a lot, she's an atheist, she's very liberal, and she always gets into trouble. That's why we stopped talking to her, you know."

"I know." *I know that's bullshit, and I'm going to find out the real reason.*

"She scoffs and mocks the church, and I just . . . Joni, be careful. I know you think this is some fun road trip, but this is really serious. She's a threat to your salvation if you're not careful. Actually, you may be in just the right position, now that I think of it. Maybe you can reach her! Maybe you're the beacon of light she needs to get her life right with God."

"Maybe." *I'm not going to proselytize my aunt.*

"Just don't let her convince you to do something bad, Joni. She can be a bad influence if you let her. Tell me about this club she went into."

"It was sketchy." *Why the hell did I say anything?*

"Lot of weirdoes hanging around?"

"I didn't go in, so I don't know. But the motel was terrible. Had a weirdo banging on the door next to mine."

"What!?"

"I think a drug deal was going down. He seemed like he was drugged out or something." *Shut the fuck up, Joni!*

"Was he black? He was black, wasn't he?"

"No, Mom. He was white."

"Oh. Well, even so . . . Did he have a knife? Or a gun?"

"He had a cup with ice in it. That's all I saw."

"Oh, God, Joni. You really should have gotten someone else to go with you on your trip. You know, people waste their lives . . ."

Joni tuned the rest out. She knew it by heart.

I need to tell her what Dottie did. She needs to know Dottie was the one who saved the day.

But Joni couldn't bring herself to tell her mom anything. That was how it had always been. She figured it was easier to let her mom think she'd won this round rather than arguing. But Joni felt a pang of guilt that was somehow more real than anything the Blue Ghost could conjure up.

I hate myself. Why can't I speak up?

". . . speaking of which, will you be back in time for Violet's birthday party?"

Joni tuned back into the conversation.

"Oh, yeah. Of course. I should be getting back on July 6, if all goes well. I'm hoping to find a souvenir from out west to give Violet."

"Any ideas?"

"Not yet. I'm waiting to see what they have out there first. I want it to be something special. Turning eighteen should be special."

"Well, I'll let you go, but you think about what I said. Be careful, alright?"

"Alright, I will."

When they hung up, Joni buried her face into her pillow and screamed. She felt tears welling up and bursting onto the pillow.

Why can't I say what I want to say to her? Why do they always have to assume the worst about people like it's no big deal? Why can't I be myself like it's no big deal for once?

She clutched the pillow and squeezed tight, angry at herself.

I need to talk to them. I need them to understand. I'm tired of hiding who I am to them. I'm tired of hating myself.

It wasn't long before Dottie returned with the food. "You hungry?"

Joni sat up and exhaled. "I'm starving."

Dottie set a take-out box on Joni's bed and climbed onto the other one. "Well, you're in luck. That one doesn't have mayonnaise." Joni opened it to find a cheese-and-turkey sandwich with lettuce, tomatoes, red onions, and green peppers on it, and French fries on the side. There were even two packets of ketchup for her consideration.

Either Dottie didn't notice that Joni's eyes were red from crying, or she chose not to say anything. Joni was glad that she didn't ask.

"Dottie, this looks amazing."

"My pleasure. You're welcome to a bite of mine if you want. It's an egg-and-cheese sandwich that's been smothered with mayonnaise. Lots and lots of mayonnaise. In fact, I have two packets of mayonnaise for my fries if you want one."

"No thanks," Joni said, grabbing her sandwich. "Mayonnaise is a product of the devil." She bit into the warm, melted cheesy sandwich and chewed away the fear of heights, fear of parents, fear of moral righteousness.

How do you tell loved ones they are hurting you and everyone around them?

7

Joni's phone alarm went off at seven o'clock. She got out of bed, wiped the sweat from her forehead, and threw some clothes on. Dottie barely stirred. The morning sunlight was starting to seep through the crack in the window curtains.

Almost immediately the phone conversation from yesterday came back to her. She tried to shrug it off, but the scene kept replaying in her mind like a movie turned up way too loud and on repeat. Every word she'd said echoed in her mind, making her wonder when and where she could have answered more honestly . . . or avoided the discomfort altogether.

Joni went downstairs, careful to grab a keycard and shut the room door behind her. On the lower floor was a common lounging area through some glass doors with small tables and stools to sit at. To the left of the lounge was a mini-bar with the options of cereal, bagels, assorted cream cheeses, toasted bread, doughnuts, oranges, milk, juices, and coffee. A small line of people shuffled along for the continental breakfast. There was an elderly lady and a middle-aged man ahead of Joni in line. The man wore a black-and-red plaid shirt and was telling a corny joke to someone on his phone while holding a half-eaten powdered doughnut.

"Knock-knock . . . Stacy . . . Stay seated!"

The elderly lady tried to figure out how to work the juice dispenser.

Joni grabbed a bowl and put some doughnuts in it. She poured herself some coffee. Grabbing a plate, she set out two bagels (one for her and one for Dottie), two packets of cream cheese, two plastic butter knives, and two napkins. Sitting down at the table, she began spreading the cheese on one of the bagels. Since Dottie was still waking up, Joni decided to go ahead and eat her food.

She'd had a dream. It starred her mom driving a car. Joni was strapped down to the passenger seat with asylum bed-straps while her mom laughed maniacally and drove ninety miles-per-hour on the side of a mountain cliff. Right when they reached the edge of the road, her mom transformed into the Blue Ghost. She was still laughing but with a distorted laugh and blood-soaked fangs bared. Joni screamed, worried for her safety, worried for her soul, shouting apologies for ever questioning Pastor Greg, but the Blue Ghost only laughed as if to say, "Too late!" When the Blue Ghost inevitably drove off the side of the cliff, they flew right into a tornado made of rainbows. It carried them and landed the car on a beach.

Could use that for the story.

Her nerves were a bit calmer than they had been yesterday, but the phone conversation with her parents still gnawed at her mind. With some shame and distress, she distracted herself by biting into one of the bagels which was warm from the toaster.

Focus on something else. Focus on your story. Look for ideas.

As she sipped her coffee and restarted her morning brain, her creative writing cogs started turning. Out of the corner of her eye, she saw that the woman was still figuring out the juice machine. The woman turned to a nearby employee and asked, "Where does the milk come out?"

The employee said, "That's the juice dispenser. It only gives you apple juice and orange juice. The milk is in that silver container next to it."

"Oh. Thank you. I thought I was missing something." The lady found the milk and poured some into a paper cup.

This lady. Why is she out here in Okemah? What prompted her to drink milk? Maybe she's got a condition or something. Too much sugar in juices for her. Joni shifted her sleuthing to the bearded man in the plaid shirt. "As I was saying," he said into his phone, "a car is a conceptually different concept."

The hell is that supposed to mean? Is that an expression people use? The man went on for a few minutes in great detail about the inner workings of a car's engine and how much thrust his engine had, but while Joni ate in peaceful silence, all she really got from the conversation was, "My car is bigger than yours."

A woman needs milk. A man loves cars. Maybe the woman is travelling. Kinda like me.

That idea had potential.

What if she's trying to write a book, like me? And has to travel across the country to get inspiration?

It had the right spark of something good. In Cate's book, *One More Thing Before You Die*, Joni had read about how a good writer would create fictional stories that were based in part on something in reality. If she created a character who followed the same long, winding road of I-40 as Joni did, it might work. But what would she do?

Joni continued chewing, thinking about that. *Making it her goal to write a book might come off as uninspired. I don't want to write a Mary Sue.*

Before she forgot, she grabbed her phone and punched in a note. *Story idea: include lady who can't find milk and burly man who loves to brag about his car size. Make as Freudian as possible. The more phallic references, the better. Include the phrase 'pulsating and thrusting engine' somewhere.*

She gulped down her coffee, threw away the trash, and took the rest of the breakfast back to the room. It was fairly cool outside now, but she knew it would get hotter as the sun climbed. Right now, the sun glowed yellow from just over the horizon. There were a few purple clouds left in the distance, but the blue sky was brightening up considerably. A gentle breeze had set in.

At the top of the stairs, Joni stared out at the sunrise. *What if the land gets high up again? Can I handle it?*

Back in the room, Dottie was lazily packing. "You know what sucks?" she asked Joni. "The morning. It always comes when you're not ready for it, whether you like it or not. You can kick and scream, but it don't care. It's kinda like hornets that way."

"I brought you breakfast," Joni said, setting the bowl of doughnuts and spare bagel down for her aunt on the dresser.

"Thank you, child," Dottie said. Joni went over to the sink. She grabbed a bar of soap and wrapped it in a washcloth. Running it under some hot water, Joni said, "I'm sorry about freaking out yesterday. I guess I just can't handle heights as well as I thought I could." She rubbed the soapy cloth across her face, washing away the oil and nighttime grime.

"Well, you might want to come to peace with it pretty quick, considering where we're heading."

Scrubbing her eyelids with the cold, soapy towel, Joni said, "I know. The Grand Canyon is a giant hole in the ground. Big holes will be easy compared to large mountains."

"No, I mean—"

"I know, Dottie. Horseshoe Bend is also a big canyon. I'll be fine. If I'm standing on my own two feet, I feel better."

"Not the canyons, honey. The Colorado Plateau."

Joni stopped scrubbing her face and turned to face Dottie. "The what?"

"The Colorado Plateau. Didn't your parents teach you geography?"

Joni froze. "I thought the desert was flat?"

"It is in a sense. It looks flat, mostly. But you're going up a giant plateau. You don't realize it because the area is so flat, but you'll actually be several thousand feet above sea level. Where are we stopping today?"

"Santa Rosa." Joni felt that same, dreadful feeling of dizziness returning but worse. The idea of climbing the largest mountain she'd ever climbed was too daunting to imagine. She looked out the window at the flat horizon. *So huge I don't even realize it?* Suddenly Joni couldn't see a flat landscape, but rather suspected the entire land was tilted at about one degree of an angle. *Unnoticeable only if your equilibrium is fine. God, it's too early for this.*

"Oh, Santa Rosa? Okay, we won't hit the plateau today. We'll hit it tomorrow, but like I said, it's so flat here, you don't even notice."

It was a small relief to hear that they wouldn't hit it today, but no matter what Dottie said, Joni would notice it. *I'm so used to living in valleys and foothills where I'm about two-thousand feet above sea-level anyway and can see the definite mountains around me that it's become my center. If my center changes—like it is here—then my balance gets off. I have to rebalance.*

Joni shuddered and tried to push the thought from her mind. Everything felt in slow motion now. She grabbed her keys in slow motion. She grabbed a cooler in slow motion. It was as if her will to move on with the trip had cracked. Her desire to balance and lose the light-headed dizziness outweighed the thrill of the adventure. *No. I have to keep going. Too far now.* Joni said, "Well, we better start packing. Long day."

"Just a sec, Joni. I think we should talk about something first."

Joni froze. She wondered what fresh hell her aunt was going to spring on her now. Dottie sat down on her bed and motioned for Joni to do the same. Joni sat the cooler back down and sat on the opposite bed.

"What's up?" Joni asked.

"I didn't want to say anything," Dottie said, "because I wasn't sure if I was imagining it or not, but last night when I came back with the food, you looked like you'd been crying. You sniffled a few times last night, and hell you still look a bit shook today. What happened? Is it the heights? Are you that afraid of the heights?"

Joni looked sheepishly at the floor. Before she could stop herself, she gushed the truth. "I am scared of the heights, but that's not why I was crying. I was crying because I called Violet, and then my parents interrupted the conversation to lecture me."

"Oh. Lecture you about what?"

Joni shrugged her shoulders. "About everything. About going on this trip, about taking you along, how I should've listened to them."

Dottie thought for a moment, then asked, "How did it make you feel?"

Joni felt like an idiot, but somehow telling Dottie the truth felt comforting. "Miserable. I felt like I wanted to tell them to stop it, just leave me alone. I didn't tell them about how you called the police at the other motel. I feel like I should have. I feel like I didn't stick up for you enough, but I wanted to. I don't know, I just froze. And I kinda hate myself for it."

"Why do you care what they think, Joni?"

Joni shrugged. "I don't know. They're my parents. I mean, I hate the things they taught me and expect of me, but I still love them. I can't not completely disregard them. It's just not that simple."

"Oh, yes it is."

Dottie stood up and sat down beside Joni. To Joni's surprise, she put her arm around Joni and hugged her tightly.

"How old are you, Joni?"

"Twenty-four."

"Yeah. Listen, you don't need anyone's permission to live your life. Because I guarantee that no one will ever give you permission to live it the way you want to. It's your life. When you die, they're not going to be there telling you what you ought to do or what you should have done. Do you trust yourself?"

"Yes," Joni said.

"Then that should be enough," Dottie replied.

"But it's hard to. They always want to know why I don't go to their church or why I invited you. I feel like I have to constantly hide who I am around them because they'll freak out if they learn that I'm not walking in-step with their weird little cult."

Joni looked down at the floor, embarrassed. She hadn't been prepared for such an emotional conversation so early in the morning.

"It can be hard to stand up to people, especially if they're loved ones," Dottie said. "But really, you only get one life. That's it. You can't go around following orders from them your whole life. If tiptoeing around them is hurting you, then say so. Be honest with them. How they react is on them, not you. It's your life, Joni. Not theirs. Not mine. Just yours."

Joni swallowed back some saliva that had built up in her throat. She took a breath. Of course, she knew her aunt was right.

"You think I should confront them with all this?"

"After what you told me yesterday, it's pretty obvious you're hurting. I think you should. Stand up for yourself. And I think you shouldn't feel guilty about it at all. Life's too short to spend it hurting because someone else wants you to hurt."

Joni said nothing but nodded her head.

"Joni, you're a smart kid. I think we both know you can trust yourself and your own judgment on things. Hell, you arranged this whole trip by yourself and reached out to me! The weird aunt! That took guts. So I'm just going to say that you don't need anybody's fucking permission to live your life. The only person you need permission from is yourself. Now Joni, do you give yourself permission to enjoy your life without shame or permission from anyone else?"

Joni knew the Blue Ghost was raging nearby, but somehow Dottie's words made him seem less of a threat and more of a spoiled child throwing a tantrum. Joni nodded. "Yes. I give myself permission."

Dottie smiled and patted Joni's knee. "How do you feel?"

Joni smiled. "A little better."

"How do you feel about standing up to your parents?"

Joni thought for a moment. "A little better. You're right. It's my life, not theirs. I shouldn't have to worry about what they think."

"When do you want to talk to them?"

"I think . . . I should do it in person. Maybe sometime soon after I get back. Not right away, though. Maybe sometime after Violet's party."

"Alright. And what are you going to do for the rest of this trip?" Dottie asked.

"I'm going to enjoy myself like I've never enjoyed myself before. I am giving myself permission to enjoy my life."

Dottie smiled. "Atta girl." Her aunt stood back up. Joni smiled and wiped away her tears, feeling her aunt's words had rejuvenated her better than any coffee she'd ever had.

"Hope you're excited," Dottie said, grabbing her suitcase. "You'll finally get to see some desert today!"

Ever since she was little, Joni had always imagined what the desert looked like. From her earliest days watching cartoons, she had vague ideas of giant sand dunes, buttes, and cacti. In fact, she had no idea what to expect. As they pulled out of the motel parking lot and hit the road, Joni noticed again just how much less green the land looked here.

Dottie switched out the old CD with another from her favorite violin master. This album had a much livelier rhythm to it. The early nineties rap influences were undeniable, and there was a female choir in the background of some of it. Joni enjoyed the sound of scratching records mixed with a unifying violin background.

"I need to learn more about this Lukaas Bennett guy," Joni said, happy for a distraction from the seemingly endless stretch of road that disappeared into an invisible vanishing point of grass, road, and sky. "I'll have to find his songs when we get back home."

"He was a genius," Dottie said. "Had two degrees in music composition and theatre. He was able to translate the emotions of the stage into the music he wrote."

"Was?"

Dottie looked out the window at the ever-rising sun behind them. "He died."

"He did? Oh no. How old was he?"

"He was thirty-three. Too young."

"How'd he die?"

Dottie looked up at the ceiling, as if trying to recall. "Um . . . It was a car wreck. A drunk driver hit him head-on going down the wrong lane. Lukaas tried to swerve out of the way, but the guy was so drunk he was swerving all over the place, going about seventy. Killed them both."

"Man. That sucks. He has such good music. He could've been a star with these sick skills."

Dottie looked at the road, then her knees. "Yeah."

"And you discovered him at a concert?"

Dottie smiled. "Met with him after the show, too."

"Wait, you got to meet him, too?"

"Oh, yeah! He was a really good guy."

"That's so cool. I wish I could meet a celebrity."

Dottie chuckled. "He wasn't like a superstar or anything. He never hit it big, but he did have two professional albums under his belt. This one's his first one, actually. He was a local artist, too. He taught music at the college and created it in his spare time. Music was his life. He died too young, though."

"Well, Dottie, I think his music is pretty cool."

"I think so, too, Joni."

Dottie pulled out a cigarette and blew smoke out the window. The flat grasslands zoomed by fading into the horizon where they met the bright, blue, cloudless sky. The beats of violin and drums fell into rhythm with the bumps on the road. At ease with herself, Joni turned her thoughts toward her book.

Maybe I can use that. Okay, don't steal your aunt's idol. But maybe my girl can still die too young. Not by cancer or anything, but maybe the book she wants to write . . . no, not a book. Maybe the thing she wants to do is big, like really big. And maybe tragedy strikes that stops her. Like the tragedy is that something hit her before she could do some good. Maybe. That could work.

Dottie sensed that Joni was deep in thought. "What are you thinking about?" she asked.

"Just thinking about my book. I have some ideas but nothing concrete yet. Just trying to sift through them all, see what sounds best."

"Hmm," Dottie said. She smoked her cigarette in silence for a few moments, then said, "What's your book about?"

"I don't know yet exactly. I just have a lot of ideas."

"Like what?"

Joni thought for a moment. *What the hell, why not.*

"It's all disjointed. I'm thinking maybe it's about a girl who wants to do something big. Like, big with her life. I don't know what yet. I was thinking maybe she writes a book, but I don't like that idea. Anyway, before she can do something big with her life, tragedy strikes. She dies before she can finish it."

"Okay," Dottie said slowly.

"Some other ideas I was tossing around included her going on a trip, travelling the country. I might not use that one though, since that's too similar to me right now. I can work in a lady who has trouble finding milk and a hurly-burly man who loves to talk about the size of his cars."

"Those are random details," Dottie said. "What's the girl's name? What's she like?"

"That's what I need to figure out," Joni said. "I don't know who this girl is yet. Maybe she's not a girl. What if she were a boy? No, never mind. I don't want to write about a boy."

Dottie laughed. "I guess I'm getting a front row seat to the writer's process, aren't I?"

"I guess you are. Sorry, I don't have a more interesting story ready yet."

"Well, let's work it together," Dottie said. "Pretend you're a casual consumer with ten dollars to spend. What sort of book do you want to read?"

Joni thought for a moment. "I'd want it to have some adventure. It can't be a preachy, moralistic book. I mean, no one wants to be entertained with anecdotes about how awful they are."

"True," Dottie said. "Okay, so adventure! Let's say Girl goes on a trip across the country. Why? Why is she travelling?"

"Let me think," Joni said. "She could have family out west. Maybe the lady having difficulty finding milk is her mom. Or maybe her mom needs help. Hmm . . . Maybe her mom is the one who dies? Or just has issues? Like maybe she's too old to take care of herself. Maybe her dad ran off chasing trucks or something. Yes! Dad is a total douche."

"Alright, sounds like you're starting to get something cooking," Dottie said.

"If I were to root it all in some sort of reality," Joni said, "maybe she's estranged from her parents a little. Kinda like me."

"Estranged in what way?" Dottie said.

Joni wracked her head for more memories.

Memories. Memories are the key. Thus sayeth Cate. Chapter twelve. "Memories are your greatest secret weapon. Pull them out, dissect them, and use them for spare parts."

"I could use myself as an example. Sort of like a jumping off point for the character. I'm kind of estranged with my parents. I mean we still talk, but not about anything honestly. Actually, scratch that. I don't want her to be an avatar for my thoughts and feelings about fundamentalism. I want her to have a more adventurous element to her."

"Probably a good idea," Dottie said. "I read a book one time with this really annoying scientist who was clearly just the author's mouthpiece. He was always correcting everyone and acting smarter than everyone, and the author clearly loved him and devoted whole chapters to this guy's ramblings. It was so smug and annoying. I could practically hear the author jerking himself off with glee."

"Oh God," Joni laughed.

Dottie shrugged her shoulders. "I'm just saying."

"I think those are called author surrogates," Joni said. "Yeah, no, I wanna avoid that."

The road took a right, then a left, then kept going straight. The road's speed limit was seventy-five. The landscape rose slightly, blocking out the view of the relative flatness just beyond the top of the surrounding hills. Just over the hilltop to their left, however, the white, spinning blades of a windmill came into view, standing out in contrast to the blue sky. As they neared the top of the hill, another windmill appeared beside it, then another, and another. As they crossed over the hill and saw more endless flat land, Joni was taken aback by how many windmills there were. They seemed to stretch on for miles away on either side of the road, like soldiers awaiting battle orders. What would have been a lush, green, flat pasture was now fully decorated with windmills. Some blades spun slow, some spun fast, and others not at all.

I've never actually seen windmills in real life, Joni realized.

What surprised Joni most of all was how sleek and modern they looked. These weren't the rusty, weather-beaten clunkers she'd expected and seen in so many old pictures and illustrated editions of *Don Quixote*. These were tall, shiny, and surprisingly skinny. The blades looked more like giant airplane propellers.

"Maybe I can include a windmill in my story," Joni said. *No, not a windmill. Maybe some kind of structure, though.*

It was a mesmerizing sight, but after crossing over a bridge above a small creek, it became flat again. The gray road beneath them vanished into a distant blurry line where the grass and sparse trees all seemingly met. Some of the natural flow of grass would be interrupted by patches of bare dirt and rock. Joni noticed some hills here and there in the distance. Reminding herself that it was all flat and a simple matter of perspective, she drove steadily on.

Every once in a while, she'd notice a farmhouse in the distance, but the trees were becoming increasingly rare, and those tired colors were still getting more and more tired of being green. The hills were more apparent in the distance. Some looked more like small rocks that had popped out of the earth with minor landslides underneath them.

"You got a name for your character yet?" Dottie asked.

"I think so. Claire. I like that name."

"Does that name have any meaning?"

"Not really," Joni said. "I used to know a Claire in college. We weren't like best friends or anything. The name just seems right for some reason."

After driving a little further, Joni noticed that her fuel was starting to look a bit low. "I hope they have a gas station soon," she said. "There doesn't seem to be too much out here."

"No, there really isn't," Dottie said.

As the noon sun started its downward descent, Joni saw less and less green and more and more brown. The grass became thinner, more spread out, and rocks and dirt appeared more and more frequently. Joni rolled down her window and stuck her hand out. It was hot outside, but the wind felt nice against Joni's skin.

"There's an exit up here. Might have gas," Dottie said, fumbling with the GPS. "I'll try to pick up some smokes. I'm about out."

"Cool."

When they reached the exit, they were dismayed to see that it had no gas station.

"Maybe the next one?" Dottie suggested.

"How far is it? We only have about a quarter of a tank left."

"Five miles."

"Well," Joni said, "that'll have to do." But when they passed this exit, it also did not have a gas station.

"I really hope we don't run out of gas," Joni said. "It looks hot out there, and I do *not* want to get stuck in tornado country pushing a car."

Dottie laughed. "Joni, everything west of the Atlantic Ocean is tornado country. We just happen to be in the heart of it all. Anyway, the next exit is in three miles."

More and more distant hills on either side of the road were starting to look like rocks poking out of the ground. Their tops were getting flatter, and instead of being covered in grass, they seemed to be bare and collapsing with dust and rocks.

When they reached the exit, they were relieved to discover a gas station. Dottie bought cigarettes while Joni pumped the gas. *I better start hitting gas stations when I see them. This must be the part where you go hundreds of miles before hitting another one.*

She screwed the fuel cap back on and went inside to use the

restroom as Dottie came out. "Bathroom," Joni motioned as Dottie nodded. When Joni saw the bathroom, she saw a sign stating that it was for paying customers only.

Of course. Well, I could use some caffeine.

After a delightfully relaxing piss, she bought a soda using a spare five-dollar bill she had in her purse. Back on the road, Joni listened to the hypnotic hum of the car going about seventy miles. Dottie reclined her seat and stared at the ceiling. "Wanna keep working on your story?" Dottie asked.

I have no fucking idea what my story is going to be about.

"Sure," Joni said, then sighed. "I realize I don't have any good ideas just yet. Maybe a dying girl, maybe she's a writer, maybe she's traveling. But these just don't feel right to me."

"Why's that?" Dottie said.

"They feel too safe," Joni said. "Like . . . okay, you remember me talking about the Blue Ghost?"

"I remember."

"It's like I want to think more creatively, more adventurously, but then I keep getting that feeling. Like when I wrote that mummy story and my parents deleted it and got the youth leader over. It made me feel guilty, and now it's like I've got some sort of mental barrier preventing me from being more creative."

"Joni," Dottie said. "What did I say about waiting for permission?"

Joni took a deep breath. "I'm the only one who can give it."

"Right. So tell this Blue Ghost to go fuck itself. What sort of story would Joni write if there was no shame or guilt attached to it? You can write about anything in the world."

Joni thought for a moment. "Maybe something with the supernatural."

"Ah!" Dottie smiled. "Now that sounds interesting."

"Yeah. It does." Joni knew she needed to think about it further, but it felt good to admit what kind of story she wanted to write. The Blue Ghost didn't seem as big as he usually did.

The sun was shining a little to the left of Joni's vision now. *Time to break out the shades.* Joni pulled the lid down on her windshield storage compartment and took out her sunglasses. With the glasses, the sky was tinted and the glare not quite so harsh. Rocks decorated the ground for miles around them now. The grass had largely been replaced by sparse shrubs and bushes.

As late afternoon began to set in, they crossed into New Mexico. Supported by two huge columns was a big, yellow sign suspended above the highway that read *WELCOME TO NEW MEXICO – LAND OF ENCHANTMENT*.

"Dottie! We're in New Mexico!"

Dottie smiled. "Feel good about giving yourself permission yet?"

A wave of inspiration hit Joni. "Hell yes! I've officially gone further west than Mom! I've always dreamed about this place. Like, is it all desert? How dense is the rattlesnake population? I honestly have no frame of reference for this place other than that it's the home of Katherine Stinson!"

Dottie cocked her head sideways at her babbling niece. "Who?"

"Katherine Stinson!" Joni said delightfully. "Famous early aviator. People always talk about Amelia Earhart, but everyone forgets about Katherine. She was a famous stunt pilot and the first woman pilot to carry mail. Actually, she did a lot of cool things."

"She lived here?"

"Santa Fe, I think. We won't get to see her old home, sadly. But hey! So what! History and stuff! It's the desert!"

They pulled off at a rest stop not far beyond the state sign. Getting out of the car, Joni was surprised by the temperature. It was hot, but not as humid as Oklahoma had been. Inside the station, Joni used the restroom, then took a few brochures back to the car while her aunt also went. As Joni sat in the car, barely able to contain her excitement about this state, she noticed a tiny dust devil just beyond the protective gate of the parking lot. It started small, but as it travelled west in front of her car, it steadily got bigger. It couldn't have been fifteen feet away.

I've never seen a dust devil before. Damn, it spins fast. I wonder how big it'll get before it sizzles out? I wonder what would happen if I put my hand in it? I read they aren't as powerful as tornadoes, but still . . .

The sudden thought of tornadoes killed her joy and made her straighten up and look behind her. There was nothing but a slightly raised hill of brownish-yellow shrubbery and the road. No other cars were out. The anxiety was trying to make a comeback, and Joni hated it. The joy of making it this far had tasted so good.

Taking off her sunglasses, she realized that the sky was still incredibly bright blue with only a few clouds in it. She decided to roll the windows down.

When Dottie came back, Joni took a deep breath. "How much further to the hotel?"

"Two hours," Dottie said.

"Good."

8

The wind swept through the open window and blasted Joni's hair wildly as they sped along at seventy miles an hour. Dottie leaned over to her niece. "I don't know if you want to do this, but it looks like we might have some opportunities to do some sight-seeing tomorrow."

"Really? Like what? More desert?" Joni laughed. She loved this new and unusual landscape. The scenery was tan and rocky for miles all around, spotted with green and yellowish plants. Dirt roads running adjacent to the highway stretched away to distant houses and towns. They passed a hitchhiker once and a work zone with men repairing a bridge, but that was about it. There seemed to be nobody else on this long, lonely stretch of road.

"Well, there's a famous meteor crash site we could go visit," Dottie said. "You get to walk right into a massive crater. It's called the Barringer Crater. Looks like it's a ticketed thing. You gotta pay to get in."

"Hmm. How massive are we talking?"

Dottie chuckled. "You really are freaked out by heights, aren't you?"

Joni shrugged apologetically, then said, "Sorry. I'm just learning this about myself. I mean, it might be cool to see a meteor crater, but I don't know. The idea makes me a little uncomfortable. Let's stand right where a giant rock smashed into our planet. Maybe someday, an even bigger rock will smash into the planet and kill us all."

Dottie laughed. "God damn, child. Buzzkill, much?"

"Sorry. What else is there?"

Dottie scrolled through her phone. "There's the Petrified National Forest. It's on the way to Flagstaff. It's a park, but they've got lots of cool sights. They've got the Painted Desert, petrified rocks. Fossilized trees, I think. Or what's left of them, anyway. Newspaper Rock. It's got a lot of old petroglyphs on them."

"That's the one," Joni said. "We should go see the Petrified National Forest. I want to see the petroglyphs."

"It's ticketed, too. And it looks like they don't want you to take any rocks or fossils with you, either."

"I can understand that. Because of erosion?"

Dottie continued scrolling on her phone, reading a website's information. "Looks like you'll be haunted by the ghosts of a thousand Native-American spirits if you steal."

"Say what now?" Joni said, bewildered.

"This website says that when people steal the petrified wood and rocks, they invoke the wrath of an ancient curse. People have claimed to have seen visions of angry buffalo at night, so they return the wood to lift the curse."

"That's very weird," Joni said. "Still, I think I'll just take lots of pictures instead."

"Hallucinogenic fossils," Dottie said. "Asteroid craters and now hallucinogenic fossils. What the fuck."

The shrubs and greenery dotted the landscape like a minefield. In the distance, Joni could see rocky hills rising again. It felt very western now, and Joni realized that her own expectations of what the desert would look like were all based in fantasy. This land was anything but bare. It was rocky, dusty, and decorated with the last standing warriors of flora. They were gray, brown, and yellow, but they were still here.

"Those are some pretty hills," Joni said, pointing at one that jutted upwards with sheer rock walls but was almost completely green and flat on the top.

"They're called mesas," Dottie explained. Pulling out a cigarette, Dottie tried to light it, but the wind made this difficult. "Damn it, wind." She leaned over at an awkward angle to light it, cursed, and rolled up her window.

"We got an hour to Santa Rosa. Want to do anything there?" Dottie asked.

Joni had given this some thought. "I read that they have this old, abandoned church. It was built in the 1740s, but it's been abandoned and turned into an historic site. I'd like to get a few pictures of it if I can."

"That might be fun." Dottie fumbled with the cigarette again, but to no avail. "Joni, you mind shutting the window for a sec? I can't light my damn cigarette."

Joni shut her window. Dottie ignited the end of the stick, inhaled deeply, and let loose a burst of smoke. Dottie puffed again. With the windows closed, the car instantly smelled of burnt tobacco. Joni coughed while her aunt exhaled again.

"God, this is an incredible invention," her aunt said. "Want a stick?"

"I'm good, thanks," Joni said. "I'm giving myself permission to live, but I'm not a smoker."

"Suit yourself," Dottie said before lowering her window again to let out the smoke.

It was about four o'clock when Joni pulled off the exit and into the town of Santa Rosa. The road sloped ever slightly downward through the town leading to the busier section. There were buildings and restaurants on either side of the road, and the street was moderately busy with traffic. The sky was beginning to turn vaguely pink as the setting sun approached. Signs acknowledging Historic Route 66 were posted here and there. Some roads acted as offshoots from the main one and led down into neighborhoods while others led off elsewhere. One road to their left appeared to lead into a community park.

Not long after arriving in the town, Joni and Dottie checked into their hotel. Their room was the first door to the right of the suite's entrance. Inside, the room was much smaller than the previous two had been. Only one person at a time could walk between the dresser to their right and the two beds facing it. There was a flat-screen television hanging from the wall above the dresser. Joni claimed the far bed closest to the black-draped window. Dottie set her suitcase down on the bed closest to the bathroom. After dropping her bags on the floor, Joni plopped down on the bed.

"I am so tired and yet so hungry."

"I need to shower," Dottie said. "I ain't showered in three days. I can feel the sweat setting up colonies on my skin."

Joni waved her hand. "Go ahead. I think I need just a few minutes to rest." Dottie grabbed her stuff and went into the bathroom.

Joni stared up at the ceiling. The white spackled texture looked like it was drifting away from her, as if she was still driving and the ceiling was just another horizon too far to reach. She rubbed her eyes and yawned.

The thought of ascending the Colorado Plateau started to bug her again. Today hadn't been too bad, but she sensed that her fear of heights was going to return soon. Not knowing exactly what the land looked like ahead made her more anxious about continuing.

The shower spicket sprang to life in the bathroom. Dottie called out from behind the closed door, "I figured the shower out! You gotta turn the knob upside-down! The labels are backwards!"

As Joni rubbed her temples with her eyes closed, she let her mind wander. She tried to think about her story a little, but that led nowhere. Then she remembered Dottie throwing out the half-empty bottles of wine.

Instinctively, she looked at her aunt's green suitcase. She felt an urge to open it just to see what all was in there. Sitting up, she listened for her aunt. The patter of running water was interrupted by her aunt moving about in the shower. Feeling that she had at least a few moments to look, she went over to the suitcase.

Joni hesitated. *This is so wrong.*

With the shower water still going, Joni suddenly flipped open the two latches. Opening it, she caught that scent of old strawberries again. She saw what she'd expected: clothes. There was also a brown, leather-bound book sitting on top. Curious, she quickly flipped through the clothes. She tried not to rustle the clothes too much. She didn't want it to look like someone had gone through the clothes.

Feeling somewhat ashamed for idly snooping, Joni shut the suitcase and locked it. She went back over to her bed and closed her eyes. It took her a few seconds to realize what she had just seen. Suddenly, she sat up straight and looked back at the suitcase.

Oh my God, that book.

The shower was still running. Quietly moving back over to the suitcase, Joni unlatched the suitcase again and opened it. This time she looked at the brown book more closely. It had a violet ribbon bookmark sticking out of the bottom. The edges were worn and warped from what seemed to be almost exhaustive use, and the book had to have been from at least the early 90's. The leather had flaked off in many places. Joni lifted it up and debated opening it, listening for any change in the sound of the shower.

She opened it. Sure enough, there were personal journal entries written in pen and pencil.

This is it. This is her diary.

Joni had an overwhelming sense that she'd just found the metaphorical holy grail. Whatever had happened between Dottie and her parents, this book might hold the answer. This book would answer the question Joni had been dying to get to the bottom of. No more would she have to settle for, "Well, Dottie's just a liberal atheist."

Joni started to turn to the front page when something fell in the tub with a dull *thud*, probably soap. With lightning-fast agility, Joni shut the suitcase with the book inside and latched it up. Almost immediately, the shower water stopped.

Oh shit, so close.

A few moments later, Dottie stepped out wrapped in a towel. Her aunt grabbed some clothes from her suitcase, not indicating any sign that she suspected Joni had gone through her belongings.

"You wanna go see that church?" Dottie asked.

"Sure do," Joni said, sitting on her bed idly and pretending to know nothing about the existence of Dottie's diary.

"Alright. Let's fix some sandwiches to eat, then hit it up."

"Sounds good to me." Joni reached into her own purse and pulled out her camera. *Gotta read it next time.*

After they ate a meal of sandwiches, chips, and veggie pouches— Joni's stomach was throwing a tantrum by this point—they drove back and turned left through the road that ran adjacent to the park. The sky was a pinkish-purple now. The road slanted downward, making Joni weary again of coming across a cliff. Eventually, the road turned left, and they pulled onto a street that felt flat again. To their right were a few houses with fencing. To their left, however, was the abandoned church, white and collapsed against the clear, cloudless sky. It was fenced off, prohibiting onlookers from getting any closer. Joni parked on the grass at the edge of the property and got out, taking her camera with her. Dottie got out and looked as well.

Jumping the fence would have been easy, but Joni felt a strong urge not to. She decided ignoring the "No trespassing" sign would be the height of disrespect, so she decided to just look from a distance. A nearby sign read *St. Rose of Lima Chapel and Cemetery.*

It was a halting ruin of dilapidated white walls. There was no visible roof, and near the top, some jagged bricks still stuck out in defiance to weather. Just beyond what would have been the doorframe, Joni could see that grass was growing where the floor had once been. Nature was still reclaiming this church.

In front of the ruinous church was a small cemetery. Average-to-large-sized stone monuments with crosses and some angelic figures dotted the grassy lawn. Joni could almost touch one just beyond the fence.

She'd heard of ghost towns. She'd actually looked up and considered visiting some when she'd done her research. Almost all of them were a little too far out of the way for her trip, but this church was enough for her.

"It's haunting. To think that this church used to be a staple of the community," Joni said.

"Yep," Dottie said, looking on in deep thought as well. Aside from a gentle breeze in the grass, nothing could be heard. No evening crickets, no distant cars. Nothing.

"It's so quiet here," Joni said. "Like a quietness that hits your soul, you know? It's kind of eerie. Like it reminds me that everyone dies eventually. And then the earth reclaims us, just like it's reclaiming this church."

Dottie said nothing for a moment, then nodded slowly. "I know what you mean. It reminds me of that passage. Something about how we came from the dust of the earth, and so we must return? Something like that."

Joni snapped a picture of the church, but then almost felt guilty when the camera shutter clicked. It was just so silent here. It almost felt like snapping photographs at a funeral procession.

"I can't help but wonder," Joni said. "How many lives did this church help? How much of its community did it influence? Did it bring this place together? Did it tear it apart? It's just really haunting to think about."

Haunting.

One of the stories she'd worked on as a teenager came back to her. The one with the lighthouse and the girl defending it from zombies.

Oh my God. Claire could be defending a haunted lighthouse.

Then Joni laughed. Her laughter pierced through the somber quiet of the site, and it surprised her aunt. A deep passion suddenly stirred in Joni—the peaceful scenery of this dead church somehow moved her.

"Dottie, I think I just had an *aha moment* for my book."

"Yeah? What's that?"

"I could have Claire defending a haunted lighthouse. But like the lighthouse has some kind of significance to the place. Like this church. Maybe it's on an island. It's an historic lighthouse or something. I had a story sort of like that once. One that my parents deleted. It was about zombies. I don't want to do the zombies, but seeing this church just got me thinking. About how I had some good ideas, and if I'm going to try to live my life without anyone else's permission, then why not start by reclaiming a few things?"

Dottie smiled, then looked back up at the church.

"It may be haunting, but it's beautiful, too, isn't it?" Dottie said.

"It is."

Joni lowered her camera. "Dottie, do you want to get a picture together?"

Dottie cocked her head at Joni with a raised eyebrow. *Why does she always look at me like I'm trying to sell her something? It's like she doesn't trust the words coming out of my mouth.*

"Okay. Where should I stand?"

Joni smiled, running over to the car. The sun was shining at an angle so that shadows protruded in front of the church. Joni situated the camera to compensate for this and set it on the car trunk. Turning it to Dottie, she said, "That should be good where you're at. I set the timer for ten seconds."

She pressed the shutter and outran the camera's ten-beep countdown. Joni put her arm around Dottie's back. Dottie slowly put an arm around Joni's shoulder. They both looked at the camera and smiled.

"I always hated holding a smile for the camera," Dottie said through grinning teeth.

"It won't take long."

She's so rigid. Like she isn't used to hugs or something. I feel like I'm taking a picture with a marble statue.

The camera snapped the picture.

"You want another one where I pose like a saucy debutante?" Dottie joked, raising her right hand in the air and thrusting her hips to the side.

Joni laughed. "If you want!"

Dottie posed like a saucy debutante, and Joni made finger guns with a goofy face. After the timer went off, the camera snapped the picture. "That'll be one for a photo journal. A legendary photo for the ages," Joni said.

"Nice camera," Dottie said. "Does it record video?"

"It does," Joni said. "I actually have an old tape camera back home. I debated bringing it, but this one does video, too, so I just left it. This one's way better, anyway."

They looked at the viewfinder to examine the photos they'd just taken. They laughed at their poses and decided to do another silly one.

Back at the hotel, Dottie was lying down on the bed closest to the bathroom, eyes shut. Next to her bed was the green suitcase.

In the other bed, Joni had her laptop open, feeling . . . *that feeling.* It was the same feeling she'd felt whenever getting inspired from Cate Marlington's writing seminars. The feeling that the sky was merely a roadblock. Beyond space was where she wanted to be. Anything was possible. And she wanted to get her ideas typed out before they left her.

Joni didn't know who Claire was just yet. But whatever intentions Joni had when she'd first thought of her story, she'd now come to realize they were just shackles holding her back from writing the story she wanted.

This would not be some boring character study about a daughter learning to care for her mother. This would not be about some hurley-burley man with an unhealthy obsession for cars beating his chest and learning to be kind to others. This would be an adventurous story with a ghost and a haunted lighthouse. Claire was going to have to defend the lighthouse somehow from either a ghost or something else.

Joni typed her thoughts out as quickly as she could. *What the church taketh away, Joni taketh back, motherfuckers!*

Then she remembered the diary in the green suitcase, and the will to write faded. Drowsiness overtook her, and as she settled in for the night, her mind wondered what secrets the diary contained.

9

The next morning, Joni felt good showering. She'd gotten quite a few things figured out about her story and now felt that it was finally starting to take some shape.

Her thoughts soon turned to Dottie's diary and how it might hold the answer to why Dottie was disowned by the family. An idea to try to read it began to form in Joni's mind. She'd already tried asking Dottie directly what had happened, but her aunt said she didn't know. Joni didn't believe this, but she figured the truth was probably too painful for Dottie to go into. The diary was her only option left for solving the mystery. Rinsing her hair, she imagined what the defining moment might have been.

Maybe she got pregnant out of wedlock. Oh shit, what if she got pregnant and then got an abortion? That would definitely do it. Hmm. Could also be something stupid. Like she mooned them or something. A funny image of Dottie smoking a joint and sticking her bare ass at her parents came to Joni that almost made her burst out laughing.

That would have been hilarious.

As Joni exited the shower and got dressed, Dottie returned from the front lobby with some doughnuts and bagels for breakfast. "They ain't got any milk in the vendor. Says they're all out," Dottie complained. "I want some damn cereal."

"We can pick up some in Flagstaff when we get ice," Joni said. "The ice needs replenishing soon, especially now since we're in the desert."

Dottie threw her arms up. "I need a smoke."

Soon they were back on I-40 with nothing but the sounds of Lukaas Bennett on the speakers and desert all around them. The wild brush looked uniformly uninterested in trying to be exotic now. It was content enough just to be present.

"You seem chipper this morning," Dottie said, enjoying her first cigarette of the day. "You enjoying giving yourself permission to live?"

"I am," Joni said, smiling. "I actually got some writing done last night."

"Cool beans!" Dottie said. "What'd you write?"

"Well, I decided to explore making it about a girl named Claire who has to defend a lighthouse. When I was a kid, I wrote the one about zombies attacking a lighthouse, but I don't want to do zombies. So I started thinking about what else I could do. And then it hit me: why not have her defend the lighthouse from a bunch of crazy fundamentalists? Use what I know, right?"

"This story is starting to pique my interest," Dottie said. "What kind of fundamentalists we talking about? Christian? Generic religious?"

"I'm still figuring those specifics out," Joni said, "but I started drafting sort of the local history of this lighthouse. I think it's going to be on an island where these religious people have lived for ages. The lighthouse is sort of the job no one wants, and Claire gets stuck with it. She's eighteen years old, just finished her apprenticeship or whatever, and . . ."

She thought for a moment. "I'm toying with making them think she's a witch and that's why they attack the lighthouse, but I'm not sold on the idea yet. Maybe she really is a witch but like a good one who actually helps them without them knowing it, but their blind religious fanaticism makes them hunt her down. But I don't know. I'm just toying with the idea."

"Wow! It sounds like you're off to a good start with your story," Dottie said. "And doesn't it feel good to not care whether someone thinks it's righteous or not?"

"It does feel good," Joni said. "Really good."

In the distance, the horizon ran very nearly straight from left to right, but every now and then on either side of the road Joni saw those flat, upended hills where the land had seemingly fallen away.

"What did you say those tiny mountains are called? The flat ones?"

"Mountains?" Dottie said, squinting. "Those little rocky cliffs with the flat tops?"

"We're not in the Rocky's, are we?" Joni asked, getting alarmed.

Dottie laughed. "Not even close, sweetie. Those are called mesas."

"Hmm," Joni thought, getting a little anxious. She clutched the steering wheel, prepared for the roadside to unexpectedly drop several hundred feet on either side of her. This land looked old, like something out of a movie about dinosaur excavations. Her mind went from worrying about heights to wondering how many dinosaur bones lay hidden under the road forever entombed and never to be found. How many had she driven over since leaving South Carolina?

The road took a sudden turn through two somewhat mountainous-looking white cliffs of sheer, dynamited rock. When the road started steadily going up, Joni clutched at the wheel, not daring to let go. She held her breath, too scared to relax. At that exact moment, a semi-truck driver appeared behind them in her rearview mirror. He didn't seem too keen to slow down.

"Oh shit," Joni said quietly.

Dottie, sensing her niece's unease, turned off the music.

"You look tense, Joni."

"I'm good!" Joni blurted.

"You sure? You want me to take over?"

"I'm good!"

She felt the sweat collecting underneath her hands again. She was dismayed by how quickly her enthusiasm had been dampened by her fear of heights. She began to imagine all the horrible ways they could die.

What if my hands slip? What if we nosedive off a cliff? 'Flat' my ass. There's mesas, hills, mountains. Meteor craters the size of lakes! And now there's a semi behind me. Great. I can either die by cliff-diving or die by semi-truck.

Anytime the road bent or rose even slightly, she felt disoriented. The road became one lane. They passed a brown sign that read HISTORIC 66 and pointed toward the cliffs.

"I thought we were on Historic 66?" Joni said.

"This is I-40. It replaced the old 66," Dottie said.

"But that sign. Is 66 in the cliffs? Are we going to drive up those cliffs? I don't see a turning lane anywhere."

"No, Joni, we're not driving up the cliffs. It's okay. You'll be alright."

When the road came out of the valley of small cliffs, it was above the treetops. They were at least ten feet above trees.

"What the actual hell!" Joni said, now breathing heavily. "We're above the tree line, Dottie."

"Sweet baby Jesus, here we go again," her aunt said, shaking her head in annoyance. "Look, we're not that high up. It's alright. This ain't no worse than anything you got back in Greenville."

Joni continued to breathe heavily. She gripped the steering wheel tightly, too afraid to take her eyes off the road ahead of her. The semi-truck driver passed her and was soon way ahead of her.

When they began to pass through Albuquerque, her fears became almost unbearable. At one point, their GPS told them to continue down a particular exit. When they reached the exit, however, the GPS fixed itself and indicated that they had taken a wrong turn. When it redirected them to an exit so they could turn around, they found that the exit was *CLOSED FOR REPAIRS—TRY ANOTHER EXIT!* This led them to yet another closed-for-repairs exit, and another. That the road itself was on a raised bridge surrounded by even higher bridges did not help Joni's anxiety. Joni's breathing became more frantic. She felt her skin grow hot and her heart beat faster. Finally, their GPS gave up and indicated that they should turn around whenever possible.

"You okay, hon?" Dottie said.

"Goddamn it, goddamn it, goddamn it," Joni kept repeating quietly.

They finally found an exit to pull off of. She eventually found her way into a grocery store parking lot. She parked near the back end of the lot far away from the customers and took deep breaths. There were patches of clouds in the bright blue sky, but Joni could only stare at the steering wheel.

Just breathe.

As Dottie readjusted the GPS coordinates, her aunt said, "The Painted Desert is only about three hours from here."

"I thought you wanted to go to the Petrified Forest thing?" Joni said, feeling the pressure mounting.

"It's part of it. You wanna go?"

Joni sighed. "Dottie, I'm really scared of heights."

Dottie blinked at Joni in disbelief. For a moment, she turned her head to look out the front windshield, as if trying to think of something to say. Then, she turned to her niece and said, "Why did you take this trip, Joni?"

Joni kept breathing heavily, trying to reorient herself. "Try new things. Get some writing inspiration."

"Joni, we are heading to Flagstaff. It's nearly 7,000 feet above sea level. That's higher than Mount Mitchell, the tallest mountain peak in the Appalachians. Honey, we are ascending the Colorado Plateau. But guess what? It's all so gradual that everything looks flat!"

"Oh, God! Why'd you have to remind me?" Joni felt the color drain out of her face and into her bladder. *I have to pee.*

Dottie suddenly pointed at Joni. "Alright, you know what? Move. Get out!" To Joni's bewilderment, Dottie threw off her seatbelt, got out of the car and marched over to the driver's side. "Out!" she shouted again.

"Why?" Joni asked.

"Get out! I'm driving."

Joni awkwardly took off her seatbelt and got out. Dottie plopped into the driver's seat while Joni reluctantly went over to the passenger's seat. Getting in and strapping on her seatbelt, she looked over at Dottie.

"Are you sober?"

Dottie laughed and started the car. "Plug in the Painted Desert. We're gonna have some fuckin' fun today."

Joni, hesitating at first, did as she was instructed. *Okay, breathe. Breathe. Breathe. You can trust her. You can trust her.*

"It's about three hours out," Joni said. Turning to her aunt, and in the vain hope she could get out of this one, she said, "Do you think we'll have time to make it to the motel in Flagstaff before dark? I mean, I didn't exactly see if they had late check-in or not."

Dottie laughed. "Joni, you need to lighten the fuck up. You keep trying to play it safe, and eventually your life'll run out without having done anything." With that, Dottie took off. Joni frantically tried to read the directions off the screen, but the GPS was once more rerouting.

"I don't know where to turn!" Joni said, exasperated.

"Relax, little grasshopper," Dottie said. "I know my way. I've been out here before, remember?"

"Well, yeah, but—"

"Just trust me," Dottie said, now cackling and driving fast-as-fuck in the slow-as-hell lane. To Joni's surprise, Dottie was able to reconnect with I-40 west, and they were once again staring at endless miles of desert road and the occasional mesa.

Dottie had one hand on the steering wheel like some hotrod from the fifties. With her other hand, she reached into her purse and pulled out the other Lukaas Bennett album. With stunning agility, Dottie swapped the discs and began playing his second album, which Joni now saw was titled *Don't Die*.

How appropriate, she thought.

As an upbeat violin solo began, Joni leaned over and noticed that her aunt was going eighty miles an hour. The road here was seventy-five. Instinctively, Joni pressed her foot down on an imaginary passenger's brake pedal and grabbed the door hanger. *If you run into anything over seventy, you're dead.*

"Going a little fast, don't you think?!"

Dottie rolled down both front windows. "Ah! Feel the breeze!" her aunt said, flicking her cigarette out and draping her left arm over the doorframe.

"Don't you think we should slow down a bit?"

Dottie shrugged. "Nah. Some places out here let you go ninety."

"But what if we hit something? What if a tire blows out?"

"Here's an idea: *what if it fuckin' doesn't?*" Dottie said. "You can't live your life in constant fear, Joni. Yeah, there could be a nail on the road just waiting to pop our tires. Then again, there might not be. Whatever the case, we're gonna enjoy the moment because life is short, life is precious, and this is our time to be self-indulgent. It's summertime, baby!"

Joni stopped trying to reason with her aunt, and instead focused on regulating her breathing.

"Man, this thing has much better pick-up than my old wagon did,"

Dottie remarked. "This is a nice little car. Seems to get pretty good gas mileage, too."

"I bought it my senior year of college," Joni said, trying to engage in conversation long enough to distract herself from her fear.

"New?"

"Used. The original owners outgrew it when they had a kid, I think."

"Their loss," Dottie said.

When three hours had passed, their exit showed up on their right. A brown sign indicated the exit led to the *Petrified National Forest Park*. After a short drive onto the exit ramp, the road began to wind slightly. Joni had never seen so much sky before. The ground was mostly yellow and brown.

Before long, they drove through the ticket booth. After purchasing the tickets, they continued driving a short distance until they reached the small visitor's center. While Dottie went to grab a brochure from a nearby stand outside the visitor's center, Joni decided to fill the tank up since the center had its own small gas station. This turned into a slightly more complicated ordeal than she figured it would. The station used old-fashioned pumps that didn't have debit card readers. Joni had seen them before but never actually used one. Getting out of the car on wobbly legs, she went inside the station and asked the attendant with vivid embarrassment how to use the pumps.

"Oh! You just tell me how much you want to put on the gas."

Had it been any other day, Joni would have calmly done the math to figure out a reasonable amount to charge. Gas prices had fluctuated between stations, and at this point in the desert gasoline averaged about two dollars and sixty-something cents. Her car took about twelve gallons. Having surrendered her car to Dottie, ridden in said car for too many hours, and agreed to go explore the desert with possible mesa-scaling involved, she was in no mood to mentally calculate exact dollars and cents times twelve.

"Twenty-five dollars, I guess," Joni said, hoping it would be right enough.

"Alrighty! Which pump?"

Joni mentally kicked herself for making this exchange even more awkward by not checking first. "Let me go look."

She figured a quick look out the window would do, but the pump was so small that her car was actually blocking the number from her view. Awkwardly, she went outside and looked at the pump to determine that it was pump 3. Returning, she told the attendant that it was pump 3. The attendant rang it up and said, "Alrighty! You should be set!"

Finally, she went back to the car to pump the gas. Dottie had returned and was now waiting patiently in the driver's seat with the window down, looking through a brochure she'd found.

"Dottie, do you mind if I drive this one?" Joni asked as she pumped. "I'd like to take it slow."

Dottie sighed, looking at Joni to see if her niece was being serious. When she saw that Joni was, she handed her back the keys and sighed getting out of the car. "Just don't freak out on me, okay? How much I owe you for gas?"

"Just twenty-five."

After finishing the gas and getting into their seats, Joni took off down the road. It definitely looked like miles of more desert, but she noticed that the scenery to her right was hillier. After quite a few minutes of driving, they finally reached a pull-off to the right where they could park and take in the view of the Painted Desert. What Joni saw almost made her collapse in her seat.

Just over the lip of the hill, which was defined by a small wall of stone, was a vast expanse of hilly desert that seemed to sprawl out nearly a hundred feet below them. Some hills looked red and purple while others were sandy-brown and white. The hills appeared smooth and humbly majestic. In the distance, she spotted some clouds. In the middle of the hills, a large cloud covered them with a shadow. Aside from a gust of wind hitting her ears and smacking her loose strands of hair against her face, there was not any other sound.

Joni felt nervous standing so close to the edge. This wasn't helped when Dottie decided to stand on the stone wall and say, "If anyone wanted to kill themselves, this would be a good place to do it."

"Oh my God, Dottie! You're gonna fall!"

"I ain't gonna fall. I'm just gonna get some good pictures." Dottie pulled out a small point-and-shoot camera and began taking pictures. Joni watched nervously as her aunt tempted fate in various and disturbing ways, such as leaning over to snap a picture of some unseen part of the slope or turning around and leaning back to take a selfie.

"Be careful. It's pretty far down," Joni said.

"This is nothing."

As her aunt continued to snap pictures, Joni kept a safe distance from the edge. Something about the curvature of the horizon was making her lose her balance. She wasn't used to it being so flat. She wondered how her character Claire would react to such a sight.

It is gorgeous.

As they got back in their car, they took off further into the park.

If that was the worst of it, Joni thought she might be fine. But when the road wrapped around to the left, it swung a little too closely to the edge. With no guardrail there, that sinking and disorienting feeling came back. Against all reason, it felt as if she were being pulled off the edge. She clutched the steering wheel.

"Oh God," she said.

Ahead in the near distance, the mesa seemed to rise even higher. She knew she was safe going slow and not actually driving off the road, but the anxiety didn't care. Joni felt nothing but fear as she inched forward in the car. Despite being on a perfectly even track of road, she felt as if the car would slide off the mesa and fall hundreds of feet to end in a violent explosion. She could sense the tiniest of rotations in the steering column, the pull of gravity on her tires.

The path curved around to the left again, giving them a wide-open view of the Painted Desert. Dottie said, "Wow! It's so colorful for being a bunch of rocks and dirt." Joni, however, couldn't enjoy it. The path climbed higher as it swerved around, giving her the sensation that they had nothing behind them to catch them if they fell, nothing to stop them if the car engine shut down or the brakes snapped, and they rolled backwards.

Fuck anxiety.

Joni started to quietly cry. Dottie looked at her niece with wide eyes.

"You alright?"

Joni couldn't stop herself. "No, damn it! I can't do this!"

"Then let me drive," her aunt said calmly.

"No! I need to be in control!" It sounded stupid in her own ears, like she was a toddler throwing a tantrum. But it didn't matter. She had to be the one to fight against gravity pulling them sideways, even though she knew in the back of her brain that it wasn't doing that at all.

They pulled off onto an overlook and parked. Joni breathed deeply as she set her head against the wheel.

"Just give me a minute. My nerves are gone."

Dottie waited patiently, hardly moving. "If I may ask, is there a reason you don't want me driving?"

Joni took a moment to catch her breath. She tried to find the words to convey to Dottie what she was experiencing. She knew none of it would make any sense to Dottie, but it was terrifyingly real to her.

"I feel like we're going to slide off the mountain." Joni looked at Dottie for the condescending look of doubt. What she got was one raised eyebrow from her aunt.

"Mesa," her aunt corrected. "We're on a mesa."

"Whatever! If we fall off it, we die. Or break lots of bones. Either way, I'm scared of heights. I feel like we're going to fall off, like we're being pulled over the edge by some invisible force of gravity. I know that sounds stupid and impossible, but it's where I'm at right now. Okay?"

Dottie held up her hands. "I hear you. Take your time. Don't need to jump down my throat."

"I'm sorry. I just . . . I'm freaking out right now." She felt sorry that Dottie had to see her outburst, sorry that they'd come so far only to discover that she had trouble adjusting to heights. She also sensed disappointment. Not so much for Joni being afraid of heights, but rather for not simply trusting Dottie to take the wheel and drive them.

Wiping away the tears, Joni said, "I'm not crazy, Dottie. I promise. I'm just scared of heights, and I didn't realize it."

Dottie shook her head. "You don't have to apologize for it, Joni. Fear of heights is a real thing. It's called *acrophobia*. I'm just curious why you don't just let me drive. Heights don't bother me."

"I know, I just . . ." *I have no excuse. I just have to overcome this. I have to. Try new things. Take chances. That's what this has all been about, right? Go with it. I can do this. Just breathe.* "Look, it's not you, Dottie. It's me. I have to overcome my fear. I know it's weird. I just have to do this."

Without much enthusiasm, she pulled out of the overlook. Turning right to continue down the road, she clutched the wheel and cocked her head to wipe the sweat from her forehead on her sleeve.

"Okay, I'm driving up the mesa. Gonna do this," she said.

"Just keep your eyes on the road and don't look at the sides," Dottie said.

The road continued to rise. Joni's heart beat faster, feeling that imaginary tug of gravity. *It's not real, it's in your head. It's not real, it's in your head.* "Let's go out in a blaze of glory," Joni joked. "Falling off a mesa would be a great way to go out."

Dottie wasn't amused. "My offer still stands. Otherwise, please don't kill me."

"Okay. Sorry." Joni was relieved to discover that the road flattened out and veered further into the heart of the mesa away from the edges. This began to calm her nerves considerably.

Dottie relaxed enough to pull out the brochure guide she'd picked up at the visitor's center. "So just a few more miles and we'll be at Newspaper Rock," her aunt said. "The rocks are covered in petroglyphs."

"Neat!" Joni said, eager to distract herself from the fear of heights.

"What the hell is a petroglyph? I thought those were only in Egypt," Dottie said.

"No," Joni said. "Those are hieroglyphs."

Dottie referred to her phone. "Says here that they might be as old as two-thousand years. No one knows exactly what they mean."

The road stretched on until they came to another parking lot to their right. Once Joni parked, they got out and walked down a little walkway to another overlook. In passing some of the other parked cars, Joni was surprised to see a South Carolina license plate. The familiar blue and orange graphic with the palmetto tree warmed her heart a bit. *If someone else can do it, so can I.*

There were a group of people standing near the railing that separated the walkway from the edge. The people were looking and pointing. At first, all Joni saw was more desert with a large cluster of collapsed rocks and cliff-side some twenty yards away. Sagebrush sprouted in-between the rocks below. Getting out her camera, Joni zoomed in on some of the blacker rocks that stood out from the otherwise dusty-orange ones.

That was when she saw the petroglyphs. Little squiggles of orange stood out on the blackened rocks, conveying what looked like aliens from another world. Some looked like circles with dots in them, others looked like bizarre symbols, and one in particular looked like a character straight out of a poet's nightmares, snorting up some squiggly lines.

Joni felt a desire to study this language more, but time was pressing them to move on. Dottie pointed and said, "That one looks like an elephant-man snorting crack."

One of the other tourists, a woman of about fifty and wearing a white visor, pointed at the rocks. "There's a snake down there!" she said in a thick, Southern drawl.

Her teenage daughter carefully ambled up to the fence to peer down while her younger son leapt onto the fence without any concern for gravity. Joni's heart leapt up, fearing he might fall over and smash into the broken rocks below.

"I don't see shit!" he said.

"Get your ass down from there!" she said.

Maybe she's their grandmother? Joni thought.

"It's right there, where the shadow meets the two rocks. You see the ones I'm talking about? The ones lying right on top of each other? Right there."

Joni and Dottie leaned over. "You see anything?" Dottie asked her.

"I see shadows and rocks. No snakes." As they continued looking, Joni realized that her fear of heights was beginning to subside. She started to feel a little less anxious and a little more grounded.

After they took a few pictures, they got back in the car and turned around. The desert was very scenic, but they still had a ways to go before reaching the motel. As they came back down the mesa, Joni still took it slow on the curve back near the edge. To her surprise, it was a little easier to manage this time. Perhaps it was because she was on the inside of the road instead of the outside, or maybe because she was used to it more.

Just keep thinking happy thoughts. Keep your eyes on the road ahead only.

As they passed the visitor's center, she was surprised to see that no one was there to check her car to make sure they weren't smuggling fossilized forest out. It didn't matter, though. Joni had no intention of taking rocks, and it wasn't out of a fear of being stalked by a phantom buffalo. It was because it felt like doing so seemed disrespectful, and Joni didn't want to be that asshole.

Back on I-40 and heading west, Dottie turned to her niece and said, "What'd you think?"

"It was beautiful," Joni said.

"Yes, very beautiful. To think we could've missed all that beauty, too," Dottie said.

True.

10

"Alright, we're officially in Flagstaff," Dottie said as they took the exit. "Elevation is over 6,000 feet."

"Really?" Joni said, disturbed by the idea. Two giant mountain peaks dominated the skyline to their right as if holding back the otherwise purple, cloudless sky. "I see mountains right there. We're not going up there, are we?"

"No! Jesus Christ, Joni! How many times do I have to tell you? Colorado Plateau! We've been going up so gradually, you don't even realize how high we are!" Dottie lit a cigarette and laughed to herself. "Going way up there. Yeah right. Like they'd put a major highway up on a cliff like that."

As they drove to the motel, Joni kept her eye on the two massive peaks. Joni thought she detected some snow on the very top of one of the peaks. *They are gorgeous, the way the trees cover it like a blanket and then disappear for a few bald spots.*

They reached the motel and checked in just as the stars were beginning to appear in the darkening sky. Their room was very comfortable, and Joni felt the ache of constant driving. Dottie immediately took a shower. Plopping back on her bed, Joni turned on the television. Some crime drama about jaded cops dealing with a drug deal was on. A man got shot. One cop was holding his partner.

Dottie started humming in the shower. Looking out the window, Joni could see the two mountains hovering over the city like sentinels sent from on high to lord over the earth. The sky was now dark blue, and the stars seemed to be much clearer here than back home.

Then Joni remembered the diary.

Turning over to look at Dottie's side of the room, Joni was dismayed to see that the green suitcase wasn't there. *Did she take it with her into the bathroom?*

Rolling back over and disappointed, she fluffed her pillows up on the bed and lazily watched the cop drama. She was too tired to write anything, and since the suitcase wasn't there, she couldn't sneak a glance at Dottie's diary. Her mind idly turned to thinking about what gift she could get for Violet's birthday. She knew it would depend on what she found—and could afford—once she got to the Grand Canyon, but having an idea of what sort of gift to look for would help.

Could get her something cool, like drums made from animal skin or something. Might be expensive, though.

Later that evening, Joni drifted in and out of sleep. The windows let very little light in, so the room was almost completely black. As her eyes adjusted to the darkness, she rolled over to see Dottie asleep in her own bed, facing away from Joni. Between the two beds on the floor was the green suitcase. The diary inside of it, Joni wondered if she could somehow discreetly unlatch the suitcase and sneak a glance at the diary without stirring her aunt.

It was so dark though, and the slightest sound might wake her, so Joni lost her nerve and shut her eyes instead.

What's in that diary?

The next morning, Joni showered, threw on jean-shorts, a red t-shirt, her sunglasses, her shoes, and looked up at the mountains. She gave them a mental salute and thought to herself, *Lot of beauty outside my little bubble. I'm terrified of the heights but fuck it. I'm going to see one of the greatest landscapes in our planet's history. Today, I live.*

The ice in the cooler with their water bottles had mostly melted, so they dumped the water in the tub before leaving the motel. After turning their room key in and hitting the road again, Joni and Dottie stopped at a gas station for gas, coffee, milk, cereal, and ice. Dottie poured the ice in the water bottle cooler. Joni replaced the empty water bottles, put the milk in the cooler, shut the trunk, and hopped back in the driver's seat.

Pulling out of the gas station, the road took them on a series of turns through the town. Where there wasn't a forest of ponderosa pine, there was a building or stretch of houses on either side of them. Always standing out against the clear blue morning sky were those almighty peaks. Joni admired their beauty but was also terrified the road would somehow have them drive up there. At one point, the road out of Flagstaff took them down a fairly steep hill that ended with a red light. Other than that, the driving was relatively flat. As they left Flagstaff behind, Dottie snapped a few pictures of the mountains.

"It's gorgeous out here," Joni said.

"You doing okay? I mean, better than yesterday?" Dottie asked.

"Yes!" Joni exclaimed. "I'm just reminding myself that it's all pretty flat here, with a few mountainous exceptions. We're just really high up on a plateau, and being able to see over the bushes and mostly sky just gives me the sensation of being really high."

Dottie shrugged and looked back at the mountains. "Well, whatever works for you. You're doing fine."

The unexpected compliment made Joni smile. "Thank you."

They passed open fields with cattle feasting on grass. They passed deer and what could have been elk grazing in the distance. Pine trees replaced the shrubbery. Joni rolled her window down. It felt liberating to let the rush of wind thrash her hair about. Dottie let her hand catch the breeze as well. With Lukaas Bennett playing a delightfully warm melody, along with the cool, relaxing wind Arizona was throwing their way, the day couldn't be more encouraging.

"We don't have to listen to this if you don't want," Dottie said. "If you want something else or quiet, you know, we don't have to listen to Lukaas Bennett."

"No, no, I like this. The music matches the weather," Joni said.

After a left turn, they found themselves in the desert again with some shrubbery. They crossed a few bridges with dried-up riverbeds underneath.

"Mini-canyons," Dottie said.

About an hour later, they were driving through the main town of Tusayan. The road was better paved than the one running through the desert had been. It rose steadily toward and disappeared into a range of distant trees that dominated the horizon. On either side of the road were restaurants, hotels, businesses, and buildings.

Feeling their stomachs rumble, they stopped to grab a quick lunch (burgers and fries). Happy to take a break from chips and veggie pouches, Joni was a little shocked to find that a small burger and soda cost her almost fifteen dollars. Dottie ordered a much larger burger and soda and ended up paying an additional seventeen dollars. Dottie paid for it all to make up for the gas Joni had gotten at the Painted Desert gas station.

When they finished eating, Dottie threw her trash away and said, "Ready for the Grand Canyon, kiddo?"

"You bet." With that, they hopped in the car and continued driving up the street. Soon the buildings became scarce and were overtaken by trees. The road bent slightly left but kept mostly straight. Either side of the road was now flanked by pine trees. It was all still very flat, but according to their GPS, the entrance to the park would be approaching soon. Joni found herself falling behind a camper going about ten under the speed limit, which was just fine by her.

When the entrance to the park appeared, the road split into several lanes that ran under the arches of the admissions booths. Joni pulled into the one that might have been designated for people with all-year passes, but the lady at the booth graciously helped her purchase a regular pass and sent them on their way.

The road progressed through masses of pine trees under the occasional glimpse of sky, but Joni drove five under the speed limit out of fear that the road would suddenly turn and send them flying off into the canyon. She wondered when the massive hole in the ground would show its face. *I really hope we don't end up driving alongside the edge.*

Her fears were unfounded. They found the village and their lodgings without seeing any bluffs or canyons. Once they got checked in, they went and found their room. The room had no air conditioning but did have a ceiling fan, two beds, a large flat-screen television, and a large dresser.

Setting her stuff down on the bed closest to the window, Joni pulled back the curtains and looked outside. As the light poured in, she was pleased to see nothing but forest in the view. Some squirrels darted across the ground and up a tree. According to her research, elk and mountain lions could also be spotted here, but Joni didn't see any.

"Think we'll see any elk or mountain lions?" she asked Dottie, who was bringing in the last of the food coolers and her green suitcase. Dottie set the cooler on top of the dresser under the television and said, "Elk, yes. Mountain lions, maybe. The last time I came here, I didn't see any mountain lions. You know what they say, though. Stay away from both, and if you run into a mountain lion, make yourself look big and make lots of noise."

Dottie set the green suitcase on the bed closest to the bathroom.

Joni raised an eyebrow. "Somehow I don't think that'll stop a mountain lion from trying to eat me."

Dottie shrugged. "It's an official stay-safe tip. Kinda like running in zig-zags if you meet a bear."

"Umm," Joni said with increasing skepticism, "I think these are made-up safety tips. The only one I think that's been proven is don't feed wildlife."

"What?" Dottie said, applying sunscreen lotion to her bare arms now. "I feed wildlife all the time! At home, I'll throw the birds some expired bread. I feed the squirrels some food, too."

Joni grabbed the sunscreen lotion and applied it to her skin. The lotion was cool and smooth to the touch. *Good thing I didn't forget to bring this. The sun would've cooked me alive.* Joni had to remind herself how deceptive the weather could be out here. The altitude was much higher than they were used to back home, which meant that the air was a lot cleaner and less humid. At the same time, feeling comfortable could lead one to forget about the sun's ultraviolet rays, so sunscreen was a must.

"You ready?" Dottie asked, smiling.

"Yes! Let's go!" Joni said. She grabbed the keys and got two water bottles out of the cooler. Handing one to Dottie, she said, "Thanks for being my navigator."

Dottie waved a hand. "Thanks for not disowning me forever!"

Smiling, Joni led the way out. Locking up the room, they hopped in the car and took off. The road continued winding through a forest of pine trees and shrubbery. Joni kept a lookout for any sudden cliffs, but they never appeared. A view of the sky became wider as the trees receded to make room for intersecting roads and turnoffs. Finally, they found the visitor's center.

Parking in one of the large parking areas, Joni and Dottie got out. The sky was a vibrant blue all around them, broken up only by the line of trees shielding them from view of the horizon. Further up the incline before them, the parking lot met a sidewalk leading to the visiting area. Many people were walking on this sidewalk, and many others were returning to their cars. Joni and Dottie followed the sidewalk to a group of signs, and the signs pointed them in the direction of the canyon. They walked through a large courtyard of gift shops, information centers, and restrooms.

They passed a fairly alarming, multilingual sign that read in bright red letters *Do Not Feed the Squirrels!* It had a circular graphic of information displaying a squirrel, a flea, and a hand with a nasty-looking bite taken out of it. It explained information about ravenous squirrels that had an appetite for human flesh, especially if a person fed them. It also expressed caution of their fleas.

"Well, shit," Dottie said. "Guess I'm done feeding squirrels. That bite looks nastier than a skunk's asshole."

Joni and Dottie continued beyond the sign down the paved walkway. All around them were visitors who were just as eager to glimpse the canyon as they were. Some kids were running back towards them, excitedly exclaiming how huge it was. To her right, she saw more squirrels eyeing her before scurrying off into the thickets. A crow to their right chewed on a plastic cup. She moved towards it, which made the bird hop away. She grabbed the cup and threw it away.

"Someone just threw this cup on the ground," she said. "Was the trash can really too out of the way for them? I mean, it's literally right here."

"What a jackass. May the villain choke on plastic," Dottie said.

The path continued. Then the trees became sparser. At first, it looked as if they were looking straight up into the sky. Then, as the edge came into view, Joni slowed her walking. *This is it.* People were gathered near the edge, cell phones out and taking pictures. A man told his family, "Smile!" As they came near the fenced edge, Dottie let out a gasp. "My God, I'd forgotten completely."

Joni froze in her tracks, dumbfounded by the sheer size of the canyon. Distant, sprawling mesas and cliffs stretched out before her as far as she could see. After taking in the thin, blue haze of the distant mesas, she was able to discern the rocks and crags on the sides of them. There was so much detail to take in as the massive landscape stretched far below out of sight. The lower mesas were covered with what looked like green shrubs. The green seemed uniformly flat and spread out. On the higher mesas, she was able to see the outlines of trees against the far, hazy, blue sky.

Joni remembered having a similar sensation the first time she'd ever seen the ocean before. It was like looking into the gulf of space on Earth. She grabbed a nearby tree to steady herself. The view was so overwhelming that she felt as if she were going to fall over the edge, even though the edge was some ten feet away and shielded by a metal fence.

Getting out her camera, she said, "Wanna take a picture, Dottie?"

Dottie stepped up. "Maybe we could ask someone around here to help take it for us." As if on cue, a woman stepped away from the edge and asked them, "Would you mind taking our picture?"

"Sure!" Joni said. The woman handed her a camera, and then she and her husband posed in front of the fence. Behind them was a clear view of the canyon. A Utah juniper tree was stationed to the right of them and created a nice, natural portrait. *I envy how comfortable they feel standing that close to the edge with their backs.*

"On three. One . . . two . . . three!"

The couple smiled as Joni took the picture. "Thank you!" they said. "Would you like us to get a picture of you and your mother?"

Dottie laughed. Grabbing Joni by the shoulder, Dottie pulled her niece close. "Sounds like a swell idea! Sure! Come on, daughter!"

"Sure thing, Mom!" Joni said, also laughing. Dottie's jovial attitude was infectious, and Joni smiled for the woman taking the photo. After the lady took the picture and handed the camera back, she asked, "Where are you from?"

Joni said, "We're from South Carolina."

The woman's eyes brightened. "Oh, okay! My in-laws are from there. They live in Greenville."

"Really?" Joni said. "That's where we're from!"

"Wow! What a small world!"

"Where are you from?"

"We live in San Francisco, but I was born in Thailand originally."

"Wow! Cool! Well, thank you so much for taking our picture!" Joni said.

"No problem! Thank you! Have a good one!" With that, both parties went on their way. Joni and Dottie continued walking left down the trail, stupefied at how vast the canyon was. The longer she looked, the more details Joni realized. At first it looked as if wild greenery had overtaken one giant, flat mesa far below. Then she was able to make out that there was a long walking trail running through the greenery. There was even a barely noticeable man walking it. *How'd he get way down there?*

Beyond that, much further below in a deep gorge, she was just able to see a thin band of the Colorado River. Getting out her camera again, she zoomed the lens on it just to make sure.

That's the Colorado, alright. Should've signed Dottie up for some whitewater rafting.

There was something surreal about watching condors soar through the sky a hundred feet below where she was standing. Even more peculiar was watching little squirrels pop their heads up over the canyon wall to scurry up trees or into the brush. Joni kept her distance from the fence, feeling too anxious to get any closer to the edge. One thing that didn't help was watching little kids run beyond the fence and jump up and down.

Are they crazy? Do they want to die? Where the hell are their parents? Turning, she found the mom and dad, standing there with cameras out by a grove of trees and telling their kids, "Smile!" *Oh, okay. They're endorsing this? Is there a trail I'm not seeing?* She was curious, but she didn't feel comfortable approaching the fence to look over. That falling sensation was back and even worse than when they'd been at the Painted Desert.

Moving on from what was sure to be a disaster in the making, Dottie and Joni continued taking numerous pictures.

"Oh, look at those people!" Dottie said, pointing ahead.

Down below in the canyon, a large stretch of rock extended

outwards. The bulk of it seemed to be resting on a rather fragile-looking mound of sheer rock-wall. On top was a broken-up, rocky flat-top. Dozens of people were standing on top of it, seemingly oblivious to the fact that a few mere steps to their left or right would send them plummeting hundreds of feet to their deaths.

"Wanna go down there?" Dottie asked, pointing at the flat-top.

"Nope. That is a well-rounded, fast-as-fuck *hell no*. I thought we couldn't leave the trail?"

"Nah, I'm pretty sure we can go down there," Dottie replied.

"Have at it, Dottie. I'm good."

The trail opened up onto a natural lookout. The ground was pure stone, but at least this had a well-defined, fenced-in area. As she and Dottie descended onto the platform, Joni felt that incredibly shaky feeling in her knees. Only this time, there were about a dozen or so people behind her waiting for her to go down the steps. Clutching the railing at an awkward angle, she tried her best to give them space, but they didn't seem to take the hint that they could move around her.

Great, now I'm holding up traffic again.

When she got down there, she felt more comfortable staring into the gorge than turning her back to it. As she awkwardly clung to the fencing like a spider, she took in every detail. Every rock. Every bush. Every color. Every layer. She even saw that the same two kids from earlier were running along a little walkway she hadn't seen before.

As she stood there absorbing the scenery, another condor soared and landed on one of the rocky outcrops. Peering closely, she saw that it had a number clipped to its wing. Getting out her camera, she zoomed to get a clearer picture. She was able to snap it just before the bird took off again. As the bird flew away, she examined the photo. She was able to make out the number 23.

I'll have to look into that later.

On their way back to their room, she said, "Well, Dottie, we made it. I couldn't have done it without you."

"No problem. What's the agenda for tomorrow?"

"I want to write. I want to sit and write tomorrow morning, try to get some ideas figured out. Since we're here for two days, you could do whatever you wanted to while I wrote. Maybe tomorrow we could go see the canyon after lunch. Oh, we should also go look for a gift for Violet, too. Can't forget that."

Dottie nodded her head. "That sounds reasonable. You mind if I take the car, then, while you're writing?"

"Sure. Just don't drive it off a cliff."

Dottie laughed. "Deal."

When they got back to the room, they broke out some sandwiches and fruit pouches for dinner. Dottie turned a Humphrey Bogart movie on the television. As she ate, Joni tried to process the visuals she'd experienced that day. The canyon had been so much larger than anything she'd ever seen before. But that fear of heights was also gnawing at her. She felt that if she kept her distance from the fencing, then she could manage it. Then again . . .

We drove all this way. Maybe I should try looking over the fence just once, just to say I did it. Face that fear. Give myself permission to be a little bold.

As they watched the movie, Joni noticed the green suitcase out of the corner of her eye. It was lying on the floor next to Dottie's bed. Joni wondered if she might finally be able to sneak a glance at the diary while her aunt would be out.

The next morning, Joni took a shower. Dottie called out in the hallway, "I'm heading out to the canyon! You need anything?"

"I'm good! Drive safe!"

"See you later!" Joni then heard the front door shut.

She felt a little wobbly in the shower, as if she were on a boat rocking to the waves. She placed her hand on the wall to stabilize herself. *Whoa, Joni. Keep your shit together.* She felt her feet cement to the tub.

When she got out of the shower, she wrapped herself in a towel and went immediately to the front door. Looking out of the peephole, she didn't see the car.

She's gone.

Joni went over to the green suitcase and unlatched it. Dottie had thrown some dirty clothes haphazardly in with the clean clothes, but Joni carefully looked through each of them. To her dismay, the brown book was nowhere to be found. Joni closed the suitcase and looked around the room in the hope that Dottie had left it out in the open somewhere.

It was not in the room. *She must have taken it with her.*

"Damn it," Joni said, standing up and feeling annoyed. *She took it with her. That was my best chance to read it.*

Resigning herself to this setback, she got dressed while her laptop booted up. Looking out the window, she saw a large, brown lump with antlers resting in a shaded area of the woods. Moving to the window for a closer look, she saw that it was an elk.

She watched as its ears flicked, and its snout wiggled. Its massive sides expanded and contracted as it breathed rhythmically. She thought of how at peace it seemed. Despite not having an exact home to call its own—this was, after all, a national park with lots of people walking around like they owned the place—it was the lord of its own life. It ate as it pleased, it drank, it mated. It just lived.

Moving to her bed, Joni opened the computer file for her untitled book project and stared at the disjointed notes she had so far. She had the character's name, the setting of a lighthouse on an island, and a town of religious zealots attacking the lighthouse. Now, she needed to make some sense of it all.

Joni typed in the obligatory 3-act structure parts including the inciting incident and denouement. Then she took it a step further and split the second act into two parts. Then, underneath the Act 1 exposition, she simply wrote *Claire becomes a lighthouse keeper.*

Joni thought for a moment. She recalled some details from her lost mummy story to see if she could reuse anything from that. Her mummy story followed Barbados who rode a camel endlessly through the desert to save an archaeologist named Teresa (his love) from being sacrificed to the mummy and allowing it to live forever. He pushed his camel too hard, rode it too fast, and the poor beast collapsed on him in the middle of a sandy, lonely desert. The camel died, and Barbados lost his friend, but he had to push on to save his love. The final chapters would have dealt with Barbados's epic midnight ride through the desert to rescue Teresa before the mummy killed her.

There's something there, Joni thought. *What if Claire has to protect someone she cares about in the lighthouse? Maybe the townspeople go all Frankenstein on the lighthouse with pitchforks and torches because of the other person, not Claire.*

Joni typed her thoughts out underneath the story structure section. *But why would they attack the other person? What did the person do?*

Joni wracked her brain trying to think what would work best. Then the idea came to her, and it made her laugh how simple the solution was. She typed it out before the thoughts could leave her.

Later that afternoon, Joni and Dottie split a pizza for lunch at the lodge dining hall. As they ate, Joni told Dottie about the progress she'd made on the story.

"I decided to make it about a haunted lighthouse."

"Ooh, haunted! Nice," Dottie said, pouring some parmesan cheese on her pizza. "What will your parents think about that?"

Joni laughed. "Who the hell cares? It's my story!"

"Good girl. I've raised you well!"

"So it's haunted by a ghost. I was trying to think of what sort of religious community this island is made up of, and I think I might lean more into them being just really superstitious of anything that isn't traditional or out of the norm. Kinda drawing on religious fundamentalism but not being so heavy-handed about it, you know? And I figured that if they're superstitious, what better thing to be superstitious about than a ghost? So by the end, they'll end up attacking the lighthouse because of the ghost, and Claire has to defend her."

"The ghost is a girl?"

"Yep. It took me some back-and-forth thinking about it, but I decided that it's going to be a young adult mystery story. Claire has just become the lighthouse keeper. It's kind of the job no one else wants, and she just sort of ends up stuck with it. On her first night as the new lighthouse keeper, she discovers a spirit who dwells in the lighthouse. At first she's scared, but then she discovers that this ghost is actually just a fun-loving dreamer who means well. Claire befriends the ghost and enjoys her company each night as she tends to her duties. As the story goes on, she learns more about the ghost—I don't have a name for the ghost just yet, but it was a girl when alive—and comes to realize that the ghost can't leave the lighthouse because of some unfinished business. The ghost doesn't know how she died, so Claire sets out to find out."

"I see," Dottie said. "Sort of like trying to fill in the gaps. Does the ghost not remember what she was doing before dying?"

"Not exactly," Joni said. "She's bound to the lighthouse because it turns out that's where she died, but Claire has to figure out what happened exactly. So she basically investigates in her own little discreet way, and that's how we get sort of a window into the small-town politics of this island. She learns a lot about the people and how their superstitions and biases turn otherwise good people into secretly horrible people."

"I like this idea," Dottie said. "It seems like you're drawing from experience without being over-the-top with it."

"Exactly. That was one thing I was struggling with: how much do I use before I'm just writing my own life story? One of the things that's important is that Claire keeps this friendship a secret because she knows how freaked out the townspeople would be if they learned there was an actual ghost in their lighthouse. And of course they find out at almost the same time that Claire learns the truth. She discovers that the ghost is actually the previous tenant who died after falling out of the tower. But remember, the ghost has no memory of this. She doesn't know what happened, who did it to her, or why. That's the unfinished business: once she learns what happened and why, then she can pass into the afterlife and be at peace. Claire comes to learn that the mayor pushed her out the window. The mayor is the one who killed her."

"Oh shit! Does she learn why he did it?"

"Yes. Money. I think money. For now, anyway. He wants to build a new lighthouse with an electric light—I'll have to do some lighthouse research here probably—but the tenant refused to give up her family lighthouse and is the key owner who wants to turn it into an historic landmark, meaning he can't have it demolished. With her out of the way, no one could stop him. So he kills her and makes it look like an accident, clearing the way for the local government to seize the lighthouse."

"That's a neat twist. But if she's a ghost, why can't she just, I don't know, float away or something?" Dottie asked.

"So I decided that because she has no memory of the incident, she has that unfinished business and so remains attached to the lighthouse. She can't leave it until she learns the truth. Sadly, this also means that destroying the lighthouse would vanquish the ghost, and the murderer would get away with his crime. That's where the town storming the lighthouse at the end will come into play, right as Claire learns the horrifying truth and reveals all. I'm still figuring out the details in places."

Dottie swallowed a bite of her pizza, then said, "Sounds like your story is really coming along, Joni. That's really awesome. You want me to read it when you finish it?"

"Would you want to?"

"Sure, yeah! I think it's really neat to watch you go from having no idea to suddenly you've got this really creative story, and now even I'm interested in reading it. Sounds like it'll be a good one."

"Thank you," Joni said, turning her attention to her own pizza.

"I could never be a writer," Dottie said. "I don't think I have the patience for it. Reading is hard enough to find time for, but writing? That's completely out of my ballpark."

Joni shrugged. "You just gotta find what you love to do."

"Yep. I mean, I'm trying to be better about reading," Dottie said. "I used to read a lot more when I was younger, but the older I get, the harder it is to find time. Or maybe not, I don't know. I'm less motivated, I guess. Anyway, this is damn good pizza."

Joni smiled at this rare self-reflection on Dottie's habits. She wondered if she might try to ask Dottie again about what happened with her parents, but Joni decided to just enjoy the pizza instead.

After lunch, the two drove back to the canyon. There were a lot of people, and the sun was high above in the clear sky. As Joni and Dottie walked the length of the edge, Joni spotted a gift shop.

"Let's check this shop out."

"To find something for Violet?" Dottie asked.

"Yeah."

They went inside. The shop was dimly lit, contrasting with the brightness outside. The space was crowded with racks of postcards, shelves of hand-weaved blankets, pottery, some spears and bows, trinkets here and there. Joni scanned the aisles looking for the perfect gift.

A totem. Something Violet can look at during those rough college all-nighters and be reminded that she's got someone rooting for her.

Observing a spear that was suspended across a low-hanging door frame into another section of the shop, Joni grimaced at its two-hundred-dollar price tag. Moving over to the display cases, she saw smaller items that seemed more within her price range. She spotted a balancing eagle.

"Maybe Violet can use this as a totem for college," she said, picking it up. This one was slightly larger than her hands combined and had been painted black and brown. Its accompanying perch was a miniature tree extending out of a desert mountain—a trinket no bigger than one of her hands.

Yes, this seems right.

After purchasing the balancing eagle and having it gift-wrapped, Joni and Dottie left the shop and continued strolling further down the walkway. The canyon descent was about five feet to their right, and Joni was beginning to feel a little dizzy again.

"So we got another day here, right?" Dottie said.

Joni nodded. "The rest of today, and we leave around noon tomorrow. Maybe a little after."

"Then where are we off to?"

"Well, next we head to Cortez."

"Colorado?" Dottie asked, looking past Joni to survey the canyon.

"Yep. I've planned a roundabout trip that will allow us to go see Horseshoe Bend first, then get back onto the main road and get to the motel at a reasonable time."

The path suddenly dipped down onto a short tier of stone steps. The protective fence to their right ended, and Joni was faced with the dreaded feeling that a simple gust would send her toppling over the side. She quickly traded places with Dottie so that her aunt was closer to the edge than she was.

Dottie laughed. "You know, I'm starting to think that you don't like me, Joni."

"Sorry. Edge. Scary," Joni said, trying to stay focused on the path while knowing fully that she was missing a spectacular view to her right. The trail led up and up to a distant mesa. A jogger in yellow spandex came past them. Joni gravitated left off the trail to give her room. As she ran past them, Joni couldn't help but wonder if the jogger had a death-wish.

One bad trip is all it takes.

"I'm not sure where this fear of heights is coming from," Joni said. "I guess I just haven't had all that much experience with heights before."

"Have you thought about exposing yourself more?"

Joni gave Dottie a double take. "Say what, now?"

"Expose yourself more."

Joni raised an eyebrow as they continued walking. "I should get naked?"

Dottie laughed. "Expose yourself to more heights. You're freaking out now because you aren't used to the heights. But after a while of some exposure, you'd become used to them. And I bet you'd be able to handle even bigger heights after this."

Joni didn't want to even think about bigger heights. The discombobulation of being on the Colorado Plateau had all but sent her into shock. Now, as they were walking and the guard rail ended—exposing them to *one bad trip and it's all over*—Joni found herself walking slower and reaching out to lean on anything she could, like a tree or a shrub. She tried to focus on something, anything else.

What's in Dottie's diary? Am I in it?

Joni gave it her best, but the height was too much for her. They found a bench just to the left of the trail for her to sit on. Joni clutched the seat and slowly sat herself down. Against all her reasoning skills, she felt as if she might accidently slip and fall to her doom. Her aunt sat down beside her while Joni caught her breath. She rubbed her temples and tried to reorient herself.

Why am I having so much trouble with this?

Dottie patted her on the back.

"You wanna turn back yet?" Dottie said.

Joni hadn't expected her to do this. Even more, she hadn't expected to feel a pang of emotion hit her as Dottie patted her back.

"Sure. Let's go to that spot where everyone catches the sunset and sunrise."

Joni felt disoriented, but here was her aunt, who'd been estranged from her for most of her life, rubbing her back to make her feel better. This simple gesture brought her more warmth than she'd felt in a long time.

It reminded her of the late nights with Amy, when they'd stay up late discussing their hopes for the future, their frustrations of college life, and their mutual distaste of mayonnaise. It seemed an eternity ago to Joni now, and she could barely relate to her college self anymore. Amy had left her in the dust some time ago, but here was Dottie who had nowhere to go in a hurry and seemed genuinely concerned with making her niece feel good.

On the way back, they found a water fountain and replenished their bottles. A sign next to the fountain explained that the water came from natural springs in the canyon. It also urged guests to drink frequently. Joni took a giant gulp and felt her lungs soak up the water like dried sponges.

They walked nearly two miles back. The canyon was on their left now, and they walked past the point where they'd parked. Joni was on the inside of the path, looking past Dottie at the sheer size of it all. One mammoth mesa extended out towards the rest of the canyon like a leading battleship, signaling the other mesas to prepare for the wear and tear of the day. The path ultimately led to a cluster of rocks where many sunset-watchers had already begun gathering. Some teenagers were on their phones, as were their parents, but all Joni could do was sit down and watch in awe.

As Joni stared at the massive mesas, she saw more condors soaring far below her. One seemed to hover there like a drone looking for some place to land before diving down and settling on a tree branch protruding from a ledge on the distant mesa. The mammoth mesa before them now glowed a deep red, catching the sunlight like a fly-net. The sun went down, down, down, until finally it was nothing more than a distant glow.

Joni looked over to her left. In the distance, the last rays of the sun filtered through a range of trees and leaves, creating a halo of purple, red, and yellow. It looked like something out of prehistoric times. Just below that was a large, jagged rocky outcrop, supported by a flimsy-looking column of ancient mesa. Even as she watched, rocks tumbled down its side to the distant, unseen bottom. There were dozens of tourists walking all over the top, jumping, skipping, running, posing for selfies, and standing at the very edge with their backs to the void below.

Fuck that noise, Joni thought. *If they want to tempt fate like that, they can go ahead.*

All those people made Joni wonder just how stable the outcrop really was. She imagined the worst-case scenario of a landslide. The outcrop collapsing, followed by the rest of the canyon crumbling and dragging everyone down to the depths . . .

Joni shuddered at the thought, feeling very anxious of the height again.

Early the next morning, Dottie went for a jog down the same path (so as to avoid the rush of tourists) while Joni sat on the rock-cluster again. The sun peeked over the top of a distant mesa before her, casting a crown of yellow over the dim, blue canyon. She watched, mesmerized by the sight. With her camera, she snapped a few pictures.

As she took in these final moments with the canyon, she thought about everything. About what she would say when she confronted her parents. About how following their advice would have made her miss out on this breathtaking view. About how she had begun to let go and embrace her life without waiting for permission. About how the Blue Ghost had seemingly vanished into nothingness. About her fear of heights. About what was in Dottie's diary. About how this was supposed to be the trip that reunited her and Amy and all their friends, and how Joni was the only one here.

And it somehow didn't bother her as much as it used to.

Joni stood up. There was a break in the crowd at the fencing, an open spot waiting for someone to approach it.

Now or never.

She took deep breaths, planting her feet firmly on the pavement. Her legs felt like they weighed a ton, her heart beating faster and faster, but her soul begged to see what lay beyond the fence.

Give yourself permission.

Slowly, she walked over to the fence. It felt almost like a funeral march to her legs, but she was determined to do this. She reached out and touched the cold, iron fencing. Some light rust on the railing reassured her that she had something tangible and firm to hold onto. Tightly gripping the fence, she pulled the rest of her body slowly to the edge and looked down.

The rocky cliff dropped down and away to the lower mesas. She slowly looked up to glimpse the distant mesas again.

I fucking did it.

11

"I gotta pee," Joni said.

It was about three hours later, and they were on the road driving through the desert. The landscape had been mostly tumbleweed and gray bush-strewn country for much of that time. The soil looked sandy and orange. Here and there in the distance were mesas, and the road often took them over what had probably once been riverbeds some millions of years ago, but there were no exits or good makeshift restrooms anywhere to be seen.

Dottie glanced at her phone briefly. "Horseshoe Bend is only four miles away. Do you think you can hold it? Maybe they have restrooms."

"It'll have to do." Joni exhaled to relieve the intense bladder pressure that threatened to burst her open like a balloon. *Why didn't I go before we left?*

"Think you could go behind one of these rocks on the side of the road?"

"They're not tall enough. Besides, I don't want to tick off a rattlesnake."

Dottie laughed. "I doubt you'll encounter a rattlesnake."

Joni considered pulling over and going under one of the small bridges they were about to cross, but then realized that if a snake was bound to be anywhere in the desert, it'd be under a shaded bridge.

The next few miles were absolutely agonizing as Joni felt the pressure of her bladder build. It was now a race against time to find a bathroom. The entrance to Horseshoe Bend finally appeared on their left just off the road. It was a giant parking lot filled almost entirely with visitors. Huge RVs and campers that took up a lot of space made it difficult to drive quickly through the narrow lanes between the parked automobiles. Joni turned left towards the far end of the parking area where there were fewer cars. To her dismay, there were no bathrooms in sight. There was not even a portable one.

"I'm going to die," Joni gasped, trying not to hit a group of people and their kids who suddenly walked in front of her car.

"No, you're not. We'll figure this out!" Dottie said. "Maybe when you park, you can go in front of the car."

"No. I need a bottle. A cup. Something, anything. I'm not going in front of people. They'll have me arrested for indecent exposure!" Joni felt beads of sweat start to form on her forehead.

Dottie laughed. Annoyed, Joni looked at her travel mug. It still had about half a cup of tea left in it. She hated the idea, but she knew she was out of other options. As she parked the car near the far end of the parking lot (there were only two other cars parked nearby to their right), she quickly began unzipping her pants.

"I gotta go, it's coming out," Joni said.

"Let me get out first! I'll keep watch," Dottie said, hastily removing her seatbelt and leaping out of the car. Shutting the door, her aunt went and stood near the trunk. Joni quickly grabbed her mug, tossed the remaining tea outside her door, and closed the door again. Making one final check that she was clear, Joni threw her seat back and positioned herself above the mug.

God, this is so humiliating. My poor tea mug.

Out of nowhere, a couple walked right past her car. It was as if they had materialized out of the desert itself. There was no car they were coming from. The man, probably about late twenties with a buzz cut, walked within five feet of her window. Joni slouched down further to try to hide herself from the couple. They weren't paying any attention to her, but she still felt embarrassed and busted.

When she finished, she zipped up her pants and poured the contents out on the ground outside her door. Getting out with the mug, she looked for a garbage can. There were none. Locking the car, she headed to the trunk and opened it.

I know I'm going to tell my parents off for their evangelical bullshit, but pissing in their graduation gift isn't exactly what I had in mind.

There was Dottie's green suitcase along with Joni's own bags. Setting the tarnished mug in the deep recesses of the trunk, she grabbed two water bottles from the cooler, closed the trunk, and looked at Dottie who was smiling and looked ready to start laughing.

Dottie asked, "Have a nice piss?"

Joni felt flustered and red in the face. "I feel much better now, yes. Let's never speak of this again."

Together they walked across the parking lot, skirting in-between parked cars and campers and dodging moving vehicles. They followed a large group of people making their way to the trail that led to the bend. Before them, Joni saw a large desert hill that was speckled with more dry bushes and gray weeds. It seemed to rise towards the sky. There was no sight of Horseshoe Bend from here. At the start of the trail was a park ranger. They approached the woman.

"Do you have water bottles?" she asked sternly.

Joni and Dottie both held theirs up.

"Good. It's really hot today, so we're not letting anyone up without water. It's about a three-fourths of a mile hike to the ridge. Don't overexert yourself. Drink your water. Thank you for coming!"

And with that, Joni and Dottie were off to see Horseshoe Bend. The trail was much dustier than any of the ones they'd used at the Grand Canyon. Here it was largely orange-brown sand with some rocks here and there. On either side of the trail, wilderness had been left to its own designs: mostly gray bushes with the occasional pink Sclerocactus flower or spiky, green Utah agave thrown in to give the appearance of trying.

When they reached the top of the hill, the sight improved dramatically. Joni saw that only about a half-mile away was the ridge, and she could make out the tip of the canyon. Gathered on a large collection of rocky outcroppings were dozens of tourists walking about and taking pictures. Joni wanted to remember it forever, so she took a photo as well. It was odd how the landscape looked from here. The trail went down to meet the distant bend, but across the vast valley was the protruding rock wall that created the "horseshoe" shape, and that made the other side appear to be rising back up towards the sky. Joni felt that bizarre sense of falling again, but this time, it didn't seem so bad. After braving the Grand Canyon's edge that morning, Joni felt bolder about these desert heights.

"The sand is burning my feet," Dottie said. She was wearing sandals.

Beyond the lip of the overlook's rocky edge, the massive drop was much larger than what she'd expected from looking at photos. The Colorado River, dark green and sleek, snaked its way around a sandy bank far below them. Across the expanse of water was the sandy bank that bowed before the almighty protruding rock wall. Joni saw a crash of water here and there, and there was even a boat riding the river, but it all seemed so small and insignificant next to the majestic canyon hovering above and all around. The rock wall opposite her that helped form the horseshoe-shape was brown and red, speckled with green shrubs here and there. Cracks and lines ran down at an angle right towards the stream.

One brave soul who looked to be in his twenties climbed upon the outermost rock ledge and turned his back to the drop to take a selfie. His girlfriend, standing closer to Joni, laughed and said, "You're such a dumbass."

He laughed. "Yeah, but I'm an awesome dumbass!"

Joni snapped a picture of the distant boat and suppressed a laugh. *Maybe I should modernize my story just so I can include that line in there.*

Not too long after, they were on a two-lane road driving through dusty, red country. Tumbleweed and cacti flanked the road on either side, but various mesas and buttes dominated the landscape. The sky was clear blue with only a few clouds decorating it.

Within a few hours, they reached Cortez. The main street was surrounded by various hotels, restaurants, gas stations, and car dealerships. They eventually found their hotel, and after checking into their new room (which was submerged just below street level and gave them the perfect window-view of the underside of parked cars), Dottie elected to shower.

Joni got out her laptop to write, but as soon as she heard her aunt turn on the shower, her attention went immediately to the green suitcase over on Dottie's bed. Joni tip-toed over to it, then waited. She wanted to see if her aunt would unexpectedly step out of the bathroom to find some final accessory she'd forgotten, but it didn't happen. When Joni heard the distinct snap of a shampoo bottle closing in the shower, she leaned down.

This is so wrong. But I need to know the truth.

Pulling the two latches aside, she carefully opened the lid, this time ready for the smell of cotton and old strawberries. After shoving aside some crumpled shirts and jeans, she found the diary. Listening again for any sign of her aunt stepping out, she grabbed it. Flipping it open, she saw that the first entry dated back to January 1987. *Whoa, this thing is old. Guess she doesn't write much.*

Joni flipped to the end of the diary. The last ten or so pages were empty. Then she found an entry from the previous day. It wasn't long. It read:

"Day two at the Grand Canyon with my niece! Tried taking a hike, but Joni flipped out. She's a great kid, but my God is she high-strung. Terrified to death of mesas. Poor child. Wait until she gets to Mesa Verde and sees how high that goes! And she thought the Painted Desert was high! Hopefully she doesn't get us killed. Anyway, lovely desert scenery. Four stars. Would visit again. Wish you were here. Yours, D."

Joni felt a sudden wave of panic set in. *What does she mean about Mesa Verde? How high is it?* Ignoring the panic for a moment, she flipped back a page. The previous entry was a little longer and had been written about a month ago when Joni first called Dottie about the trip.

"Woke up again. Out of beer. Went to the DMV. The usual shit. Some dick in a shirt and tie came in and demanded to get a better ticket number. Flashed his business card like I cared. Told him I didn't control what numbers the machine gave, and he'd need to wait. He called me a bitch for not giving him a better number and cussed everyone else out while he was at it. Then he spat on the floor, then left. I got to clean up his spit and apologize to the other people waiting. So like I said, the usual shit. Got home. You know, I really almost did it this time. I had everything ready to go. Then guess what happens? Well, my niece calls me out of the blue. Says she's going on a trip out west and was wondering if I'd like to go with her. Damn it, I was so close. But I figured what the hell and agreed to it. Alright! It'll be just the two of us! I'm glad to see that she hasn't completely abandoned me like her asshole parents. Laura, you naive, fucking asshole. So, yeah. Joni and I will be heading west in a few weeks. We're gonna see the Grand Canyon and some other

places she mentioned (I forgot where all she said). It'll be fun to go out there again, I think. Frankly, I'm just glad I get to see my niece again. God, it's been years. Still, I'm on my guard. She might truly be her mother's daughter, and this could be some sort of trap. Like a spiritual guilt-trip or something. Guess we'll see. Yours, D."

Joni listened again for her aunt, then focused on the entry. *What does she mean by 'I really almost did it this time'?* She then wondered if her aunt had learned to trust her more now that they'd been on the road for so long together.

The more Joni mulled it over, the more it made sense. Dottie had been open with advice but mostly a closed book on personal details ever since starting the trip, and she had a good reason: Joni's parents. Up until she'd gotten in Joni's car and left for the west, Dottie had no way of knowing that Joni was not swept up by the fundamentalism that had so enraptured her parents. Indeed, once she'd learned this, her aunt had lightened up a little.

But still, there was that wall. That mask. Joni recognized it because she'd lived it too: putting on a happy face to keep the peace around her family when she was really hurting. She wondered if there was some other way to let Dottie know that Joni trusted her, and she could trust Joni.

She knew that her parents disowning Dottie had to have hurt, but without knowing why they'd done it, there was no way to know how badly it had hurt. She was sure this diary was the key to figuring it out, but she'd been reading now for about as long as she dared. Her aunt would be finished soon. At first Joni thought about taking pictures of the entries on her phone to read later but decided that there'd be too much of a risk of Dottie discovering the photos.

She flipped through the pages quickly, taking note of the dates. It appeared that Dottie didn't write too often, usually only about a month or two apart at times. There seemed to be one point where she stopped writing for about three years, with one entry dated for August 25, 1996, and the very next one dated October 12, 1999.

Could something have happened there that might be useful? Joni flipped back to those pages. She found the entry for October 12, 1999 and began to read.

"It's been a while since I've written. A lot has changed. I work—"

The shower water shut off.

Joni heard her aunt pulling back the shower curtain and grabbing the towel from behind the closed door. She hastily shut the diary, put it back in the suitcase, set the shirt and jeans back on top, closed the lid, and latched it shut.

Hopping back onto her own bed as if nothing had happened, Dottie's words about Mesa Verde came back to her. Feeling anxious, Joni used her laptop to look up the elevation level of Mesa Verde. To her utter horror, she discovered that the park rose to about 8,500 feet.

At that moment, Dottie came out of the bathroom. "You wanna get some dinner? Or do you wanna shower first?"

"I'll shower when we get back," Joni said, feeling suddenly woozy. "Let's get something to eat."

They found a Thai restaurant. It was dimly lit with clean tables, and it wasn't going to break the bank. As a bonus, the atmosphere was quiet. These were all things Joni wanted right now as her mind raced to cope with how high up they would be going the next day.

"This is delicious," Joni said. "It tastes like a plate of paradise." She'd ordered satay with chicken, various sauces, and toast. Dottie was busy spooning out some wonton soup, savoring the plate next to it with stir fried rice, egg noodles, Chinese broccoli, and chives with crushed peanuts.

"Amen," Dottie said. "I do believe this is the best meal we've had since we've been on this trip. No offense to your sandwiches, of course."

"None taken," Joni said. "Thai beats my sandwiches any day of the week. I know there's some Thai restaurants in Greenville, but I haven't had a chance to check them out."

"You'll have to put that on your to-do list. I've been to one. It was pretty good."

"Yeah. Which one? Do you know where?"

Dottie thought for a moment. "I can't remember if it was one on Haywood or Woodruff. Somewhere out there. It was pretty good."

"I'll have to check it out, then."

Dottie wiped some soup from her mouth with a napkin, then said,

"You did pretty well today at the bend. Seemed like you handled the heights well, I mean."

Joni nodded. "I think stepping up to the Grand Canyon edge this morning helped a little with that."

"I think so too!" Dottie took another spoonful of her soup. "You ready for Mesa Verde tomorrow?"

Joni sighed. "Yes. I think so. I just learned earlier how high up it is. Still wrapping my head around that. I want to do it. I just need to ready myself mentally."

Dottie nodded. She eyed her niece skeptically. "We don't have to go there if you don't feel comfortable. Of course, you could just let me drive. That might help."

Joni's heart raced again, wrestling with too many emotions at once. She knew that this was her opening, trusting Dottie to steer the car while she relaxed and faced her fear of heights. *Maybe Dottie needs to feel trusted by you before she opens up.* But it meant putting her whole life in the hands of Dottie.

"Um . . . uh," Joni stammered. This entire trip so far had disabled Joni from being able to trust the ground beneath her own feet, and now they'd be higher up than she'd ever been before. She knew she had to face her demons. *If I can't even trust my road trip companion to drive, let alone summon the courage to drive up this thing, how am I ever going to find the courage to face my parents?*

"Just saying," Dottie pressed on, "if I drove, and I'm not scared of heights, you could sit safely on the inside and take in the scenery. Maybe even enjoy yourself for a bit."

Let go.

A second thought, louder and more invasive, broke through. It was the Blue Ghost, who had also been looking for an opening.

You're gonna die tomorrow. You'll freak out. You'll drive off the cliff. Your aunt might do the honors. Crash, burn, roll, die, die, die. And scene.

Dottie looked back down at her plate.

She needs my trust.

"Okay," Joni said finally. "I wanna go." After a moment, she added, "And I think you should drive."

Dottie looked up with utter surprise. Handing over the car keys,

Joni said, "You should drive us back to the hotel, too. I'm exhausted. And I need to chill the hell out."

Smiling, Dottie took the keys and said, "That's the spirit!" She then continued eating. In-between bites, Dottie began hyping up Mesa Verde. "I've never been, but I know it's going to look gorgeous. And I think you'll be able to really enjoy the scenery with me driving. I've been enjoying the scenery as your passenger, but I think it'll be good for you to enjoy some of it, too."

"I've enjoyed the scenery, too," Joni said.

"But now you'll be able to do it without worrying about driving," Dottie said. "I feel like a spoiled child getting to be your companion on this journey. I think the least I can do is let you enjoy some of it, too."

"Well, you have been covering the gas mostly, so that's helped," Joni said.

Dottie waved her hand. "That's nothing. Happy to do it." After another moment, Dottie looked at Joni again with a pondering look. "You know, Joni, I need to ask you something."

"What's up?" Joni's throat caught. *Does she know I've been trying to snoop through her diary?*

"When you called me up last month, it was pretty unexpected. Not gonna lie, you were the last person on earth I expected to get a call from. Now I've been having fun, don't get me wrong. But I was wondering. You went to college. You made a lot of friends, right?"

"Yeah," Joni said, relaxing a little. *Okay, this isn't about the diary.*

"Why'd you ask me to go on this trip? Instead of your friends?"

"I guess I just wanted to distance myself from my parents' fundamentalism as much as possible. Maybe try to make amends. Apologize for what they did."

"That's why you invited me," Dottie said. "But was that your first idea? Did you not ask your friends first?"

Joni hesitated. Dottie was just curious, but the reminder of her old college friends brought back the pain.

"I did actually invite them," she finally said. "But no one responded. Like no response whatsoever."

"Oh. Really? Not even a 'Thanks but no thanks' or anything?"

"Nothing."

"Oh, I see," Dottie said. "That sucks."

"Yeah," Joni sighed. "I mean, honestly, it's been like this for a while, tell you the truth. We all used to be like a close-knit family of friends in college. But after we graduated, everyone just scattered, and I don't get to see them anymore. Some of them got married and had kids."

"Did something happen? Other than graduating, I mean?" Dottie asked.

"I have spent many days wondering that myself," Joni said. "Some days I figure it's just a part of life. You have friends for a season, and then you all move on and fall out of touch. But then . . . then you remember how close you were, and you start to recall these little moments where you wonder if you said something wrong or did something that hurt them without realizing it. And you wonder if the reason they stopped talking to you was because you did something like that without realizing it."

"Did you?" Dottie asked.

"I don't know. Maybe," Joni said. "I had a friend named Amy throughout college. We met as freshmen and became partners in crime, basically. Best friends. We took a lot of the same classes, stayed roommates throughout the whole time, all that jazz. And we were really good friends. Sisters, practically. She helped me through my breakup with John. She listened to me as I explained why I thought he wasn't a good fit for me, she listened when his whole group started spreading rumors about me."

"Were you in a sorority?"

"No, nothing like that. Just really good friends. She was there when I went through wanting to leave Elohim Creation Salvation. We'd stay up late while I explained all the reasons I didn't like it there, and she'd listen and be comforting about it. I mean, I told her things I didn't feel comfortable bringing up to my parents. You remember that counselor I told you about? The one who told my friends to get married?"

"Oh yeah," Dottie said.

"That was to Amy. Our senior year, Amy slept with her boyfriend

Frank. When she told me, she was crying ugly tears. She felt so ashamed and guilty. She kept going on about how she'd betrayed her future husband and was walking in sin. At that point, I was personally done with virginity culture, and I remember thinking, 'Hey! You're doing better than me in that department!' but I didn't say that to her for obvious reasons. I mean, I grew up in that same mindset. I knew where she was coming from. So I tried giving some advice as best I could. I told her that she needed to talk with Frank about their relationship, maybe set boundaries if it was moving too fast, maybe call it off if she wasn't comfortable, anything to calm her down."

"Right. Sounds like good advice."

"Well, she decided to go see that counselor guy instead. Frank went with her, just as guilt-wracked as she was about it. The counselor hears their story and tells them to get married. Apparently he said something like it was better to unite as one than to live with sin in both their lives, giving only part of their hearts to whoever they married instead of a whole one to each other. Some creepy bullshit like that. When she told me, I was shocked, and I knew that advice was wrong."

"So what'd you do?"

Joni sighed. "This is honestly where I wonder if I screwed up. I should have said something. I should've said, 'What the hell are you doing? Forget this counselor. The hell does he know? Stop feeling guilty for doing something your body is naturally inclined to do. Just move on. If you feel bad about it, don't do it again. But don't get married because some creepy counselor is trying to guilt you into it. That's a terrible foundation to start a marriage on.' But I couldn't say any of that. I had to be the supportive friend and help her. She clearly seemed happy about getting married. So I just said, 'Well, if that's what you really think best. If it's what you want.' And not long after we graduated, Amy and Frank got married. It was a beautiful wedding and all, but I can't help but feel that I let her down that day. Like deep down, she knew I told her what she wanted to hear instead of what she needed to hear. And I wonder if she secretly resents me for it."

"Well, she's married now, right? Do you know if it's an unhappy one?"

"No, I don't know," Joni said, "but that's where I debate it in my mind. Like, yeah, I feel I should've been more honest with her. But then I also look at the fact that her husband Frank works at the same church that John is now the youth pastor at with his wife. And I see pictures of them all hanging out on social media all the time. Amy, Frank, John, and John's wife. His wife has a name, I forget. Don't get me wrong: I'm glad to be forgotten by John. But Amy! What the hell? It's like she's forgotten me too. Like she's forgotten all the horrible things John did to me. Or that Frank was part of the ministry group that spread those rumors about me. It's like all those nights we spent talking and her helping me get past John never happened."

"Jeez, watching your best friend slip into the same toxic group you were trying to get out of must've really sucked," Dottie said. "Do you think maybe she just wasn't aware of the traps the same way you were?"

"Maybe," Joni said. "I've thought about it a lot. I mean, I used to try and arrange meet-ups more when we were just out of college, but we just kept talking less and less. We were growing apart more and more. Tia got married, then Elin got married and didn't invite me, and then Chris got married and now they've got a kid, and each time, no one would commit to meeting up. After a while, I just got so depressed about it, wondering if I had said something or done something wrong, but no one was talking back. And I didn't want to say anything in case I was just imagining it and inadvertently create an actual problem. So eventually I just gave up trying to hold onto those friendships."

Dottie looked down at her own plate. "That really sucks when you have a good friendship that ends like that." After a few moments of silence, she added, "Laura and I used to be closer, but then that damn church came in the picture and . . . well, you know. Now I'm disowned. You know, it kind of reminds me of one of the last times I saw you. We took you trick-or-treating. Do you remember that? Going trick-or-treating with me?"

"Vaguely," Joni said, recalling the memory. "Yeah, when I was the ninja. I think."

"Yep! You had a blue ninja costume," Dottie said. "You were about three years old, I think. Your mom was there, and so was your dad. '91 or '92, I guess. I remember you were all smiling and having a good time getting candy. You were pretty hyper, too!"

"I was about to say, I was bouncing off the walls, wasn't I?" Joni laughed.

"So we were going around the neighborhood, and we found this one house that was all decked out with scary monsters spray-painted on it. Lots of cool Halloween decorations. So we went up to it—"

"Oh my God, I remember that house!" Joni said. "It was a house with like a blue demon coming out of the flames!" Although her memory existed mainly as fuzzy images, she would never forget the dark, purple sky and the house that had a spray-painted graphic of a blue demon coming out of flames on the garage door. And her parents talking to some man in a shirt and tie.

"Probably, I don't remember much there," Dottie said. "All I remember is when we got to the door, some old dude came out carrying a Bible and started yelling at us for practicing witchcraft. Then he said Halloween was an orgy of the devil, and your father had a responsibility as man of the house to discipline you and your mother or some shit like that. Said we were all going to Hell. You know, the usual fearmongering."

"I remember them talking, but I don't remember what they said," Joni admitted. "I just kept wondering where the candy was."

"I tried to get you to walk with me to the next house, but your mom and dad seemed spooked by what the asshole was saying and kept listening! All I kept wondering was why he went to the trouble of decorating his house with so much detail just to trick people into listening to his self-righteous yank-fest. Eh . . . your parents bought into it, and they wanted us to go home right away."

"Huh," Joni said. "I guess that makes sense. That would've been the only time we celebrated Halloween. I never went again. Violet never even got to go trick-or-treating."

Dottie cocked her eyes sympathetically. "Yeah, it's a crying shame you missed out on so much. It was around that time, you know, when it happened."

"When what happened?" Joni hoped this was the answer she was seeking.

Dottie stared blankly, as if looking at some dark memory rather than the table in front of her. "When your parents disowned me. Kind of like you, I thought Laura and your dad had my back. But then they turned on me, too, and now I'm dead to them."

Joni decided to try asking directly once more.

"What happened? Why'd they disown you?"

Dottie chewed on her Chinese broccoli, swallowed, then said, "I don't know."

The mask Dottie had put up to conceal her feelings was undeniable, but Joni didn't push. *She knows exactly what happened, but she must have her reasons for not wanting to share it. Guess I'll have to try the diary again.*

"If I ever have kids," Joni said, "I'm taking them trick-or-treating. I'm letting them decide if they believe in God. And I'm letting them wear yellow sandals if they want to."

Dottie laughed. "Whoa, now. Slow down. Yellow sandals might be too much freedom for them to have!"

Joni laughed. "Just for that, I'm going to let them read books with magic and zombies, too!"

As Joni tried to fall asleep that night, her anxieties returned. The heights of Mesa Verde, the truth behind Dottie being disowned, facing her parents and being honest about their fundamentalism . . . so much was racing through Joni's mind. And now she was letting her aunt take the wheel as they would scale the highest park of the trip.

The dinner was great, though, Joni thought.

12

Joni awoke feeling the anxiety in full force. It was just past eight in the morning when Joni reluctantly rolled herself out of bed and went to take a shower. Even with the soothing stream of hot water coursing through her frazzled morning hair, her stomach was tight. The thought of how high up they'd be going in about an hour had sunk in overnight, and now she wondered if she had made the right choice in trusting Dottie to drive. The water felt less like a relaxing shower and more like a rip current pulling her out into the tumultuous ocean.

I have to let her do this. For her trust. And to face my fears.

About an hour later, they arrived at the park entrance to Mesa Verde. When Dottie pulled up to the ticket booth and purchased their pass, Joni still wasn't feeling good. The road seemed to curve away towards unseen heights.

"The road goes up to an elevation of almost nine-thousand feet at one point," the man at the ticket booth said. "Drive slowly, but don't stop at the overpasses. The roads are kind of narrow and there's falling rocks. It should take you about forty-five minutes to get there."

"Sounds good!" Dottie said, taking the tickets and driving on.

Just accept this.

Joni rode in the passenger seat. Dottie sat behind the steering wheel and accelerated up the path. The road was already rising steadily, flanked on either side by Douglas-firs and pine trees. It twisted and turned about as much as it had at the Grand Canyon entrance.

Joni felt as if she had stepped into another dimension. Her instinct was to evaluate how high up they were and how well Dottie was driving, but she found herself unable to do either. Her anxiety was at such an incredible high that she felt somehow disconnected from reality. The trees blocked her view, but soon the feeling that gravity would pull her off the side of the cliffs ahead returned.

Joni's breathing quickened. "Okay, I can do this. I can do this. I can do this."

Dottie laughed. "You're going to remember this day for the rest of your life. You want some music to relax to? Or are you burned out on violin yet?"

"I think some Lukaas Bennett would go a long way to help, actually," Joni said. Dottie hit the play button on the CD player, and soon a violin solo with jazz background accompaniments battled the anxiety for Joni's attention.

"I love music when driving up a cliff," Dottie said. "Keeps me distracted enough to not drive off the side!" Dottie laughed as Joni stared with wide eyes.

If you can face this, you can face anything, Joni thought. *Face this, face anything.*

Joni tried to remind herself of the joys of seeing vast landscapes. She clutched her armrest so tightly that her fingernails began to hurt. Allowing herself a moment to pull her hand up, she noticed that her fingermarks were embedded in the mesh covering.

Forcing her heart to breathe more steadily, she looked ahead. Before them, Joni saw that the road wound left and up around a massive mesa wall that rose what looked to be several hundred feet high. She took some solace in the fact that the entrance to the park had started at around an elevation of six-thousand feet above sea level, so another couple of thousand or so feet would be gradual as well.

I am going to enjoy this, damn it.

"Bring it on. I can do this. You can do this, Joni," Joni said out loud, partly to reassure herself and partly to let Dottie know what she was feeling.

"Just remember they had to get cranes and machinery through here to pave all this road. This is a cakewalk!" Dottie said, suddenly driving faster.

"What are you doing?" Joni said as they started passing the trees more quickly.

"I'm going the speed limit, child. It's thirty-five through here."

"This is not thirty-five, Dottie!" Joni said, alarmed and breathing more rapidly again.

"No? Then what is it?" Dottie asked.

"You're going . . ." Joni looked at the speedometer. Her aunt was indeed driving only thirty-five miles an hour. "But this feels like we're going a hundred. We're gonna fly off the side."

"That's because you've been driving like a slow-ass this whole vacation!" Dottie laughed. "You got used to driving slow-as-hell. Now it's time to drive fast-as-fuck! But within safe reason, of course." Dottie sipped her coffee and continued driving as casually as if they were heading to the grocery store.

Joni regulated her breathing and reassured herself. *Put it in perspective. We'll be fine. Dottie is a good driver. When's the last time you heard about someone flying off a mesa in a car? It's rare. Won't happen. We'll be fine.*

The road ascended the raised mesa. Some ways ahead Joni could see the road take a sharp right to continue up the mesa's side. When they reached the turn, Dottie took the turn slowly and expertly. Joni silently thanked her aunt for being a good driver, and suddenly recalled their first night together in Jackson. Joni smiled at the thought that this same aunt who'd been so comfortable with having a one-night stand with a total stranger was also a very responsible driver. Joni realized that this was one of those moments Dottie had mentioned where she'd made an unfair judgment against her aunt. It was a judgment that didn't even make sense in hindsight: one's ability to drive a car has nothing to do with their decision to bang strangers.

Wanting to right her prejudice, Joni said, "You're a very good driver. Thank you for driving."

Dottie waved her hand. "You just relax and enjoy the scenery. Aunt Dottie's gotcha!"

Before too long, the road curved a sharp left, again rising steadily with the flat and ever-receding top of the mesa. As they turned, Joni saw a small overlook to her immediate right where several tourists had pulled over to view the land. It was impressive to see how high they were, and Joni thought about asking Dottie to pull over, but another thought invaded the moment of peace. *If everyone pulled over, the combined weight could collapse the side of the mesa and you all fall to your death.*

The Blue Ghost was riding in the backseat. That nightmare hadn't left just yet. Maybe God would finally punish her here on the cliff-side for going against her parents. Joni ignored this thought and grounded herself by taking stock of everything: Dottie's slow and rhythmic driving, the landscape receding more and more the further they drove, the city far below that looked more like an oil painting now . . .

Feeling that same desire to consume as much life as possible that she'd felt her last morning at the Grand Canyon, Joni forced herself to turn her head and look out the driver's side window. Once she got over the initial jolt of surprise at their height, she had to admit it was a beautiful sight. She felt like she was touring a fantasy movie: there was a sweeping valley dotted with shrubs and faded greenery, obscuring a flat land that stretched beyond the edge of sight for miles all around. As Dottie turned a sharp right again, Joni turned to look out her own window, the edge just inches from her. She now saw even more flat land that steadily rose up into other mesas.

Joni slowly leaned forward and rested her head against the window, allowing herself to stare death in the face. There was something exhilarating about it—terrifying, existential, surreal, heavenly—whatever. Joni had never felt more alive than she did at this moment. There was fear, there was the Blue Ghost screaming from inside her soul—but it all seemed muted now. She trusted Dottie to deliver them safely to the park, and with the knowledge that nothing bad would happen, she decided that it truly was a sight worth scaring the hell out of herself for.

Even the signs that read *"DON'T STOP—FALLING ROCK"* did not bother her much now. Joni imagined the Blue Ghost giving up, folding his arms grumpily, then leaping out of the car and plummeting thousands of feet to his death.

Good riddance.

"It's funny, but this kind of reminds me of the first time I went to the beach," Joni said.

"How's that?" Dottie replied.

"The first time I went, I must've been two maybe? I remember running out to the water as it receded. But I didn't know how waves worked. I just thought that's what the water did. But when the waves came crashing back at me, I ran screaming in terror. The waves knocked me down. I got water and sand all up in my eyes and sinuses, and I cried. Then mom cleaned me up and told me to watch the waves. Then, once I got the pattern down and figured out how it all worked, the waves were no problem, and I fell in love with the ocean."

"I see. So you weren't scared of it anymore?"

"Yeah. Once I got used to it, I just wanted to play in the ocean all day. Explore the sand under the water, look for seashells and sand dollars. I just wanted to explore it as much as I could. And I'm kind of feeling something similar here. These heights are freaking me out but getting used to them helps."

Joni broke out her camera to take some pictures. She wanted to capture the memory of this place as much as possible. The mesas were endless, and she suddenly wanted to explore them all. They had caves and lost cities hidden beneath the trees. Joni wondered who had lived there. The height was now a minor inconvenience. She felt that she had become an explorer once again, just as she had that day at the beach many years earlier.

The road curved onwards, turning left, then right, then left again, ever ascending. Eventually the road leveled out, and Joni saw the flat land sprawled out all around far below. It was much greener than Joni thought it would be. A nearly flat expanse of green was met by a cloudy, blue sky. The road began moving away from the side and into the heart of the mesa. The trees and shrubs returned on either side of the road, obscuring the height as the road led them deeper into flatter terrain.

Joni leaned back from the window and patiently observed the landscape for another fifteen minutes. Occasionally they passed signs directing them to the cliff dwelling zones. As they pulled into the parking area to visit the cliff dwellings, Dottie turned off the music. She parked the car, turned it off, and looked at Joni.

Joni looked back. "That was fun. Thank you for driving."

Dottie shrugged. "Thanks for trusting me."

They wouldn't have time to take the guided tour of Cliff Palace, but that didn't matter. Joni and Dottie walked down the trail from the parking lot that led to a flat-rocked overlook. Metal railing embedded in stone protected them from the edge. Immediately beyond the overlook was a massive, natural valley. The land swooped down and rose just as dramatically across the gulf to an even higher elevation. Joni was impressed with how much green this place had. A shattered blanket of trees and shrubs decorated the valley, interrupted by white rocks and cliff-sides.

To their left, the valley stretched onward and out of sight, curving away behind the massive wall the platform they were standing on was a part of. Closer to them, however, they saw that the mesa wall had a large alcove naturally scooped out far below. Situated in this cavernous opening was the ancient village called Cliff Palace. The sandstone ruins gleamed white from the sunlight. Even from this height, the village looked impressive. Joni noticed a tour of people being led by a guide through it. Looking onward, she noticed people climbing large, wooden ladders beyond the village to reach the top of the mesa where the parking lot was.

Part of her yearned to climb the ladders, but another part of her just wanted to observe from a distance. There was a gulf of trees and rocks between their lookout landing and the village built into the side of the cliff. On the ceiling of the massive cave over Cliff Palace, Joni could make out long stretches of blackened rock. She recalled reading something about how the fires of the people who once lived in the caves would billow out and blacken the cave ceiling.

Joni snapped a few pictures, trying to capture the sheer magnitude of the valley. Turning around to snap some of the opposite cliff, she noticed an elderly woman sitting in a rolling chair situated near the railings. The woman wore blue jeans and a white t-shirt covered in paint marks. A collapsible easel was set up on a tripod before the woman. In one hand was her color pallet, and in her left hand was a brush. She was painting a watercolor of the landscape.

Joni thought about how she could include this moment in her story. *Maybe there's a woman who paints watercolors of the ocean, and she imparts some important information to Claire about the ghost.*

On the way back, Joni drove. She wanted to be sure she could still muster the courage back down. She could, and she found it easier to drive back. She took her time driving slowly and carefully. Despite being closer to the edge this time, Joni took some comfort in knowing that they were descending in height. Dottie grumbled about the line of cars collecting behind them, but Joni didn't care. Slower was her speed, and she was fine admitting that. To compensate, she pulled off in the lookouts along the way to allow the caravan behind her to pass. Once they'd done so, she pulled back out onto the road.

"Sorry, Dottie," Joni said. "I may not be fast-as-fuck, but I'm certainly not slow-as-hell anymore."

"No, you're still slow-as-hell," Dottie said. "But at least you're moving. One's own pace is better than no pace at all."

Once they were back on the road, it was around two o'clock in the afternoon. The motel was about three hours ahead in a town called Monte Vista. As the road began to straighten up and flatten out, Dottie informed Joni they would be traveling through the San Juan Mountains.

"Think you'll be okay?" her aunt asked.

Joni was silent at first. Then she smiled cheerfully. "Let's do this."

The mountains were larger than the ones she'd driven on in Tennessee, but they were nothing compared to Mesa Verde. What made Joni more nervous was the change in weather. Overcast clouds rolled in and began to mist up the windshield. The rain fell so sporadically that she found herself fighting with the windshield wipers. If she let them run on the slowest setting, they would scrape against her windshield with an irritating rubbery sound. If she turned them off completely, the raindrops obscured her vision. It was annoying, but she found a way to make it through with only a flimsy guardrail to her right.

The road took a sharp left, then it took a sharp right up through the mountains. It was mostly wet, blackish-gray cliff-sides, but collections of pine trees and waterfalls were scattered throughout the area. The road swooped through tall, dark peaks. The rain fell a little steadier now, but it wasn't too bad.

At one point the road made it through the tall peaks, and they found themselves on the side of a mountain again. This time, the wall was to their left. To their right, there was no guard rail, but the shoulder at least extended a few feet before gradually descending a hillside. All before her and down that hill was a ghostly forest of pine and fir interwoven with wisps of fog and mist. The trees were all a uniformly dark green that contrasted with the dark gray sky. Joni's anxieties spiked up but left almost as quickly. She was more inspired by the height than afraid of it now. Here was another sight of true beauty. Dottie took a few pictures, and before Joni knew it, the road was running just barely above a long stretch of forest.

The road eventually squeezed into just one lane, but the high drop to her right leveled out until they were once more on flatter land. Fortunately, there was no traffic behind her. As the sky began to dim more and more, Joni noticed a river and some campsites just beyond the first several rows of trees to her right.

I made it through the mountains. I conquered the mountains. I can tell my parents I don't accept fundamentalism anymore.

Then Joni remembered the diary, and how she still hadn't discovered why Dottie had been disowned. Her sleuthing hadn't uncovered much yet, so she started thinking of how she could sneak another reading. She knew Dottie usually took a shower in the evenings, so that might be her best chance.

She would get her chance to read it that very night.

She had no idea how horrifying the truth really was.

13

They reached the motel in Monte Vista around six o'clock. When they checked in and stepped into the room, they were stunned by its overwhelming decor. Everything was dressed up with a deer theme. No less than three deer heads were mounted around the room on wood paneling. Deer antlers were mounted and molded into a large, black television that looked like it was from 1992. The light switches had deer painted on them. The window curtains depicted deer drinking from a river. There was a painting of a deer hanging up. There was only one king-sized bed, and its top blanket depicted deer frolicking in the forest. Even the pillowcases had deer on them.

Going into the bathroom, they found even more deer designs: a deer-themed toilet covering, a deer rug, deer shower-curtain, deer antlers mounted on the wall above the mirror, deer-themed toothpaste, and deer wallpaper.

They were surrounded by deer.

"Oh my God," Dottie said. "You think there's enough deer decor?"

"A choice was definitely made, and they went all in on it," Joni said.

"Why'd you get a room with only one bed?"

"Oh, shit. Um," Joni said, looking at the bed again. "I forgot it had only one bed, actually. I think this was the only place I could afford around here, and they only had this one room available. Sorry."

Dottie shrugged, setting her green suitcase on a chair next to the bed. "Well, fair warning. I kick and have been told by several people that I like to steal the blanket."

Joni couldn't help but feel the mounted heads were all watching her. It was as if they knew what she was planning to do and were just staring with silent contempt. The battle between feeling guilty and feeling creeped out made Joni shudder.

Dottie stretched and yawned. "I'm hungry."

Joni flopped down on the bed and exhaled from her exhaustion. Pointing to the dresser with the TV, she said, "Keys are on the dresser. You should go get some food."

Dottie grabbed the keys. "I was thinking tacos. You wanna come with?"

Joni waved her hand. "Would you be okay if I stayed here? I'm exhausted."

Dottie shrugged. "Alright, cool."

"Tacos sound good."

"Be back in a bit!" With that, Dottie left.

Joni waited a moment until she heard the car door shut, which was parked right outside the room. When she heard the car pull away, Joni sat up in bed and leaned over to the green suitcase.

This is it.

After a moment's pause, she opened the suitcase. She fumbled through a few layers of clothes and found the diary. Turning to look at the door, she realized that she couldn't tell if Dottie had locked it or not. Rising, she went to go make sure it was locked, then returned to the bed to read the diary. As she opened it to the first page, the spine made a crinkling sound as the old glue strained opened.

The first entry was dated January 11, 1987. *She's been writing in this thing for a long time,* Joni thought. She began to read.

"Well, this is pretty neat! I got confirmed as a member of Elohim Creation Salvation Community Church and they got me this journal to keep my prayers and thoughts in! Greg Yontz is the pastor. He seems like a really nice man, very Godly. Laura's boyfriend, Tim, invited us. You can really feel God's presence here! I was searching for a good place of worship, a place to belong. I think I've found it! Dottie."

Joni had to read the entry a second time to make sure she was understanding it correctly. She felt as though she'd been transported to an alternate dimension. She couldn't even fathom reading it in Dottie's voice. *Dottie was a Christian? And she went to Elohim Creation Salvation?*

Joni's mind went in many different directions. She wondered if maybe Dottie stopped going to Elohim Creation Salvation and that's why her parents disowned her. Or maybe she stopped being a Christian, and that was why. *What happened?* she thought as she started reading the entry for June 11, 1987.

"I'm noticing how to be mindful of God's plan in the simplest of things. It's funny, but I was standing in the grocery line today and it wasn't moving. I started getting irritated, but then I remembered what the pastor said about Psalm 37, how we need to be patient and still. I realized my attitude wasn't going to help move the line along any faster. Maybe the cashier was having a rough day. Me yelling wasn't going to help, so I took a deep breath and forced myself to just wait patiently. Sure enough, the line started moving again not long after, and my frustration subsided. I'm trying to accept patience in other, more important areas of my life, too. I haven't found Mr. Right yet, which is also frustrating, but I truly believe it's because God has the perfect person down the road for me. I just need to be patient. Dottie."

She scanned through the next few entries. It seemed that in her early years of writing, Dottie had been very enthusiastic about church and God. Several entries mentioned lessons she'd learned in church, interpretations of Bible verses she'd considered, getting involved with the cleaning crew after the services, and so on. She'd sometimes write up to twice a week. Dottie was just as enthusiastic about church then as her parents were now.

Joni flipped a few pages ahead, looking for the three-year break she'd noticed the night before. She read the entry for March 4, 1989, which was her parents' wedding day.

"Tim and Laura got married. It was beautiful, of course. It was a little awkward, too. She's really showing the baby belly now, but at least they're trying to make the best of it. I was the maid-of-honor. I've never seen Laura so happy. I wish them both a happy life together! Dottie."

It had been about three minutes since Dottie had left for food. The entry after her parents' wedding entry was April 11, 1989.

Joni's birthday.

"Laura gave birth. Cute little baby Joni Ann Arable was born weighing eight pounds and is 21 inches. She cried for a while but fell asleep. She's so adorable. I hope they raise her right! The sight of her makes me want to have one of my own. Dottie."

Joni tried imagining her aunt holding her as a newborn, smiling and making cooing noises. Although she had no recollection from such an age, the idea broke Joni's heart. These words showed an aunt who had been full of love for her family. That Dottie clearly cared for Joni long before Joni even knew who she was brought a tear to her left eye. *So why did Mom and Dad disown her, then? They were on speaking terms at this point.*

The next entry was dated April 29, 1989.

"Took up volunteer work at the shelter this weekend. It felt very rewarding, like I was truly doing God's work instead of just singing about it. It felt good to actually serve people. One of the other volunteers is a guy named Lukaas Bennett. He's two years older than me and can play the violin. He's really nice and, dare I say it, kind of hot? He actually gave me a ticket to his concert at an art museum downtown! Oh yeah! Dottie."

Joni thought for a moment. *I thought she said they met at one of his concerts?*

October 5, 1989.

"Went to Lukaas's benefit concert. He really kicked ass tonight! The couple next to me were shocked to learn that I was his girlfriend! Ha!"

Joni's mind was blown. In all the long, unending miles of travel they'd spent listening to Lukaas Bennett's music, Dottie had never once let on that she'd dated him.

Five minutes.

She flipped through the next few pages, most of which seemed to focus on her budding relationship with Lukaas. There were fewer mentions of Pastor Greg and the church and more descriptions of Lukaas and listening to the music he made. Joni knew that by either late 1992 or early 1993, her parents would have disowned Dottie. Jumping ahead a few pages to see if the diary mentioned anything in that period, she landed on October 31, 1992. It was the day Joni went trick-or-treating, and they got yelled at by the man who had decorated his house.

"I took my niece trick-or-treating with Tim and Laura tonight. We came to this house that looked really cool, but it got weird real fast. Turns out the homeowner was this really intense Bible-thumper who wanted to damn us for celebrating Halloween. I took Joni to the next house, but Tim and Laura just stood there and listened to the man. Aargh, it was so aggravating! I just want to tell them sometimes

that just because someone says they are Christian doesn't mean they know what they are talking about all the time. Kept going on about the occult and witches and damnation. It was just weird. They took Joni home after that. It was so weird. It's just trick-or-treating, guys. Dottie."

Joni flipped a few pages more. She read the February 4, 1993 entry.

"Moved in with Lukaas last weekend. Finally got somewhat settled. I'm officially out of Elohim Creation Salvation. Thank God! Today I went to withdraw my name and formally resign my duties. Didn't have to speak to Greg. Instead, I talked to Burgens. She gave me that same dirty look, the one that says I'm the whore. Whatever. They're all liars, and I will never forget that. But Tim and Laura. God damn it, this hurts so fucking much. How could they? I told them everything that cocksucker tried to do with me, and they turned it on me. Asking what I was wearing and if I had somehow given him the wrong impression. How fucking dare they? Whenever I get a moment to myself, I curl up. I can still smell his disgusting breath. I cry myself to sleep. I can barely eat anything without feeling sick. Oh God, I've lost so many friends and I didn't do anything. Dottie."

This is it, Joni thought to herself. *She left the church. Someone tried to do something with her. Something sexual? They thought she was a whore. Classic victim-blaming, not surprising, but why? Who is she talking about here?*

Joni flipped back a few pages towards the Halloween one. She landed on the November 8, 1992 entry. In this one entry, the puzzle finally came together. Joni's throat caught.

"I'm writing this down while the details are still fresh. I have never felt so violated in my life. I feel so used, so dirty. Pastor Greg and I were in the kitchen, cleaning up after service and everyone had gone home. We were alone. I was bagging the trash up when he leaned on the fridge really close to me. He said, "Dorothy, you've been on my mind a lot. You're in your late twenties. You must be lonely." I said I was fine. Me and Lukaas are going as strong as ever. He said, "Yeah, but he's an atheist. How serious can that be? You're a Christian. He's not. He's not here. I'm here. You're here. He's not. Must be kind of lonely to be with someone who doesn't share your greatest joy of Christ's salvation." I tell him it doesn't bother me. I'm getting a weird feeling now. Then he says, "But you must have urges. Urges that might be better fulfilled by a fellow believer. Maybe I can help you." I didn't want to think he was suggesting what I thought, so I said nothing. Pretended to ignore him. He stared at me for a while, then said, "Come on, Dorothy. If you're

willing to sleep with an atheist, why not have a little thing with me? It could be our secret." I'm freaking out now. I couldn't believe what he was saying. It felt surreal and horrifying. I was scared now. He continued whispering and looking around the corner to make sure we were alone. "Come on. We're all alone here. What do you say?" He's a married man with two kids, so I said, "It's a sin, Greg." He then said, "I won't tell anyone if you won't. Come on, let it happen." He already had his shirt untucked and partially unbuttoned. He put a hand on my shoulder, but I pushed it away and said, "No. Sorry, I can't." I left. I'm so ashamed now. I feel like I need to take a shower. I don't know if I can go back. I can't look him in the eyes anymore. Not after this. Who can I talk to? He's the pastor. Everyone loves him. Who would believe me? Lukaas wants to kick his ass. I told him no, let it go. It's almost midnight. He hasn't called or anything. I don't know what to do. Do I tell Laura and Tim? Dottie."

"Oh my God," Joni said, feeling as if the entire world had just collapsed in on itself.

Pastor Greg propositioned my aunt.

She felt her heart beating faster now. She was too stunned to keep reading for the moment. This was it. This was the missing moment she'd been looking for, and it made her sick to her stomach. Pastor Greg, a married father who was viewed as a moral servant by his flock and had once chastised Joni for telling ghost stories, had propositioned her aunt, and Dottie was the one who paid the price.

Her mind raced back in time, searching for something, *anything*, that had ever been said about this. She couldn't recall anything that either her parents or other church members had said. The only person she knew who ever publicly questioned Pastor Greg's morality had been Mr. Bridges, but that happened years after this incident with Dottie, and he'd been harassed by the church for it.

There was so much that didn't make sense. *The pastor trying to cheat on his wife? At Elohim? His career would've been over.* Joni kept thinking, wondering how he ever got away with it. Dottie had no reason to lie, especially to her personal journal. *Has he tried to seduce other women? Does his wife know?*

The reality started to dawn on Joni, and it made her grow angry. *I bet it did get out, and his sheep defended him. They'd blame her. Of course they'd do that. That's why that lady gave Dottie that look. That's what they all did. They blamed her for it.* She continued reading to see if this was the case.

Six minutes.

December 3, 1992.

"I tried once more to get Laura on the phone, but she ain't answering. I went over there, but only little Joni answered the door. She got her dad. Tim said that I'd tempted Greg with immorality. And because I was a wicked sexual deviant who goes out with Lukaas (his exact words were "with that liberal druggie"), they didn't want that influence around their home. He told me never to come back there. So I guess the rumors are true: I'm dead to them. Their pastor tries to fuck me literally, then he fucks me figuratively. Convinces them all that I tried to move on him and tempt him instead of the other way around. I know this because Jeromy, the associate pastor, came by and tried saying he'd pray that I'd ask forgiveness for tempting the pastor and be released from my impure desires. Said it might be best if I not come back until I'd made things right with God. I told Jeromy to go fuck himself and shut the door in his face. Lukaas made me tea and got me some chocolate. Damn, this fucking hurts. Dottie."

Joni flipped a few pages more, eager to find anything else. She had her answer as to why her family had disowned Dottie, but she wanted to know more. She wanted to know why they had been so ready to cast out their own family member in defense of this horrible pastor.

February 14, 1994.

"I got married today! Lukaas and I tied the knot at the Botanical Gardens. The service was pretty short. Nancy officiated."

Joni had to look up from reading to comprehend everything she was learning, her mind overwhelmed with shock. *This whole time . . . Dottie didn't just love the guy's music and personality . . . she'd been married to him! Why didn't she tell me they were married?*

Ten minutes.

April 11, 1994. Joni's fifth birthday.

"Lukaas finished his new album recording today! He's going to start touring it in June. His first gig for it is in Asheville. We've been redecorating the place. So many Bible study books with nothing to say. So many memories! Ha-ha—to the thrift store with ye! We finished getting rid of all the extra crap, repainted the living room, reorganized the study, retiled the kitchen, and painted the bedroom. It's light blue now instead of that eggshell white. Well, off to the thrift store!"

As Joni skimmed through the next few pages, she caught glimpses of Dottie's life with Lukaas. One thing that seemed remarkable was how happy she seemed in these entries, especially when compared to the ones with the church in them. She wrote about going to the state fair, volunteering at the children's food drive, hiking through Bryce Canyon, and partaking in the great Shovel-Out (in which volunteers helped clear a mountainside road that had been blocked by a rock fall avalanche). There were virtually no mentions of the church or her parents to be found in these entries, and Dottie seemed more like an adventurer hungry for life.

On July 8, 1995, Dottie remarked about Violet's birth. It was the first mention of her family in a while.

"Laura had another kid. Would be nice if I could come visit her, but whatever. Mom called to let me know that they named her Violet Ruth, after Grandma. She told me to go visit them and make amends. I had to remind her that that ship set sail, and it's up to Laura. Mom said she knows, so at least she gets it. I hope they don't turn out like their parents. I miss little Joni. So full of life and curiosity! Of course, it's just a matter of time before they squash that out of her. Oh well. Dottie."

Thirteen minutes.

A few pages later, after much talk about touring the country and going to music gigs with Lukaas, Joni found the entry for August 24, 1996.

"Lukaas died."

Joni felt a pang of guilt for reading this. She'd known this inevitable end was coming, but she didn't realize just what it meant for her aunt until now. *I'm not looking for answers now. I'm just invading privacy.* Still, she wanted to read on.

"Lukaas died. I have no words. Here's the newspaper on it."

Beneath this brief description was a faded newspaper article cut-out and taped to the next page.

Two drivers were killed in a head-on collision Thursday, August 22 at 2:30 PM. The accident, it has been determined, was the result of a drunk driver. Joshua Kacz, 57, was driving when he lost control of his vehicle and veered into the oncoming lane. Lukaas Bennett, 33, was driving the other car. According to eyewitnesses, the cars slammed head-on into each other. Bennett died upon impact. Kacz was rushed to the hospital where he died two hours later. Kacz is survived by his wife, three children, and three grandchildren. Bennett is survived by his wife and parents.

Sixteen minutes.

The entry for August 25, 1996 was very brief.

"Lukaas's funeral. Laura didn't come."

And that was it. The entry didn't say anything else. It didn't have to. Here was the gap where Dottie hadn't written in over three years.

The next entry started on the next page. The date was for October 12, 1999. Joni realized that being disowned by her family and having a funeral for her husband where her own sister didn't even attend had everything to do with the gap in writing. She felt the anger building up inside her, but she read on.

This entry was much longer than the other ones.

"It's been a while since I've written. A lot has changed. I work at the DMV now. Moved into a lower-rent apartment. The neighbors are okay. The crazy ones almost always get arrested and are no longer a problem after about two months. I still volunteer when I can, though not as much. I almost burned this book. Too many memories. I reread it and realized that I should fully explain what happened. Not that anybody'll ever read it.

"It all goes back to that damn church. That god-damned fucking church. I'd actually forgotten that this journal came from them when I first joined. My life went on after the pastor made a move on me. Christ, it was seven years ago, and I'm still talking about it. He pulled his strings and got the whole congregation to hate me. Even though he was the one wanting to have an affair, not me. He was the one looking to cheat on his wife. Somehow that was my fault. I led him on, they all said behind my back. I'd made moves on him, they said. He's still with Cheryl, so obviously she took his side of the story. I guess.

"After Lukaas died, I tried calling Tim and Laura. Nothing. I spoke with Andy and Carrie, who left the church shortly after Lukaas died. They said the pastor could kill a man in cold blood, and his closest staff would cover it up, spin it so he came out looking like a hero.

"It burns me that one man can exploit the ignorance of so many people and grant a little of his power over those closest to him to keep them all in line. The man is a professional con-artist, but that's not part of my life anymore. It's not what really hurt me. What really hurt me was that I lost my sister to it. I lost my nieces to it. She's so wrapped up in it that she thinks common sense and reason are from the devil. That's why they never visited, never answered my calls, never called back.

They shut the door on me.

"That's why they weren't there for Lukaas's funeral. When I was with him, I found true happiness. He loved me for who I was, not for the way I fulfilled some biblical example. I had a family of my own. When he died, it was like losing that joy of family all over again, and this time, when they didn't come to the funeral or so much as send a card offering condolences, all I had was hatred for them.

"I was so mad and hurt and furious that I threw away every memory of Laura. Photos of us as kids, cards I'd kept from childhood, right into the fireplace. Fuck her. Fuck them. I wasn't the one who would be dead to someone. She was dead to me. All of them. Her husband especially. He was the one who led her to that psychotic place. I guess it's a good thing her kids didn't get to know me too well, because I can only imagine how fucked up that would be for them to go from having an aunt to not having one. I doubt I'll ever get to meet little Violet anyway. Joni's probably about ten now. She's probably forgotten all about me, she was so little. Man, they are going to have a rough childhood, and it breaks my heart.

"At first, I let my anger drive on each day. Then I settled into routine. Having no family except Mom became ordinary. I may update this journal every so often. Better than doing nothing. If I stop writing, it means I finally did it. I'm better now. I could care less about my sister or her husband. I do not want to live my life in perpetual anger. It's way too short for that. But I'll never forget you, Luke. My heart still beats for you, and you give me strength daily. Yours, Dottie."

Joni's mind was torn in many directions at these revelations. Part of her mind wondered what was meant by, *"If I stop writing, it means I finally did it."*

Does she mean suicide?

She couldn't believe that after all this time on the road listening to Lukaas Bennett's two albums, Dottie had not once let on that she'd actually been married to him. Not once let on that she'd been a member of—and hurt by—her family's church. And when she was in the moment of greatest need, her parents had ignored her. Closed her out.

Then Joni felt the anger at her parents burn like never before. *What about being a good steward? Helping the weak, those in need? Loving others? What kind of bullshit theology would require one to actively hurt one's own family?* Not the Jesus Joni was taught about. Joni felt in that instant that if her parents were in that room with her, she would punch them both in the face.

How dare they. How fucking dare they. Burning my stories, letting old men body-shame me, telling me what's right and wrong. All the while they were killing my aunt with their hatred. Killing her with their judgments, with their disgusting devotion to that abusive fraud.

If she had been worried about confronting her parents and taking off the mask before, that was all gone now. She would confront them and unleash all the hell they'd bestowed upon her, upon Violet, upon Dottie for years. She had been angry before, but this was an unknown hatred. Joni was terrified of it, reveled in it. She wanted to flee it and embrace it all at once. In her furious state, she didn't hear the car door shut or Dottie opening the motel door.

Joni turned to look just as the door was opening. It all seemed to happen in slow motion. There was no hiding what she'd done. Dottie opened the door, looking directly at Joni as if she'd known what her niece was doing before opening it. Her aunt's eyes were wide with fear, anger, and shock.

Joni put the book down, but it was too late. Her aunt, carrying a bag of tacos, had seen Joni with the diary. A wave of panic shot through Joni, wondering what her aunt would say or do.

Dottie stood there for a moment, not saying anything.

"You little bitch," she whispered.

Without warning, she threw the food onto the dresser and stormed over to the suitcase. Joni moved out of the way, leaning awkwardly onto the bed, but it wasn't enough. Using her whole body, Dottie shoved Joni further away from the suitcase. Her aunt slammed the suitcase shut, locked it, and yanked it off the chair.

"Why the hell were you going through my stuff?!" It didn't sound like anger. Her voice was tinged with fear, maybe desperation.

"I—" Joni tried to answer.

"You what!? What!?" Dottie slammed the suitcase on the floor and glared at Joni. Joni was horrified at how furious her aunt was. It seemed so unnatural for her. She moved and breathed like a feral cat backed into a corner.

"How much did you read?"

Joni opened her mouth to answer.

"God damn it, Joni, how much did you fucking read?"

"Most of it," Joni finally said.

For a moment, Dottie said nothing. She simply glared at Joni, jaw vibrating with rage, cheeks twitching with violence, fear seething through her narrowed eyes. Joni could hardly believe how much like her mother Dottie looked now, with her trembling hair, piercing eyes, tightly drawn jaw, trembling fists.

"I'm sorry," Joni said. "I was just curious."

"About what," Dottie said, more a command than a statement.

"About what happened. How come you never told me?"

"Told you what." Another command.

"About you and Lukaas. How come you didn't tell me you were married?" Joni found a little more courage. "How come you never told me my parents didn't attend his funeral? How come you never told me about the pastor and what my parents did?"

"Maybe because it wasn't any of your goddamn business!" Dottie shouted, letting the anger punch the oxygen out of the room. "Fuck's sake, Joni. I can't believe you did that! Holy shit." Dottie ran both hands back through her hair, exasperated. "Well, great. Hope you got your questions answered. Don't expect anything else from me." Dottie yanked a small bag of tacos out of the food bag, grabbed the suitcase, and headed for the door. "Enjoy your fucking tacos." She slammed the door behind her.

Joni heard the car door slam. Dottie was eating in the car.

Joni's stomach was knotted so tightly that she wasn't sure she felt anything at all. The shock and anger she'd felt reading the diary had been replaced by guilt and horror at the sudden venom her aunt had displayed. There were many times growing up when Joni or Violet had failed to live up to some fundamentalist standard and been punished for it, such as using the Lord's name in vain, or getting caught watching a television show with some profanity, or wearing a sleeveless shirt in public. This time, however, she knew that she'd actually screwed up. She'd trespassed on someone else's private life. She'd stolen a very personal and secret story from her aunt.

She'd broken her aunt's trust. Joni knew that despite her outward devil-may-care attitude, Dottie had demons just like everyone else.

Her demons weren't all that different from Joni's.

Joni, realizing that whatever trust she'd built up with her aunt had now just been completely shattered, began to cry.

What have I done?

14

If Dottie's silence made Joni uncomfortable, things were made worse since their room had only one bed. Joni took a shower, not finding much solace in the warm water streaming down her face. The knot in her stomach hurt now, and she knew that the rest of this trip would be mired in either awkward silence or vicious yelling. Either way, they had a long, stressful journey home ahead of them.

When Joni left the bathroom wrapped in a towel, she found Dottie already back in the room asleep on the side of the bed closest to the window. Unfortunately, that was also where Joni's bags were, which contained her sleeping clothes. Annoyed but not feeling she had any right to disturb her aunt at the moment, Joni went back into the bathroom and put on the clothes she'd driven in all day. They reeked of grimy car sweat, but Joni didn't see any other option. If she disturbed her aunt's sleep, there was no telling what Dottie would do. Joni hadn't thought it possible for Dottie to turn so violently red and venomous in such a flash, but she had done just that.

Joni quietly crawled into the bed on her side, trying not to make any noise. The bed creaked under her added weight, but Dottie didn't stir. Joni tried to pull up some of the blanket, but Dottie had wound herself like a corkscrew with most of it, leaving only a little triangle of corner for Joni.

At first Joni slowly lifted one of the extra pillows and cuddled it for warmth, but this proved too cumbersome to get comfortable. Dottie may have been asleep, or maybe was just ignoring Joni, but her body language said that she was not going to show mercy tonight.

Joni knew she had no right to complain, so she grabbed her pillow and lay down on the hard, deer-themed carpet floor. She grabbed her other pillow off the bed and used it as a cushion. It was an uncomfortable set-up, but Joni felt like she deserved it.

She kept all these secrets from me. She never told me about her and Lukaas. This whole trip, we've been listening to his music, and she never once told me that he was my uncle. God, I've fucked up.

Joni felt ashamed. She knew she'd had no right to read it. She knew that there was a reason Dottie had kept those details a secret from her. She'd wanted to know the truth of it all so desperately, but it had come with a cost. All the trust she'd gained in letting Dottie drive the car—it was all undone by this act of betrayal.

And then Joni's anger turned towards her parents.

She wanted to scream into her pillow. She wanted to punch it, throw it against a wall, and cuss them out. Make them apologize for the lives they'd stolen from her and her sister.

Their blind devotion to Pastor Greg had not only covered up what they had spent their whole lives preaching to her was an unforgivable sin, had not only led them to shun a family member, had not only kept Joni and her sister from enjoying a normal life with normal friends having normal human experiences, but had also led them to completely and utterly destroy her aunt's heart. As bad as forcing her to grow up around self-righteous, privileged religious hypocrites had been, Joni found their refusal to attend Lukaas's funeral to be the worst sin. In Dottie's moment of greatest need, they had shut the door and spat in her wounds.

Very Christ-like, Joni thought sarcastically.

She tossed and turned all night, miserable with knots in her stomach and a thousand thoughts. She was angry at her parents, angry at herself.

Before, when she was going to tell her parents off, she felt as if she would fly at them like a train running off the tracks. Without Dottie's support, though, she felt she would be flying blind. All that confidence from overcoming the mesa.

Gone.

The next morning, Joni awoke to find Dottie already waiting in the car, bags packed. Joni sat up, massaging the crick in her back from sleeping on the floor. She then got dressed into new clothes, quickly packed her bags, grabbed a fruit-pouch to substitute for breakfast, and took her belongings to the trunk. After she turned in the motel key, she climbed into the car.

Dottie was in the passenger seat and staring idly out the window. Joni started the car, then sat back. Dottie said nothing and neither did Joni. It was a painful, awkward quiet.

I hate the silences you can hear.

"Hi," Joni said finally.

Dottie made a non-committal grunt. After an awkward silence, her aunt said, "Where to today?"

Joni got out the address. "A hotel in Junction City, Kansas." She handed the address to Dottie, who then plugged it into her phone's GPS.

"Take a left, then ten miles, the road is on our right." Dottie said nothing more.

Joni pulled the car out and drove, following the directions.

"Did you want to get breakfast somewhere?" Joni asked.

"No."

"Okay."

Nothing more was said.

As they turned onto the main road that would last several hundred miles, Dottie still had said nothing, had given no indication that she even wanted to talk. She hadn't even started playing any music. Instead, her aunt just kept looking out the window. Joni didn't press for conversation, knowing that the guilt-trip was all for her.

Around lunchtime, when their gas started running low, Joni grew nervous. They had been flanked by rolling hills of tall wheat fields and grass for about two hours now, and there seemed to be no exits anywhere. There were no billboards advertising gas stations. The clear blue sky had only a few white, puffy clouds. She couldn't even pull off to the side of the road to look one up because there was no shoulder. The edge of the road just dropped a few feet, and the tall grass began. It really was a claustrophobic road, as if the crops would rush the car at any second.

"Could you look up a gas station?" Joni asked after working up the courage. They hadn't said a word since that morning.

Dottie didn't answer, but instead started typing on her phone. A few minutes later, she said, "There's a left turn in about twenty minutes."

Joni looked at the gas, happy that Dottie was at least giving her directions. The dial seemed to indicate that they could probably make it another twenty at least.

The turn itself appeared suddenly between two more fields of tall grass. After almost missing it, Joni took the turn to find a series of back roads and eventually some neighborhoods that finally led her to a pay-before-you-pump gas station. Joni went in, put down twenty-five dollars (she wasn't about to ask Dottie for gas money anymore), bought two soft drinks, and went back to the pump. As she started to pump, Dottie went inside to use the restroom.

Flies were everywhere. They buzzed in Joni's eyes, on her hair, and tried to fly up her nose a few times. She swatted at them as she filled up her car. The heat was also a bit stickier than it had been in the desert. Somewhere in the back of Joni's mind, she sensed the Blue Ghost telling her that this swarm of flies on a hot, humid day was an added punishment for her snooping. That anything the diary said about Pastor Greg was a lie, and Joni was irretrievably lost because she questioned her parents' authority. When Dottie returned, Joni put the nozzle back up, and within moments they were back on the road.

Except for the humming tires on the road, it was silent.

While Joni drank her refreshment at intervals, Dottie didn't touch hers. She didn't even acknowledge the gift. She just continued to stare out in silence.

Not being forgiven is the worst part.

The road stretched onwards into an unending oblivion of farmland. The place was much hillier than Joni thought it would be. The sky was vivid blue, and the land was covered with golden grass. As they turned around a long bend, Joni saw thin, white windmills tearing through the air. As they reached the top of the hill, she saw what looked like an ocean of them on either side of the road. Rows upon rows of windmills stretched into the hilly distance and out of sight.

It was mesmerizing, but Joni could only think about her aunt, who stared out the window and said nothing.

It was about six o'clock when they finally reached the two-story hotel in Junction City. Joni turned into the parking lot and was horrified to find a very run-down place that reminded her of the *Pick-Me-Up Lounge* back in Jackson. The hotel sign had completely collapsed to the ground. It was only thanks to the GPS that they found the hotel at all. The parking lot looked like it had recently been broken up by a jackhammer. All of it was reduced to sections of either overly cracked road or tiny rubble.

The only available parking space was next to a beat-up truck decorated with Confederate flag bumper stickers. Directly before them were a row of rooms, but to their left was a glass door entrance to a larger section of building that looked as if it needed a card key to enter. Parking to the left of the truck and stepping out, Joni's foot came down on a half-empty can of beer. Some of the drink foamed out the top of the can and splashed her sandals. *Please, God, don't let this be another Pick-Me-Up Lounge.* Joni went into the hotel to check in while Dottie remained in the car.

There was a long white counter with nobody behind it. Scuff marks marred the white walls, and the carpet was torn up in places. Some wires dangled loosely from one section of ceiling near the doors. Joni saw a cockroach skitter across one of the tables.

No. Just no. I can't right now.

A tall, stout woman with curly red hair on her cell phone came out of the door from behind the front desk. As Joni handed her the reservation information, the hotel clerk began typing on an ancient computer that looked straight out of 1983. Then the clerk started yelling at the caller on the other end of her phone in a raspy, smoker's voice.

"No! Damn it, Barbara . . . I don't know . . . Well he got her knocked up! I don't know! Now she's wanting me to pay for the kid, and I'm pregnant! I can't do it! Bob's going into town next week to get the tractor fixed . . . I don't know! The chickens got loose . . . I said the chickens got loose! . . . Yeah. I know! . . . And now she's wanting to go and join the cheerleading team. And I said to her, 'Honey, you can't be driving a tractor and cheering at the same time! What about Billy's football practice?' . . . I know! That's what I said! I said, 'Krissy, you gotta prioritize better, girl.' She just ain't never gonna learn."

Joni felt like she was being kicked while down. Between the long awkward car ride and now this colorful private conversation, she was thoroughly exhausted. She just didn't have the strength to think about what she was hearing. The clerk took a break from complaining into her phone to tell her that the room would be through the glass door and immediately to the right.

Joni went outside to the car and began unpacking. Dottie grabbed her stuff and followed her, not saying a word. Joni could feel her aunt's eyes boring into the back of her skull. They walked onto the paved walkway and headed left to where the glass door was. On the door was a sign that read, "No Smoking, Loitering, or Prostituting in the parking lot." Once they entered through it, they discovered a large, velvet-carpeted area with a giant swimming pool. The air smelled of old chlorine. There was a family of two parents and their kids, splashing and laughing in the pool. As large as the pool area was, it was also surprisingly dimly lit. A few fluorescent lights were positioned around the large pool, and that was it. *It's hard to breathe in here.*

They unlocked the room immediately to their right. *Great. We're right next door to the loud swimming pool.* Joni was not enthused, but still took a little solace in the fact that there was a family here having a good time. *Might not be as rough as I thought.*

The room walls were yellow. The bed blankets were yellow and decorated with questionable stains. The carpet was shag, and the whole room smelled like a can of bug spray. When Joni set her bag on one of the cushioned chairs, the cushion sank a few inches. Broken. She ran her finger across the brown fabric of the chair. It felt sticky and a little wet.

It's humid from the indoor pool, Joni thought.

Using the bathroom was difficult because its fluorescent lights flickered like something out of a horror movie. The flickering was headache-inducing, so Joni turned off the bathroom light and had to go in total darkness.

Once again, there was only one bed. Joni checked under the bed blankets to make sure there were no bugs in it. The white sheets underneath looked refreshingly clean.

Dottie said nothing. Her aunt grabbed a few fruit-pouches, a bag of chips, a water bottle, and a pack of cigarettes. As Joni began charging her phone for the next awkward day-long car ride, Dottie walked out the door.

Joni stopped unpacking.

She doesn't want to see me. She doesn't want to talk to me.

This was worse than any passive-aggressive behavior her parents had aimed at her growing up. Dottie was shunning her. Joni knew, however, that her aunt had every right to give her the cold shoulder. Even though she hadn't meant to, Joni had broken that trust and hurt her aunt.

Joni ate a bag of chips, paced around the room, and contemplated what to do. She hated this silent treatment. She hated not being able to talk to someone. She didn't feel like calling her sister. She didn't think she was close enough to anyone from work to call them. *Maybe Emily, but that might be kind of weird. We're not that close.* And she certainly wouldn't be able to talk with any of her college friends.

She was alone, and that was the most terrifying thought of all.

Joni sat on the bed, trying to think of what to say, how she'd apologize. Dottie didn't seem like she'd be receptive to an apology. She didn't even acknowledge the soft drink at the gas station. The last Joni had seen, it was still sitting in the car.

Joni thought and thought until finally she made her decision. It was the least she could do to try and talk with Dottie, explain things. She wasn't sure how successful she'd be, but she knew they had to fix this. Without fixing it, she wasn't sure she'd have the courage to stand up to her parents. *If I can't admit when I did something wrong, how can I call someone else out on it?* she thought.

Joni got up and left the room, closing the door behind her. Walking out of the pool area, she stepped into the parking lot. To her surprise, Dottie was seated on the curb, smoking a cigarette. The bag of chips was empty and weighted down from the wind by the water bottle. Despite the large sign right behind her that read, "No Smoking, Loitering, or Prostituting in the parking lot," it was pretty obvious that no one cared.

Joni sat down beside her aunt. Neither said a word. Dottie puffed. Joni was silent for a moment, then did what she had to do.

"I'm sorry I looked in your journal, Dottie. My family always kept things hidden from me. They never once told us why we stopped talking to you. They just said it was because you were atheist and swayed by the world. That's their answer for lots of things, so I didn't buy it. I wanted to know the real truth. I felt like family shouldn't keep secrets like that. Or hurt each other like that. I'm sorry for betraying your trust, and I know I have no right to ask for forgiveness. I just wanted to know."

Joni felt like an idiot when Dottie didn't say anything. She knew she could have phrased her apology more gracefully, but she really wasn't sure what else she needed to say. Dottie simply took another puff of her cigarette and said nothing. They sat in silence for a few minutes, watching the traffic on the road pass by. Joni began idly thumbing a loose piece of gravel on the curb next to her. Neither said a word.

Then Dottie broke the silence by saying, "They said they disowned me for being an atheist?"

"Yeah," Joni said.

"That's hilarious."

"Why?" Joni asked.

"I'm not an atheist."

Joni didn't say anything for a moment. She hadn't expected Dottie to say something like that. To her surprise, Joni realized that she'd been under the impression Dottie was an atheist this entire time and hadn't really questioned if that were true. "You're not?"

Dottie snubbed out her cigarette on the curbside. "Jesus Christ, Joni."

Joni, sensing her aunt's growing agitation, was confused. "What?"

"You're still using their words for it. Quit seeing the world through their lens and start trusting your own. When you die, their beliefs aren't going to save you. When you get into trouble, their doctrines aren't going to help you."

Joni thought about that for a moment, relieved that Dottie was at least open to a conversation. "So you're not an atheist?"

Dottie chuckled again. "Define 'atheist' for me."

"I guess it's someone who doesn't believe in a deity."

"Yeah. No, I'm not an atheist."

"An agnostic?"

Dottie rolled her eyes and finally looked at Joni. It had been the first time she'd looked at Joni since catching her with the diary. "Jesus gave three main commands," Dottie said. "*Love God. Love your neighbors. Love your enemies.* That last one, I'm not so good at, but that's what I try to live my life by. I may not live like a puritan, but then again, I don't really think Jesus wants us to. I mean, isn't that the point? That we're not perfect?"

Dottie got out another cigarette, lit it up, puffed. Then she continued. "Ever notice how every time the Pharisees brought a sinner before Jesus to condemn them, he always made them reflect on their own sins? That's what I mean. The church wants to build walls and perfect everyone who doesn't meet their standards of biblical interpretation, but they really need to be building a mirror. Reflect on how they really treat others. Reflect on their own arrogance. They need to realize that true faith isn't some message approved by powerful rulers to control the weak."

Dottie angrily sucked on her cigarette. Joni could sense that Dottie was trying to control anger, but whether it was anger at Joni or anger at her parents or just fundamentalists in general, she couldn't tell.

Dottie continued. "That's why I left that church. Haven't been to another one since. My faith isn't dependent on what others think. Yeah, they tried to guilt-trip me with some bullshit about 'corporate worship' and 'God-ordained leadership.' But I find that trying to love others and God has been far more fulfilling. And yeah, I don't know if he's really there or not. Maybe he's just some sky bully made up to control people. I don't know. I like to think he's really there. By accepting that sort of faith, I've found God to be so much bigger than the Bible we've tried to lock him up in."

Looking Joni directly in the eyes now, Dottie said, "I came out here with you when you asked me because I wanted to reconnect with my niece. I'm glad to see that you're not like them. You're a good kid,

Joni. But I'm very pissed at you right now, and yeah, what you did really hurt me. That was really fucked up. I kept those things secret because they were mine to keep." Dottie looked back at the traffic and continued with her cigarette. "I'm sure I'll forgive you eventually. But not today. I can't. It's . . . I . . . not today. I'm allowed to hurt, too." With that, Dottie stood up and went back into the hotel room.

Joni looked at the empty bag of chips and cigarette butts Dottie had left on the ground. Whether she meant for Joni to clean up after her or just wanted to leave a comment on the hotel's shoddy conditions, Joni wasn't sure. Deciding to do the responsible thing, Joni began collecting the trash to throw away. Here she discovered that Dottie had finished off the drink Joni had bought her at the gas station.

15

Joni didn't feel it would be wise to attempt further conversation, so they ate a small dinner of sandwiches and chips in silence, turned out the lights, and went to sleep. Sharing the same bed again, she gained a little more bed space than the night before, but Joni clung to the edge as close as she could, not daring to disturb Dottie.

The night was only intermittently disturbed by the playful shouts and splashes of the family who were still cavorting about in the swimming pool. The last thought Joni had before letting sleep take her was how little sense it made to put a swimming pool in a carpeted area.

When they checked out of the hotel the next morning, it looked even dumpier than it had during the evening. There were no working lamps in the parking lot, and everything was dark in the morning gloom.

What followed was yet another day of almost total silence from Dottie. Aside from the occasional glance at the directions and a brief utterance of where to turn next, Dottie said nothing and stared out the window.

The silence was what killed Joni. As she thought more about how she had betrayed Dottie's trust, Joni sensed the Blue Ghost again. This time, she felt the old feeling again that she couldn't shake him. The anxieties, the shame . . . it was all returning.

You dishonored your parents by going with her. You never should have done this. You're going to Hell. Even reminding herself what her parents had actually done didn't ease her mind. The shame kept building until she felt absolutely miserable. All she could do was keep driving and remind herself that these anxieties were nothing more than lies.

The rolling hills and plains of tall grass in Kansas gradually gave way to flat plains and more raised roads with no shoulders to stop on.

There was another situation in which the gas started running low without any exits in sight, but just before Joni had to ask for directions from Dottie, an exit with a gas station appeared, and the problem was solved.

Before long, trees started lining the roads more consistently. The landscape reverted from the golden, grayish colors of the west to the greener flora of the east. Around two o'clock, they stopped at a rest stop near Ferguson, Missouri. In the stall Joni used, she saw something lying on top of the toilet paper rack.

It was one of those Christian witnessing tracts she'd grown up reading.

There on the front cover was the faceless Blue Ghost in all his glory, pointing at the reader. Joni saw that this particular tract was titled "Gay is NOT Okay!" She flipped through the 24-pages of anti-gay propaganda filled with stereotyped illustrations of gay people—all of whom were depicted as overweight male bikers in short shorts and leaning in to kiss other men. At the end, a very white American-looking Jesus came to tell them they were all going to Hell for the sin of homosexuality, and the men all repented and vowed to read the King James Bible.

We are definitely getting closer to home, Joni thought, taking the tract and tossing it into the trash bin.

When they finally arrived at the hotel in Benton, Illinois, Joni was relieved to find that it was much nicer and cleaner than the one in Junction City. It also helped that there wasn't a carpeted pool area right outside their doorway.

Dottie still wasn't talking. Thankfully, there were two beds here. Dottie promptly unpacked, claimed the one closest to the door, and turned on the television.

"I'm going to get some food," Joni said, grabbing her keys.

"Okay."

"Would you like anything?" Joni asked, hoping for some sort of conversation, however small.

Dottie didn't speak at first, but then finally said, "No, I'll just have a sandwich and chips."

Better than nothing, Joni thought.

The next day—the last day of their long trip—had them driving southwards through the Appalachian Mountains. The majority of the day's trip would be spent in the mountains. Joni felt a little more confident about it. These were much smaller than the cliffs at Mesa Verde, and she didn't get too perturbed when bends in the road suddenly revealed hundred-foot drops.

The difficulty started when they crossed the Tennessee line. Almost immediately, it started to rain. Joni's visibility was reduced to the wet, black road ahead, the dark green and gray mountains around them, and the gray vapors shrouding it all. To their right was a guardrail between them and the cliffside, but thankfully the cloudy mist blocked out how far down it went which gave Joni some sense of safety.

What really made things scary was the semi-truck driver. Joni drove in the right lane at fifty miles an hour, which was five less than the fifty-five speed limit. The semi-truck driver behind her barreled down on their car and blasted his horns before violently swerving into the next lane to get around her. Just as quickly, he swerved again into their lane, almost sideswiping them in the process.

"Jesus!"

Joni slammed her brakes as the semi-truck almost immediately slowed to about forty miles an hour. In her mind, they would rear-end him and likely be hit from behind, and there would be no avoiding an accident here on the mountainside. To her astonishment, they were able to slow down quickly enough to avoid a collision, but Joni was on full alert. Now they were stuck behind the semi-truck driver who was going even slower than she had been going.

Dottie, clutching the grab handle, said, "What the hell was that?"

"An asshole who can't drive," Joni said.

The semi-truck driver apparently came across someone else who was going too slow for him, for he once again blared his horns, careened into the next lane—almost taking another car with him—and zipped ahead until he was far out of sight.

A little while later, traffic slowed down until it came to a complete stop. The rain was coming down faster now, and Joni could see dark, gray mist moving through the valley to their right. As they inched forward, the road wove in-between tall mountain peaks covered with dark-green trees. The peaks were cloaked in low-lying clouds, and Joni felt some comfort in being surrounded by mountains again.

Joni eventually saw what the problem was. The semi-truck that had passed them was now lying on its side in the median to their left, completely out of the road. Spilling out of the collapsed trailer were some couches, now soaking wet and muddy. The driver, wearing a black-and-red plaid shirt with jeans and a ball cap, was yelling at a police officer and throwing his arms in the air, shouting. There were no other damaged cars to be seen, and everyone on the road was slowing down to observe the spectacular mess.

"Huh," Dottie said. "Karma's a bitch, ain't it."

Joni didn't reply. She wondered if this scene was a sign of things to come for her life.

The rain had ceased by the time they crossed over the South Carolina border. It was now around eight o'clock at night. They had driven most of the day, and Joni was feeling beyond exhausted. It was around eight-thirty when she finally pulled into the parking lot at Dottie's place.

"Can I help you carry anything?" Joni offered.

"I've got it," Dottie said. "Thanks, though."

Joni felt worse than ever. Talking and even offering thanks was a step forward, but she recognized it for what it was. Dottie had once again put on the mask. That Dottie felt she couldn't trust her niece made Joni feel even shittier. Joni got out of the car.

"Dottie, thanks for being my travel companion. And for everything you taught me. I really appreciate it."

Joni knew it was a weak attempt, but she didn't know what else to add. For a moment, neither of them said anything. Dottie was silent looking at the ground and holding her suitcase and purse. Finally, she nodded and said simply, "Okay. Thanks for having me."

Without another word, Dottie closed the trunk and left for her apartment. Joni stood in the parking lot for a moment, wanting to cry, wanting to scream, but ultimately resigning herself to the inevitable truth.

I'm on my own.

Around nine o'clock, she finally pulled back into her own driveway. The neighborhood was darkly lit with only a few streetlights to guide her. There was the familiar oak tree in the center of the flat front yard, left of the driveway. She parked under the metal awning and then followed the half-sunk, broken up stone path to her front door. Joni was relieved to see that windows hadn't been smashed, and the door hadn't been kicked open.

Doesn't look like I was robbed. That's good.

She went inside and set her bags and suitcases in the living room. Walking down the hallway towards her room, she checked the bathroom and all the closets to make sure she was truly alone in the house. At last, she made it to her bedroom where she stripped off her travel clothes and put on clean pajamas fresh from her dresser.

Turning off the lights, she fell onto her bed and embraced her pillow like an old friend. That night, she had nightmares about telling her family who she truly was.

16

It was the next day.

Joni, at her desk near the front door, stared at her open laptop. The outline to her story was displayed before her. To her surprise, the story elements she had assembled played out better than she initially thought.

Claire becoming the new lighthouse keeper, Claire meeting the ghost who is bound to the lighthouse and cannot leave it because she does not remember how she died, the mayor being the killer because he wanted to stop the person from turning the place into an historical landmark, Claire solving the mystery . . . the story was progressing. As Joni had outlined it, the story read like a decent young-adult mystery novel. However, Joni felt that amidst all the sleuthing and supernatural fun, it still lacked some key ingredients.

"Nobody has any character," Joni said aloud, hoping that by hearing her own voice the answer would magically come to her.

She looked out the window in front of her desk. With the curtains pulled aside, she could see the clear, blue sky of July. There were a few clouds. A cardinal skittered about on the windowsill outside, and then it took off. Joni pondered where it would go, hoping that would give her an idea.

They're a superstitious island town. But why?

Violet's birthday party would be the next day, and Joni already had her sister's birthday gifts (the balancing eagle totem and a birthday card) sitting on the kitchen counter behind her ready to go. As her mind turned from her book to celebrating her sister's eighteenth birthday, she began to think about her parents.

I could add the religious implications. But I don't want it to be specifically Christian. More like a generic 'This is God's way' and 'Ghosts have no place in our belief system' sort of thing.

Joni started typing. She imagined Claire's parents as being people-pleasers, much like her own parents. *The mayor,* she decided, *will be in love with his power and uses the town's superstitious nature to hold onto that power.*

She paused. *What are their superstitions?*

Inevitably, she found inspiration thinking about her own family. *They believe in family tradition. Women must marry an upstanding and rich gentleman by . . . let's say age 25. 24.* She continued typing. *Yeah, 24. There is no room for magic on this island.*

Joni typed faster now. *Maybe they drove out the island natives many years earlier because they feared them, thought they practiced magic or something. Claire can discover this. Definitely something a xenophobic group would do.*

The more she wrote, the more she thought about her parents, and the more that sinking feeling crept back in. She knew that going to the birthday party would be unpleasant. For whatever reason, the party would have not just Violet's friends, but their parents and other church family members there, too. There would be an expectation of an upright Christian atmosphere.

Joni could already see the scenario playing out. Someone would bring up some political or moral issue. That would lead to them insulting and ridiculing people they deemed to be "of the World," followed by congratulating themselves on their moral superiority, and eventually they would see Joni wasn't partaking in the circle jerk. Because they had no boundaries, they would start asking Joni for her thoughts on the topic, or why she wasn't laughing with them, or if she even understood what was at stake. The conversation might then turn to where Joni was going to church nowadays, and why wasn't she going to Elohim Creation Salvation instead, and did she have a Godly man in her life, and why didn't she have a Godly man, and so on.

Joni couldn't imagine a scenario playing out that didn't involve her telling them the truth: that she didn't agree with their bigotries, that she didn't go to church, that she would never return to Elohim Creation Salvation, that she was happier without a Godly man in her life, and that her romantic life was none of their business. But it was her sister's eighteenth birthday party. She had to go.

I don't want to turn Violet's birthday into my own little soapbox. It's not the right time.

She knew a conversation with her parents would have to happen eventually. She hadn't forgotten what they'd done to Dottie. She felt an anger deep within her core thinking about the trauma they'd forced on her aunt. But her nerves collapsed when she thought about how she, too, had hurt her aunt. She needed Dottie on this one, but she knew it was impossible.

A fresh wave of guilt clutched at Joni's stomach, making her curl up into a ball on her chair and sit with the shame. *Why didn't I stop reading? Why did I have to keep reading?*

She wanted to call Dottie and apologize again, but she knew this was a bad idea. *She said she was allowed to hurt. I need to respect that. I fucked up, and Dottie'll forgive me in her own time. If at all.*

She was on her own. Dottie wouldn't be there to support her. Violet still had to live in their parents' house and play the part for a little while longer, so getting her support was out of the question (even though Joni knew she had it).

I can't pretend to be someone I'm not, she thought. *But I also don't want to start something at this party.*

She started typing again, forcing herself to focus on her story. *Once they learn about the ghost, they want to burn the place down because they think it's ungodly. They want to send the ghost back to Hell.*

Joni stopped typing. She knew this idea opened up all kinds of possibilities for Claire as a character, including struggles with moral dilemmas, obedience to God and parents, and accepting a truth that her community astutely denied—making not only an unpopular choice but also a potentially deadly one.

But there had to be an emotional catalyst for Claire and the ghost. Something that bound them together. Some big twist that justified the whole journey. Joni typed some more.

The Ghost turns out to be her aunt who had been shunned by her family for marrying a farmhand instead of a government official. She married for love instead of family tradition, so her family disowned her as an embarrassment. It's a family lighthouse, so maybe Claire volunteered to take up the mantle once her aunt gave it up. She loves the lighthouse and wants to take care of it. Ships and the sea fascinate her.

The ideas kept coming to Joni, faster and faster now.

The lighthouse has long been said to be haunted, so Claire is taken aback when she discovers an actual ghost there. A smart-ass, wisecracking ghost. Claire quickly makes the connection that the ghost is her aunt. The ghost says she can't depart in peace until she learns how she died, which she can't remember. Claire tells her that it was reported she died slipping on water from a rainstorm and fell down the tower to her death. The aunt ghost says there must be more to it because she is still here. Claire decides to investigate and try to help figure out the truth.

Joni stopped typing, realizing that she could have a moment to show Claire screw up and instantly regret it, much like she had when Dottie discovered her with the diary.

As she interviews people, Claire is the one who accidentally reveals the ghost to the townspeople, who want to then destroy the lighthouse and burn it because they fear the supernatural. This is bad because this will kill the ghost who must remain bound to her place of death or depart forever. She will depart before she can learn the truth.

Joni tied it all back to the mayor's guilt.

Claire discovers that the greedy mayor did it to stop her from pursuing having it made an historical landmark that he couldn't tear down. He has a financial deal to replace it with a new, modern electric one that will make him a lot of money. No, scratch that. He wants to put in a bank that has agreed to cut him some profits in exchange for building it. He already has assurances that her parents wouldn't stand in his way of tearing the lighthouse down. He claims the bank is needed for their growing population, but he doesn't mention that he'll get profits from it. Every time he interacts with Claire, he is trying to make sure she will not stand in his way. Eventually, she starts getting death threats. She eventually discovers what the mayor did and why, but she accidentally reveals she has been helping a ghost, which turns the villagers against the lighthouse before she can share the whole truth.

Joni sat back in her chair, reading over what she had. There were missing details, gaps in how it would progress from beat to beat, but the overall sequence of events was in place. She already saw certain themes emerging: lust for power, woman vs. society, and hurting what we try to help. As she stared at the whole of Claire's journey, she began to see what sort of meat she could use to fill out the skeletal outline with later.

It's not about finding the killer. It's about family, honor, and love.

Joni scrolled to the end of her story outline and revised it a little.

The townspeople burn the lighthouse down, forever releasing the ghost of Claire's aunt before she could find peace.

It hurt her to be so cruel to her character, who would now be modeled after her Aunt Dottie. But she had been cruel to Dottie without meaning to be. She had betrayed her aunt without meaning to, and now she had to live with that.

Joni recalled a passage from Cate Marlington's book. "To be a writer is to be cruel. You are a ruthless, unforgiving goddess of your own world. You're a sadist now, so break out the torture devices and make your characters suffer. They will want to fight back, so keep torturing them until they defeat your devices and ultimately overcome their obstacles."

Overcome their obstacles.

Joni typed out the new details, fleshing out her outline from five pages to six, and then to eight, and finally to twelve.

Reaching a stopping point, she realized how much she had written, and how quickly, too. As she read through it again, checking (and rechecking) the plan, that seed of paranoid Christian fundamentalism was now so thoroughly integrated into the story that she couldn't imagine it any other way. Claire's conflict wasn't only with a money-hungry mayor and understanding the supernatural, but also in wrestling with her own beliefs and standing up to the xenophobia of her community.

You're going to burn in Hell for all eternity.

Like an intruder sneaking up from behind her, the Blue Ghost was suddenly there and whispering in Joni's ear. *You thought your aunt cared about you? She has misled you down a path away from the Lord. Now you're a sad, confused little soul. And you have betrayed your parents. Betrayed the Lord your God. Do you think His salvation is still for you? Do you think he will welcome you with open arms anymore?*

Joni started breathing heavily, the anxiety mounting. *No,* she thought. *I screwed up by going behind Dottie's back, not for disobeying my parents. They are the ones who should be asking forgiveness here.*

She closed her eyes and rubbed her temples, trying desperately to ignore the Blue Ghost, to ignore all the years of indoctrination that screamed to her that she mustn't go against her parents or their church. Joni folded up into a ball on her chair again, letting her emotions sweep over her.

God, I fucking wish Dottie was here, she thought. *I fucked up. I'm so angry at my parents for what they did, but I hurt her too. I didn't mean to. But now she'll probably never talk to me again. I feel lost, so fucking alone. My friends are gone. Dottie's gone. I feel like I have no one left. God, it's so tempting just to go back, admit the church was right, shut-up, and put on a happy face. At least it was a community. But I can't go back. They hurt people. They hurt me. God, I don't even know if you're real. I'd like to believe it. Some days, I'm not so sure. I've never been so terrified in my life. I don't know what the hell I'm doing. I'm afraid of what will happen when I pull this mask off. I feel so torn when I put all that next to the person I am. I'm not a bigot. I'm not a fundamentalist. And I feel so left for dead by my friends. I feel like I'm on my own no matter what I do.*

Joni knew what standing up to her parents meant. There would be ugly words and accusations of blaspheming. There would be distancing and possible shunning. There was not even a remote chance they would surprise her by realizing their mistakes, apologizing, and attempting to be better people.

Joni tugged at her hair, defeated. Just as she was about to continue once more at fleshing out her story outline, Joni recalled what Dottie had made her promise to do back at the motel in Okemah.

Give yourself permission.

She looked back up out the window. A bumblebee flitted about the windowsill outside, smacking into the glass a few times but always landing back on the wood to continue exploring. Much like the bee, she realized that she'd been smacking her head against a glass wall for no reason, too.

It's my life. Not theirs. I don't have to make a big confrontational speech. I can just be true to myself. Wiping her eyes, she sniffled and felt as if someone had just turned on the lights in a pitch-black room.

I don't have to start anything with them. It's Violet's birthday party. But when they ask why I'm not laughing at their jokes or agreeing with their beliefs, I can be honest with them. I don't have to lie. When they ask where I go to church, I can be honest with them. If they still haven't taken the hint and start pushing me to come back to their church, well that's on them for starting something. I'll let them know exactly why I won't be coming back. I'll tell them all about sweeping Pastor Greg's behavior under the rug, and how they stepped all over Dottie, and how they shamed me about my body and how my yellow sandals gave some old pervert an erection, and how they're a toxic group that hurts others.

She'd be alone, but she had Dottie's advice to help her at least. She didn't want to ruin another birthday party for her sister, but she also owed no one an explanation for why she was going to live her life her own way. If they had a problem with it, that was on them, not Joni.

She looked at her computer screen once more. She typed: *Claire's aunt's name is Dottie. As Claire investigates, Dottie helps her believe in herself more.*

17

The next day around four in the afternoon, Joni grabbed the present, hopped in the car, and took off towards her parents' house.

The drive normally took about twenty minutes with light traffic, but for Joni, it wasn't long enough. The twenty minutes were nearly gone before she realized that she'd forgotten to turn some music on. Hitting the play button, she was surprised to discover that Dottie had left one of the Lukaas Bennett albums in. It was the *Don't Die* album. Before she knew it, she was pulling onto the street where she'd grown up.

The driveway sloped up a slight hill to her parents' two-story house, and it was already packed with trucks, cars, and at least one motorcycle. Some of the guests had begun parking in a makeshift row in the front yard which was freshly cut and green as a crayon. Not wanting to get blocked in by other cars in the driveway, Joni pulled up to the curb on her right at the bottom of the hill.

After parking, she grabbed Violet's present and card from the passenger seat. She noticed the album case for the Lukaas Bennett CD in the passenger door bin. She grabbed it, put the CD in it, and stuffed it into her purse.

Why not? she thought.

Getting out, she instantly caught the familiar scents of suburban Greenville that she'd grown up with her whole life: soil, acorns, and new paint. She walked up the driveway to the house. Raucous laughter emanated from inside that confirmed the presence of what Joni assumed were many of the churchgoers.

When she got to the front door, someone from inside spotted her through the window and opened it before she could knock. It was an older man wearing spectacles and a button-down shirt with a vest that seemed rather thick for late July. "Hello? You here for the party?"

"Yes," Joni said.

"Alrighty! Right this way!" the man said. He held the door open and motioned for her to come inside. As Joni entered, he asked, "Are you a friend of Violet's?"

"Um, no, I'm her sister. I'm Joni—" The man gave a look of joviality but was overcompensating for it.

"Oh! You must be Joan! Violet's mentioned you several times."

"Joni," she repeated.

"Sorry! Jody, right this way. If you go down the foyer and take a right, you'll see the kitchen table. That's where they're setting gifts."

There's no way Violet invited this ass. He's here because of Mom and Dad.

Joni thought he smelled like a Bradford Pear tree in Spring, and his breath had a hint of hot sauce and tortilla chips. Him assuming an authoritative presence with her instantly made her feel like a stranger in her parents' house. Her childhood home was alien now, tainted with years of guilt and a foreboding sense of unwelcome. His smile might as well have been concealing fangs.

From the foyer, he led her down a short hallway that opened up into the living room where many teenagers were gathered talking and laughing. Some Christian rock music played on a CD player on a table near the stairwell opposite Joni. Banners and party decorations draped the walls and furniture. Violet was seated on a couch with her friends. Seeing her sister Joni, Violet set down her cup on the living room table and jumped up to greet her.

"Joni! You're here! Finally! The party can really start!" Violet hugged her sister tightly and whispered, "Please, God, change this music to something cool."

Joni laughed. "Seems like you got started without me!"

She felt someone tug at her shoulder, as if pulling her away from hugging her sister. Turning around, it was Bradford Pear guy, ushering her to the kitchen. "Come this way!" he insisted, pulling her by the shoulder towards the kitchen where several other adults were conversing quite loudly.

Why is he touching me?

Joni casually moved her arm away from his reach as they entered the dining room. The kitchen and dining area were connected to the living room on its left. The dining room was first, situated with a table of eight chairs (beyond the original four wooden ones) for the party. Further on was a serving counter that divided the dining room from the kitchen, where her parents were busy conversing and prepping food. A few of the familiar elders were seated at the table, talking. As Joni set her gift with the rest on the table, Bradford Pear announced her arrival. "Look who's here!"

"Joni!" her mom said, stepping away from the sink where several dishes had gathered. Her mom moved through the crowd and gave her a hug.

"Hey, Mom!"

"So glad you could come home! I see you've met Mr. Harris. He's the new Youth leader. And this is his wife!"

Her mom indicated to a woman wearing glasses who also smelled of Bradford Pear in Spring. Her dad, busy flipping burgers and rolling hot dogs on the stove, called from the kitchen. "Hey, Joni! You're just in time for dinner!"

"Hey, Dad!" Joni said.

One of the men her dad was talking to turned to face her. He was an older man with white hair and beady eyes made darker by black, blocky glasses. It was Mr. Northen.

Joni immediately averted her gaze, trying to avoid eye contact with him. She suddenly felt conscious that she was wearing shorts and a purple shirt with short sleeves. She felt a shiver as the thought that no matter what she wore, he might start creeping on her. To her frustration, she noticed that when her dad approached her, so did Mr. Northen.

God. I don't want to go through this again.

Squeezing past a distracted Mrs. Harris, her dad gave her a hug.

"Have fun out west?"

"I did! It was life-changing."

Mr. Northen gave some unasked-for commentary. "Oh, I remember this little thing, all right!" He pointed a finger at her. It looked like a cleaned chicken bone. "You remember me?" he asked with a crooked smile that revealed two rows of yellow-stained teeth.

Fuck you, asshole.

"Uh, yeah, sort of," Joni stalled, looking for an escape back into the living room where her sister was. Mr. Northen bellowed a rather ear-splitting laugh. "Oh, she remembers me!"

"Joni, you remember Mr. Northen, the deacon?" her dad said.

Mr. Northen jokingly slapped Mr. Arable on the back. "She remembers! I set her straight! Yes, I did! I remember she tried walking into church one day wearing those blue sandals like it was nothing!"

"Yellow sandals," Joni corrected before she could stop herself.

Shit. Shut-up, Joni. Get out.

"Yellow sandals! That was it!" Mr. Northen kept laughing. "Yellow sandals! She wore these yellow sandals to church like it was no big deal! She thought she'd skimper on in, trying to tempt the fellers, but I set you straight, didn't I?" He pointed the bony finger at her with a sincere smile, as if the incident had been some source of comic relief to him for years.

God, he smells like a donkey's ass.

"I pulled her aside, I did, and I told her she ought not dress like that! She sure did stop wearing those yellow sandals after that, didn't you, missy?" He clapped his hand on her shoulder and left it there. Her dad had already begun making his way back to the kitchen.

Don't touch me, you fucking pervert.

"I don't really remember," Joni said, awkwardly maneuvering out from under his hand. She felt a sick knot beginning to form in her stomach that started to bubble with anger.

Not here. I'm here for Violet, not myself. I'll address this at a better time.

Mr. Northen laughed again. "She's just like your wife, Tim! Always forgetting!" Her dad and Mr. Northen shared a belly-laugh. "Well, I'm glad you were there to teach her!" her dad said from the kitchen.

Joni turned to leave when Mr. Harris decided to join in. "How old are you, Jody?"

"Twenty-four," she said, getting desperate for an escape. She wished Dottie was there.

"Twenty-four, huh? What do you do?" Mr. Harris pressed.

"Well, right now, I'm working at—"

Mr. Northen interrupted again. "Twenty-four? It might be time to get out those yellow sandals again, girl! Get yourself a handsome young man! Why ain't you got a man, yet? You seem good-looking enough to land one!"

"Rick, the guy running sound? He's twenty-five. About her age," Mr. Harris mused.

Joni took a subtle yet very deep breath.

"Timing just isn't right," Joni said. Before anyone else could comment on her, she said loudly, "Hey Mom, I'm going to go see Violet!" She waved as she parted through the crowd of adults. Mr. Northen tried saying something else that elicited laughter from the adults, but she'd had enough.

Back in the living room, Joni walked past the stairs and television set to her left towards the fold-out table situated under the corner windows. It was covered with chips, salsa, napkins, plates, soft drinks, tea, cups, and a cooler of ice. Next to the table and opposite to the television set and dining room entrance was the fireplace where some teens were sitting. Behind her and facing the table was the couch where Violet sat with some friends, chatting. Joni grabbed a plate of barbecue chips and poured herself some sweet tea.

She set her food down on the edge of the fireplace mantle next to a guy friend of Violet's she didn't recognize. He had short, auburn hair and a slim, athletic build. He was wearing a blue shirt and jeans. He didn't seem interested in talking to anyone, so Joni turned to her sister. "Hey Violet, I'm going to get some music. You got any CDs in your room?" she asked.

Violet gave her a thumbs-up. Joni moved past the laughing group of teenagers standing in the middle of the room. She started heading up the stairs, which were situated to the left of the food table.

"Hey, hey, hey! No going upstairs!" someone called to her. "Gotta stay down here! Nice try! Come on! Stay where we can see you!" The caller started snapping his fingers, beckoning her away from the second floor.

I'm not your fucking dog, and this isn't your fucking house.

She didn't have to turn around to know it was Mr. Harris trying to tell her where she could and couldn't go. "Hey!" he called again, but she ignored him and continued up the stairs.

I give myself permission to do as I please.

In Violet's room, Joni was reminded of her own room from when she grew up here. The room had no visible displays of rebellion. The usual Bible verses etched on the dresser-mirror, a Bible placed neatly on the corner of her computer desk next to a bookshelf stacked neatly with books, and a small shelf for CDs. All this was on the wall adjacent to the windows, where her bed was situated against the wall underneath. Opposite the bookshelf was the closet, closed and likely just as clean as the rest of the room.

Violet still lives here. She still has to wear the mask.

Joni knew the tricks. Wondering if Violet did, she grabbed the bottom pillow off of Violet's bed. Reaching inside the pillowcase, she felt the hardcover, leather-bound journal she knew would be there. *Don't read this,* she thought.

Joni moved over to the CD shelf. Every album was either a Christian artist or a collection of classical pieces from the greats: Mozart, Beethoven, Tchaikovsky, Saint-Saëns, Chopin, Wagner, Vivaldi . . . Nothing offensive.

I wonder.

Squatting down to study the books on the bottom shelf, Joni started pulling the books away from the back of the shelf, exposing the white-painted back. She got to the middle of the shelf doing this when she found a folded-up picture. Checking to see if anyone was at the door watching her, she unfolded the picture.

Hey, it's that guy at the fireplace! In the picture, the teenager with auburn hair and Violet were holding hands, smiling at each other under a tree.

Joni put the picture back and shoved the books back into place. *Of course. They only want courtship here, not dating. That'd be too normal, so you're having to hide it, aren't you. Poor Vi. Hiding secret boyfriends and diaries.*

As she stood up, she scanned the CDs once more, hoping she'd find something to replace the monotonous Christian music that droned downstairs. She didn't see anything. It was all Christian music, and she knew Violet liked other things.

Probably on her MP3 player somewhere. But where is that?

Then she remembered. She reached into her purse and pulled out

Lukaas Bennett's album. *Well, it's instrumental, so they can't really complain.*

She walked back down the stairs with the CD in hand. "How about a little violin?" she said to Violet, who was talking to the mystery boy in the picture now at the fireplace. Violet shrugged and said, "Sounds cool!"

Man, if they are an item, they sure are keeping it on the down low. Smart.

Joni went to the CD player and turned off the album. As she switched discs, Mr. Harris approached her. "Hey, I was calling you," he said. "Don't go upstairs. We want to keep the teens down here. It sends the wrong message if anyone goes up there." He walked away as if his point had been the final say on the matter.

"I think you'll be fine," she said anyway, not caring if he heard her or not. But then Mrs. Harris approached her. "Oh no! Turn that back on! We're enjoying that! It's an album with all the latest hits!"

"We're just switching the tunes. A request from the birthday girl! Here's a little Lukaas Bennett for you!" Before turning back to the CD player, she caught a glance from her mom in the dining room who looked as if she'd just heard a bee flying around inside. The violin music began, and Mrs. Harris seemed taken aback and slightly confused. It was as if no one had ever acted contrary to her wishes before.

I am giving myself permission to disregard these weirdos.

As Mrs. Harris went back to join the deacons and other parents in the dining room and kitchen, Joni sat back down to enjoy her chips and tea at the fireplace. The boy from the picture on her right was working on his own plate of salt and vinegar chips with a lemonade. Violet, still sitting next to him, was listening to a redheaded girl on the couch who Joni didn't recognize telling everyone a story about her family's trip to Jamestown. To Joni's left was a guy with swooping blonde hair, laughing with a brunette girl about basketball.

I don't recognize any of these kids.

"Joni, who is this? This is beautiful," Violet said.

"This is Lukaas Bennett. He was a violin player before he died." She leaned in. "He was also Aunt Dottie's husband. Our uncle."

Violet's eyes widened. "I didn't know Aunt Dottie was married!"

Joni laughed. "Oh, there's a lot we didn't know about Aunt Dottie.

I'll tell you about it later."

She heard Mrs. Harris scoff from in the dining room. Out of the corner of her eye, she saw the woman talking with her mom at the doorway. Mrs. Harris said, "I mean, isn't this why we homeschooled our kids? So they wouldn't have to be exposed to trash like this?"

Joni almost choked on her chips at that. *Seriously? That's our uncle you're talking about.*

Mrs. Arable nodded her head. "It just amazes me what the kids listen to these days. You can't turn on the radio without someone singing about doing drugs or killing a cop."

"Or having interracial sex," Mrs. Harris added. "We truly live in a morally bankrupt society. And this music is just another example."

It's a fucking violin solo. Get over it.

"Joni! Show us pictures of your trip!" Violet suggested.

"Yeah! Where'd you go?" asked one of her friends.

"She went to the Grand Canyon!" Violet said.

Joni nodded, getting out her phone. "And I went to Mesa Verde, and Horseshoe Bend, and drove through a lot of desert."

"What's Mesa Verde?" one of Violet's friends asked.

"I'll show you," Joni said, pulling up her photos on her phone. "It's basically an old mesa with cliff dwellings. Like actual abandoned, stone villages that were built into the side of the cliffs."

"Cliffs?" said one of the girls. "Were there mountains out there?"

"Oh, yeah," Joni said. "And mesas. Big ones."

"How big?"

"Bigger than the Appalachians. Driving up Mesa Verde actually takes you higher than the tallest mountain in the Appalachian range."

"What's the tallest Appalachian mountain?" the girl asked.

"Mount Mitchell. I think it's over 6,000 feet high. But Mesa Verde gets to be almost 9,000 feet."

The teens exchanged looks of wonder and incredulity as they tried to picture mountains bigger than the ones they had grown up with. To them, Paris Mountain was the almighty sentinel they were most familiar with.

Violet snuck a smile at the auburn-haired guy. He winked back. Joni pretended not to notice.

The teens gathered around her to look at the pictures. As Joni flipped through her photos, showing and explaining them to the circle of Violet's friends, she kept an ear out for the conversation between her mom and Mrs. Harris. It had definitely taken an odd turn.

"And you know, Laura, it's entirely our fault."

"Oh, yes."

"Because we were rebellious, too. We listened to our rock music and not our parents, and now we're reaping the seeds we sowed. The music and movies today are so laced with immorality, and Pagan influences, too."

"Oh, yes," her mom repeated, nodding her head.

"What are Violet's plans?" Mrs. Harris asked in a tone that suggested concern.

"She wants to go to college. She wants to study music," her mom said.

Mrs. Harris laughed. "That's interesting. But that's more of the problem, you know. Girls shouldn't be so concerned with education and degrees. What happened to the good old days of wanting to be swept off our feet by some accomplished young man? You know, there's plenty of young men in our choir. Just saying."

The conversation was just loud enough for everyone to hear without drawing all the focus. But Joni recognized the passive-aggressive nature of it, so she spoke to Violet just as loud. "I think it's awesome you want to study music, Violet. You want to learn how to conduct? Or play? Or what?"

"I want to compose," Violet said, smiling to be so subversive to Mrs. Harris's wishes. "We need more music in the world. It's a language everyone understands."

She heard, too. Vi's going to be alright.

Mrs. Harris was now engaged in a much quieter conversation with their mom, though she still kept looking at the CD player as if it were about to explode into flames and release thousands of tiny violin devils.

"Hey, everyone! Dinner's almost ready, so why don't we go ahead and do presents?" her dad suddenly called from the kitchen. One of the other deacons, a slim man in perhaps his mid-forties, was leaning on the bar-counter that divided the dining room from the kitchen. He got up and began positioning the presents to make a space for Violet at the table.

"Violet! Let's do presents!" Their mom waved her in.

"Woo-hoo!" Violet exclaimed as she and her friends got up to go into the dining room. As Joni put her phone away, she saw Mrs. Harris go over and casually turn the music off. The youth leader's wife then picked up Lukaas Bennett's album case-holder and examined it. Not wanting to make a scene, Joni resisted the urge to go over and take it away.

Mrs. Harris set the case-holder down a little too forcefully and walked towards the kitchen. Joni darted over to the player, ejected the disc, put it in the case, and slid it back into her purse. As Joni walked towards the increasingly cramped dining room, she overheard the two deacons in the secondary dining area by the front door.

"I can't believe they actually still sing 'Happy Birthday' and do the cake thing."

"I know. It's a Pagan tradition, you know, but no one seems to care."

"That's right."

Joni was now standing behind one of the deacon's wives, and as Joni tried to get a glimpse of her sister and friends gathered around the table, she couldn't help but wonder why all of these people were here. It was one thing to bring along adults whom you felt made a difference in your eighteen-year journey. It was another thing for those adults to make the party all about them. And right now, they weren't letting Joni be with her sister.

Violet opened her presents. Joni could just barely see over Mr. Harris's shoulder. The first present her sister opened was a leather-bound diary with a matching pen. "It's so you can record your journey after high school!" Mrs. Harris explained. "I used to keep one, and I use it every day to illustrate lessons with the youth. Helps me remember that time in my life!"

The next gift was a pair of yellow sandals from one of Violet's friends. "Nice! I can use these when we go to the beach!" Violet exclaimed, hugging her friend. Joni could sense Mr. Northen hyperventilating over that one.

Then Violet received a few gift cards and money, a small refrigerator, a microwave, a collapsible clothes hamper, and various other college necessities. One friend had been gracious enough to get her an overhead lamp for her desk.

"I remember you said you needed one," a teenage voice said. Joni suspected it was that boy, but at the back of the group, she couldn't see beyond the heads of all the adults and teens gathered in the dining room.

"This one's from Joni. Where is she? Where's Joni?" her mom said.

"Back here!" Joni called.

The adults finally began clearing a path for her so she could join her family. As she moved into the kitchen, she saw that the wrapping papers had been collecting in a pile on the floor next to Violet making it impossible to stand next to her. The smell of barbecue and hot dogs permeated the room, and Joni realized how hungry she was.

She took a place next to her mom, who beamed brightly at Violet. Mrs. Arable seemed so happy that she put an arm around Joni. It caught her off guard. Joni didn't question it for long. She enjoyed it. It had been too long since either her mom or dad had shown casual affection like this. It was good to be held by her mother.

But Dottie . . .

Joni pushed the thought out and focused on the moment. Violet read the card and pulled out the wooden eagle totem. "Aw, this is adorable!" Violet said. "I could put it on my windowsill."

"It's handcrafted, too," Joni explained. "When you're off at college, you can keep it as a little reminder of home."

"Thank you! That's really neat! Where'd you get it?" Violet said, setting it with the other stuff.

"At a gift shop at the Grand Canyon."

"Oh, you'll have to show us the pictures of that!" her dad said.

The next gift was shaped like a book. "This is from Mr. and Mrs. Keele." One of the middle-aged deacons and his wife stepped forward. The man said, "We figured since you were graduating, this would be helpful in discovering the next step of your journey."

Violet opened it. Joni suppressed a laugh. It was the same thing they had given her several years earlier when she'd graduated from high school. It was a copy of *The Divine Calling of Woman: Putting God First* by Dr. Adam F. R. Morris and a few other men. His name was the most prominent though. In that book, they would go on to inaccurately describe the tendencies of women, why women had no business speaking in church, why it was immoral for women to get an education or hold a job, and why they had been designed for the sole purpose of having sex with men and making babies that could pass on their family names. *Can't believe they got her that. What dicks.*

Violet didn't know that yet. Although Joni had mentioned the story to her several times, she was sure her sister didn't realize this was the same book.

"Thank you! I'll have to read this," Violet said.

"Read it before you go to school," Mr. Keene said. "It's really helpful and enlightening."

Oh, I bet.

With presents out of the way, Mr. Arable declared that it was time for dinner. "Alright, everybody! We've got some barbecue and macaroni and cheese and some greens, so if everyone wants to gather around, we'll say a prayer to bless this food. Then everyone can get in line and serve yourself. Brother Harris, would you like to ask the Lord's blessing?"

"I'd be honored," Mr. Harris said.

As everyone bowed their heads, Joni looked down but didn't close her eyes.

"Father God," Mr. Harris began, "thank you for this wonderful day and chance for us to be together as we celebrate young Violet Arable's eighteenth birthday. Father God, we know the things you have in store for all of us, and they are all good, and we pray asking that you keep watch over young Violet as she enters new realms of womanhood. We ask that you keep her strong in her faith, which has been so inspirational to all her friends and family around her. Lord, we ask that you . . ."

Sweet Jesus, get to the food, dude.

". . . watch over her and guide her towards an everlasting biblical womanhood."

"Amen," Mr. Northen said.

"Amen," another deacon added as if trying to compete with Mr. Northen's volume.

"And Lord, we also pray for the sanctity and well-being of our world. We ask that you would heal it, O Lord, and just lead people to you, O Lord. Lead the fallen to you. Lead the wicked to you. Lead those who have gone astray from your fold back into your herd, O Lord."

He's still talking.

"Father God, we ask that you lay a hand on Pastor Greg, as he prepares . . ."

Why the actual fuck are we talking about Pastor Greg now?

". . . his message for Sunday. Father God, watch over him and guide him as he does what no other pastor in this state, in this country, has the will to do. That is to serve you, unflinchingly, and to follow your will."

"Amen! Praise God!" a deacon said.

"Praise God!" another deacon added.

"Praise *Jesus*," Mr. Northen corrected.

Whatever happened to 'Don't babble like hypocrites who love to be seen'? Why are we not eating yet?

"And Father God, we also ask that if there be anyone here who does not yet know you, that you would impress upon them to come forward that they may know you. We pray that you would lead them toward the light and out of the cold, dark pleasures of the world."

You know what else is cold? The damn food!

Mr. Harris waited for anyone to come forward and accept Jesus. When no one did, he remembered why he had been asked to pray in the first place and finally got to the food. "Father God, we ask that you bless this food and use it for the nourishment of our bodies. We remember that our bodies are your Temple, O Lord, and so we ask that you keep this time together holy as fellowship should be. Keep our conversations pure and honorable. We ask these things in your Almighty Name, amen."

"Amen!" everyone said. They all began lining up to serve themselves the food.

"I say we let the birthday girl go first!" Mr. Northen declared.

"Sure! Violet! You and your friends go first!" their dad said. Violet sidestepped the discarded gift-wrapping and made her way into the kitchen. One of the deacons gathered the wrapping paper and stuffed it into a large garbage bag. Mrs. Arable took the garbage bag and set it beside the fridge in the kitchen. "We can use this for the trash," she said.

Joni grabbed her food. There were plenty of leftovers for all the guests, so she didn't feel bad taking two hot dogs, a scoop of corn, and a handful of celery sticks. When she finished filling up her plate, she went back to the living room.

She discovered that all the seats had been taken up already. In addition to the teenagers, several of the deacons' wives had moved in here. As she looked around the room for a place to sit, her dad called from the dining room. "Hey Joni! Sit with us! Tell us about your trip!"

Turning around, she realized that the only seat left was at the dining room table with her parents. And Mr. Northen. And Mr. and Mrs. Harris. And another old deacon she didn't recognize. *How many deacons are at the church now?*

Bracing for impact, Joni went to go join them. As she took her seat, she imagined the Blue Ghost sitting superimposed over every last one of them.

I am giving myself permission to go fast-as-fuck now.

18

Mr. Harris set his tea down. "So your parents tell us that you visited the Grand Canyon. That's really very fantastic!"

One more adverb and maybe I'll believe you're sincere, Joni thought.

"Yes," she said, avoiding his piercing gaze. "I went with my aunt." Joni was seated where Violet had sat opening presents near the kitchen serving counter. Unavoidable due to seating, Mr. Northen and the older deacon she didn't recognize ended up on her right. The older one's face seemed to have a perpetual frown and disgruntled glare molded into it, and he looked like an angry, wrinkled prune. To her left were the Harris's. At the other end of the table opposite her were her parents.

"Did you drive or fly?" Mrs. Harris asked.

"We drove. We drove one way through New Mexico to get there. Then we drove a little north so we could see other places. We saw Horseshoe Bend too, then drove east through Colorado. We saw Mesa Verde, then drove through the San Juan mountains. It was beautiful." She lifted her hot dog off her plate.

"Where all did you go?" Mr. Northen asked before she could take a bite.

I literally just said where.

"Horseshoe Bend, Mesa Verde. We saw lots of places."

"What's Horseshoe Bend?" Mrs. Harris asked.

Joni set down the hot dog. "It's this place a little north of the Grand Canyon. The Colorado River bends around this cliff in sort of a horseshoe formation. It's really neat. I'll show you the pictures." She pulled up the photos on her phone and let them pass it around. While they swiped and looked, exclaiming at the amazing picture quality, she bit into the hot dog before anyone could ask another question. She relished the torn meat mixed with ketchup and mustard as it made its way towards her empty stomach.

I really should've eaten more today besides carrots and hummus.

"What's Mesa . . . what did you call it?" Mrs. Harris asked.

"Mesa Verde," Joni said, setting her hot dog down and swallowing her food. "It's a gigantic mesa where people used to live in cliff dwellings. Like villages and huts built into the sides of cliffs. Here, there are some photos in there I can show you." She took the phone and found the pictures of Mesa Verde for them.

"Wow," Mrs. Harris said, examining the photos. "How do you suppose they did that?"

"From what I read, no one knows for sure," Joni said. "They know they had to carry objects and tools and supplies up these huge wooden ladders, and I think they said something about climbing in foot-wedges up the cliffs, too. They were there for a long time, and no one is really sure why they left. Probably a major drought or famine. It is the desert, after all."

"Tell us about the Grand Canyon. What was that like?" her dad asked.

"It was . . . big." Joni took a spoonful of the corn as the others laughed. "It was just huge. Huge doesn't even begin to describe it."

"Can you imagine how that thing formed?" Mr. Harris asked. "Just imagine. It's so deep. And vast."

"We know how it formed," Mr. Northen said. "The earth was flooded. It rained for forty days and forty nights. That was all it took. Bam. Grand Canyon."

Be yourself.

Joni looked up at him and chose her words carefully, wanting to enlighten rather than anger.

Here goes.

"Actually, it was created over many millions of years. The Colorado River would flood every now and then, shifting dirt and creating large canyons. Eventually, we got the Grand Canyon as it is today."

No one said anything. Even the Blue Ghost was looking at her in shock. She could sense the worried look in her parents' eyes, but Joni simply picked up a carrot and ate it as if she had just told them the sky was blue.

Mr. Northen spoke up. "Well, that sounds like public school education to me."

"The *devil's* education," the other, perpetually disgruntled deacon said.

"Millions of years old," Mr. Northen continued. "We know the earth ain't no millions of years old, and you know how we know? The Bible tells us otherwise. Look, it's just over 6,000 years from the time Adam was alive. We know it because if you add up all the time from when the Hebrews were slaves and how long it took each King and patriarch to have children and how long from then until their exile, there's no way the Earth is nowhere close to millions of years. Come on, child! You're supposed to be the smart college girl!"

"Amen," said the other deacon, eyeing Joni as if she were a dangerous wasp.

Ignoring Mr. Northen's use of a double-negative, Joni continued. "I don't know. I'd have to look into that for myself more. The Canyon shows different layers of sediment that span several million years each."

Mr. Northen laughed. "Well, they sure did a number on you in that liberal college! Can't even use logic or reason no more! Millions of years old!" He laughed. "What'd you major in, anyway?" Before she could answer, he added, "Not science, I hope!" This garnered laughter from around the table.

"English language and literature," Joni said, feeling her cheeks turn red and the anger rising within. She caught her parents' glances. *Not here. Not today.*

Mr. Northen threw his hands up in the air, astonished. "English! I didn't think that was even something they taught anymore! English!" Everyone around the table laughed again. Joni said nothing.

"You know," Mr. Harris said between bites of a hamburger, "I am finding that more and more of the youth who go to college are buying into the old earth lie."

"It's liberal brainwashing," her dad interjected. "Once they took God out of the schools, common sense and morality went afterwards."

"And we just stood by for so long and did nothing," her mom

added.

"Well, we take a stand, but it's not enough," Mrs. Harris said. "We need to go further. The silent majority just doesn't get invested as much as they need to."

"It's a shame," her dad continued. "People act like they love God, but do they really? I mean, if we really loved God, we would take an actual stand. We ought to be marching in the streets, going straight to the top, and demanding they remove this atheist garbage from schools. We ought to be locking up these atheists for indoctrinating kids. Teaching them to think and vote like a liberal and accept homosexuality. I mean, Leviticus 20 tells us exactly how we ought to handle homosexuality. Maybe that sounds harsh, but seriously. I mean if we were to truly follow what God wants, then we shouldn't be afraid to speak up."

Joni remembered exactly what Leviticus 20 called for and was horrified to hear her dad speak this way. She couldn't keep silent on it.

"Are you saying that we should kill gay people?"

Her dad held a hand up. "I'm not saying that. I'm just pointing out that we live in such a politically correct society that people are too afraid to stand up for God and what's right."

"Amen," Mr. Northen and the other deacon said in unison.

"Amen," said Mr. and Mrs. Harris after that.

But you did say that. You just referenced Leviticus 20. That's literally what it calls for.

Joni felt surrounded by venomous snakes looking to strike. It was as if her dad didn't even realize that he had, in fact, just advocated for murdering people. Her mom was still looking at her with that subtle glance as a warning to Joni to not embarrass them in front of the guests. Joni decided to keep quiet, suddenly feeling in danger herself. *He wasn't always like this,* she thought. *They've gotten more extreme.*

"Look at it this way," her dad continued. "When we die, we're either going to meet Him as our Lord or as our Judge. When I die, I'm going to be held accountable for my actions. What am I going to tell God when he asks, 'You know what I said to do with homosexuals. Why didn't you? Why did you let your neighbor continue to sin when it was wrong?' I mean, what will I say?"

"That's true," Mrs. Harris said. "You know, my calling as a wife is to submit to my husband. And one day, God'll call on me to account for whether I was a good wife who submitted to her husband or just did my own thing without his authority. And there's no hiding anything from Him. So I just have to make sure I keep myself walking within those biblical guidelines."

"It makes me sad to think," Joni's mom said, "about how so many young people don't even know those biblical guidelines anymore and are just living every day for themselves, not worrying about what they'll say when they're face-to-face with God."

"Well, one problem I see is how so many of them don't even believe in God," Mr. Harris said. "The millennial generation has stopped coming to church. Mostly, not all, but a lot of millennials. And it's getting worse. Pretty soon, there'll be no young people to take up the call."

Her dad set his drink down. "Millennials are a lost cause. They're so used to having everything handed to them that they don't even understand the importance of saving their souls. Lazy, entitled brats. They think God is dead. God isn't 'hip' enough for them. That's why they're leaving. Because the church doesn't play the kind of music style they like, or because the rules are too hard. They'd rather be in the world where God isn't seen as something cool."

"What do they know?" Mr. Northen said, spitting flecks of chewed corn dangerously close to Joni's plate. She scooted her plate away from him about an inch. "They grew up with the Internet! They don't go outside anymore! They play video games and think that the nice house with a car and dog and wife and kids just gets handed to them! Well, they're in for a rude awakening. Wait'll they learn about the second death."

Everyone except Joni laughed. Joni sat staring silently at her plate, not eating anything else. Hearing them talk made her sick to her stomach. She felt as if she were eating food laced with arsenic.

"And look at the world it's created," her mom continued. "You can't even mention God in public without getting sued. Can't preach against the sin of homosexuality because that's not politically correct anymore! All we want to do is show them the love of Christ, but this world hates His name."

There is no 'love of Christ' in your church. There's only hate and a desire to harm others.

"What do you think, Joni? You're awfully quiet." Mrs. Harris caught her off-guard.

"Sorry . . . what was the question?" Joni asked.

"Why do you think millennials are leaving the church more than any other generation?" Mrs. Harris asked.

Joni gave a thoughtful "Hmm" to buy some time to think.

It was the moment of truth. The Blue Ghost was back with the gates of Hell at his side. *I can't be passive. I have to be honest with them.* She looked up, and then an idea came to her.

It's not really them I'm attacking, but the culture that raised them, and the warped beliefs it's created. They may confuse the two, which I get. I was in that boat once, but I was able to change. Be loving, be understanding, but be honest.

"I think they are leaving the church because they don't see any good in it," Joni said.

Joni might as well have just announced she'd killed someone. It got really quiet in the dining room. Her dad stared at her with wide eyes—perhaps in embarrassed shock—while her mom had a look of worry and confusion. This wasn't *their* daughter talking. Not the way *they* had raised her.

The Harris's seemed just as confused and taken aback. For a moment, Joni was aware of the laughter and talking going on in the other room. Christian music was playing again. Accepting that she had firmly and publicly established that she did not agree with them, Joni finally took another bite of her hot dog and ignored the awkwardness at the table. *I didn't do anything wrong. Just stating an obvious fact.*

Mr. Northen broke the silence. "Huh? What's that?" he said, as if to try and trip her answer up by making her repeat herself.

You heard me, creep.

"I'm sorry?" she said, flipping his tactic back on him.

"Why aren't they coming to church, you say?" he said, eyeing her carefully. Behind those beady, brown eyes was a warning: *Wanna try again, young lady?*

Joni calmly sipped her drink and set it down, then looked directly into his eyes. "Millennials are leaving the church because they don't see anything good in it."

Hear me that time, asshole?

"Not our church," the older deacon protested.

"Yes, your church. Most churches, but your church, too."

I'm not backing down. You asked, so here's my answer. Deal with it.

"How is that?" Mr. Harris said. "In what way don't they see good in it?"

She had to choose her words carefully if she was going to get the point across. *Use language they respond to.*

"They see a church that claims to save souls, preach the Gospel, bring believers together and all that. That's fine. But they also see a church that condemns people. A church that condemns gay people, people with different beliefs, people who care about the environment. And then a church that gets involved in government to try to enforce those beliefs on others. I mean, you were just now talking about how we should be killing gay people."

"Oh, that's not . . . that's a bunch of bull," the disgruntled-looking deacon said. "Homosexuality is a sin. They can't argue with that! The Bible clearly says that."

"They see how the church responds to things like abused women, abused children, even abused men," Joni continued, ignoring the deacon's attempt to derail the point. "They see a church that claims to love all but really could care less about people except to get their money."

She snuck a glance at Mr. Northen, who didn't look happy about anything she was saying. Before she could continue, the other deacon interrupted. "What are you basing this on?"

They're getting defensive now.

Out of the corner of her eye, she could sense the shock and embarrassment of her parents, but she continued, trying to remain calm and rational.

"A personal story. I was . . . I had a friend in college. She was dating this guy. He was training for Christian ministry. But he didn't really love her. He just wanted to make out with her all the time, lust after her body, and used her to get a good social standing with his church buds. He would spend Sundays and Bible studies lecturing others about purity, and then spend his evenings getting handsy with her. Total hypocrite. But he didn't pay attention to her interests, desires, or needs. He just needed a trophy wife to cook for him and give him kids one day. She was just a prop to him."

Mom and Dad must be mortified right now. Good.

"She didn't like this," Joni continued. "She didn't want to be his trophy wife, so she called it off. Now that should've been the end of the story, but his church buds intervened and started pressuring her to stay with him. She refused. The ex-boyfriend joined in, constantly pressuring her to get back with him. She ignored his calls after countless times explaining why—and let me stop there. Why did she have to explain all over again? Why wasn't she allowed to break up with him? All the intimidation, fear, and doubts about all this led her to get advice from the Christian counselor, who sadly also joined in on pressuring her to get back with the guy."

"That doesn't sound like pressure to me," Mrs. Harris said. "If so many people are telling her to get back with him, that could've been God handing her a sign." The others murmured in agreement.

I actually feel sorry for you, Mrs. Harris.

"She had already broken up with him. She didn't want him! She knew it was a disastrous relationship, but that didn't stop her ex or his friends from constantly bothering her. Anyway, she keeps telling him no, no, no, until he finally leaves her alone. But then he and his buddies started going around to all their mutual church friends and their girlfriends and telling them she was sleeping around. That she cheated on him. Just started straight up lying about her. I mean, real husband material, right? Suddenly the girls from her Bible study stopped talking to her and started meeting elsewhere without telling her. She lost a lot of friends all because he didn't get his way and decided to smear her reputation as payback. But the damage was done. And that whole system of abuse was enabled by his church friends and even the Christian counselor."

"I don't think that's fair, Joni," her Dad chimed in, his tone indicating that he was firmly on the deacon's side. "That's just one bad dude. You can't blame all of Christianity on that. Besides, it sounds like she put herself in that situation. If she didn't like him, she should've stayed away from him."

"Yeah! I don't see the problem. Sounds like she was asking for the unwanted attention," Mr. Northen added. "Have to say, young lady, you ain't proved your case."

Joni looked at the man fully now, not afraid of him anymore. "Well, you asked what I thought, and I have to say, y'all's responses are exactly the sort of responses that led her to stop trusting the church."

"She should've come to *our* church! Our counselors wouldn't have done such a thing!" Mrs. Harris said, frowning and looking disturbed by the story. Joni looked down at her plate.

Okay. Here we go.

"This probably won't be easy to hear, but it's the truth. She actually *did* go to the church. To Elohim Creation Salvation." Joni looked back up, looking at the distraught faces with no intention of looking away from them.

They need to hear this.

"She spoke with one of the counselors there. Two of them. They told her the same thing you just said. 'Get over it. You shouldn't have put yourself in that situation. Maybe you were wearing something that gave his lie some truth.' That's what they told her."

Joni took a sip of her drink, letting the silence around the table say it all. "Who was it? Your friend," her mom asked. "I only remember you coming a few times during college. I don't remember you bringing a friend."

Joni, not wanting to reveal that this story had actually been about her and John, waved her hand to feign forgetfulness. "It was a long time ago. The point is that this is what millennials see. For all the preaching of Jesus' word and love, the church has made it clear over and over that they stand with hateful beliefs and extremist identities that have nothing to do with what Jesus taught. They could hear someone express the same ideas as the sermon on the mount and think it was liberal propaganda. It's hard for people to believe in a God whose people create more problems than they solve."

"Oh, they're just railing against God because their parents were godless themselves!" the other deacon said.

"No," Joni said. "The church jettisoned logic when attempting to justify its corruption, so it never changes. Instead, it blames victims. Says it's their 'sins' that brought the problems. And so the church never takes responsibility. So it's no wonder people have trouble trusting church people. And keep in mind, I'm just talking about people who are open to the idea of believing in God. This is to say nothing of the people who already find it difficult to believe in the mere existence of a God they can't see or have any evidence for. That's another big reason people are leaving the church, too. It just smacks of a system of control enforced by old-world superstitions."

"Well what about *you*?" Mr. Northen asked, clapping a hand on her shoulder. His hands were clammy, hairy, and bony. She felt like a great, big skeleton was touching her, and she didn't like it. "Where do you go to church now? You're a big, fancy, educated, millennial yourself. Where do you go to church now?"

She knew that her absence at their church had not gone unnoticed by either the deacons or her parents. She also knew that not returning to it spoke volumes to them about her feelings towards it.

They want to hear me say the words so they can pounce.

But at that moment, all she could think about was how Mr. Northen had his hand on her shoulder and hadn't removed it.

"Alright . . . first, let go of my shoulder," she said in a half-joking manner to keep the already tense mood light. She repositioned herself so that Mr. Northen's hand fell away. Facing the others, she said, "So I haven't really found a church, honestly," she said.

"Haven't found one? You've got one! You just ain't been to church in a while!" Mr. Northen said, patting her roughly on the back again. She felt a shiver run down her spine. She sensed that he was trying to feel her bra-strap.

"Take your hand off me," she said quietly. No joking tone this time. She was dead serious and staring directly at Mr. Northen. No one seemed to pick up on this exchange, for the other deacon quickly added to Mr. Northen's comments, "I ain't seen you in a while, either!" The others nodded and whispered in agreement, but Joni wasn't focused on that. She continued staring down Mr. Northen, who looked somewhat unnerved for a moment. He removed his hand casually, pretending as if the exchange hadn't actually happened.

"Why don't you come to church anymore, Joni?" the older, disgruntled deacon asked. She still had no recollection of who he was or when he had ever been there.

"Well, you know, between work and trying to survive. Paying bills after college, not to mention student loans. It's been tough to find one I—"

"Shoot, Joni, you don't live but twenty minutes away," her dad said. To everyone else, it sounded as if he was just trying to encourage her to come back to their church where it was safe and godly. But Joni picked up on that subtle crack in his tone, that unmistakable attempt to steer the conversation towards a place where his daughter could not continue embarrassing him and his wife. "Surely you can get up on Sunday and make the drive. It's practically halfway between you and us! Not even ten minutes' drive from where you live!"

"Well, I just—"

"I think your daughter's a true millennial, Tim!" Mr. Northen said loudly, overcompensating with an obnoxious laugh. To Joni's annoyance, the rest joined in.

"Well, you can say that again," her dad said, looking down at his own food and picking at it with a fork.

"I know we didn't teach her these things," her mom said, smiling uncomfortably.

"No, *we* raised her right. It's that college education," her dad said, laughing along. "Teaches them to be gay socialists, teaches them to be afraid of church. Gets them so confused until they can't discern right from wrong. Maybe we ought to look into Violet's program more closely."

"I agree. That's a good idea," Mr. Harris said.

"Ain't that right," Mr. Northen said. He started poking Joni on the shoulder in an accusatory manner. "Fancy college degree, but no brains!"

It was like the end of those tracts where the Blue Ghost always said, "Depart from me, ye cursed," and sent the protagonist to Hell.

Only now, the Blue Ghosts—all of them—were laughing at her. Her pain was only a punchline to them.

And for the fourth time that day, Mr. Northen was touching Joni. As her own parents joined in with the laughter and ridicule of everything Joni had gone through, Mr. Northen's prodding fingers made her snap.

Jumping up from her seat, Joni said, "Get your *fucking* hand off me, you pervert."

The laughing stopped.

She shoved Mr. Northen's hand away and glared at him.

"Joni!" her mom said.

"Remember yourself, young lady," her dad said. "Ya'll may use that language with your college friends, but not under my roof." Mr. Northen had a crooked smile as if he were getting called out for sneaking a cookie from the cookie jar.

"Joni, go outside," her mom said, trying to stop the tension. "I think you should go outside for a little."

"If you ever touch me again," Joni said, ignoring them and pointing at Mr. Northen, "I'll kick your fucking nuts so hard they fly out your goddamn mouth." Mr. Northen's smile faded into an angry scowl. Staring his eyes down without backing down, Joni felt her face flush red with rage.

Everything was quiet. All eyes were on her. Even the living room had gone quiet except for the music playing. Before anyone could break the silence, Joni grabbed her purse and stormed out of the room.

19

Joni sat sideways behind the wheel. The car door was open, and her feet rested on the asphalt. Crickets had gotten started with the late afternoon chorus of chirps across the street. Someone a few houses up the road had just mowed their lawn and left a sprinkler on. She stared as a dirtied stream carrying blades of grass now slid down the road beside her car towards an unknown destination.

Her stomach was wound so tight and her head throbbed with so much anger that she grabbed her keys. It would be so easy to put the keys in the ignition, drive fast-as-fuck, and never look back. But she knew she had to talk with her parents. As gratifying as it had been to tell Mr. Northen off, they had to know the truth. The mask was off, and she was not backing down this time.

Joni kicked a pebble out from under her foot. Drawing her knees up to the edge of her car doorway, she wrapped her arms around them, completely aware of each heartbeat and trying to regulate the sick feeling that threatened to overwhelm her. Her stomach burned with unease.

I wish Dottie was here.

She heard the front door swing open from up the hill behind her. Looking back through the passenger-side window, she saw her mother storming across the lawn towards her car.

Here we go.

Straightening up, she let her legs rest back on the pavement. Her mom came around to her side of the car. She leaned down to look at Joni, her face deadly-serious. It reminded Joni of her face when she'd yelled at her about the ghost story at Violet's birthday sleepover.

"What was that all about?" her mom snapped.

"Mr. Northen wouldn't get his hands off me," Joni said. "He kept touching me."

"Joni Ann," her mom continued with that tone Joni hated so much—the tone that suggested *she* was the one out of line. "Could you not simply have asked him to stop? Did you really have to cuss him out in front of everybody? In front of Violet's friends?"

"I did ask him. I asked him politely. Two times. He heard me, and he ignored me. He kept poking me and touching me." Joni felt her anger rising, but she did her best to keep it under control.

"He was just trying to talk to you," her mom countered. "There was no need to fly off into a rage like that. And then to use that kind of language in our house? No. You knew better than that. Could you not have excused yourself or done something else?"

"Normally, I might agree. But he deserved every word of that, Mom. He's always been a creep. He knew what he was doing. He had no right touching me."

Her mom then pointed back at the house. "Our friends from the church are in that house. They see our oldest daughter acting like a little rebellious child. Do you know how that reflects on us?"

Joni glared at her mom in disbelief, looking her directly in the face. "Who cares what they think? Do you know how it reflects on you when you make excuses for pervy old men?"

Her mom threw up her arms in exasperation. "You just have to make Violet's birthday parties all about you, don't you?"

"Oh my God," Joni said. "What are you talking about? He was touching me and had no right to! I called him out on it. If anyone should be embarrassed right now, it's him. Your church friends can just get over it."

Her mom looked angered by that, but Joni didn't withdraw her glance. She wanted her mom to see that she was resolute, and no guilt or shame would make her back down.

The front door opened and closed again. This time, she saw her dad approaching the car, and he was walking fast. He looked ready to explode. When he came around to her side of the car, he looked only at her mom.

"She say anything yet?" he said, his voice full of barely contained rage.

"She's making it all about herself again, Tim."

"No, I'm not! I just told that creep—"

"What were you thinking, girl? You thought you could use that kind of language in my home? Embarrass us like that in our own home? I don't care what sort of language your aunt taught you. You know we don't tolerate language like that in our home."

"You wanna talk about my aunt now?" Joni said, feeling her blood rise and her cheeks redden with anger. She glared at her dad. "Okay, let's talk about Dottie. Did you know she had a husband?"

"Joni," her mom said, "don't try to change the subject. You used—"

"No, you want to stick up for the pervert? You wanna bring up my aunt when I was perfectly willing to just keep to myself? Fine. Yeah, Dottie had a husband. We had an uncle! He died. Did you know that?" She looked at her mom, who looked shocked by Joni's outrage. "Yeah, your sister was married. Did you know that?"

"Don't talk to your mother that way. We didn't raise you to act like this," her dad said.

Reel it in. Dial it back.

Taking a deep breath, Joni continued a little more calmly, looking down again at the moving stream of grass on the street under her car. "I learned what Pastor Greg did to Dottie. And I learned what the church did to her." Looking back at her parents, she said, "And how you two just shut her out and went along with it."

"You have no clue what you're talking about," her dad said. "You were too young to know what was happening back then."

"We stopped talking to her for a good reason," her mom said. "We didn't want her influence around you."

"What? What are you talking about?" Joni said. "The pastor made a move on her and then swept it under the rug. And the people at that church, including you two, helped him! What does her influence have to do with anything?"

"You just had to take a road trip with her," her dad said. "Now she's all in your head, isn't she? Made you think you could come here and start cussing like a sailor in our house. In front of the church guests, Joni! Do you know how that makes us look? Now nobody's gonna want to come back here. They're gonna think we teach evolution and public school atheism now. Do you know how this will affect Violet?"

"I don't even know where to begin with what you just said," Joni replied. "This all started because Mr. Northen wouldn't stop touching me. He's a pervert, okay? He's a pervert. He was a pervert back when I went to that church, and now he thinks he can just keep touching me. You should be glad that's all I said to him."

"He is not a pervert, Joni. Stop saying that. You're all twisted up and confused. He was just trying to show you how the things you were saying were not biblical," her mom said.

"Exactly," her dad added. "You were the one going on about evolution and how evil the church is. Just had to make it all about Joni. Showing off her really smart college degree or whatever you were doing. Again, do you know how that reflects on us? When our oldest daughter is saying these things?"

"Let me make this perfectly clear for you," Joni said, feeling her temper rising again. "I don't give a damn how this reflects on you. I really don't care what those church people think. Okay? I haven't for a long time. They asked me questions, and I gave honest answers. Would you rather I had lied to them? I didn't start any of this, so stop saying I'm trying to make things about myself or that I'm confused or whatever."

"Joni—"

"He wouldn't stop touching me, Dad. He was trying to feel my bra strap! What was I supposed to do? Respect my elder and not question it? He's a sicko."

"And I told you he was just trying to talk to you!" her mom said.

"It doesn't matter!" Joni said. "I told him to stop, and he didn't! That should be enough. He has no right to touch me! I don't want him touching me! He's a creepy old man. Always has been. Going on about my yellow sandals when I was just a kid, and—"

Joni couldn't find her words. Her anger was so great that her brain couldn't process the right words fast enough.

Her dad sighed loudly. "Why would you do this, Joni?"

"Do what? Stand up for myself?" Joni knew what he meant, but she wanted to hear him say the words.

"They're officials of the church. Deacons and leaders. You cussing them out in our home, talking about evolution, bashing the church—and on your sister's birthday, no less—we didn't raise you this way. You didn't get these ideas from us. You're all confused."

"Stop saying I'm confused," Joni said. "I'm not confused."

"We need to get back to the party, Tim," her mom said, looking down at the asphalt with her arms folded.

"It's alright, Laura. I handled it," her dad said. "I apologized and told them she went on this trip with her aunt, and now she's speaking like a sheep and that's why she's acting this way."

Joni stopped herself from punching her dad. "What the fuck would you know about my aunt?" she snapped.

"Joni!" her mom exclaimed.

"Excuse me?" her dad said, taken aback.

"Pastor Greg wanted to fuck her, and she said no. So he spread lies about how she came onto him. And you two just went along with it. You shunned her. You disowned her because your precious Pastor Greg couldn't possibly be lying about your own goddamn family member."

"Language, missy!" her dad warned. Her mom was covering her ears now, shaking her head, face scrunched up and ready to cry, and it almost pained Joni to see her like this. She'd never seen her mother on the verge of tears. She felt guilty knowing she'd caused her mother to start crying. But Joni couldn't forgive them. Not for what they had done to her or to Dottie.

"Greg lied about her. And the church she loved turned on her," Joni said. "When she needed us most, when she desperately needed to see Christ's love, you basically told her to get lost. You weren't there for her wedding. You weren't there to comfort her when her husband died. You weren't there."

"Joni, you are so out of line right now," her dad said. "It's almost hilarious how off-base you are. Your aunt was the one who tried to seduce the pastor, for starters. When she told us her version of the story, we went to the church to confront him. Asked him if it was true. And guess what? Greg told us the true version. His wife and several of the deacons were there as he said it. You can ask them. We all heard it from his mouth. *She* tried to seduce *him*. Okay? She was single and looking for something to satisfy her sinful urges. She thought she could tempt the pastor. She was just a lying slut who felt guilty about her sin, and now she wanted to blame him."

"Don't call her that word," Joni said. In the back of her mind, she sensed the Blue Ghost trying to work a gnawing doubt into her mind that maybe Dottie had lied about the whole thing, and maybe her parents were telling the truth. But Joni quickly pushed the thought from her mind. She realized that they'd gotten a crucial detail wrong.

"She wasn't single or looking for action," Joni said. "She was in a loving relationship with a man named Lukaas. And of course, Greg would say that she was lying if his wife was right there!"

"You can't trust her," her dad said. "She was an atheist posing as a church-goer who wanted to bring a good man down, plain and simple. She was the liar!"

"If only you'd never left the church," her mom added, "you wouldn't be acting like this."

Fuck you, we're doing this.

Joni took another deep breath. "I only spent about two weeks with Dottie. But in that short time, I learned something very important. My aunt has more love of Christ in her than anyone in that church combined."

Neither of her parents said anything, too stunned by what Joni had said.

"That story I told at dinner? That was my story. Not a friend. Me. That happened to me. I was the one who broke up with the guy. And what happened when I tried to call it off? His church buddies hounded me, stalked me, called at all hours of the night demanding I change my mind. Saying I was doing the devil's work breaking up with him. He did the same thing. Because that's what Jesus would do, right?"

"Joni—" her dad said.

"No! I came back to your church looking for help on what to do and got told by the counselors to just stick it out, pray about it. Just settle for fucking garbage! Who cares how I felt? The poor preacher boy needs a trophy wife to prove he's a goddamn saint!"

"I'm not gonna ask you to watch your language again," her dad said.

"Your church hurts people," Joni said. "It hurt me. It hurt Dottie. It hurts anyone who questions its pastor."

"What are you talking about?" her mom said.

"More melodrama," her dad said, sounding tired. "Wants to live for the world. She's just trying to make this about herself. We need to get back to the party before they leave."

"About me?" Joni said in disbelief. She pointed back at the house. "What about when they kept mocking me just now? Kept saying I had a fancy education and all that shit? I didn't ask for that. You just had a creepy old pervert touching up on your daughter, Dad! In your own house, Dad! Why the hell are you taking his side on anything? Because your church expects it? Just like they expected you to sweep Greg's infidelity under the rug and blame Dottie? Your sister, Mom! And you were just okay with that!"

Her mom reached up suddenly and slapped Joni across the face. Before Joni had time to register the sting, her mom was already burying her head back in her hands, fighting tears. Her dad took her mom in his arms, then shot a nasty look at Joni. "How dare you, Joni. You see what you've done? You happy? You've made Violet's birthday all about you."

"She's an atheist," her mom said between tears. "She's a liberal atheist, just like Dottie. I can't do this again."

"It's okay, Laura. It's okay."

"I'm not an atheist," Joni said, rubbing her cheek.

"Could've fooled me," her dad snapped. "No follower of Christ would ever talk the way you have today. No one going to church would speak the way you have today."

Joni sighed. "Probably not. Good thing I stopped going."

Her dad held her mom, who was crying. Neither were looking at her now. She thought about starting her car and just leaving, but that felt like the wrong move.

"You stopped going? So all those times you said you were going to a different church was just a lie?"

"Yes," Joni said. "Because when I was hurting, you kept acting like Pastor Greg's church was the only pathway to salvation. His church hurt me, too, though."

"We cared deeply about you," her mom said. "We raised you to be a beacon of light for this world, smart and wise. We will not condone your atheism. We will not support you in this."

"Why didn't you tell us you were struggling with any of this?" her dad said. "We could have gotten you biblical help from an actual Christian instead of letting you get your head all warped from liberal idiocy."

"I told you. I went to the church, and it told me to settle for something harmful. Christianity was hurting me. And you guys have made it very clear over the years that we don't question it. But I can't follow that anymore. Just going with whatever the Bible says hurt me."

"Our church always follows biblical guidelines."

"Dad," Joni said, "I just heard you talking about how we should be killing people in the name of God."

"I was just making a point," her dad said. "I wasn't saying we should really do that."

"Then maybe you should think more carefully about what you say," Joni said. "But honestly, how could I expect you to do that? That idea is in the Bible. I believe that idea is absolutely wrong and evil. I can't follow that. And honestly, if I had any serious confusion about that idea, I would never trust Pastor Greg or anyone at Elohim Creation Salvation to guide me with advice. Not after how those church people seemed to agree with you at the dinner table. Not after how the church handled my situation with John. Not after how they convinced you and Mom to destroy my creative writing stuff or force me to pray in front of you like some prisoner interrogation. Or how they shamed me for the clothes I wore growing up. I hear the phrase 'biblical guidelines,' and all I think of is people trying to control me. I won't abide by that ever again. You may not like to hear that, but that's who I am, and I won't apologize for that."

Her dad was silent for a moment. Then he asked, "So you're an atheist now?"

Joni shook her head. "More like an agnostic Christian. Some days I think I might still believe. Other days, I'm not sure. I don't have it completely figured out."

Her dad scoffed and her mom wept. "Christ," her dad said. "This cannot be on us. We did everything right. All because you can't take some spiritual advice from a man who, by the way, has served at this church since before your mother and I were even married."

"I don't care if he saw Jesus leave the tomb. You let that pervert shame me because I wore yellow sandals," Joni said. "He tried feeling me up, but even now you're taking sides with him because he's a leader in your church."

"Stop it, Joni."

"You once destroyed everything I wrote because of some fundamentalist fear of books. Because the church told you that magic was evil—"

"It is evil, Joni. You'd know that if you read your Bible."

"They were fantasy stories. They were harmless, and you knew that deep down. And then you both terrorized me into praying for forgiveness in front of some weird church leader."

"Joni, stop it. I've heard enough of this pity party."

"I'm not sorry for who I am," Joni pressed on. "You asked me, and I told you. Plain and simple. I never once tried to make this about me."

"I don't even know you anymore," her dad said. "You're not the daughter we raised. Mr. Gallows was right. That college education was a waste on you. Never should've sent you to school. It turned you into a worldly sucker. You got a taste of the world, and now you're a sucker for it. Just wanna live for the pleasures of the world instead of God. And now you're hanging out with your aunt, so no surprise that you came home with such a rebellious attitude. Can't even suck it up and go apologize."

"Did you listen to anything I just said?" Joni asked. "I don't know why I have to be the one to say that just because you have Jesus in your heart doesn't give you the right to bully or terrorize other people."

Joni felt the pressure behind her eyes and felt that salty sensation burning the bottoms of her eyes. That salty burn was now stinging her cheeks. Joni wiped away her tears, realizing she had failed to contain them some time ago.

"I'm not going to apologize for telling a creep off. I am not going to apologize for standing up for what I think is right. And I'm not going to apologize for being myself. I'm done with that."

"Don't worry about apologizing. It's not going to do you any good now," her mom said, letting anger show in her voice. Wiping her hands clean of tears, her mom balled up her fists and rested them on her hips, staring defiantly with venomous eyes at her daughter.

They were the same eyes Dottie had shown when she caught Joni reading the diary.

That look.

It finally sunk in for Joni what was happening. The tears were the realization of what they would have to do. The scrunched, angry eyes were the doubling-down on what she believed. Just as she'd been taught. Just as her dad had been taught, who was now also staring grimly at Joni.

No one said anything for a minute. Finally, her dad whispered, "You need to leave, Joni. Now. And don't come back."

She turned in her seat and started the ignition. Joni shut her door, not looking at them or saying goodbye. She saw them go stand behind a blue car out of sight of the house windows so they could recompose themselves before returning to the party.

The party.

Joni felt unburdened yet also awful. She hadn't expected to have this conversation with them today, yet it happened. She felt relieved that the mask was off but incredibly anxious about what was next. Was she to be disowned as Dottie had been?

She pulled away from the curb.

Joni sensed her anxiety evolve into a sort of intensity that was almost surreal and circling around to comical. She imagined the Blue Ghost ripping off his own mask to reveal a purple snake-like monster with fangs gnashing and flaming eyes burning with rage. She didn't know if she should feel terrified at how definite this break had been or relieved that she no longer had to hide her true self.

Sit your ass down and shut-up, she thought of saying to the Blue Ghost. Almost immediately, she imagined the beast retreating like a whipped puppy.

Part of her wanted to go back and hug Violet farewell. She had wanted to enjoy more of the party. But instead Mr. Northen had forced her to take the mask off. She'd held up the mirror. Her true self had hijacked the mood of the party.

No. I refuse to feel guilty about this. This is on them.

She drove on down the road as darkening skies fell.

20

"You seem glum today, Joni," Emily said, sweeping up the floor under the coffee maker. It was Monday, July 8—Violet's actual birthday—and Joni was back at work. She leaned back in her chair and rubbed her eyes.

"What makes you say that?" Joni ran a hand through her hair, looking at the computer screen. She was updating the inventory on products that *Chemical Supplies and More!* had in stock. After a few hours, the chemical codenames started to look like a bunch of binary nonsense.

"You seem quieter than usual," Emily said, stooping to sweep the dirt into the broom pan. Joni's office was really more of a corner with a desk and computer. In her area, there was also a vending machine and a shelf of long-forgotten files for clients who had not ordered anything in over twenty years. To the left of Joni's desk was an open doorway that led directly to the communal kitchen with a counter, sink, refrigerator, and table where everyone gathered for their lunch breaks. Emily dumped the dirt into the trash can under the sink and slid the broom and dustpan back into the slender broom closet. "Methinks you're planning something wicked. You going to spike the coffee?"

Joni chuckled. "I had a fight with my parents yesterday."

"Oh, dear." Emily leaned on the doorway and folded her arms. "Everything okay?"

Joni sighed, trying to remember if she had just updated the quantity list for item #013362 or #013361. "It's a long story, but basically, we had a falling out. I had to tell them once and for all that I was my own person with my own beliefs and values and . . . and they didn't take it too well."

"That must really suck. I'm sorry," Emily said. "It must've been rough. You just got back from a really cool vacation, too, so I was wondering why you weren't your usual, chipper self."

Joni shrugged. "They're very intense church fundamentalists. They specialize in sucking the life out of people. I just didn't want any part of that anymore."

Emily grabbed Joni's empty coffee mug and walked over to the maker. "You gotta do what you gotta do. You're living on your own, though, right? You weren't still living with them, right?"

"Yeah. It gets lonely sometimes, but at least I have my own place."

Emily laughed. "I remember the day I finally moved out of my parents' house. I was like, 'Yes! Thank God! Freedom!' Okay, so I miss them sometimes. It was nice having meals made for you. But at the end of the day, I had to be my own person too, you know? Couldn't exactly be a logistics director when your parents want the lights out and everyone in bed by nine, you know?"

Joni nodded. "You know it's true. That's pretty much it. I just can't stand behind a group that hurts people. Oh, thank you." Emily brought Joni a fresh cup of coffee with steam rising. Joni took a sip from the green mug, enjoying the sensation of her dry throat soaking up the hot torrents.

Ah, le nectar des dieux, she thought.

"So, yeah. I'm not on good terms with them now."

Emily nodded, standing in the doorway and working on her own fresh cup of coffee. "Joni, I'm really sorry. It's never easy standing up to parents, is it?"

"I guess not. Hey, thank you for the coffee! You didn't have to do that."

Emily shrugged. "It's what friends do. Let me know if there's anything I can do, okay? You're a good person, Joni. Don't feel guilty about what happened, and definitely don't feel ashamed for standing up for yourself. Okay?"

Joni nodded. "Okay."

As Emily walked back to her own office, Joni sipped her coffee and stared back at the screen. Chemical #013362 was highlighted. She checked her hard paper inventory notes and saw that she had corrected it already. She moved onto product #013363, sipping her coffee.

I wish I could be as kind and loving as Emily.

Later that evening, Joni pulled back into her driveway. Getting out, she locked the car and headed inside. Once in her kitchen, she opened the fridge to see what she could make for dinner. She found some cheese. Next, she opened the cabinet, where she found some bread and an unopened can of tuna.

Tuna melts it is.

She assembled the ingredients, turned the oven on, and set the tray inside. Impulsively, she checked her phone. There were no missed calls or voice messages. No attempt to do the conversation over or throw in some final jabs.

I'm not going to call them. This is on them.

Joni went over to her computer and put Lukaas Bennett's album in the disc drive. As the violin music started playing, she went over to the couch and ate her tuna melts. Once she finished her tuna melts, she lied down and looked at the ceiling, just taking in the music and thinking on everything that had happened.

I need to get this CD back to Dottie.

The clock turned 6:53.

I should try to call Violet. Try to at least apologize for what happened.

Joni called her sister but reached only the recording to leave a message. Hanging up, she rubbed her forehead, feeling a headache coming on. She wondered if Violet was mad at her for what had happened.

Probably.

But she couldn't imagine Violet disowning her the way their parents would. Violet had nearly the same reservations about Pastor Greg that she did, but their parents also had more strings on her as well. They controlled Violet's ability to go to school at this point. Scholarships or no, they had no legal obligation to physically drive her or support her financially in any way. And since Violet had no car or license of her own, managing the move herself would be nearly impossible. Most of her friends were the children of parents who felt that women had no place in college, so hitching a ride from friends (who had also been deprived of driving training) was out of the question for her. While Violet still lived in their house, she had to play by their rules.

I don't blame her if she is ignoring me. I fucked up. I ruined her party.

Another idea came to Joni. If Joni was officially an "other," their parents might fear that Violet could be influenced by "Joni's ungodly ways." They would do what they could to prevent another child of theirs from going astray.

What if they forbid her to talk to me while she's still living there?

Joni spent the evening washing some dishes, reading a book, and revising some notes in her story outline. By around ten, no one had called or left messages. She checked her e-mail. There were countless ads for travel options and agencies, a dozen notifications of people liking her photos online, but nothing from her family.

I'm not going to lose sleep over this.

Joni went to bed after typing new details in her story outline. She clarified the point that Claire couldn't leave the lighthouse without perishing forever. This way, the ghost had to stay put for a reason instead of just because the plot said so.

Eventually, she turned her brain off for the night and climbed into bed. She wanted more than anything to talk to someone about what had happened. There had been a time when she could have gone to Amy, or Elin, or Tia maybe, but those days were long gone. Without Dottie to talk to, Joni felt more alone than ever.

The next day at work during her lunch break, Joni checked her phone. Still no messages or missed calls from her family. She thought about driving across town to their house to confront them, but she decided there was no point in wasting that much gas just to create an awkward face-to-face situation again.

Wednesday was pretty much the same as Tuesday. A massive order for an overseas construction crew came in that depleted over half their stock of water-proofing lubricants. Joni inspected the barcode numbers of each barrel that was shipped out and had to log into the system which barrels were leaving. There were over two-hundred barrels that needed to be properly logged in. As Joni neared the end of her database managing, she checked her phone again. Still no texts, messages, or missed calls.

Thursday and Friday were no different. Joni went to work, laughed with Emily over lunch, went back to work, and her phone never once rang.

It wasn't until Saturday that Joni received anything resembling clarity on her family situation. Sitting on her front porch, she typed away at her story. She had begun a draft of the first chapter. The sky was blue, birds tweeted, and every now and then a car would drive by. Winds carried the scent of fired up grills and nearby family cookouts from elsewhere throughout the neighborhood. As she typed out the remaining paragraphs of her first chapter draft, her phone buzzed.

Picking it up, she saw that it was a text message from a strange number she didn't recognize. It had the right area code, though, so she opened it. The message simply said, *This is Violet. Meet me at mall food court at 6 if you can. Much to tell. You've been disowned by parents and I'm trying to sneak around that. This is a friend's phone.*

Waves of gratitude and pain swept over Joni. She was glad to see that her sister was covertly fighting for autonomy and wasn't going along with the family's shunning nonsense. Violet was her own person. Whatever personal journey she'd been on, she knew how to be sneaky and not get caught.

On the other hand, there had been a sort of comfort in thinking that her parents were simply upset and would eventually get over it. Having in writing the words *You've been disowned* made it real. Her stomach turned.

She was really on her own now. Joni set her computer aside and rested her face in her palm, wrestling with the emotions.

Later that evening, Joni parked in the mall parking lot on the side far away from the food court. She didn't mind this. She looked forward to a stroll through the mall before meeting with Violet.

Haven't been here in a while.

Joni walked in through a shoe store department. She took a down-escalator to the main area of the mall. When she made it to the food court, she looked for an empty table to sit and wait at. *There has to be at least three-hundred people here*, Joni thought. Violet, with her straight, brown hair and slender build would blend in with almost any of them. Joni scanned the crowds for groups of teenagers, but that didn't help. Most of the crowds were teenagers, many with slender builds, and even more with brown hair.

Joni almost texted Violet that she was there when she remembered that her sister had been using a friend's phone, and almost certainly wouldn't have it still. *She probably used it because they're watching her phone, making sure she doesn't contact me.* Joni got out her phone just in case another message had come through. None had.

Joni waited about six minutes. She was about to go wandering again to look for Violet when her sister finally showed up. Violet broke free from a group of teenage girls and scanned the food court. When Joni noticed her, she stood and waved. Violet spotted her and came over. Before sitting down, Violet gave Joni probably the tightest hug the two had ever shared.

"Ugh, it's been one hell of a week," Violet said before letting go and sitting down.

"I am so sorry," Joni said, sitting back down. "Vi, I'm sorry I screwed up your birthday party. Again. I really didn't mean to."

Violet waved her hand as if there was nothing to apologize for. "No, you didn't ruin anything. But what happened? All I know is I heard you cuss, and then apparently you said you hate the church and everyone in it. That's what Mom and Dad said, anyway."

Joni rolled her eyes. "They cornered me at the dinner table, Mom and Dad and those church people. They all asked my opinion why millennials weren't interested in church. And I was just honest with them. Meanwhile, Mr. Northen kept putting his hands on me, being real condescending with me, telling me I was a dumb, college millennial."

"Eww," Violet said. "I fucking hate that guy. He's always given off a weird vibe. I can't wait to get out of here."

"Yeah. I asked him to stop, and he didn't, so I blew up at him. That's when I cussed him out. We went outside and they hounded me some more until I let them have it. Told them everything. About John. About Elohim Creation Salvation—God, what a fucking mouthful of a name. About their church members. They probably weren't ready to be called out for their crap, but they needed to hear it. Anyway, Mom cried, and she slapped me. Dad got upset. They told me to leave."

Violet's eyes widened with disbelief. "Jeez."

"I'm really sorry, Violet."

"What for?"

"Ruining your birthday party. This was supposed to be your week, and I really wasn't expecting them to force this conversation so suddenly. I wanted to wait a little bit, maybe after you'd left for college, before talking with them."

"You didn't ruin anything," Violet said. "Everyone had fun. I knew something was up, but Mom and Dad pretended like everything was okay. They didn't tell me until everyone had left what happened. Their version of it, anyway."

Joni sighed. "I'm guessing their version left out the part where Mr. Northen kept putting his hands on me."

"Yeah. Well, you've been shut out," Violet said. "Just like Aunt Dottie. I only found out yesterday, but the deacons told Mom and Dad to shun you and stop giving you support. They're not to talk to you or help you in any way. And they are going to follow through with that, I'm afraid. They won't talk to you, call you, visit, or anything. They think you're too swayed by new-age values and worldly influences. They think this will teach you to question God."

"What about you? Are they trying to get you to stop going to college?" Joni asked.

"No," Violet said. "Not yet, anyway. They did say they wanted to look at my college program again. Probably want to make sure it's a good enough Christian program or something. But they did sit me down and say that I had to avoid you too, not give you any help."

"Fuck," Joni said, turning in her seat to see if anyone was watching them. "So you're not supposed to be here talking to me now, are you?"

Violet nodded. "If word gets back to the deacons that I'm here right now helping you, they'd freak out. But you know what, who cares? I'm eighteen now. Going off to college soon. Pastor Greg doesn't rule my life. I'll be out of there too, and maybe someday I'll have to have the same unpleasant conversation with them that you did. Of course, I'm still dependent on them now for things, like getting to places, driving, a phone, and all that, so . . . God, how did you do it?"

Joni shrugged. "I just played by the rules until I could escape. And honestly, I regret doing so. I missed out on so much because I played along. I wore the dorkiest clothes and didn't make many memorable friends. I can't help but think that if I'd stood up sooner, maybe Mom and Dad wouldn't be so blind to the abuse that church causes. Maybe they wouldn't be so wrapped up in it."

"Maybe," Violet said. "Yeah, they've definitely gotten worse in the last few years. I told you about that weird purity intervention they did when I went to prom, right?"

"Oh, yeah."

"Like, what even was that?" Violet said, looking over her shoulder. "It's so weird, Joni. I just want to get out and live a normal life."

"I remember feeling like I was walking on eggshells all the time. Is it hard having to follow all these new rules?" Joni asked.

"I get by," Violet said. "I feel like I'm walking a balance beam all the time, but I can do things without them knowing. Like, you know, this." She indicated her meeting with Joni at this particular table. "I figured they were going to tell me not to talk to you anymore, so good thing I used someone else's phone to reach you first."

"That's good. Did they tell you I'm an atheist, too?"

Violet nodded. "I'm curious what led you to become one."

"I'm not an atheist. That's the thing! Beyond all reason and logic, I'm not. I still believe in God. Well, somedays, anyways. I think I might be agnostic if anything. I don't have scientific proof for you that God exists. I won't pretend I do. Maybe He's there, maybe not. I don't know. I'm still figuring things out. But it's because of that belief that I also feel I have a moral obligation to set things right. I don't believe having faith in God means you get to exploit people. That's what their church does. That's what a lot of the Christian culture does, and I don't like it. If I get shunned for that, so be it. I'd rather die a caring person than live as a complacent jackass towards people."

Violet nodded. "I agree, but listen, Joni. Keep a watch out, okay?

I did some research on that whole incident with Mr. Bridges. I found his article online. When he wrote that opinion piece, he started getting harassed not long after. They found out it was some guys working on behalf of the church. Pastor Greg denied being involved, and they couldn't prove he gave them the orders to go after Mr. Bridges, especially once he fired the guys. But obviously the whole thing was about shutting down criticism of Pastor Greg. Just remember this is a big community church you've drawn a line with. They have connections everywhere in this area. Please be safe."

"I will," Joni said, feeling her stomach tighten again. "At least it's not the eighties. The church was much bigger back then."

"God, Pastor Greg would've been in his twenties," Violet said, nodding. "Yeah, it's not as big as the glory days, but it still has a lot of followers. Oh, before I forget, the parents changed my phone so I couldn't contact you. Let me see your phone real quick."

Joni handed it over. Violet dialed a number, her new phone rang, and she handed Joni's phone back. "I'll save your number as *Spiritual Guidance Hotline*," Violet said. Joni laughed, unsuccessfully shaking the nervous feeling that they were being watched. "In case they decide to snoop through my phone."

"Cool. So every time you call, I'll just respond like an automated machine with daily spiritual wisdom quotes," Joni said. Imitating a robot, she joked, "Thou shalt not question Pastor Greg."

Violet laughed. "Alright, I need to head back. My friends are probably wondering why I'm taking so long in the bathroom. I said I'd meet them at the pretzel stand. Take care of yourself, okay? We'll catch up more when I get to college. You still gotta tell me about your trip and Aunt Dottie and everything!"

"I will. Thanks for letting me know, Violet," Joni said, reaching over to hug her sister. "When you get to college, don't date a douchebag."

"Deal," Violet said.

A few days later, Joni went to check her mailbox. She'd just gotten home from work. Aside from an insurance ad mailed to Ms. Margot Kensington (the former resident), Joni was startled to discover three issues of porn magazines from different publications. The covers were graced by voluptuous women with price bubbles covering their nipples. Joni quickly looked around to see if someone was playing a prank. She saw no one.

"What the fuck?" she said to herself.

She went inside and looked at the covers. *Is it supposed to be a joke? Is someone trying to screw with me? So juvenile.*

She flipped through the magazines to see if there was a message stuck in-between the pages. When she didn't find any, she tossed the magazines on her kitchen table and stared at them, baffled. Looking closer at the address box on the covers, a wave of panic hit her.

The magazines had been mailed to her—Joni Arable—specifically.

That's my name. That's my address. But I didn't order these.

Unsettled, Joni went to her computer and logged into her bank account. *If someone hacked me, it should show up in my bank statement.* The statement didn't show anything from recently, so Joni scrolled through the entire statement. After scrolling through a year's worth of statements, Joni found no suspicious purchases.

She sat back, somewhat relieved. *Who sent me porn?* She figured someone, probably from the church, had done it to spite her or screw with her. Joni scooped up the magazines and stored them in a blank folder. After storing the folder in the top drawer of her desk by the front door, she went to the window and looked out. The family across the street was loading up into their minivan with their kids. Other than that, there was no one. No one was openly staking out her house.

I wonder.

Joni pulled out her laptop. Elohim Creation Salvation posted their Sunday services on their official website each Monday. One Sunday had passed since the argument between her and her parents. *My parents are actively involved in that church. Pretty well-known members. I wonder.*

If this had been a coordinated attack from the church, then Joni was sure there would be an accompanying passive-aggressive sermon aimed at her. Not in the hopes that she'd come back, but rather to discourage any others who might get the idea to question authority.

The sermon had the usual format. Eight minutes or so of opening worship songs, a stinger video with a woman's personal testimony about how great the church was for helping her father get off drugs and find Jesus again. Then there were some welcoming announcements from the youth leader (it was Mr. Harris, who seemed highly animated with bright, wide eyes and wild arm movements). Then some more worship songs, none of which Joni had ever heard. Finally, after nearly twenty minutes, Pastor Greg took to the stage. The lights came up to show his tan skin, balding head, swimmer's build, and fatherly wire-rimmed glasses. After his exuberant declaration of, "Good morning!" the entire auditorium erupted with applause.

Joni had to admit that even in his late fifties, Pastor Greg had kept his body in great shape.

Joni clicked her way through the sermon, looking for key moments in which he might say something. She stopped the video at a point in which Pastor Greg was staring quite intensely at the audience, but he continued to talk only about the 144,000 in Revelation. The camera never showed too much of the audience, but Joni knew there had to be at least six hundred people in attendance. There was an odd moment where he focused on signs during the last days.

"It will be a time when sons and—don't miss this, folks— *daughters*—will turn from the truth and rebel against their parents!" he said. "And look at what we're seeing now! Millennials think they're too smart for God! Millennials think God isn't hip or cool enough. But the joke's on them. God's got another thing coming for them."

The audience laughed. Joni shut the computer and wanted to puke.

The next day, Joni hopped in her car and went to work at the lab again. Today, she was tasked with alphabetizing a very long, two-drawer cabinet with customer folders dating back to the nineties. Over the years, people had casually thrown files and folders in no particular order into the drawers, and now Joni had to undo over fifteen years' worth of other people's bad habits.

She started by simply pulling out all the folders and stacking them into the piles based on what letter they started with. *Jackson goes on J, Dustin goes on D . . . goddamn, this is monotonous.*

As she continued stacking the folders in piles, Miranda Colbertson came around the hall quickly. Miranda, a woman in her late forties, was the Human Resources manager. She usually spoke to Joni only when it involved either cutting her hours, cutting her benefits, or cutting her pay.

Maybe she's come to cut me a slice of cake this time.

"Joni, do you have a moment? I need to talk to you in my office."

"Alright," Joni said, setting a stack of folders down and following Miranda towards her office. They climbed a flight of stairs and turned right. Stepping into Miranda's office, the smell of moldy filing boxes was replaced by a strawberry-scented air freshener. As Joni took a seat in one of the leather chairs facing Miranda's desk, Miranda closed the door. "I'll shut the door so we can talk privately."

Privately? Joni felt another knot tighten in her stomach. *Am I about to be fired?*

Joni clenched her seat with her fingertips, bracing for the worst, when Miranda sat down at the desk and faced Joni. She folded her hands like a teacher about to explain a punishment.

"Joni, I received a call a little bit ago. Someone complained about you."

Confused, Joni said, "Complained about me?"

Miranda nodded her head. "They called and said they spoke to you on the phone about an order you messed up? They said you cussed them out and yelled at them. Is this ringing a bell?"

Joni's eyes betrayed her surprise at all this. In the entire year she'd been with the company, she hadn't used a phone to contact a customer. Not once. This was largely due to the fact that customer service wasn't part of her job.

"I have never talked to a customer on the phone, Miranda. Never." Joni leaned slightly forward in her chair, confused and wondering what was going on. "Are you sure they said me? *Me*, specifically?"

Miranda nodded. "They said they spoke with Joni Arable on the phone. Are you sure? You've worked closely with the Quality Assurance department. Did you ever place a call or take a call for any order? Maybe when Emily stepped out of the room for something?"

Joni shook her head. "I've never placed a call or taken one. I've never called anyone outside of work, either. I've always just logged the quality tests in the database. Sorry, Miranda. I've never spoken with anyone or had any sort of yelling match with anyone. Ever. Who was this? What did they say?"

Miranda sat back in her chair, more at ease. "They said they ordered twelve drums of acetone, and they only got four. They said they called and spoke to a service rep named Joni Arable. They *specifically* named you. They said you registered only four drums and refused to acknowledge their original order of twelve. They said when they read their order to you, you started cussing them out. You apparently said to them, 'Burn in Hell! Kiss my ass!' Told them they could go suck your . . . well, you get the idea."

Joni frowned and cocked her eyebrows. "That doesn't even sound like me. Did they have a purchase order number? What were their names?"

"Well," Miranda said, "I was hoping to get that from you, actually. When I asked them that, they told me to not bother. They would order from another vendor and would never buy from us again." Miranda leaned forward in her seat. "And you're saying this did not happen? Ever?"

Joni held up her hands at a complete loss. "Miranda, you know me. I don't interact with customers. That's Emily's job. You know I'm like the quietest person in this building. I can't stand confrontation. I mean, the fact that they didn't give you a name or an order number should be proof enough that it was a fake. And I can't imagine Emily doing that, either."

"Well, I'm glad it's a lie, I guess," Miranda said. "Of course, I believe you, Joni. What they were describing certainly didn't sound like you. Or Emily. Not at all. I was really hoping you could tell me who would make up such a thing, though."

Joni sat back in her seat, suddenly gripped by a realization. "Actually, Miranda, I think I can think of someone who would do something like this."

Miranda cocked her eyebrows. "Really? Who?"

Joni sighed. "It's complicated. And I can't be sure who specifically is doing it or even if it's the group I think it is. I may as well tell you what's been going on."

Joni proceeded to tell Miranda the whole story: how manipulative her church had been, how abusive her Christian clique had been in college, how she'd left that scene, how she spent years trying to speak to her parents, how she'd been forced to speak honestly about it, and how her family had disowned her. She also described how that church handled disobedient members, and how she'd been disowned.

"And now, I think that church is trying to intimidate me or something. I don't know. It's not to teach me a lesson. It's more to warn their congregation of what'll happen if they leave too, I guess. And they'll do anything to get the point across, even dragging people into it who have nothing to do with it. See why I left it? Crazy people."

Miranda sat back in her seat. "Alright. Next time someone calls to complain about you, I'll check if they have an actual number and name. If they don't, I won't bother you with it. Just make sure you stay away from making contacts—and I know this sounds unfair because we trust you, but just to be safe and cover our bases—don't call or take calls from customers. I know you haven't, which is good. Just keep that up so they have nothing on you. And Joni, I would recommend that you keep a record of all this in case it continues. If it continues, call the police."

Once she got inside her home later that evening, she locked her door. She looked out the windows to see if anyone was lurking around her house. When she saw no one, she grabbed her phone. She hesitated, then dialed her mom.

Four rings straight to voicemail.

Of course.

"Mom, it's Joni. We need to talk. I think I'm being stalked. Please call me back."

She left a similar voice message for her father whose phone also went directly to voicemail. She looked out her windows but still didn't see any suspicious people.

The next morning, Joni went about the same routine: showered, dressed, surfed the morning news online while munching down cereal, and out the door by 7:30. This morning, Joni was greeted by yet another unpleasant surprise. As she started her car and began to back out of the driveway, her car immediately started bobbing up and down, shaking. She stopped the car.

"What the hell?" she said, setting it in park and climbing out. She checked her side of the car, making sure she hadn't run over something. Looking under the car, she didn't see anything. Joni walked to the other side.

Her right rear tire loosely clung to the wheel. It was flat, but there was a very clear and definite jagged tear across the side of it. Someone had slashed her tire.

"You gotta be kidding me," she said, taking out her phone. She quickly snapped a picture of it and called Miranda. As she told Miranda why she would be late to work that day, she quickly looked around the bushes and behind her house to see if anyone was hiding out. Once again, there was no one.

Cowards.

"Joni, call the police," Miranda said on the phone. "Tell them what you told me. Don't change your tire just yet. Let the police look at it. Just come in when you can. If you can't, that's fine. Just let me know, okay? Take care of this first."

Joni did as instructed. While waiting on the police, she got out her spare tire, jack, and wrench. When the officer arrived, she told him what she had found, showed him the slashed tire, and explained that she hadn't heard anything during the night. The police officer inspected the rest of her vehicle for damage. "Sometimes when this happens, the person'll cut your brake hoses, too. But you say you were able to stop fine, and I don't see any damage to them here."

He inspected the other tires too. "Yeah, these are fine, too. Sometimes they put nails or tacks in the tires to mess them up, but they didn't do that here. Looks like they just took a knife or something and cut a hole in the one. Your other tires are fine."

He turned to face Joni. "And you think this might be a stalker?"

"Yes, sir."

The officer took out a clipboard and began filling out his report.

"Is there anyone who you think might have done this? Any enemies or people who are upset with you?"

Joni hesitated. "I have an idea of who might have done this, but I don't have any evidence, really." She explained the situation with her parents, reliving the whole drama once more. "I don't have proof that their church is behind this, but that's the sort of church it is. They punish anyone they view as a threat. Me not going and explaining why I don't go puts me on their bad list. I might give their congregation bad ideas or something. Anyway, I don't know if the church itself is behind it or if someone going there is behind it. My parents wouldn't do this. They disowned me. They want nothing to do with me."

"What's the name of the church, Ms. Arable?"

"Elohim Creation Salvation Community Church," said Joni. *It really is a mouthful just to say the whole name.*

"Really?" the officer said, surprised. "That's where I go."

"Oh," said Joni, feeling cornered.

Joni didn't know this officer. Was he a genuinely good man who knew the law and would enforce it, knowing fully that it could potentially involve charging his pastor? Or was he corrupt? Would he give the church a free pass, writing Joni off as merely a disgruntled ex-member who probably deserved the slashed tires?

"Well, like I said, it could just be people acting as individuals or it could be coming from higher up. I don't know, but that's what I'm sensing. Whoever did it also sent me porn magazines the other day, addressed to me like I'd ordered it, and placed a fake complaint against me at my work."

"Did you keep the magazines? As evidence?"

"Yes, officer." She went inside, grabbed her folder, and showed them to him. "If you need to, I can give you the number to my work's HR rep for the whole story about the fake phone call complaint."

The officer finished taking notes and said, "Would you like some help changing your tire, Ms. Arable?"

Joni said, "Thank you, Officer. I think I've got it."

"Well," the officer said, "here's what you should do. Keep a record of anything that counts as harassment. Any threatening e-mails, any letters, take pictures of anything that gets damaged. Keep a record of it all. Keep an eye out for any suspicious cars that drive by. Check your windows. Make sure you're not being spied on. Usually perpetrators who do this like to escalate the problem until they get caught. If you have a camera, set it up. If not, maybe look into a few good home security systems. I mean, you can just go online and find them. Or go down the road to the hardware store. They've got some options there. Just keep an eye out for anything suspicious. We've got this report on file now, so if anything comes up, just call us back. We'll see how to proceed from there. Sound good?"

"Yes, sir."

"Alright. You have a good one, Ms. Arable."

After Joni replaced the tire with the spare, she drove into work. Irate and frazzled, she parked the car when she arrived and got out her phone. She dialed directly to her mom's voicemail, not wanting to talk but to leave her own message.

"Hi, Mom. Someone slashed my tires last night. Thought you should know. Joni." She pressed *END* forcefully and threw it on the floor. Resting her face against her palm, Joni took a moment to calm down. It was already ten-thirty, which meant she would be docked two and a half hours' pay.

Great. Someone slashes my tires, and I'm the one who has to pay. Pay for new tires, pay for lost time. My parents get to throw me under the bus, and I get to do this alone. Just like Dottie.

Joni thought about her aunt. The events of the night she got caught reading her diary came flooding back to her, and she felt the shame all over again. Joni wondered if this was how Dottie had felt all those years ago when she'd been disowned. Had she felt out of options like this? Had she felt this isolated? She wondered what Dottie would have done to cope with being cut off from her family.

Probably had some fun.

When she went inside, she found Emily who was busy printing out a certification of quality sticker. Joni went up to her and said, "Emily, I need a friend. You want to go out for a drink sometime?"

Emily smiled. "I could absolutely go for a drink. Friday night sound good?"

***

Later that evening after work, Joni discovered yet another nasty little surprise. When she checked her mailbox, she discovered a roadkill bird carcass sitting on top of the mail.

"What the fuck!" she exclaimed. It was only then that she noticed her next-door neighbor was out trimming his hedges only ten feet away. She noticed him pause in the trimming to look at her. Feeling embarrassed, she decided to include him in on the problem.

"Excuse me, did you notice anyone at my mailbox today, sir?"

The man, who appeared to be in his sixties, shook his head. "Sorry. I just got out here. Is something wrong?"

"Yes," Joni said. "Someone put a dead bird carcass in my mailbox."

The man's eyes widened. Setting down his yard clippers, he walked across her driveway and came to inspect the mailbox. When he saw the mangled, black-feathered corpse, he shuddered a little. "That's disgusting!" he said.

"Yep. It is," she said.

That night, right before Joni went to sleep, she turned on her porch light. She took out her old mini-DV tape camcorder and set up the tripod at the front door. With the lights off inside, no one would be able to see the camera pointing out of the front door window at them. It only had an hour's worth of available recording time, but maybe that would be all she needed. She plugged the camera charger in, hit record on the camera, and went to bed.

About an hour later, right as she was drifting off, the sound of smashing glass startled her back to consciousness.

The bedroom was dark, and only the moonlight shone through her window. Sliding her legs over the bedside, she got up and tip-toed to her bedroom door. She grabbed the old, wooden baseball bat placed next to it and opened the door. Creeping as silently as possible down the hallway, trying not to make the wooden floors creak, Joni held the bat up, anticipating some intruder to leap out and attack.

What she found instead was just as scary. The large window to her living room had a gaping hole in it. A rock sat in the middle of the floor with a trail of smashed glass behind it. Some light bounced off of the shards, alerting her to the damage. Surveying the rest of the house to make sure no one was inside—all the doors were locked—Joni finally turned on the light to see the entirety of the damage.

Someone had clearly thrown the rock through the window. When it came through the glass, it bounced off the television. That explained why the flat-screen was both turned at a slightly awkward angle and now had a white scrape mark across the top of it.

Through the window, Joni saw ghostly strands of white dangling from her gutters. Looking out the front door window, she saw that no one was there. As her eyes adjusted to the dark, she noticed the white strands were also dangling from the oak tree in the front yard.

Toilet paper.

"Did I really just get TP'd? Is this the fucking 90's?" she said aloud to herself.

Stepping outside, Joni saw the extent of the damage. The tree in her front yard was covered with toilet paper. The house was draped with it. She almost missed it, but upon returning inside, she noticed that several more porn magazines had been placed near the door. Looking at them, she saw that these were also addressed to her specifically. Seething with rage and feeling violated, she marched inside. Slamming the door shut and locking it, she turned on all the lights in her house. She started a pot of coffee and got to work.

I will not live my life in fear. If they wanna play games, they'll learn the hard way not to fuck with Joni Arable.

Before calling the police, she went over to her camcorder. It was still on but had gone into sleep mode and was no longer recording. *Used up the whole tape. Hope I got something.* Joni rewound the tape and started it at the beginning. She looked through the rectangular LCD screen.

Much of the tape simply showed a quiet and silent front yard, so she fast-forwarded it and kept her eye on the screen. Around the forty-minute mark of the tape, however, she saw that two teenage boys approached from the street on the left side of the screen with a plastic tub. Setting it down near the tree, they pulled rolls of toilet paper from the tub and began throwing the rolls over the tree. This took about five minutes. Both seemed to be athletically built and had pretty good throwing abilities. They both wore hoodies and what appeared to be bandana masks that obscured their faces. Most of the time, they stayed largely in the shadows.

Then they hid behind the tree and watched the porch for a little bit. They appeared to be conversing quietly about something—probably trying to determine if it was safe to go on the porch—before finally one of them worked up the nerve to sneak up. This guy had the magazines in hand and was cautiously surveying the windows. He walked up quickly but with a pose that was ready to bolt if he needed to.

He stepped onto the porch. He paused, trying to scan the windows for signs of movement. Standing back up, he set the magazines next to the door. Briefly, he pulled his mask down to catch his breath, then put it back up. Joni's eyes widened.

She recognized him as the blonde kid from Violet's birthday party, the one who'd been joking about basketball. Even with the hoodie and cartoonish-looking bandit scarf, she recognized his blonde hair swooping down to one side, and that smirk seemingly engraved on his face.

The boy ran back to the tree. It took a few minutes, but eventually the boys started looking around for something. Eventually one of them found something and picked it up. *Is that the rock they threw?* The boy set the object down next to the tub. Then the boys started throwing the toilet paper around her house.

Here the tape ended.

She remembered the incident with the man in Jacksonville, Tennessee. She remembered feeling so scared to even consider bothering the police. Now, however, she knew she had every right—and moral obligation—in the world to do so.

Joni grabbed her phone and called the police.

By the time Joni had explained the situation to the police and shown them the tape, the sun was beginning to rise. She had gotten no sleep, and it was about time to go in for work. A different police officer from before said she would contact the church to find these two youths and deal with them.

Joni went back inside, wanting at least thirty minutes of rest before her alarm would go off.

The police contacted Pastor Greg himself about the incident and discovered the identities of the two boys. The message had been sent: *Don't fuck with Joni Arable.* She decided to tune into his sermon that next Sunday to see if the incident was alluded to at all. *I'll be shocked if it isn't,* she thought.

As Joni watched his sermon unfold—laying down on the couch with her laptop propped against her lap—it began and continued like all of his other sermons: self-congratulatory descriptions of people coming to Jesus, lead-ins to Bible verses, the occasional pop-culture reference, and a steady dose of ethos and pathos with very little logos.

Then he got onto a message of prayer. "Look," he said to the congregation, "I'm going to say this once and move on. Once, loud and clear, got it? Listen, it's this: When you encounter a disagreeable person, pray for them."

The audience applauded.

"If someone criticizes us," he continued, "let them! Just bless them and move on. If they are so afraid of God's will and they'd prefer to burn in Hell with their worldly-thinking, let them! If they think ordering porn and disobeying God are better than enjoying the promise of eternal life in Heaven, let them! We don't need to fight them. We don't need to throw stones at them. We don't need to go TP their houses. We need to pray for them. Pray for their souls."

Even more applause.

Joni shut the video off and stood up. Setting her laptop on the coffee table, she walked over to the television stand. On it was a picture of her family. It was one they had taken at an Easter service about four years earlier, probably the last one they had ever taken as a whole family. She grabbed the frame and slammed it to the ground, stomping on it and kicking it. She shouted at the top of her lungs before falling onto the couch facedown. She buried her face into a couch pillow, crying.

It's so unfair. He gets to mix half-truths with lies, and everyone thinks he's a man of God. I try to help my parents see the harm they do, and I get disowned.

She grabbed her phone. Seething with anger, she started to dial her dad's phone number. She didn't know what she would say. Maybe she wanted to cuss them out for homeschooling her, for teaching her that critical thinking was dangerous, for letting their church intimidate and harass their daughter, for raising her to be ashamed of her own body, for enabling a creepy old man's fetish with yellow sandals.

Joni clutched her phone, not hitting the call button. She spotted her car keys on the counter. She thought about driving over there and telling them all this in person.

Then she looked at the mirror hanging above the stove in the kitchen. Walking over, she recoiled a little at how fierce she looked now. Her eyes were wide with rage, eyebrows arched with pain and focused hatred. Her cheeks were flush with red, and her jaw trembled with violent rage.

Dottie's words came back to her: *You don't need anybody's fucking permission to live your life.*

She set her phone down on the counter, calming down a little. She relaxed her jaw muscles, she softened her eyebrows, and she wiped away her tears.

Give yourself permission to enjoy your life without shame.

Joni looked out the window. A car drove by. And just like that, she decided not to call or drive over to her parents' house.

I am done trying to be the daughter who saves them. I said all I needed to say. If my safety really means nothing to them, if my life really means nothing to them, then fuck them. I get to say who stays in my life, not them. They don't get to disown me. I get to disown them. It's my life, and it's too damn short to try to please them.

She grabbed her car keys. She knew who she needed to see.

Across town, Joni parked her car outside of Dottie's apartment. Getting out of the car, Joni was surprised to see Dottie smoking a cigarette on one of the benches outside. She walked up to her aunt quietly and sat down beside her.

For a minute, neither said anything. Dottie exhaled some smoke, watching some yellow jackets scurry about on the ground. The traffic from the road passed by with roaring engines and cars driving both fast-as-fuck and slow-as-hell. Joni finally spoke.

"So this is what it feels like to be dead?"

Dottie didn't take her eyes off of the bees.

"Yep, pretty much."

Joni looked at the yellow jackets now too, not bothering to move her legs or even caring if she got stung. "It's a weird feeling. There's pain but also freedom."

Dottie looked at Joni, then offered up her box of cigarettes. "Want a smoke?"

Joni looked at the box and took one. "Sure. Thanks."

Her aunt took out a lighter and lit it for her. Joni sat back and inhaled deeply. Then she started coughing violently and put the cigarette out. "I'm sorry. This is disgusting. I can't. How do people smoke this shit?"

Dottie looked at her niece, chuckling. "Well, at least you tried it for yourself."

Joni sighed. She looked up at the sky. There were a few clouds, but none of them made any discernible shapes. "What do I do now?" she asked.

Dottie took another puff, and then blew out the smoke. "Pray and live. When you're dead, it's all you can do, really."

Neither said anything until the sun went down. When the sun disappeared behind the trees, Dottie said, "Come inside. I'm making omelets for dinner."

Fall of 2014

21

No way, she thought. *Is this it?*

Joni sat at her desk, staring down at the unopened letter from another publisher. She'd read over twenty rejection letters so far, but this one was different. It was in a manila envelope that seemed to contain a packet. Had it been a rejection letter, it would have been an e-mail or a simple sheet of paper folded up in a regular envelope. Unsure what to expect, Joni began to tear away at the sealed tape.

Outside, the last of the leaves had turned yellow and were barely hanging onto the naked tree. The road was damp, and the November air was cool. The thermometer in her window read 68 degrees Fahrenheit. It was Saturday.

She tore off the top of the envelope and pulled out a thin stack of paper. Her heart stopped, not daring to hope this could be what she thought it was.

She read the letter.

Dear Joni,

Thank you for submitting your manuscript entitled Lighthouse of Eternal Pictures. *I want you to know that your submission is exactly the sort of story we are looking for. Within the opening sentences, I was hooked. I wanted to know how Claire would escape her village's fascist wrath. The character dynamics are very strong, and it comes through in your writing. Having grown up in a fundamentalist situation myself, I could relate to everything Claire was going through. Our staff is excited about the possibilities of this book and believes it can be a bestseller.*

If you have not found another publisher, we would like to make you an offer by accepting your request to help publish your book. The papers included with this acceptance letter are documents detailing the publishing process, some editor's notes, and a draft version of our offered contract.

I will call you in the afternoon on November 10 to discuss your decision. In the meantime, please review the editor's notes. We hope to work with you and get your story out there.

Sincerely,

Faith Thompson, Managing Editor

There was additional contact information, but Joni read through the letter again, just in case she had missed some bad news in there somewhere.

She hadn't.

It had been a long time since she'd experienced this sort of euphoria. It was as if she had been chained to a slow-moving boat, and someone had finally taken the shackles off. Not only that, but they'd given her the engine to get out of there.

She didn't know who to tell first. Dottie? Emily? Jerry or Benjamin, both of whom she'd met through various social gatherings with Emily and her sister Rachael? Joni paced around the house excitedly to find her phone. Once she found it, she texted Emily. Then Jerry. Then Rachael. Then Benjamin.

She considered calling Violet. Violet was now midway through her sophomore year of college and had found ways to gain her own independence. She paid for her own phone now, and the sisters were finally free to talk again.

After the two stalking boys had been caught, the police contacted Pastor Greg to see what had happened. The ensuing investigation revealed that the two boys had acted on the requests of Mr. Northen. This not only led to Pastor Greg giving a passive-aggressive sermon about dealing with critics, but also led to the two boys being excommunicated, issued restraining orders from Joni, and sentenced to community service hours. Mr. Northen denied any such instructions, claiming that his "open musings about disappointment in the girl" had been misinterpreted by the youths. He was given a simple warning about inciting destructive acts with delinquent youths. He now knew better than to mess with her in the future. While Joni was sure it was only to head off any legal trouble—after all, they had acted on his teachings—she felt safer.

Violet had been distraught to find out what Michael—her blonde friend—had done. She apologized to Joni on his behalf about two months later when she was well into her first semester as a college freshman.

"I admit," she'd said when she finally called, "I only just found out. That's horrible what he did. I honestly didn't think he was the sort to do that kind of thing."

"Honestly, I'm angrier at the adults in his life. He was just acting on Mr. Northen's orders," Joni said. "It's the self-righteous leaders who play innocent. They're the real problem here."

The sisters shared a laugh.

"Well, at least I made new friends here," Violet said. "This crowd doesn't seem as eager to trespass against people they disagree with."

That conversation had taken place just over a year ago. She texted Violet the news. Then she called Dottie.

"Dottie, what time do you get off of work?"

"It's Saturday, child," her aunt said on the phone. "The DMV isn't open today," Dottie said. "Why? What's up? You discover scotch yet?"

Joni laughed. "I have something to share with you. I'm coming over in person to show you."

"Well, feel free to keep me in suspense!" Dottie said, laughing. "What is it? Will I like it? Is it something weird? Wait, are you pregnant?"

"No, not pregnant," Joni said, grabbing her keys and the envelope. "You'll love it. I promise."

She threw her shoes on and ran to the car.

A few minutes later, she was at Dottie's apartment, knocking on the door. Deep bass beats emanated from a nearby apartment. Dottie opened the door, and Joni was greeted with a blast of cigarette smoke.

Joni came in. The familiar white walls with some pictures of her aunt and Lukaas were still there. The blinds to the small, backdoor patio were shuttered. The dull, brown couch was to her right in the small living room. The kitchen light was on with a calculator and some paperwork scattered on the table. Dottie was paying some bills.

When Dottie shut the door, she commented, "My next-door neighbor has been blaring some shit music all day. I'm protesting by making this entire wing smell like an ashtray from which there is no escape."

Joni handed the envelope to Dottie. Dottie looked at it suspiciously, then back at Joni. "You drove all this way to show me a fucking envelope?"

"Read it," Joni said, failing to conceal her giddiness. Dottie smiled and opened it. When she read the letter, her eyes widened. "Oh my God, Joni. Holy shit, you did it!"

Dottie hugged her niece. "I'm so fuckin' proud of you, kiddo."

"Thank you," Joni said, overcome with exuberant emotion. Smiling, she said, "You wanna go somewhere for dinner tonight? My treat."

Dottie looked pleased. "Sounds good to me! Thanks! Anyplace special you have in mind?"

"I was thinking we could do that Thai place we went to. Haven't been back there in a while."

"That sounds good! I just need to finish some bills." Dottie indicated the pile of papers on her table. "Even the vampires need to eat."

Joni smiled. "Also, I haven't told you this yet because I wanted to wait until it was ready to go. But I wanted you to know that I'm dedicating the book to you."

Dottie looked taken aback and confused, staring incredulously at Joni. "Really? Why me? What'd I do?"

Joni replied, "Well . . . because you saved my life."

Dottie stared at her niece, then back at the letter. She sat down on her couch and looked sheepishly at the coffee table. "That . . . I . . ." Dottie had no words and was fighting the losing battle between tears of joy and tears of great regret.

Joni sat down beside her aunt. "I love you, Dottie. You're the best aunt anyone could ask for." Dottie sighed, trying to hold tears back and let a little more laughter into the room. Something like a snort with tears happened instead. Dottie wiped her eyes.

"I love you too, Joni. Thank you for saving my life as well."

THE END

A very special thank you to Amanda Chandler, Katrina Makkouk, and Lori Franklin.

About the Author

STEVEN BAILEY was born December 3, 1988 in Marietta, Georgia. He graduated from Anderson University in 2011 with degrees in both English Secondary Education and Theatre. He taught high school English for ten years before leaving teaching to focus on writing full time. He currently lives with his wife Anna in North Carolina, where they enjoy hiking the mountains, creating art, and biking together.